HEALING STONE

PRAISE FOR *HEALING STONE*

"This book has heart—big, insightful, full-of-forgiveness kind of heart that takes us deep into the psyche of the people of a small town in Kentucky. Stone, the seventeen-year-old farm boy with healing hands, is a cipher for the times, 1955, at the dawn of the Civil Rights movement. He busts prejudicial behavior apart as surely as a thresher mowing wheat in the fields of his Kentucky farm. Mr. Booher tells a tale rich with folksy wisdom. Magic realism at its best."

MAUREEN K. POWER
Author of *Miracle on Massachusetts Avenue*, member of Science Fiction and Fantasy Writers of America and Codex Writers Group

"Brock Booher's latest offering, *Healing Stone*, is a gem of the storytelling craft. The tale is at once engaging as well as inspiring. Laced with rich imagery as well as meaning, *Healing Stone* teaches lessons that lift one from the backdrop of 1950s Kentucky into the world we live in; where character, love, and hope can make a difference—and where miracles can still happen."

STEPHEN J. STIRLING
Author of *Shedding Light on the Dark Side* and *Persona Non Grata*

"We talk a lot about books that haunt us, and often that's a bit of an exaggeration. Not so with *Healing Stone*. I found myself sneaking it back out after I was supposed to be in bed, and discussing it with friends and family after finishing it. . . . A wonderful blending of small town charm with historic family drama and a large dollop of the fantastic. The kind of book you can recommend to almost anyone!"

SUZANNE WARR
Content editor for Red Adept Publishing

HEALING STONE

BROCK BOOHER

SWEETWATER
BOOKS

AN IMPRINT OF CEDAR FORT, INC.
SPRINGVILLE, UTAH

This is a work of fiction. The characters, names, incidents, places, and dialogue are products of the author's imagination, and are not to be construed as real. The opinions and views expressed herein belong solely to the author and do not necessarily represent the opinions or views of Cedar Fort, Inc. Permission for the use of sources, graphics, and photos is also solely the responsibility of the author.

ISBN 13: 978-1-4621-1394-1

Published by Sweetwater Books, an imprint of Cedar Fort, Inc.
2373 W. 700 S., Springville, UT 84663
Distributed by Cedar Fort, Inc., www.cedarfort.com

LIBRARY OF CONGRESS CATALOGING-IN-PUBLICATION DATA

Booher, Brock, 1963- author.
  Healing stone / Brock Booher.
    pages cm
  Summary: Abandoned at birth in a small-town Kentucky graveyard, seventeen-year-old Ezekiel Stone Maloney is content with the simple country life until a tragic accident awakens a dormant gift inside him--the power to heal.
  ISBN 978-1-4621-1394-1 (perfect bound)
  [1. Healers--Fiction. 2. Farm life--Fiction. 3. Kentucky--Fiction. 4. Self-actualization (Psychology)--Fiction.] I. Title.
  PZ7.B64488He 2014
  [Fic]--dc23
                                    2013034843

Cover design by Kristen Reeves
Cover design © 2014 by Lyle Mortimer
Typeset and edited by Melissa J. Caldwell

Printed in the United States of America

10 9 8 7 6 5 4 3 2 1

This book is dedicated to my parents, whose stories inspired me to begin, and to my wife, who believed I could actually finish.

ONE

❧

I got Rusty as a present for my tenth birthday. Otis Wilburn, a colored man over on Coe Ridge, owed my Daddy some money, and the pup, supposedly the son of a pedigreed hunting dog, was paid as interest. At ten years old, I didn't know a thing about pedigrees, fancy hunting dogs, or settling debts with colored folks, but the pup's coat was the color of rusty nails. So I named him Rusty. We were inseparable until the summer of 1955 when I turned seventeen. The day I discovered my gift, I saved Rusty's life, and then he saved mine.

Early that summer, I was mowing hay down in the river bottom with the John Deere. The engine whined and belched out smoke because I had it in high gear. I wanted to go fishing instead of mowing hay all day. It was late morning, just after breakfast, and the dew was still burning off. The smoke from the tractor hung heavy in the cool morning air and mingled with the aroma of fresh-cut hay. Unlike the whirling blade of the bush hog encased in a metal cover, the sickle blade of the mowing machine slid along beside the tractor, exposed and dangerous. Daddy warned me that a mowing machine operating at high speed would cut a dog's leg clean off. A rabbit darted out of the long grass ahead, and Rusty, always the hunter, lit after it.

At the speed I was going, I should have looked ahead more often like I'd been taught. Instead I had my head turned sideways watching the sickle blade slide along the ground and tear through the stand of alfalfa like a knife through hot butter. I guess Rusty had chased that rabbit back into the long grass in front of the blade while I wasn't looking. When I heard Rusty's yelp over the roar of the tractor engine and the chattering blade of the mowing machine, it was too late.

I yanked the throttle to idle and stomped on the clutch and brake. I spun around in my seat. Rusty wriggled on his side a few feet behind the blade. "Aaaooo! Aaaooo! Aaaooo!" His rapid, howling cries cut right through me, and a wave of guilt and panic washed over me.

I put the tractor in neutral, set the brake, and started to jump off, but then I remembered where I was. The last time we mowed this river bottom, I saw at least a half a dozen copperheads. I froze and searched the ground for any poisonous snakes, just like Daddy had taught me. Finding the area clear, I jumped off the tractor, rummaged through the toolbox for an old rag, and ran over to Rusty, my heart beating out of my chest.

The sight of Rusty took my breath away, and I fell to my knees beside him. Three of his paws—the front left paw and both back paws—had been severed near the ankle joint. Through the flow of blood, I could see the white of the bone and the hanging tendons. Strained whimpers had replaced his howls and yelps, and he scratched at the fresh cut hay with his only good paw. When he saw me, he raised his head and tried to get up, but I gently pushed him back down and put the rag around his front paw to stop the bleeding. The rag was useless against so much blood. The sight of Rusty's red blood against the green alfalfa hay made me queasy. I swallowed back the bile and choked back tears. Rusty twitched and shivered as his lifeblood ebbed out onto the rich river bottom ground. Wishing I could do anything to save him, I whispered a quick prayer. "Lord, please help me save Rusty."

I'm not sure why, but after I finished the prayer, I found the severed paws and set them next to Rusty. Maybe I was trying to make sense of it all, like putting together a puzzle, and I viewed the paws as missing pieces. I knelt there on one knee, stroking his head and feeling helpless, as the words of a scripture haunted me like a ghost.

About that time, I heard the squeaky frame of the Ford pickup as Daddy pulled up beside me. Billy Molony isn't my real father, but at the time I didn't know my real father, so he was Daddy to me. "I got worried when I saw the tractor stop," he said as he craned his neck and looked down at Rusty. He shook his head and let out a sigh. "I told you to watch out for him."

I hung my head in guilt, unable to look Daddy in the eye. "I was looking down at the blade instead of out front, like you taught me, and didn't see him 'til it was too late."

Daddy got out of the truck and surveyed the scene. He took off his straw hat and rubbed the back of his neck. "Well, I reckon there ain't much we can do for him. We'll have to put him down." He put the hat back over his thinning hair and said, "I'll get the rifle."

I jumped to my feet. "The rifle? Daddy, we can't just shoot him!"

Daddy just pointed at Rusty shivering on the ground.

"Look at him, son. He'll never be able to walk, much less run and hunt. He's practically useless. Besides, he's lost so much blood, he's gonna die anyway." He put his big calloused hand on my shoulder and looked up into my eyes. "It's a mercy killing, Stone." Then he pulled back his hand and started for the truck to get the Winchester that hung in the back window just above the shotgun.

I stood there in denial thinking about all the time I had spent training Rusty to point for game and flush out birds, or the hours we spent down by the river together scaring up rabbits and fetching sticks out of the slow-moving water. I wondered if it was merciful to take a life just because it was no longer useful. Daddy woke me from my trance when he cranked the bolt and chambered a round.

"Can't we at least try to bandage him up?" I pleaded.

He stood there with the rifle slung over his left arm shaking his head. "That would only make him suffer longer. You want him to suffer?"

I looked away and tried to find a reason not to put Rusty down. The scripture that had been haunting the edges of my thoughts flooded my mind: *Live; yea, I said unto thee when thou wast in thy blood, Live.* I knew I had seen it somewhere, but I couldn't remember where.

Daddy held the rifle out to me. "You ran into him with the mowing machine. I suppose you should be the one to put him out of his misery."

I looked at the dark rifle in his outstretched hands and a chill ran down my spine. I had killed wild turkey down along the Cumberland, and several covey of quail flushed out by Rusty himself. Just last year I bagged a ten-point whitetail buck, and we were still eating the venison. I had killed snakes, rats, and even a fox that was killing our chickens. But I had never killed like this.

I hesitated and then knelt down beside Rusty again as the scripture scrolled across my mind over and over. His crying had been replaced with soft whimpers, and his chest heaved up and down. I could see his eyes glazing over, and I reached out and stroked his head. I shook my head and said, "I can't do it."

"Stone, sometimes killing an injured animal is better than letting it live," he said in a calming voice. He placed the butt of the rifle on the ground beside me for me to take. "End his misery."

Live; yea, I said unto thee when thou wast in thy blood, Live. The haunting words went round and round in my head, almost audible. I closed my eyes and concentrated on the words, and then I recognized the scripture. It came from the headstone where Sheriff Pace found me as a baby.

I felt my scalp begin to tingle. It started at the base of my neck and worked its way up until my entire head felt like it was host to some personal lightning storm. Tiny bolts of power struck with random accuracy. Each jolt of electricity flashed inside my mind and momentarily lit up a vision of what I should do. I could see my hands reattaching the paws to the legs, like snapping the final pieces of a puzzle into place.

As if the sensational electric storm in my head wasn't enough, my hands began to burn. It wasn't painful like the time I burned my hand on the wood stove, but it felt more like the time I had a fever, and my mama caressed my head with a cool cloth. My hands felt like living torches of spiritual energy.

I knew what to do without thinking, almost as if possessed by some spirit, but I knew it wasn't an evil spirit because it wanted me to do good. I remembered the verse from Matthew, "By their fruits ye shall know them," and gave in to its urgings.

I reached out and took Rusty's front left leg in my right hand. My left hand picked up the corresponding paw. I put the two together and recited the scripture in a whisper. The burning in my hands increased, and the tiny lightning storm raged even more. When I dared to open my eyes and look, the paw had reattached—skin, tendons, bone, and all.

I heard Daddy mumble something, but I was so focused on saving Rusty that I ignored him. I grabbed his back right leg and the severed paw and shoved them together with hot hands. I closed my eyes and whispered the scripture again with the same result. Without hesitation, I repeated the process for his other back leg. My hands burned like hot coals. The storm inside my head raged and tingled from my forehead to the base of my neck.

When I finished, the power gathered in my chest and burned inside of me like some sort of ointment. I let out a scream, and all at once, it flew away like a dove. I fell over onto my side, out of breath. I thought my eyes were open, but the world was dark. I could feel the grass stubble against my cheek and the warmth of the climbing sun on my arms. I heard Rusty stir and whimper. Then I felt his cold nose and warm wet tongue on my face.

"Dear God," murmured Daddy. I felt his rough hand on the back of my neck like he was checking for a sign of life. "Stone, are you okay?"

I rolled over onto my back and stared up at a dark world, unable to see. I reached out and felt the short hair of Rusty's reddish-brown coat. "I think so, but I can't see anything."

"Just stay there while I put the rifle away." I heard his work boots rustle through the freshly cut hay.

Rusty had started licking my face again. I reached out and found his front left leg with my hand. I cupped my hand around his leg and followed it down from the knee. It felt as if he had never been injured.

"Let's get you to the truck," said Daddy. I felt his strong hands grab underneath my arms. "Do you think you can stand up?"

"I think I can stand, but I can't see a blamed thing."

"You still can't see?" he asked in a worried voice. He picked me up and put me on my feet. "Just hold on to me."

"Daddy," I asked, "is Rusty okay?"

"Well," said Daddy with a deep breath, "I ain't never seen anything like it. His legs are good as new."

Daddy threw my arm over his shoulder and led me to the seat of the truck. I could hear the John Deere still idling. I could feel the sunshine on my skin. My mouth was dry and chalky. The smell of fresh-cut hay hung in the air. All my senses seemed to be working, except I was blind as a bat.

"Do you have any water?" I asked. "I'm thirsty." I heard Daddy grab the quart jar he used as a water jug, and he helped me get a drink. Still dazed at the events that had unfolded, I asked, "You mean, I healed Rusty?"

He was silent for a moment. When he answered, he spoke reverently like he was at church. "You healed him, Stone."

I sat there stunned and confused but was happy that Rusty was okay. I blinked, and I could see dark shapes and forms, like I was looking at the world through an old brown liniment bottle. I blinked again, and I could see the sunlight on the green hay. I squeezed my eyes shut and tried to focus. When I opened my eyes, I could see Daddy with his khaki pants and white shirt standing in front of me holding his jar of water.

"I can see." I jumped out of the truck. "I can see!" Daddy's face lit up and he gave me a big hug, but then he released me quickly and stood back staring at me. I could see the worry on his face. I had seen his furrowed brow hundreds of times before as I watched him care for my older stepbrother, Leck.

Rusty nuzzled me with his big, wet nose and began licking the dried blood from my hands. I looked down at his shiny brown fur and yellow eyes. His tail was wagging like a catfish out of water. I knelt down and hugged him. I grabbed his front left leg and examined his paw—it was as good as the day Daddy brought him home. I looked up at Daddy, and he stood there watching Rusty and shaking his head. I said, "Maybe we should give him something to drink."

I cupped my bloody hands, and Daddy poured the water. Rusty drank until the water was all gone, and then he licked my hands clean. After that, he must have smelled that rabbit again, and he raced off into the tall grass jumping and looking. I stood and watched him in silence. Daddy pulled off his hat and scratched his head. The John Deere still sat there idling. We both stood in silence for a few minutes trying to make sense of it all.

Finally, Daddy turned to me and put a hand on my shoulder. He looked up at me and wagged a finger in my face. "Don't say a word about this to nobody. Understand?"

I nodded in agreement, and he backed away. I wasn't sure how I had healed Rusty, why that scripture came rushing into my head, or if I could ever do it again. Yes, I agreed with Daddy. I needed to keep this to myself until I could understand it.

"Do the words, 'Live; yea, I said unto thee when thou wast in thy blood, Live,' mean anything to you?" I asked. "Isn't that the scripture from the headstone where I was found when I was a baby . . . you know, the one from Ezekiel?"

He looked down toward the river, away from me. "I'm not sure," he answered.

We stood in awkward silence for a few moments. He gazed at the bluff across the river, and I stared off in Rusty's direction. At last, he patted me on the back and said, "Well, you'd best finish up this mowing if you want to go fishing."

Since most of my strength had returned, I nodded obediently and shuffled over to the idling John Deere. As I climbed on, he yelled, "Take it a little slower, and watch out for Rusty." I nodded again, put the tractor in a lower gear, and continued mowing the hay. Each time I went around the field and passed that spot, I wondered what to make of it all. How did I heal Rusty's severed paws? Was it a gift from God or a freak of nature? I was a lot more careful to watch out for Rusty.

I finished mowing the hay and stored the machinery the way Daddy liked it. Usually I would have gone into the house for lunch, but I didn't want to talk to Mama, or especially Leck, right now. So I snuck into the kitchen and grabbed a couple of biscuits left over from breakfast before heading down the dirt path to the river. I hoped a few hours of fishing on the banks of the Cumberland would help me sort through the strange events of the morning. It was warmer than I hoped it would be, but the breeze was rustling through the trees. I had my red tackle box and an old coffee can pail with stink bait in one hand and my Zebco rod and reel in the other. Rusty followed along, darting in and out of the grass along the path, always hunting.

Bordered by a big sweeping bend of the Cumberland River just south of the sleepy town of Burkesville, Kentucky, our farm sat far enough off Celina Road that we didn't usually hear all the traffic heading back and forth across Neely's Ferry, but we did have an occasional hitchhiker or hobo come to the door looking for a handout. The trees grew tall on the steep banks of the Cumberland. On our side of the river, the banks were often slick and muddy. A stone bluff rose up on the other side like God had carved it with his own hand and put it there to make the river bend. I stood at the top of the bank surveying the green water for a good spot to cast my line. The swollen river of spring had deposited a fallen log on the bank and then piled sand, floating debris, and smaller branches up against it. I navigated down to the water by sticking to the sandy pathway and dodging sharp pieces of driftwood that stuck out of the jumbled pile. The limbs of an oak tree cast a nice shade out onto the river and provided a home to a family of swallows that darted in and out of the branches. I could hear Rusty scurrying about in the grass at the top of the bank.

I put my tackle box down on the sand and peeled back the tin foil on the coffee can. It was my own personal concoction of flour, chicken livers, and chicken blood thickened with a mixture of cornstarch and water. The rotten smell of dried blood and decaying chicken livers made me gag as I baited my hook. I didn't much care for it, but the catfish loved it. Out of the corner of my eye, I saw Rusty poke his head out of the pile of driftwood as soon as I baited my hook. The strong smell of blood must have caught the attention of his hunting dog nose. I adjusted my fishing bobber and cast my line out into the dark, lazy water with a splash. Then I took a seat on the sand, put a leg over my pole, and leaned back on my hands, waiting for one of those big channel cats to go for the bait.

I stared at the red-and-white bobber and reflected on the morning until something rustled in the driftwood off to my right. At first I ignored it, but the rustling grew louder and startled me enough that I turned. Coiled among the small branches of the driftwood pile not more than six inches from my hand, I found myself looking into the menacing yellow eyes of a large copperhead snake. His long scaly form with the telltale hourglass markings twisted up among the branches, and his pale yellow tail vibrated against a small pile of dead leaves.

Out of instinct and fear I started to jerk away, but I knew that any quick movement would simply startle the snake and surely cause him to strike. So I froze. For a few moments all I could hear was my heartbeat thumping so loud that I was sure it would even chase the fish away. I didn't dare move a muscle, not even to breathe. The beady-eyed snake stopped vibrating his tail and sat there with his forked tongue sliding in and out of his lipless mouth.

The fishing pole underneath my leg began to jerk. No doubt some large channel cat was making a meal of stinky chicken livers and old blood. Out of the corner of my eye, I noticed that my bobber had been pulled underwater. Startled, I started to reach for the rod and reel. Unfortunately, the movement startled the snake as well, and his yellow tail began to thrash against the dry leaves again. I held my breath as he coiled and prepared to strike. I wasn't sure whether to jerk my hand away, let the rod and reel slide into the river, or simply sit there and hope that he would calm down again. Rusty made the decision for me.

Just as I was certain the angry copperhead was about

to strike out at my right hand, Rusty came bounding down the banks and put himself in between me and the snake, barking like he always did when he had his prey cornered. I seized the opportunity, grabbed my fishing pole, and rolled away from danger. I scrambled to my feet still fighting the channel cat. I'm sure I jerked at the line more than normal, which caused it to snap, setting the big channel cat, the bobber, and the stink bait free.

For the second time that day I grimaced at the sound of Rusty's painful yelp. I turned to see the evil snake wriggling in the soft sand. I threw down my fishing pole, grabbed a big rock at the water's edge, and smashed the snake's head. Rusty pawed at a spot on his neck and whimpered. Two small drops of blood dribbled down his rust-colored fur. The yellow-eyed snake had bitten Rusty in the neck. Knowing that most dogs don't live very long after a bite so close to the heart, I scooped my loyal companion up in my arms and hurried up the banks and back along the dirt trail toward the house, hoping that maybe Daddy would know what to do. I had gone about thirty yards when I remembered how I healed him earlier. Knowing that there was little I could do for Rusty even if I got him back to the house, I laid him down on the trail. I could tell by his eyes that he was already getting weak and lethargic.

I looked down at his paws, and the vivid memory of the earlier experience came rushing back to me. I strained to remember the scripture, but a dark cloud covered my mind. I tried to speak the miraculous words I had spoken earlier and call upon the power I had used that morning, but my tongue seemed to stick to the roof of my mouth. No lightning storm filled my head. My hands did not burn. The words of scripture did not flood my mind. Thinking that perhaps I had done something wrong or was somehow unworthy, I knelt and said a prayer. I begged the Lord for mercy. I begged the Lord for help. Nothing came to me.

I knelt there in a daze as Rusty's breathing grew shallow. An ironic feeling of peace came over me, and I thought that perhaps the power to heal him had come back. I tried to utter the words from Ezekiel again, but once again the words did not come. I reached out and stroked Rusty's head, hoping that somehow contact with him would help, but once again, nothing. His eyes glazed over just like they had earlier in the day. Just like before, his life was leaving him, but this time I couldn't produce a miracle to stop it.

He died in a matter of minutes.

I knelt with Rusty's head in my lap and tried to understand. Somehow God allowed me to save his life earlier in the day but had not allowed me to save it now. I knew that everything had a season, but I couldn't understand why his life had been extended for just a few hours only to be taken again. I was angry. I was hurt. It seemed so unfair, so unjust. I stroked his head with tears streaming down my face trying to decide if I should be grateful that Rusty had saved me from the snake, or angry that he had died. Numb, I scooped him up in my arms and carried him toward the house.

Mama must have seen me coming through the kitchen window while she was fixing supper because when I got close to the house, she hurried down the back porch steps, barefooted and wearing her apron with the faded yellow flowers. When she drew close I dropped to my knees and laid Rusty down on the ground.

"Oh, Stone, what happened to Rusty?" she asked as she wiped her hands on her apron.

"He got bit by a copperhead and died," I said as I wiped the tears from my eyes.

Ada Lee Molony wasn't my real mother, but you could never tell from the way she treated me. She loved me like her own. They say few things are stronger than a mother's love, but after my years as the recipient of her compassion, I could say the same about her love as well. She knelt beside me and wrapped her frail arms around me. She was a small-framed woman who always seemed to be on the verge of sickness. By the time I was fifteen, I was a head taller than her, but right at that moment I felt like a baby swaddled up in her tender mercies. My tears flowed freely for several minutes until the well ran dry. Mama wiped my cheeks with her apron and kissed me on the forehead.

"You go to the barn for the shovels, and I'll go find Daddy," she said. "Together you can find a good spot to bury him." She rose and extended me her hand.

I sniffled, nodded, and ceremoniously pulled myself up by her hand. I stared down at Rusty, still wondering why I was able to save him from the injuries I had inflicted with the mowing machine but was unable to save him from the malicious bite of an ignorant snake. I was going to miss that dog.

I raised my eyes as Mama rounded the house to find Daddy, and saw Leck, my older stepbrother, on the back porch. He leaned against his crutches and surveyed the scene with pitiful eyes. After a moment he hobbled back into the house and let the screen door slam behind him.

Daddy and I buried Rusty down by the river in the shade of a bur oak tree. The rhythmic sound of sharp metal against soft moist earth seemed to echo off the high limestone bluff on the other side of the river as we dug a shallow grave for my friend of seven years and lowered his lifeless body into it. Before covering the body, Daddy put his hat over his heart.

"I am grateful to God that we're lowering Rusty's body and not yours into this grave," said Daddy. "Seeing as how he almost died earlier today and was saved by your hand, I reckon it was just his time."

I had no more tears left at that point and simply stared at Rusty's lifeless body in the shallow hole. His paws showed no signs of trauma from the blade of the mowing machine. I just couldn't understand how I was able to save him from dying the first time, or maybe why I couldn't save him the second time. I could feel the anger and confusion lurking in the back of my mind waiting for the chance to burst out into the open. The sound of Daddy's shovel plunging into the black soil interrupted my thoughts. In my numbness, I joined him and buried my best friend.

When we finished, I dropped my shovel and fell down on my knees beside the mound of fresh earth. I wanted to cry, but nothing came. Daddy patted me on the head, picked up my shovel, and headed back to the house, leaving me alone to mourn.

I was quiet that night at supper until Leck started pestering me about the whole thing. He had a way of picking the scab off a healing wound and making it fester again. I used to think he did it to make every-body miserable like himself, but I've since learned that the motivation was much deeper and difficult to discern.

"What happened to your dog?" asked Leck through a mouthful of corn bread. Mama always chided me when I did that, but she never said a word about his bad manners or infractions of proper upbringing. Leck had a way of getting under my skin.

I swallowed the green beans I had been working

on. "He died," I answered without looking up from my plate. Daddy was attacking a piece of fried chicken with his fingers. Mama nibbled at her corn bread. Neither of them offered any more explanation.

"That was obvious. How'd he die?"

I pushed the mashed potatoes around on my plate before answering. "Snakebite. Copperhead."

"You couldn't save him? Dogs usually don't die from that if you can flush out the wound."

I looked up at him and scowled. "He got bit in the neck. There was nothing I could do for him this time!" I blurted out.

"This time? What did you do last time?" Leck seemed to enjoy the conversation once he got me riled up.

Flustered and bothered, I said, "I saved him when he got his legs cut off, but this time . . ." The words slipped out before I realized what I was saying.

Leck tried to chuckle and bits of corn bread flew out of his mouth and onto the table. "You saved him when his legs got cut off?"

Daddy cleared his throat. Mama put down her fork and stared at me. Leck stopped chewing and waited for more.

"Ezekiel Stone Molony," scolded Daddy. "I told you to keep that to yourself. They don't know what happened earlier."

My face flushed with embarrassment and anger.

Mama gave Daddy a curious look and asked, "What happened earlier?"

Daddy wiped his mouth with his napkin and shifted in his chair. "Well, I ain't exactly sure," he said with his head down. Then he looked up and his face had a hardened expression. "Let's get one thing clear," he said, shaking his finger. "Nobody talks about this outside of this house. This is a gossiping county, and I don't want to give nobody an excuse for gossiping about the Molony family." He paused and then added, "Everybody clear?" We all nodded.

He took in a deep breath through his nose and exhaled sharply. "Today while Stone was out mowing hay, Rusty ran ahead in the tall grass and he didn't see him. Before he could stop—"

"I cut off three of his paws with the mowing machine," I interrupted. Daddy shook his head, gave another heavy sigh, and waved his hand for to me to continue.

"I cut off one of his front paws and both of his back paws with the mowing machine. Daddy wanted to shoot him and put him out of his misery, but I couldn't do it. This scripture—I think it's from Ezekiel—kept going round and round in my head like a whirling dervish, and before I knew it, it felt like a thunderstorm was going off in my head. I reached down without understanding why or how, and picked up the front paw. In my mind I could see what to do, so I did it."

"Did what?" asked Mama.

"Well," I held up my hands like two foreign objects as I continued the story, "I closed my eyes and shoved the front paw back into place. My hands burned like, like the burning bush that Moses saw, and when I opened my eyes, that paw was as good as new." I returned to pushing around my mashed potatoes and waited for everyone's reaction.

Daddy nodded in agreement and said, "I saw it with my own eyes, Ada."

"It must be a gift from God," said Mama. "How else could he do such a thing?"

"I reckon so," said Daddy. "But even then, these things are best kept private."

Leck spoke up. "Maybe he's an alien from another planet. After all, the sheriff did find him crying in the graveyard one night." He snickered.

I gave him the evil eye but wondered if there was any truth in the jab. I didn't know my real parents, and they did find me, as a baby, crying in the graveyard. Leck's proposal had just as much merit as the idea that God had somehow granted me a special gift.

"Hush that nonsense," scolded Mama. "The Bible talks about the healing gift, but it doesn't say anything about aliens from other planets."

"Well, no matter where his 'gift' came from, I think it's best to keep it a secret for now," said Daddy.

The conversation sagged for a moment as all of us tacitly agreed to Daddy's terms. Leck and Daddy continued eating, but Mama turned her excited blue eyes on me. "What did it feel like when you healed Rusty?" she asked.

I took a bite of potatoes and recalled the details of the experience. "It was like nothing I've ever felt before. I could see the miracle in my mind before it happened, like it was telling me what to do." I took a drink of my water. "My head felt like a small thunderstorm had taken over, and my hands burned. When I finished healing him, I was blind for a few minutes."

"Blind?" asked Mama.

"I had to help him to the truck. After he got a drink of water, he was fine," explained Daddy through a mouthful of food.

"Dear Lord!" said Mama.

"If you healed him the first time, why didn't you just work your magic when he got bit by the copperhead?" asked Leck.

I shrugged. I didn't have an answer.

"Maybe there was kryptonite nearby," said Leck with a chuckle.

Daddy gave Leck a stern look and pointed at him with his fork. "You see? That's exactly why this doesn't need to be talked about outside this home. People will just poke fun and laugh about it. He may have a gift, but it isn't a gift we can openly share."

"Well, we don't want him to hide his talent under a bushel," said Mama.

"And we don't want to cast our pearls before swine either," answered Daddy. "I'm the head of the house and I say we keep this to ourselves. Understood?"

I answered, "Yes, sir." Leck winked and nodded irreverently. Mama just bowed her head and picked at her chicken.

After supper, Daddy hurried into the living room to warm up the RCA radio. Leck grabbed his crutches and hobbled after him. The Grand Ole Opry would be coming on soon. I put my dishes in the sink and started after them, until Mama asked me to help her clean up after supper. After the crazy day I'd had, I just wanted to stretch out on the living room floor and drift off to sleep to the rhythm of the music on the radio, but I didn't argue and started helping her with the dirty dishes.

"You know," said Mama as she scraped the food scraps into the pigs' slop bucket, "your gift could help many people."

I started running water and put some Dreft soap into the sink. I thought about what she said, but since I couldn't seem to control my abilities, I wasn't sure how I could help anyone. I felt torn. I didn't know if I should hide my gift under a bushel or cast my pearls before swine. "I doubt it," I said. "If it really is a gift, then why didn't it work when I needed it most? If it's a gift, I don't have the foggiest idea how it works."

"How did you feel when you healed Rusty?"

I scrubbed a plate and handed it to her to rinse. "Good, I guess."

"Do you think you would feel good about something evil?"

"I guess not."

"Then it has to be a good gift."

"Then why couldn't I save Rusty from the snakebite?"

"Stone, sometimes God has a different plan. Maybe it was his time. Maybe you were able to keep him alive so he could save you."

I didn't like that answer. It didn't make sense. If I could save him once, why couldn't I save him again? I took my frustration out on the dishes and banged two of them together as I scrubbed.

"I want my dishes clean, not broken," said Mama.

"If it is a gift, then why did I get it?" I asked. "Maybe I *am* from outer space." Mama chuckled as she dried the dishes. I stopped and looked at her with my hands resting in the soapy water. "Do you have any idea who my real parents are?"

She stared out the kitchen window at the sunset and mechanically dried a plate. "All we know is that Sheriff George Pace found you crying in the graveyard on May 16, 1938." She put the plate into the cupboard and continued staring out the window like she was looking for answers to come floating in off the clothesline. "George knew we wanted more children, and he knew about my medical condition. So he brought you here for safekeeping."

It was the same story she told me when I first asked her several years ago. I thought about asking her what was written on the headstone but decided it was something I would have to go see for myself. "Did he ever look for the mother?" I asked.

Mama glanced at me and then lowered her eyes as if ashamed or sad about something. "Yes, but your real mother was never found. After a couple of years we made it official and adopted you."

I went back to washing dishes, and both of us were silent for awhile. I remembered the day I found out I was adopted. Two of my classmates in first grade, Dewdrop Hazard and Rufus Stearns, were teasing me and telling me I wasn't born. They said I had been found in the graveyard on a witch's grave. I gave Rufus a black eye. That afternoon when I got home, Mama told me the truth. She said that secrets like that can eat you up inside, and I was old enough to know the truth. Her explanation satisfied me, and after that, I never spent much time worrying about where I came from or who my parents really were. Ada and Billy Molony had given me everything I ever needed and loved me like their own. As far as I was concerned they were my parents, but today's events did make me wonder. I handed Mama the last piece of silverware, pulled the plug in the sink, and stared at the dirty water swirling down the drain, wondering if the secrets of my past could help me unlock the secrets of my gift.

"Stone," said Mama, her voice shaky. "Do you think you could heal Leck?"

I felt the blood run out of my face. "Mama, I don't know how I healed Rusty. I . . . I don't have any idea where to begin healing Leck."

"Well, just think about it." She reached up and kissed me on the cheek. "Thanks for helping with the dishes."

I acknowledged her thanks with a nod and shuffled

21

toward the living room where the radio was playing Webb Pierce's song "More and More." Daddy was sitting in the big chair tapping his foot, and Leck was lying on the couch with his crutches leaning up beside him. I slid over to the corner and stretched out on the floor. I stared at the ceiling and listened to music pour in over WSM and thought about Leck. He had left for the Korean War a celebrated local athlete and avid hunter. He returned a broken man barely able to get around on crutches. He didn't smile much, and he never had anything good to say. I tolerated him, but I didn't enjoy being around him anymore. I could feel him looking at me, and when I glanced over at him, he looked away. If I couldn't heal Rusty from a snakebite, how in the world was I supposed to heal Leck?

For the first time in my life, the questions about my past gnawed at me. I grabbed the family Bible from the coffee table and opened it up to the Old Testament. I thumbed through the pages of Ezekiel looking for the scripture that had given me the power to heal, but the day soon began to take its toll and I couldn't keep my eyes open. I decided that I would have to pay a visit to the graveyard tomorrow and read the headstone myself. Satisfied with the decision, I closed the book and drifted off to sleep to the music of Little Jimmy Dickens.

TWO

༺☙❧༻

Daddy let me sleep in Sunday mornings, if you count sleeping until six as sleeping in. I woke up on my own a little after five thirty, got dressed, and slipped out the back door. Without thinking, I whistled for Rusty. As soon as the sound left my lips, all the memories from yesterday flooded my mind, and it felt like someone punched me in the stomach. I moped down to the barn to get my morning chores done, feeling short of breath.

I washed out the galvanized metal milk bucket and one of the stainless steel milking cans with a little bleach and water and sat the rag aside. I dumped some sweet feed into the feed bucket and called, "Soo cow! Soo cow!" Jersey Girl started for the barn. When she got close, I shook the bucket so she could hear it and dumped the sweet feed into her trough. She slipped into her stall without hesitation. I pulled up close to her with the milk stool and patted her on the side. Then with the wet rag, I cleaned her teats and massaged her bag so her milk would let down. "Ready for breakfast, Rusty?" I asked out of habit. Rusty usually sat next to me while I milked, and I always gave him the first few squirts. I squirted the milk out on to the floor where he usually sat. I leaned my head against her big cow belly and lost myself in the rhythm of the milk squirting against the side of the bucket. I started crying again. I must have looked like a mess—my head against a dirty old cow, my tears mingling with her coat, and all the while yanking those teats in steady rhythm. Jersey Girl coughed and woke me from my pitiful trance.

After I finished milking, I turned out Jersey Girl and poured the milk through cheesecloth into the stainless steel milk can. While I cleaned and rinsed out the milk bucket, my thoughts went round in circles. If I did have a gift, I still had no idea where it came from, how it worked, or if I would ever be able to use it again. When I remembered how Rusty died, my confusion turned to anger. Why would God let this happen? I shuffled back to the house with the fresh milk, slipped off my boots on the back porch, and put the milk into the icebox while my thoughts went around in circles.

Leck snapped me back to reality. "See any snakes this morning?" he asked through a mouthful of food.

I ignored him and filled my plate with hot biscuits and gravy. Mama sipped her coffee by the window dressed in her flower print Sunday dress with her apron on and curlers in her hair. I shoved a fork full of breakfast into my mouth just as Daddy came walking through the door with a hat full of eggs.

"Stone, you forgot to gather the eggs," he said as he set the hat down on the counter. "Did you remember to feed the calves?"

I swallowed and answered, "I believe so." The truth was I couldn't remember any specifics from the morning's chores except milking Jersey Girl.

"Go back down and check before you finish your breakfast," said Daddy as he started to put the eggs away. "Livestock don't feed itself."

Mama looked at Daddy and started to say something, but then she just sipped her coffee and stared out the window. I looked down at my plate of food and let out a sigh. I wanted to tell Daddy I would do it after breakfast, but I already knew the answer to that comment. So I slipped back on my work shoes and shuffled back down to the barn, grumbling to myself. I found the calves bawling in front of an empty trough. I had been so preoccupied that I forgot to feed them. I fed and watered them, checked the pigs and chickens, and headed back to the house.

My biscuits and gravy were cold by the time I got back. Daddy had finished his breakfast and was sitting at the table sipping coffee. Mama was washing dishes. I put a little salt on the gravy and started eating the mixture of soggy biscuits and cold gravy. I guess that Mama and Daddy must have been arguing because the air in the kitchen felt as thick as the gravy.

"Don't tell anybody what happened with Rusty yesterday," said Daddy as he finished his coffee. "It's a private matter. Understood?"

I nodded with my mouth full. I thought I heard Mama sigh over the sound of clinking dishes.

Mama came from a long line of Methodists, so we drove into town to attend the Methodist church. She and Daddy were married there. Daddy was on the church board, but I suspect that he would have been just as happy attending the Baptist church right up the road from us. I was the last one ready, and Daddy was honking the horn when I ran out the front door with my suit coat and clip-on tie in my hand. I slid into the back seat of the '49 Buick next to Leck as Daddy sped down the lane onto Celina Road and into Burkesville.

The church parking lot was over half full when we

got there. Daddy grumbled something about not getting our usual seats and hurried into the meetinghouse. Mama smiled and greeted everyone in the parking lot as she helped Leck out of the car. I started looking for Ruby, the preacher's daughter.

Ruby Ruth Tabor had moved to Burkesville about five years ago as a scrawny girl with pigtails. William (Willy) Travis McCoy and Floyd Talbot used to tease her and call her "Ruby Runt" because she was so skinny. I always laughed a little at the name, but inside I felt bad for her. She took it all in stride and giggled at the nickname, and in the end she got the last laugh. At thirteen she started growing and for a while was even taller than Willy. By sixteen none of us dared called her by her nickname because we all wanted her to go steady with us. Last summer Daddy volunteered me to mow the churchyard and trim the bushes every Thursday afternoon. She came out every week and gave me iced tea when I was done. By the end of that summer we were dating regularly.

I spotted Ruby at the doorway of the chapel, smiling and greeting everyone as they came in like she did every week. Her chocolate eyes sparkled in the sunlight. She wore a pale blue dress with a lace collar and a matching hairpiece in her dark brown hair. Her lips were the color of strawberries and her skin looked like fresh cream. She was giving Widow Thacker a hug when I walked up with Mama and Leck.

"Sure glad you're here today, Mrs. Thacker," she said as she ushered the old woman into the building. "Well, good morning, Leck," said Ruby as she turned to greet us.

Leck responded, "Morning, Ruby. You're looking pretty as ever this morning. Don't you think so, Stone?"

I felt the blood rush to my cheeks and tried to grin to cover my embarrassment. "Yes, you look very nice," I mumbled.

"Nice? She looks good enough to stop traffic, if you ask me," said Leck as he hobbled on into the chapel on his crutches.

Mama shook Ruby's hand and said, "Good morning, Ruby Ruth. Sorry about Leck. Seems he forgot his manners after coming home from the war."

"It's okay, Mrs. Molony." She gave me a quick glance. "At least he's not afraid to compliment a young lady."

I stuck out my hand. "Good morning, Ruby Ruth. You look very nice in blue."

Instead of shaking my hand, she stepped forward and gave me a big hug. I hugged her back and pressed my face up against her silky brown hair. Her hair always smelled like Prell shampoo. I just wanted to stand there, holding her close and taking in her smell, but we were standing in the doorway of the Methodist Church. So I let her go and stepped back. She took my hands and replied, "Why, thank you, Stone. Are you coming over for dinner tonight?"

"I'll be there around four," I said with a grin.

She squeezed my hands before releasing them and then turned to greet Mrs. Maggie Owens and her daughter Hazel, who suffered from polio. I watched Ruby greet the mother and even bring a smile to Hazel's face. I reluctantly left her side and headed to the pew Daddy liked to sit on every week. He had staked a claim to the right of the altar about six rows back. He said it gave him a good view of the cross, but I suspect he chose it because of the pillar that kept Pastor Tabor from seeing him sleeping at the end of the pew. I slid in between Mama and Leck.

Daddy was talking to Deputy Sheriff Cortis Russel, who always sat on the pew behind us. He was married to Mama's cousin, Shirley Mae. "I hear that Sheriff George Pace is finally going to retire after all these years. Are you running for sheriff?" asked Daddy.

"I'm fixin' to put up signs this next week," said Cortis as he stretched his long arms along the back of his pew.

"Is anybody going to run against you?" asked Daddy.

"Just that half-blind Republican, Harold Guffey. I can beat him with one arm behind my back," boasted Cortis. Daddy laughed.

Cortis Russel was something of a hometown sports hero. When he was a senior in high school, he led the basketball team to the state finals, and now he helped coach the high school basketball team. He had the perfect athletic build—broad shoulders and thin waist—and his wavy brown hair was always combed and perfect. I never saw him with a hat on. He went away to college for a semester but then came back home and married Shirley Mae Radford, a former Miss Cumberland County. She was the closest thing to a hometown socialite, always dressed in the latest fashion and hosting local social events. Between his status and her influence, he got on as the youngest deputy sheriff in the history of the county.

"Stone, I didn't see you at the basketball gym yesterday. Where were you?" asked Cortis.

I opened my mouth to speak, but Daddy beat me to it. "I had him mowing hay down in the river bottom all morning."

Cortis nodded. "Well, this next Saturday we're going to play over in Marrowbone around nine. We could sure use your height under the basket." He gave Daddy a gentle punch on the shoulder. "If your Daddy ain't working you to death."

"Slim chance of that," said Daddy with a chuckle. "I'm lucky if I can get a half day's work before he heads down to the river to go fishing or starts shooting hoops out by the barn."

"I'll be there," I said, "unless Daddy can't manage things by himself." I smiled. Daddy just grunted.

About that time Shirley Mae walked up dressed like the cover of a fashion magazine. "Slide over, Cortis," she demanded.

"Must be nice to have boys to help around the place," said Cortis as he slid down the pew to make room for his wife. I noticed Shirley Mae bow her head and look away at the comment. They didn't have any children.

The service was a typical Sunday service. Floyd's mom, Mrs. Talbot, played the organ. The choir sang an opening hymn. Old man Riddle started to lead us in the Lord's Prayer but had a coughing fit. We pushed on through it from memory while he coughed up a lung. The congregation sang a hymn. Then Pastor Phillip Tabor stood to deliver his sermon.

"I read in the paper this week that a man by the name of George Hensley died," he began. "Some of you may recognize the name. George Hensley claimed to have climbed a mountain in Tennessee in search of spiritual gifts, particularly the ability to handle poisonous snakes without harm, as mentioned in Mark chapter sixteen. While he was up on that mountain, he encountered a rattlesnake. He knelt beside the snake and prayed aloud for the power to take up the serpent without harm. After he finished his prayer, he leapt upon the snake and grabbed it in his trembling hands. Then, like Moses, he descended from the mountain carrying that snake as proof that God had given him power from on high. With that snake in hand, he started a revival in an effort to put all of the spiritual gifts mentioned in Mark chapter sixteen on display, including the handling of poisonous serpents, and he had been astonishing audiences with his snake-handling revivals ever since.

"You are probably wondering how he died." He leaned forward on the podium and said, "George Hensley died from the bite of a rattlesnake." He paused and looked out over the congregation. "What can we learn from this? Let us read from Mark chapter sixteen."

Pastor Tabor opened the big Bible on the podium and rustled through the pages. "Mark chapter sixteen reads, 'And these signs shall follow them that believe; In my name shall they cast out devils; they shall speak with new tongues; They shall take up serpents; and if they drink any deadly thing, it shall not hurt them: they shall lay hands on the sick, and they shall recover.'"

He raised a finger to heaven and continued, "God will not be mocked in such things. Gifts of the Spirit should never be sought after for personal aggrandizement and cannot be used like circus acts to woo the crowd for show and entertainment. These gifts are rare and should be accepted with reverent heart and exercised with great discretion and wisdom."

From the corner of my eye I saw Daddy shuffle in his seat. I guess he was still awake and listening. Leck bumped my foot with his closest crutch. When I looked at him, he kept his eyes on Pastor Tabor and nodded piously. Mama reached over and patted my hand.

If I hadn't known better, I would have thought that Leck had told Pastor Tabor about me healing Rusty. It was like the sermon was directed at me, but for the life of me I didn't know how the pastor would know about my gift or why he would direct his sermon at me. The chapel felt hot and stuffy all of a sudden, and I shifted in my seat.

Now, I knew that I was a little angry with God because of Rusty. If my gift was from God, I wanted to know why it didn't work all the time. I started figuring that if God knew that I was angry, and he wanted to send me a message, all he had to do was put a thought in Pastor Tabor's head to give the sermon he was delivering right now. Was God trying to tell me something? I guess since God knows everything you don't have to tell him that you're angry with him. He already knows. You can't hide being angry with God.

Since I was wondering if God had inspired Pastor Tabor to give this sermon as a message to me, I decided I'd better pay attention. I sat up straight, put on an attentive face, and listened to the words being delivered from the pulpit as if they were a personal message from God.

Pastor Tabor continued. "Some would even argue that these gifts ended with the Apostles and were only necessary for the early Christians because they lived in times of persecution. That is an easy argument to make since we do not live in an age of miracles like the early Christians. Miracles are not as commonplace in our day as they were in theirs.

"How do we know if a gift is from God? We read in Acts chapter 19," he turned the parchment pages of the large Bible in front of him, "that God wrought many special miracles by the hand of Paul, who was converted on the road to Damascus. Paul healed the sick, spoke with tongues, and cast out devils. Once a young man fell asleep during one of Paul's long sermons and fell from the loft to his death. Maybe that's why we don't have a balcony in our church." He paused as several folks in the congregation laughed at his humor, Leck included.

"Paul even raised that young man from the dead. Truly, Paul was a holy man filled with the power of God and capable of performing mighty miracles. But we learn from the same chapter that not everybody that performs miracles is filled with the power of God. Apparently a certain Jew named Sceva had seven sons who went about casting out devils in the name of Christ. Now being Jews, they had no Christian authority. They were not ordained ministers of the Christian work. They had not even been baptized, yet they went about invoking the name of Christ. They even went so far as to clarify their lack of authority to the devils they cast out by adding the phrase 'Christ that Paul preacheth.' In other words they were charlatans, copycats, and fakes."

By now small beads of sweat had started to form on my forehead. I slipped off my tie and unbuttoned the top button of my shirt trying to cool off. Daddy gave me a stern glance. Leck sat there with a smirk on his face. Mama looked straight ahead. The skin of her face was tight, like all the muscles in her face were tense. I tried to get comfortable on the hard pew, but it felt like I was sitting on a burning log.

"What became of these Jewish imposters? One night they entered a house to cast an evil spirit out of a man. They probably burned some incense or repeated some ancient incantation. Maybe they even quoted some scripture from the Old Testament in their ritual. When they attempted to cast out the evil spirit in the name of Christ, whom Paul preacheth, guess what happened? That evil spirit spoke to them!" He pounded the pulpit, and Mrs. Talbot, who was still sitting at the organ, jumped. Several old ladies in the crowd gasped.

He raised his finger and continued in a loud voice, "And here's what that evil spirit said: 'Jesus I know, and Paul I know; but who are ye?'" He paused, then leaned forward over the pulpit and shouted, "But who are ye?"

I jumped in my seat like a hot coal had suddenly burned through my trousers and made contact with my skin. Leck suppressed a chuckle by pretending to cough. Pastor Tabor continued, his voice and cadence rising. "We see that even the evil spirits recognize an imposter when they see one. Even those possessed have the ability to discern between those with true Christian authority and a circus act. What did that evil spirit do? It tore into those copycat Jews and overcame them. It ripped their clothes from their bodies and cast them out of the house naked and beaten. Why?" He shook his finger at the congregation and proclaimed, "Because they had no Christian authority! They were usurpers of spiritual power destined to be stripped of their status among men. Brothers and sisters, beware of such imposters. Beware of those claiming to have spiritual gifts. Beware of the George Hensleys of the world that would make a mockery of the gifts of the Spirit by putting them on public display like some carnival sideshow."

Pastor Tabor gripped the pulpit with both hands and lowered his voice. "Look to those who have been properly educated, ordained, and endorsed by the church to understand and exercise those special gifts. Do not be fooled by wolves in sheep's clothing, even if they profess to perform miracles."

He closed his sermon with a scripture reading from Corinthians about love and turned the service over to the choir. While the choir filled the air with singing praises, I sat there wondering where this left me. If I had somehow performed some sort of miracle yesterday, I didn't know how, or if, I could ever repeat it. I certainly wasn't ordained or educated, and I didn't want to end up naked on the street at the hands of some evil spirit. I arrived at church a little angry at God and hoping for enlightenment. After Pastor Tabor's sermon I still didn't have any answers. I still didn't understand, but now I was scared to even bring it up to anyone who I thought might be able to answer my questions. To top it all off, I was having dinner at his house tonight.

I sat through the rest of the service trying to cool off. The choir sang. They passed the plate. Pastor Tabor invited people down to the altar. I stared at the big wooden cross behind the pulpit and thought about Rusty. After the services I buttoned my shirt, clipped back on my tie, and started to Sunday School out of habit.

"Ada, Leck, Stone," said Daddy with a scowl on his face. "Let's go home." None of us argued. We exited the chapel, piled into the car, and headed back to the farm. The ride home was quiet except for the hum of the big Buick engine. Mama made one comment about the hay in the river bottom along the road needing to be cut, and Daddy just grunted. Leck sat there looking like the cat that ate the canary. I just stuck my arm out the back window and played with the wind as Daddy drove us home. He pulled up in front of the house and shut down the car. Before anyone could get out, he said, "Now y'all understand why we can't talk about what happened with Rusty yesterday."

Mama responded, "Now, Billy, Pastor Tabor wasn't referring to Stone. He was talking about those Pentecostal snake handlers down in Tennessee."

"Ada, I've seen good men's reputations get trashed because they looked like a threat to somebody's authority. Don't you remember what happened to my cousin Jerry when he ran for the school board? His opponent spread a lie about him, and he lost the election. He was so embarrassed that he had to move over to Simpson County and start over."

"Stone isn't a threat to anyone," answered Mama. "He's just a young man."

"A young man with an unusual gift that will make some folks uncomfortable," said Daddy. "Didn't you hear the way Pastor Tabor went on?"

I was tired of them talking about me like I wasn't there. "Look," I interrupted, "maybe you're making a fuss over nothing. I only healed Rusty one time and I couldn't heal him the second time. Maybe that was it."

Leck opened his door, pulled himself out of the backseat, and started hobbling toward the house without saying anything. Mama kept her eyes on him as he struggled up the porch stairs and into the house. Nobody spoke.

Finally Daddy broke the silence. "Ada, I know what you're thinking, and I understand why you would want to help Leck, but we have to be very careful." He turned around and faced me. "Don't tell anyone about what happened. Understood?"

I nodded.

That afternoon I got to Ruby's house near the corner of High and Church streets about fifteen minutes after four and found her sitting in the glider on the front porch waiting for me. She was still dressed in her pale blue dress from church and looked as fresh as she did this morning. Her face lit up with a crooked smile as I walked up onto the porch and greeted her, "Hey, Ruby Ruth."

"What?" she said coyly. "No compliments this afternoon?"

I blushed a bit and tried to think of something original, but all I could think of was, "You look nice in that blue dress."

She laughed and said, "So I've heard."

She extended her hand, and I pulled her up and kissed her on the cheek. Her hair still smelled as fragrant as this morning, and I wondered how she could keep it clean for so long. The touch of her skin made my heart beat faster, and I felt my throat tighten. Leck was right; she looked good enough to stop traffic.

She smiled and rolled her eyes. "Fifteen minutes late as usual," she said as she opened the door. "Hope you're hungry. Mother has dinner ready." She yanked on my arm and pulled me in.

I loved walking into Ruby's house every Sunday evening. The house was warm with the smell of a slow-cooked picnic ham, a family tradition at the Tabor house. The air was always stuffy, like Mrs. Tabor was trying to trap the escaping flavor of the food she was cooking by closing all the doors and windows. The moist aroma of fresh biscuits and picnic ham hit me like a wall when I walked through the door, making my mouth water and my stomach growl.

I followed Ruby into the small dining room adjacent to the kitchen. I could see Mrs. Tabor stirring a pot on the stove. Pastor Tabor was sitting at the head of the table reading from his Bible. "Good evening, Stone," he said without looking up from his reading.

"Good evening, sir," I answered. I thought about extending my hand but didn't want to interrupt his reading. I knew better than to sit at his table without an invitation, so I just stood there with my mouth watering. The air was so thick with the dinner aroma, I was gaining weight just smelling it.

"Hello, Stone," said Mrs. Tabor as she stopped stirring and moved the pot from the burner. "I hope you don't mind picnic ham again. It's a Sunday tradition."

"No, ma'am. I love ham," I said, hoping my sincerity was obvious.

She smiled as if she was being courteous but didn't believe me. "Phillip, dinner is ready."

Pastor Tabor closed his Bible and motioned for me to sit. Ruby darted into the kitchen and I took a seat at the other end of the table. Ruby and her mother spread the Sunday feast before us and took their seats at the sides of the table. It was the same meal as every Sunday—hot biscuits, corn, green beans, mashed potatoes, gravy, and a medium-size picnic ham with the meat pulling away from the bone.

"Let us pray," said Pastor Tabor as he bowed his head. "Lord, we thank you for these gifts and ask that they may be a bounteous blessing to our bodies and souls. In Jesus' name, amen."

Pastor Tabor cut up the ham as we waited for him to bestow a slice on each of us. First he served Mrs. Tabor, who then began filling her plate with vegetables. Then he carved a slice for Ruby. I passed my plate down and he carved a thick slice for me. While I dished up some vegetables, he carved a slice for himself and filled his plate last. We all waited with our plates full until he took his first bite before beginning our own meal. The Sunday dinner scene unfolded the same way every week, like a religious ritual.

"Stone, what did you think of today's sermon?" asked Pastor Tabor between bites.

I took a bite and chewed slowly, deciding how much to say. I swallowed and said, "It was interesting." Trying to change the subject, I asked, "Have you ever seen anyone handle snakes at church?"

Pastor Tabor sat back in his chair and cleared his throat. "Snakes have no place in a true house of worship." With that, he nonchalantly cut another bite of ham as if the whole matter was settled.

I'm not one to question people in authority too much, but after the day I'd had yesterday, that answer just wasn't good enough. He hadn't even told me if he had ever seen anybody handling snakes. I stared down at my plate of half-eaten food, breathed out through my nose to try and stay calm, and decided to ask again. I mustered as much respect as I could and repeated the question. "Yes, sir, I understand how you feel about snake handling as a matter of doctrine, but have you ever seen anyone handle snakes at a worship service?"

I kept my head down, not wanting to be disrespectful of their hospitality. After all, they had been feeding me Sunday dinner ever since I started going steady with Ruby, almost three months now. Mama taught me to show proper respect in another man's home, but I wanted, and needed, some answers from God, and Pastor Tabor was the closest thing to him right now. I could feel Ruby's eyes on me when I asked the question again.

Pastor Tabor straightened himself and sat tall in his chair, but he still wasn't as tall as me and had to look up to me. "Actually, I watched George Hensley himself handle a large rattlesnake at a tent revival down in Tennessee years ago."

I looked up in surprise, and when I glanced at Ruby, she looked surprised also. "What was it like?" I asked.

"It was a big week-long revival down in Cookeville, Tennessee. Must have been twenty years ago. They started the revival by singing several songs back to back, each song louder and more jubilant than the first. The whole crowd seemed energized with electricity. Then 'The Reverend George Hensley,'" he said with a feigned respect, "preached for a while to shouts of hallelujah and

38

praise." He chuckled and shook his head. "He had the believers jumping to their feet."

I sat mesmerized at the story, not sure if I should feel the same cynical disbelief as Pastor Tabor obviously did, or a longing to see the same scene in person. I glanced at Ruby. She had stopped eating her food as well, her eyes glued to her father.

"Well, at the end of the preaching, he called up anyone that needed to be healed. Several people came up—a man on crutches, a woman with a patch over her eye, a few people carried up sick children in their arms. The reverend anointed them with oil, laid his hands on their heads, and with a loud shout pronounced them healed. At that point I was beginning to let go of my disbelief.

"After that they started the singing again, and I joined in. With the crowd jumping and singing, they brought several boxes and set them on the stage. The Reverend George Hensley danced his way over to one of the boxes, opened it up, and pulled out a large rattlesnake. Then some other people came out on stage and pulled more snakes out of the boxes. They sang and danced to the music with the snakes slithering up and down their arms. They even invited people out of the crowd to come up and handle the snakes." He stopped and took a bite of his food as if he was finished.

"What happened after that?" asked Ruby. I was glad she was as interested as me in the outcome of the story.

"Well," he began, "at first I was mesmerized and captivated, just like the rest of the crowd, but then one of those snakes must have lost the spirit and decided to bite a young woman that had come up from the congregation. It bit her right here near the elbow," he said as he pointed with his fork. "She screamed and ran out of the tent while everybody else just kept right on handling the snakes." He scooped a big bite of mashed potatoes and shoved them into his mouth.

"Phillip, don't keep these young people waiting," said Mrs. Tabor as she sliced up her piece of ham. "Finish the story."

"Yes," insisted Ruby. "What happened to the poor woman?"

Pastor Tabor pointed to Ruby Ruth with his fork and said, "She died."

"She died?" asked Ruby and I at the same time.

"If they had the power to heal, why didn't they just heal her?" I asked.

"That's what I thought," he replied. "Right then I began to see through their charade. It was all a circus act, not the power of God." He went back to eating his dinner.

"Daddy, why didn't you tell me that story before?"

"The topic never came up before."

"Well, why did you talk about it in church today?"

"I saw a flyer over in the drugstore advertising the coming of a tent revival this week. It specifically mentioned snake handling and healing the sick."

I went back to eating my dinner, but my thoughts were on the revival. I wondered if there was someone like me at the revival—someone who had a gift for healing. If there was someone, maybe they would know how to use their gift and probably understand why it didn't work all the time. I know that Pastor Tabor had told the story in an attempt to keep us from going to the revival, but it had the opposite effect on me—I needed to go.

"How's the basketball team going to be this year?" asked Pastor Tabor as he polished off his food.

I nodded and said, "Pretty good. We've already been practicing with Deputy Russel's help."

"Is it true that Cortis led the team to the state finals when he was in high school?"

"Yes, sir, and we all look up to him as a coach because of it."

"Well, he and his wife, Shirley Mae, are very generous as well. We're lucky to have them in our congregation."

"I overheard that he's going to be running for sheriff next election," said Mrs. Tabor.

"Well, he'll certainly get my vote if he does," said Pastor Tabor.

We all nodded agreement as we finished cleaning our plates. After dinner Ruby and I did the dishes and cleaned the kitchen for her mother like we always did. We usually talked a lot, but this Sunday we were both quiet. I'm not sure what she was thinking, but my mind was stuck on the thought that somebody else might have a gift like mine and be able to help me. After we finished cleaning, we went back out on the front porch and sat in the glider. Her parents were just inside the front door reading in the living room. At first we just glided back and forth and held hands without saying much. Then Ruby asked me in a whisper, "I wonder what it would be like to see someone handle a real live rattlesnake?"

I looked at her a little surprised and answered quietly, "I know I wouldn't want to do it. I've killed a bunch of copperheads while mowing hay in the river bottom." I thought about Rusty, and even though Daddy had made me promise not to tell anyone, I had to tell Ruby. "A copperhead bit Rusty in the neck yesterday and killed him."

Ruby looked over at me in shock. "Rusty's dead?" I nodded my head. "Why didn't you say anything?"

I shrugged. "I didn't really have the chance until now." That wasn't entirely true. I had passed several chances, but my mind was preoccupied with Pastor Tabor's sermon and the coming tent revival.

"Oh, Stone, I'm so sorry," she said as she put her arm around me. "Do you want to talk about it?"

I looked through the front window of the house and saw Pastor Tabor rocking back and forth in his rocking chair with the Bible in his lap. "Do you think we could go for a drive?" I asked. I knew that if I asked her father, he would say no. But she had a way of sweet-talking her father and getting her way.

A few minutes later we were driving up to Big Hill in the Buick with the windows rolled down. The road wound up the side of the bluff overlooking the town and took us to the parking lot beside the Alpine Motel. From the motel parking lot, we could see the entire town, the river, and almost all the way to Neely's Ferry. I pulled up under a shade tree and turned off the car. It was pretty quiet this afternoon with only one visiting family out taking in the view. Ruby kicked off her shoes and stretched out across the big front seat with her head on my lap and her feet sticking out the window. Her pale blue dress had slipped down her legs a bit, exposing her knees.

"So, what happened to Rusty?" she asked as she looked up at me with eyes the color of chocolate.

I looked out over the valley and remembered Daddy's warning. I looked down at her eager face, and the smell of her hair drifted up and melted my defenses. "You promise not to tell anybody?" I asked.

"Cross my heart and hope to die," she said, drawing a quick cross with her finger on the left side of her chest.

"Especially your father," I added.

She rolled her eyes. "I only tell my father what he wants to hear. It's easier that way." She reached her hand up and stroked my cheek. "Now tell me this big secret of yours."

I spent the next several minutes recounting the unusual events of the day before. I didn't leave anything out. I talked about cutting off Rusty's paws with the mowing machine, the tiny electric storm in my head when I healed him, the blindness, and how he saved my life by distracting the copperhead snake. When I started the story, she was lying down, but by the time I finished she was sitting up in the seat with her legs crossed in front of her, staring at me with her mouth open.

"So you can imagine how I felt during your father's sermon this morning," I said with a sigh.

"Do you think you could do it again?" she asked. "I mean, heal somebody?"

I thought about Mama's request for me to at least think about healing Leck. "I don't have any idea." I looked out over the valley. "I think I'm going to go to that tent revival your father mentioned and see if somebody there might have the same gift. Maybe they could help me."

"You think it was just a onetime thing?"

I shrugged and shook my head. "It's just so bizarre I don't know what to think." I looked her straight in the eye. "Don't tell anybody. My daddy would skin me alive if he knew I was talking to you about this."

She giggled like a little girl that had just learned her best friend's deepest, darkest fear and relished in it. "Sounds like our fathers are a lot alike." She stretched herself out on the front seat again with her feet out the window and her head in my lap with hair soft as corn silk falling against my legs. "Do you think it's from God?"

she asked. Her chocolate eyes sparkled with excitement.

"I don't know, but if it isn't, why did the words from that scripture keep playing over and over again in my head? It was weird." I stroked her hair and with her touch found my worries being clouded by my desires. She must have noticed the change in my face because she grabbed the back of my neck and pulled me down into a long wet kiss.

We had kissed several times before, but they were usually courteous pecks on the lips or cheek. Once or twice, when we weren't being chaperoned by her father or mother, the kisses had been charged with a little more energy, but it always felt like we were both holding back, keeping ourselves from journeying down forbidden paths. We held nothing back in this kiss. The power of the shared secret deepened the bond between us, and I felt desire run through me. I ran my fingers through her hair and grabbed her behind the head, trying to press her closer, as if that were possible. She responded to me with a hunger that I could feel through her supple lips. For a moment the desire overcame us, and all the emotional walls came down, but it was only for a moment.

In these parts, it is common for a father to have a candid conversation with a young man that wants to court his daughter. It isn't uncommon for the father to have some sort of firearm in plain view during the sit down. It sends a clear message about consequences to any young man with ill intentions. When I first asked to date Ruby, Pastor Tabor had interviewed me. He had made it crystal clear how much he valued the chastity of his only daughter. He had put the fear of God in me, but I didn't see any guns while he talked. He simply opened up the Bible and read verse after verse about sexual sin and the punishments of hell. He wasn't going to shoot me. That would have been too good for me. He was going to make sure that hell had a nice warm spot for me throughout the eternities.

I think Ruby and I both realized our predicament at the same time. She released my neck and let herself fall back into my lap as she sucked in a sharp breath. I slipped my hand from her silky hair and put both hands on the steering wheel. She giggled again and shivered like she had just heard someone scrape their nails against the chalkboard and liked it. I took a deep breath through my nose and exhaled slowly through my mouth. I didn't want to go to hell, but I could understand how folks would risk it for another bite from the apple of desire.

Off in the distance I could see the water of the Cumberland River meandering through the valley. I thought of all the fish in that river that just lived to eat, swim around, and reproduce. Was there some sort of fish society that restricted them from carrying out their urges or desires? No, I'll bet when they get hungry they just eat. When they get tired I'll bet they just go to sleep. When the mood hits them to have sex, if they have sex, I'll bet they don't try to suppress the desire in the name of some fish-society rule. Right at that moment, I wished I was a fish.

I noticed I was still breathing hard, and Ruby let out another giggle. The sun was getting low in the sky, and I knew I need to get my mind on other things or I, we, might do something regrettable. "I need to go to the cemetery," I said.

Ruby laughed and let out a sigh like she was still thinking about the kiss and knew that my comment was an attempt to keep that train from leaving the station again. She sat up and straightened her hair. She laughed again and cleared her throat as if trying to gain compo-sure. "Okay, why do you need to go to the cemetery?"

"I want to see the headstone where I was found," I said. "I want to see if the scripture running through my head yesterday is the scripture on the headstone."

She smoothed out her dress and gave me a mischie-vous smile. "Well, let's go to the cemetery."

I started the car and headed down the winding road back to Burkesville. The tires whined a little at each turn, and the surging desire seemed to descend at almost the same rate as we descended the hill. By the time we reached the flatland of the valley, I felt in control again, but I knew that a hot coal of passion still burned and would only need a bit of coaxing to make a roaring fire. I focused on get-ting to the cemetery and finding the headstone. I turned left off of Highway 61 and followed the road to the back of the cemetery next to the trees and parked the car.

"Do you know which one?" asked Ruby.

I nodded and got out. She slid across the seat and got out on my side.

"You know, you've never told me the story about how you were found," she said.

I got my bearings and started walking. "You never asked."

"Ezekiel Stone Molony," she said sternly. "Don't play games with me. Tell me what happened."

I forgot how direct Ruby could be. It was a trait I'm sure she picked up from her father. "According to my Mama, Sheriff George Pace was sitting in his squad car one night over there beside the road with his window open and heard a baby crying. He investigated and found me wrapped up and lying on the ground in front of the headstone for Opal Newby." I saw the headstone I used as a marker with the name "McCoy" in big letters and turned down the row. I knew it was about six or seven headstones down.

"Nobody came forward to claim you?"

I stopped in front of the headstone where the sheriff found me. "Nope." I stood and stared at the chiseled letters on the stone hoping for some clue to my past.

Ruby started reading aloud. " 'Opal May Newby, 1876–1938 . . .' What year did they find you? I mean, what year were you born?"

"The sheriff found me the evening of May 16, 1938."

She continued reading, " 'And when I passed by thee and saw thee polluted in thine own blood, I said unto thee when thou wast in thy blood, Live; yea I said unto thee when thou wast in thy blood, Live. Ezekiel 16:6.' " She paused and then asked, "Was that the scripture you were talking about?"

Hearing her read the words sent me back to yesterday—the blood from the wounds, the electricity and heat, the blindness. I just nodded.

"Oh, I get it now," said Ruby as she ran her hand across the top of the headstone. "They named you Ezekiel Stone because of the scripture on the headstone where you were found."

I nodded again. "Mama told me it seemed like a good name for a gift from God." I knelt and pulled back the grass that had grown up around the base of the headstone and revealed another phrase carved into the face of the stone with smaller letters. The words chiseled in the stone caught me by surprise.

" 'May your healing gift continue forever,' " read Ruby.

I ran my fingers over the carved words as if to prove to my mind that they were really there. *May your healing gift continue forever.* I chiseled the words into the flesh of my mind.

THREE

Monday morning I got up at five, like usual, and milked Jersey Girl, but this time I made sure I took care of the calves, pigs, and chickens. I didn't want to eat cold gravy again. By the time I got back to the house, Mama and Leck were setting the table for breakfast. I washed up and sat down at the table, hoping that I could drive into town to see Ruby that afternoon, but Daddy dismissed that hope with one sentence.

Right after he said amen to the grace, he added, "Looks like the hay has cured and is ready to bale." Nobody responded. We all knew what it meant. We would be spending all day baling and putting up hay.

After chores and breakfast, the real work began. I hitched the hay rake to the John Deere tractor and headed down to the field where Rusty had lost his paws to the mowing machine. I set the pitch on the rake, put it in gear, and started whisking the freshly cured hay into nice big windrows for the baler. For the most part it was mindless work: I made pass after monotonous pass along the field focusing on the placement of my front wheel and occasionally looking back to see if the windrows were even. I took advantage of the mindless task and let my thoughts pass back over the last couple of days and gather my thoughts into nice little rows, just like the rake was doing to the hay. I was adopted and didn't know who my biological parents really were. The headstone where I was found mentioned a healing gift. I had used a healing gift to heal Rusty. I didn't have the faintest idea how my gift worked. If I was related to Opal Newby somehow, then somebody in her family might also have, or know, about the gift. By the time I finished raking the hay, I knew what I wanted. I needed to find out more about my past in hopes that I could understand my gift and maybe get answers to all these questions that were suddenly plaguing me.

Daddy started baling the hay as soon I was done raking it. I put away the rake and took a break for lunch before I hooked up the hay wagon and pulled it down to the field. Otis Wilburn and his son Samuel were waiting under a shade tree at the edge of the field.

Before Leck went off to the Korean conflict, putting up the hay was a family affair. Daddy would bale the hay, and Mama would drive the tractor with the wagon. I would toss the bales onto the wagon and Leck would stack them. When we had the wagon loaded, Daddy would stop baling and help us get the hay into the barn. Daddy would throw it from the wagon into the barn loft. I would drag it to Leck, and he would stack again. That meant that I lifted every bale twice, before Leck went to Korea.

While Leck was off to war, and after he came back busted up, Daddy hired Otis and his son to help with the hay and tobacco. It always puzzled me how he got them word that we needed help. We didn't have a telephone yet. If we needed to call someone, we had to drive into town. It wouldn't have done us any good anyway. Most of the colored folks up on Coe Ridge didn't have indoor plumbing yet, let alone a telephone. Yet, when we needed help, they magically appeared. I pulled up beside them with the wagon and shut off the tractor. "Hey Otis, Samuel," I said with a grin. "Glad to see you, fellas." "Afternoon, Missuh Stone," said Otis with a tip of his straw hat. "We knowed you needed the help, and here we are." His voice was deep and rich like it started somewhere in his toes and echoed up through his whole body before it came booming out. Sometimes he would sing when he worked, and you could hear that deep baritone tune a mile away. Samuel, the only son of four left alive, smiled but didn't say anything. Although he was quiet, his smile was always bright, and he could outwork just about anybody I'd ever seen.

Both men were dressed in bib overalls and dusty old work boots. Otis always wore a white T-shirt that needed washing and a straw hat. Samuel was bare chested under his overalls and you could see that he didn't carry any extra weight on his ribs. Samuel never wore a hat. Otis was dark black with a flat nose and a round face, but Samuel took after his mother and was brighter with a sharper nose and a long thin face. Both men were a little bit bigger than Daddy, but I was taller than them both.

"Looks like yo' Daddy's got a head start," said Otis as he pulled out a pair of cotton gloves and put them on. He seemed anxious to get the job going. "We best get this hay in the barn, boys."

I started up the tractor and Otis stepped on the tongue of the wagon, then up on to the wagon bed. He usually stacked the hay on the wagon or drove the tractor. There is a certain knack to stacking bales of hay on a moving wagon. You have to tie the stack together by laying the bales like overlapping bricks in a wall. The trouble is that unlike bricks, the bales are not always uniform and need a little finesse positioning. Of course you don't usually build brick walls on an old wagon bed bouncing up and down as it crisscrosses the field. Otis had a knack for stacking.

I drove the tractor for the first load, and when we got to the barn, I took the hardest job of throwing the bales up into the barn since I was still fresh. It took us an hour and a half to get the first one hundred bales into the barn, and I estimated we had about four hundred more to go. So much for going to see Ruby tonight.

I swapped with Otis and rode on the wagon next to Samuel on the way back to the field.

"Where's Rusty?" asked Samuel.

I spat and said, "He got bit by a copperhead and died."

Samuel nodded and watched the ground pass below our feet as Otis put the tractor in high gear for the return trip to the field. "Dogs don't usually die from that. He must've been bit in the neck," he said without looking at me.

His astuteness surprised me at first, but then I remembered that he was the one who raised hunting dogs up on Coe Ridge. Rusty had come from one of the litters from his kennel. I nodded and answered, "He was protecting me. He attacked the snake and got bit up behind the left ear."

"Shame to lose such a good dog."

Coming from anybody else I might have considered the comment a veiled insult, like it was a shame to lose such a good dog saving the likes of me, but I didn't think Samuel had a mean bone in all of his body. I had heard all the stories about his three brothers and the troubles that seemed to follow them and eventually led to their untimely deaths, but Samuel wasn't anything like that. I never saw anything but quiet smiles, clear-eyed observations, and hard work out of him.

By the time we threw the last bale into the barn loft, it was almost eight o'clock at night. Mama had supper ready for us all. Daddy and I washed most of the hay off and sat down at the kitchen table. Mama had fixed chicken-fried steak smothered with gravy and fresh tomatoes and biscuits on the side. I lit into the food like a starving dog. Leck had already eaten and was sitting on the front porch. Mama must have already eaten too, because she took a couple of heaping plates of food to the back porch for Otis and Samuel and started doing the dishes.

As soon as I was finished eating supper, I headed up to take a shower. It always amazed me how much hay worked itself into the various cavities and crevices of my body. I figured that by the time I was done hauling hay all day I was hauling around at least a half a bale sticking to my skin and hiding itself in my hair, and judging by the green snot coming out of my nose, I had sucked another half bale into my nostrils. I reminded myself that it still wasn't as bad as working in tobacco as I scrubbed, purged, and washed all the hay off, and out, of my body.

I slipped on a clean pair of jeans and a T-shirt and found Leck on the front porch cleaning his M-1 rifle from the war, like he did quite often. In addition to his wounds, he brought back several souvenirs from the war, but his favorite was the rifle. At least once a week, he pulled it out of the storage chest in his room, broke it down, and cleaned as if he had fired several hundred rounds with it that week. He had never fired it once since he came home.

Daddy pulled up in the Ford truck after taking Otis and Samuel down to Neely's Ferry and plopped himself down on the top step with a tired sigh. A couple of cars passed along the road on their way to Burkesville. We all sat there under the porch light looking out into the summer night, nobody willing to break the silence. Finally, out of curiosity, I asked, "Daddy, I thought Coe Ridge was across the new bridge that replaced the free ferry. How come they always go across Neely's Ferry?" Leck chuckled like I had asked a stupid question. Daddy pushed up his hat and said, "Well, we always take the free ferry, or the new bridge now, because the roads are better and it works out in my delivery schedule. If you cross Neely's Ferry and then start hiking along the bluff to the right, you'll be on Coe Ridge. I only take the other way because it's easier on my truck. If you're walking, it's much quicker to take Neely's Ferry."

Leck had finished cleaning and polishing the unused rifle and chimed in, "Ain't you ever noticed that all the Coe niggers always walk down this road when they want to get to Burkesville?"

I knew the colored folks from Coe Ridge came across Neely's Ferry and walked, or hitchhiked, into Burkesville. Occasionally a drunk one would wander up to the house and Daddy would have to turn them around. His comment made me feel stupid and wish I hadn't asked the question, or maybe I wished that Leck wasn't around to answer it. Not wanting to admit anything to Leck, I replied testily, "No, I haven't noticed."

"You been living under a rock?" asked Leck.

"I'll show you tomorrow," interrupted Daddy. "We're delivering feed tomorrow, and Otis's place is on the list." He chuckled and grinned. "He says he needs some shelled corn for his chickens. I didn't know he had so many chickens." Leck laughed with Daddy, but neither of them explained what was so funny. I wasn't in the mood to ask another stupid question, so I hauled myself up to bed.

My sore hands woke me up the next morning. My throbbing fingers were curved into a permanent hook, and I had to practically pry my hands into the normal position. I wiggled and stretched the kinks out of them as I rolled out of bed. By the time I finished milking Jersey Girl, I had worked most of the soreness out of my fingers.

Working on the farm was expected, and Daddy rarely paid me for the hours of backbreaking labor, but he let me use his vehicles, kept me fed and clothed, and gave me a few dollars every now and then if we had a good tobacco crop or sold a few cattle. Delivering feed was different. On an average week, he would pay me five dollars for helping him make deliveries. On a good week, he might double that number. Even though I was sore from hauling hay, I didn't want to miss one of my few chances to earn a buck or two, because it was the only spending money I got.

After breakfast Daddy pulled the big Chevy feed truck around front and hollered for me and Leck. I shadowed Leck down the stairs just in case he needed my help, but he ignored me. When we got to the truck, he tossed his crutches up into the cab and grabbed the door. I waited as he tried to pull himself up into the cab two or three times until I finally just gave him a push. He didn't offer any thanks or even acknowledge my effort. In fact he seemed put out that I had helped. Daddy had the truck in gear by the time I got the door shut.

Daddy backed the truck up to the loading dock at Talbot's Feed and Implement Store and went inside. I got out and climbed up into the back of the flatbed truck while Leck stayed in the cab. It was a 1948 one-ton

Chevy with dual wheels on the back axle. We put short racks on the sides of the bed when we hauled feed, and Daddy loaded it so full it could barely make it up the hills we had to climb, but he wanted to get the most out of his time and effort.

"Well, look what the cat drug in," said a voice from the loading dock.

I turned to see Floyd Talbot standing there looking up at me from beneath the rim of his Dekalb Seed Company cap. We were in the same grade in school and went to church together, and his dad owned the feed store. Except for church, he always wore a cap with some seed company logo pulled so low over his eyes that he had to tilt his head up to see anything. Since I was good head taller than him, he was practically putting a crick in his neck just to look me in the face.

"Hey, Floyd," I answered with a nod.

"Y'all delivering feed today?"

"Yep." Even though we'd been friends since elementary school, our conversations seldom got out of the mundane banter. He always asked questions about the obvious, usually some comment about the weather, and I always answered by stating the obvious.

"Did you see the big tent going up over on Columbia Road?"

"No," I replied. That was something new.

"I guess there's going to be a big tent revival—some Holiness Pentecostal bunch they say." He looked around like he was worried someone was listening. "You reckon you'll go check it out?" he asked, almost sounding like he was referring to some circus peep show.

I shrugged and said, "I reckon I might go." I tried to sound casual. After Pastor Tabor's sermon about snake handlers and faith healers and the conversation over dinner, I wouldn't miss it. The good pastor might not be too happy to know that his sermon didn't drive any of us away from the event; it simply made us want to go even more.

About that time, Daddy came out with an invoice, and we started loading up the truck. He called out from the list and Floyd and one of the hired hands stacked the bags of feed on the loading dock. When they had everything ready in piles next to the truck, Daddy started handing me the bags according to his methodology. He knew the order he wanted to load the bags according to his delivery schedule. I noticed that he put on a bunch of shelled corn at the front of the truck. We would be going to Coe Ridge last.

The springs of the truck groaned as Daddy tossed on the last bag. We were loaded to the gills. I climbed down from the back of the truck, dusted my hands off on my jeans, and wiped my brow with my sleeve before climbing up into the passenger seat. Daddy hit the starter, slipped the truck into gear, and eased out into the street.

We stuck to the lowlands first, with the springs of the truck bottoming out and groaning as we passed over each bump with such a heavy load. We followed Daddy's usual loop and headed out Crocus Creek Road for a couple of quick stops. Then we went to Bakerton and delivered some chicken feed to Old Man Riddle, who raised a bunch of chickens. After that we headed out to the Stearns place on Lawson Bottom road.

Daddy whistled songs and we usually made small talk, except on Lawson Bottom Road. The road a narrow stretch wedged in between the ridgeline and Cumberland River that was only wide enough for one vehicle at a time. When we got to the beginning of that stretch, Daddy stopped whistling and stuck his head out the window. After listening for a moment, he honked his horn a couple of times and then listened again. We didn't hear anything, so he put the truck into first gear and eased along that narrow stretch. Daddy and Leck were staring out the front windshield. I was looking out my window and straight down into the waters of the Cumberland River. No matter how many times we drove this stretch, I always got nervous.

We made our delivery to the Stearns place and passed through that narrow stretch of road again, but this time I was looking at the rocks of the bluff instead of the rushing river. Instead of going straight back into town, we hung a right on Little Renox Creek Road and made a delivery at the Moody place. By now we were over halfway done and the truck was handling a lot easier. The truck bounced on its big springs, but instead of swaying and bobbing down the road, it ran true and even.

We came back into town along Glasgow Road, and sure enough, just like Floyd had told me, they were setting up the tent revival on the right side of the road. The open field just outside of town looked like the circus had invaded it. A gigantic brown tent was being raised smack-dab in the middle of the field with several trucks and vehicles surrounding it. A few men in khakis with white shirts were tightening ropes and unloading trucks. Most of the cars and trucks were lined up on the side of the field closest to town. At the end of the line, closest to the road, was a shiny blue-and-white travel trailer. I had never seen a travel trailer. It looked like a tin can on wheels with a couple of windows and a door.

Daddy slowed down as we drove by. Leck whistled and said, "Well, looky here."

There, in the doorway of the trailer, stood a woman smoking a cigarette. She looked tall against the small door and was dressed in a plaid dress without any sleeves. She had long black hair piled up on top of her head that seemed to fill the top half of the doorway. Daddy almost swerved off the road, and the truck rocked back and forth for a few yards. As we rolled by, I swear she looked me straight in the eye.

We stopped and grabbed a sandwich at the Houchen's market across from the hardware store, and headed across the new bridge for Coe Ridge. The Coe Colony was started by Ezekiel and Patsy Coe after the slaves were set free at the end of the Civil War. It was a rough wooded area of about three hundred acres of land, but not a whole lot of it worth farming. The Coes and their kin had eked out a living from logging, farming, and, lately, moonshining. I heard lots of nicknames for it around town—Nigger Ridge, Coe Tribe, or Zeke Town, after Ezekiel Coe. I had even been teased at school a couple of times myself for being named after Ezekiel Coe. That's when I started insisting that folks call me by my middle name, Stone.

We headed through the square and hung a left down Albany Road and over the new bridge across the river. As we crossed, Leck said, "This is the Cumberland River, and if you fell in right now, you could float downstream to our farm." Daddy chuckled. I didn't say anything and tried to ignore his dig.

We turned down Modoc Road and made a stop at the Guthrie place. We sold everything except the shelled corn, some calf supplement, and a couple of bags of dog food. "Next stop, Zeke Town," said Daddy as I climbed back in.

We hurried down the winding country road with Daddy whistling a Hank Williams tune and Leck tapping his foot to keep time. I stuck my hand out the window and played with the passing breeze. After several twists and turns, Daddy downshifted and turned on to Zeke Town Road. It was more like a washboarded and pitted dirt lane, hardly capable of passing as a road. Daddy put the Chevy in second gear to negotiate the ruts and crannies and gullies of the trail and we started uphill. We came into a small clearing as we reached the top of the hill, and Daddy stopped the truck.

"If you look through that tree line over yonder, you can barely make out our farm," said Daddy, pointing out my window. I looked and caught a glimpse of the river and the field where I had healed Rusty.

Before Daddy started the truck and put it back in gear, we heard somebody holler from the woods up ahead and off to our left. "Fiiire in the hoooole!" It sounded almost like a yodel, and you could hear it echo down some of the hollers. After the first cry, we heard someone repeat it off in the distance. They were sending out the warning that a stranger was on the ridge. When you're in the moonshine business, you need to be on the lookout for the Revenue Man.

Daddy shook his head. "You'd think as much as I come up to Zeke Town that they'd learn to recognize my truck." He put the truck in gear and started easing down the sorry excuse for a road.

Directly we passed a small unpainted clapboard house on the left. All the houses looked the same up there—pitiful one- or two-bedroom shanties with rusty tin roofs, a small raised porch, and a cook shed off the side. When we passed the first one, a couple of barefoot kids stood looking at us from the barren dirt in front of the shack. A couple of dogs jumped up and came barking after us. Up on the porch a colored man sat with his feet propped up on the railing. He was smiling and his pearly white teeth popped against his shiny black skin. He tipped his straw hat as we passed. Daddy waved.

We continued on the dirt road, dodging holes and passing by similar scenes of dilapidated structures posing as houses. Several of them were abandoned. Any vehicles in sight were old, decrepit junk heaps that looked like they could barely run. Everyone seemed to stop whatever they were doing and came to watch us pass by like we were a parade traveling through the community. People waved and watched. Dogs chased us until they got tired. In spite of the smiles, hat tipping, and waves, I always got the impression that everyone seemed leery of our intrusion. I never noticed that feeling when I came up here with Daddy as a kid, but as I got older I could sense the underlying distrust and hesitancy that hung over this isolated community. It made me uneasy.

We forded a small creek and headed up the hill to Otis Wilburn's place, and when we pulled up, I saw Samuel playing in front of the house with a German shorthair about the color of muddy water. I immediately thought about Rusty and let out a sigh. Samuel looked up, grinning from ear to ear like he knew we were coming before we got there. I waved at him as we pulled up and glanced up at the porch, looking for Otis or his wife Patsy Ann. I didn't see either of them on the porch, but what I did see took my breath away.

At the top of the rickety wooden stairs of the porch stood a tall young woman, barefoot and wearing a white cotton dress. Her skin was the color of clover honey in a glass bottle and she had her long wiry black hair pulled back away from her face. The dress fit her loosely, almost like it was too big for her slender figure, and one of the straps of her dress had slipped down on her arm, exposing the soft curves of her shoulder and hinting at the inviting curves of her chest. Her eyes were dark, burning lumps of coal in a cool, sharp-featured face. In spite of her bare feet and simple clothing, she had an intoxicating air of confidence that could be felt several yards away.

"Wonnie?" I half whispered.

Leck clicked his tongue and said, "Well, looky here," for the second time today.

Daddy didn't look up until he had parked the truck, but when he did look up at the porch, he was quiet for a moment. Then he cleared his throat like he was trying to clear his mind and hollered at Samuel, "Hey, Samuel, where's Otis?"

Samuel ran over and stepped up onto the running board of the truck. "He'll be long d'rectly," he said. "Y'all wanna pull the truck down to the barn, and I'll unload it?"

"Is that Wonnie?" I asked, unable to hide the surprise in my voice.

Samuel's grin got a little bigger. "She don't look like the little girl you used to play hide-and-seek with no more, does she?"

I blushed a bit. "When did she get back?"

"She caught the Greyhound bus up from Birmingham three or four days ago. You oughta go say hi." Then he winked. "Maybe y'all can play a game of hide-and-seek, or go swing on the rope."

Leck laughed at Samuel's comment. Daddy hit the starter on the truck, but before he could put it into gear, I had opened up the door and slipped out. When the truck cleared, Wonnie was still standing on the porch, looking like some hillbilly goddess waiting for her worshippers to pay alms at her bare feet. I was surprised at how eager I was to approach her altar and be saved myself. I felt myself drawn to her raw beauty and sensuality that bubbled up like a spring of fresh water. I had never looked on a colored girl that way, and the feeling struck me dumb like Zacharias when he saw the angel in the temple. I shuffled forward like a sinner during an altar call.

Wonnie looked up at me, puzzled at first, but then her face lit up and she jumped off the porch in one bound and came running toward me. "Zekie!" she said as she got close, and then she wrapped her arms around me in a spontaneous hug.

At first I was stiff as a board with my arms almost afraid to embrace the goddess from the porch, but I managed to fling my arms loosely around her shoulders. She had left around the time I got Rusty, and at that time, we were almost the same height. I was taller than her now, and the top of her head fit neatly under my chin as she continued to embrace me so tight that I felt every curve under that soft cotton dress.

"Wonnie," I said almost as a question. "You've grown up since I saw you last."

She let me go and stepped back. "And what about you? When I left, we were almost the same height. Now I have to crane my neck just to look in your face." She laughed, the same way she laughed when I would find her during hide-and-seek all those years ago. She turned and started walking back toward the house. Looking over her shoulder, she said, "Come sit down on the porch. You know the men are going to visit a bit down at the barn."

I understood what she meant by visit. More than likely after they unloaded the corn, Otis would pull a bottle out of his hiding place and they would all have a sip of home-brewed corn whiskey while they talked about current events. Daddy had yet to invite me to participate. He said it was best if I was a bit older before I tried any white lightning. Right about now I was more than content to be sitting on the porch talking to Wonnie.

Wonnie leaned up against the house and looked down at me. One of the straps from her dress had slipped down again. "So tell me, Zekie, what have you been doing while I was away?"

"Just going to school and helping Daddy on the farm," I said as I sat on the top step of the porch. I could hear her mother, Patsy Ann, working in the kitchen through the screen door of the shack.

Wonnie stood a little taller and said, "I graduated from Booker T. Washington High School last week. The first in my family to graduate from high school."

"Congratulations," I offered sincerely. They only had a one-room schoolhouse up on Coe Ridge, and most of the folks were lucky if they knew how to read and write at all. The nearest colored high school was two hours away in Bowling Green. If a family from Coe Ridge wanted their son or daughter to graduate from high school, they had to send them to live with a family member or a friend. After the tragic passing of three of her older brothers, Otis and Patsy Ann sent Wonnie away to Birmingham to live with a cousin and go to high school.

"So what you gonna do now?" I asked.

"I want to go up to Indianapolis and get a job, but Mama doesn't want me to go." Her eyes looked off into the woods like she was trying to see Indianapolis. "There's nothing for me here," she said with a sigh. "Except my old friend Zekie." She nudged my shoulder with her foot when she said my nickname.

I picked up a stick and began carving at the dirt beside the stairs. "Nobody calls me Zeke anymore. I go by Stone now."

"Why did you change?"

"Because . . . well," I stammered, not wanting to tell her the real reason, "I just like Stone better than Zeke. It sounds more manly."

She laughed. "And as tall as you are, you certainly look more like a man."

I blushed. "I guess we both have changed a lot since we were kids."

"We sure have, and it's time some other things started changing as well."

"What do you mean?"

She sat down across from me, and I noticed her dark eyes had become eager. "Things are changing for the colored folks these days. Folks down in Birmingham and Montgomery are saying it's time for more things to change."

At that point of my life, I had never given much thought to the way things were. Coloreds and whites had their separate lives that ran parallel to each other like the strands of wire in a fence. Whites lived alongside blacks in segregated communities, interacting as necessary, but usually only in the way the law, or society, dictated. Like the wires in a fence, I had never questioned why it was built that way. I simply accepted it as it was. Wonnie was about to change all that.

I looked up at her and could see that her face had hardened, and her eyes were black embers. "What kind of changes?" I asked.

"We're getting tired of being treated like second-class citizens in this country. Why can't I sit anywhere I want in the theater? Why can't I drink at the 'white' water fountain down at the square in Burkesville? Why do I have to sit in the back of the bus? Why can't I go to the same church as you?" She paused and looked at me through narrow eyes waiting for an answer. I looked down and carved at the dirt.

"You know why," she said, sounding like Mama when she was scolding me. "It's simply because of the color of my skin." She slid over beside me and stuck her arm next to mine. "See, Zekie. Your skin's a few shades whiter than mine, and that means you can sit down front in the theater, drink from the water fountain, and sit in the front of the bus. Does that seem right to you?"

I tossed the stick out into the yard and looked at Wonnie's face. I saw the face of a ten-year old girl again, vulnerable and idealistic—the face of someone who still believes that they can do anything in life. "No, Wonnie, it doesn't seem right to me," I answered softly.

She looked back at me as if she was looking for some proof of my statement, and then her face broke into a big grin. "One of these days real soon, I'm going to march into Burkesville and drink from the white water fountain and sit in the white section of the theater. You watch, Zekie. Things are going to change around here."

The Chevy truck roared to life down at the barn, and I stood as if the sound was my cue to leave. I looked back at Wonnie. She rested her face in her long thin fingers and her elbows on her knees. Her knees were pressed together with her bare feet splayed apart like the legs of a frog. Her face was soft again, and the contrast of the white cotton dress against her honey dark skin made her look like some colored angel that had been cast down to earth.

Daddy stopped the truck up in front of the house and shut it down. Otis and Samuel, who had ridden up from the barn on the back of the flat bed, slid off. I started to say my good-byes when Patsy Ann came out through the screen door backward and then spun around with a basket of hot corn bread and a jar of honey in her hands. "Y'all cain't go away hungry," she said, offering up the fresh corn bread.

Daddy hopped out of the truck and came around toward the porch. He opened the passenger door, but Leck elected to stay in the truck. I went and leaned up against the passenger fender.

Patsy Ann went around offering the basket of eats with smiles and nods like it was her place to please everyone. She served Daddy first. Then she climbed up on the running board of the truck and offered some to Leck. Next, she came to me and almost bowed her head as she held out the basket like an offering. After that she went to Otis, but without the deferential nods or exuberant smiles, just a simple offering of food to her husband. Then she held the basket for Samuel and Wonnie at the same time.

I watched the scene like an observer from far away, like some professor of anthropology studying the habits of the Coe Tribe in the dark recesses of Africa. I knew that Patsy Ann had behaved out of courtesy to guests, but it was more than that. She treated us like we were better than her. I realized that I called her by her name, not Mrs. Wilburn. Why did I do that when I wouldn't dare call a white woman of the same age by their name? Why did she feel obliged to feed us like some visiting dignitaries? The scales were falling from my eyes, and it gave the corn bread a hint of guilt and shame, but I choked it down.

I was quiet as we started back. Daddy focused on the road and whistled. Leck joined in, filling the cab with the smell of moonshine. I could tell he had tipped the bottle a bit more than usual. As we turned onto the asphalt road and headed for home, I interrupted their whistling duet and asked, "Daddy, why don't we have any colored members in our congregation at church? Is there some sort of law against it?"

Daddy stopped his whistling and cleared his throat like he always did when he was thinking. "No, ain't no law against it, but they have their own churches."

"What would you do if a colored family came to church this Sunday?" I asked.

Daddy cleared his throat again and shifted in his seat. "Well, I reckon I would welcome them like any other new family, as long as they don't sit in my spot," he said with a smile, trying to make light of the question, but I could see that he was nervous.

"What would you do if a colored person sat beside you in the theater or on the bus?"

Daddy cleared his throat again, but he didn't answer. He opened his mouth, but nothing came out, and he stared straight ahead at the winding road.

Leck intervened. "What did you and that nigger girl talk about while we was down at the barn?"

I had heard that word all my life and never felt it to be derogatory until that moment. "That colored girl has a name—Wonnie," I spat back.

"Okay, what did you and Wonnie," he drew out her name with alcohol-filled breath, "talk about?"

"She says the colored folks in Birmingham are itching for change," I answered. "She said they're tired of being second-class citizens just because of the color of their skin."

"Aw, heck," said Leck. "They've been living that way for hundreds of years. Ain't nothing gonna change."

"Wonnie aims to change things around here too," I stated, proud of taking her side, yet naïve to the cost of that stance. "She says she's going to drink from the white water fountain down on the square and sit in the white section of the theater."

We topped a rise in the road, and the Cumberland River and Neely's Ferry came into view. "You think she's going to make a difference? You think she's going to change things?" mocked Leck. "She might as well try to stick out her hand and stop the Cumberland River. It may seem like a courageous act at first, but in the end she's just gonna get washed away like driftwood."

We were all quiet as Daddy paid the toll and drove up onto the ferry. When he turned off the truck, Daddy looked out over the passing water and said, "She can't stop the river by herself, but the river can be stopped. You get enough men working together and they can dam that river, even control it. It took a lot of hard working men and the power of the government behind the project, but they dammed the Cumberland River. It can be done."

Leck fidgeted in his seat like he wanted to respond, but he didn't say anything. Feeling a little bolder, I asked, "Do you think colored people get treated like second-class citizens?"

Daddy pushed back his hat and looked out the window. "Yeah, of course they do, but I try to treat them fairly."

"If you think Wonnie is right, why don't you help her change things?" I asked.

He let out a sigh and rubbed his chin. "Stone, do you remember when they finished Wolf Creek Dam a few years ago?"

I nodded.

"Remember all those folks that came up out of Burnside and passed through Burkesville?"

I did remember the parade of old trucks filled with destitute dirt farmers and their families displaced by the swelling river. One of the trucks stopped by the house. The father left the old truck piled high with his family's possessions, and while several of his kids looked anxiously on, he came to the porch with his hat in hand. I remember how his hollow, sunken eyes looked devoid of hope when he asked for food. "Yeah, I remember," I said.

"You can dam that river," said Daddy, "and in the process control flooding, generate electricity, and hold fresh water in reserve for times of drought. But when you dam a river like that, it also wreaks havoc on the lives of some folks. Even though it was better for all of us, some folks got hurt in the process." He started up the truck and eased off the ferry, and we headed up the road for home.

FOUR

Friday night Ruby and I grabbed a booth at the Walgreens for a soda before we walked over to the Webb Theater on the north side of the square. We bought our tickets for *Creature from the Black Lagoon* and settled into some good seats near the end of the row in the middle of the theater. I was holding Ruby's hand and waiting for the show to start when Wonnie plopped herself down beside me.

"Hello, Zekie," said Wonnie. She had cleaned up and was wearing a plaid dress with black shoes. My mouth fell open, and before I could get my tongue untied, she reached her hand across to Ruby and said, "Hello, I'm Wonnie Wilburn. What's your name?"

Ruby graciously shook Wonnie's hand and smiled. "My name is Ruby Tabor. Pleasure to meet you." She gave me a curious glance. "Are you a friend of Stone's?"

A big white smile flashed across Wonnie's face as she pulled her hands back into her lap. "Stone," she said with perfect diction, "and I have known each other since we were children."

Ruby gave me another curious look. I felt the temperature climb at least twenty degrees in the theater. "My daddy has been hauling feed to her family up in Zeke Town since before I was born," I said.

70

"Oh, I see," said Ruby like she was talking to someone coming through the front door of the church—a polite and endearing façade.

I leaned over to Wonnie and lowered my voice, "Wonnie, you shouldn't be here. You're just gonna cause a ruckus."

Wonnie feigned a shocked look and said, "Et tu, Brute?"

I gave her a puzzled look. "Huh?"

Ruby laughed and leaned forward so she could see Wonnie. "I'm afraid Shakespeare is lost on your Zekie. Where did you go to school?"

Wonnie's face beamed and she said, "I graduated from Booker T. Washington High School in Birmingham, Alabama, just last week, with honors."

I could hear the whispers and hushed voices in the audience growing. Wonnie's presence in the white section was getting attention. I shifted uncomfortably in my seat, thinking of excusing myself and going to the bathroom. Instead I was caught between Ruby and Wonnie like a runner in a hot box at a baseball game.

"Well, you're a year ahead of me," said Ruby. "I just finished my junior year." She folded her hands together and rested her chin on them. "What's it like to live in a big city like Birmingham?"

Out of the corner of my eye, I saw Jed Mock with his pathetic attempt at a mustache on his upper lip pointing us out to the usher, Jimmy Lee Farmer. The whispers and hushed voices grew louder as both of them stared at us. Ruby and Wonnie were carrying on talking about the finer points of life in Birmingham as if they were at some dinner on the ground at church. As Jimmy Lee headed our way, I could sense the gathering storm and remembered Leck's words about getting washed away like driftwood by the Cumberland River.

The whole place got eerily quiet as Jimmy Lee stopped at the end of the row beside Wonnie. She pretended not to look up and kept chattering on about the tall buildings of downtown Birmingham.

Jimmy Lee cleared his throat and said, "This section is for whites only."

I sank into my seat with my tongue stuck to the roof of my mouth. Wonnie looked up at him and smiled. "I paid as much for my ticket as everyone else. Why can't I sit wherever I please?" she asked politely.

Jimmy's mouth dropped open, and he tried to speak, but it was like her question had knocked the wind out of him. As he was catching his breath, Ruby chimed in. "Now, Jimmy Lee Farmer, just go show the movie. When you dim the lights, nobody will even know she's here."

I stared wide-eyed at Ruby and felt my cheeks flush with embarrassment, but I wasn't sure if I was embarrassed about what was happening or my reaction to it. We were all frozen for a moment, and I was beginning to feel like that piece of driftwood still clinging to the shore as the river rises.

Jed Mock stood up with an unlit cigarette hanging from his mouth. "You don't belong down here," he shouted. "Git up there with your own kind!" He flung his arm wildly like he could somehow cast her up into the balcony with the flick of his wrist, like she was a piece of trash. The murmurs rose like rushing water, and the other boys sitting next to Jed stood and started shouting with him.

"You ain't allowed down here!" shouted Stanley Walsh.

"Go sit in the balcony, nigger!" yelled Carl Ash.

"Git!" said Johnny Hart, and then he laughed like an old mule Daddy used to have.

Jimmy Lee repeated more emphatically, "This section is for whites only."

A few angry voices had set the current in motion, and now the whole theater seemed to be in commotion like the rising waters of Cumberland during the spring floods when it pours over its banks and wipes out everything in its path.

"Wonnie," I pleaded, "maybe it's best if you just go sit in the balcony and avoid any trouble."

She turned to me and narrowed her dark burning eyes. "It is time things change around here," she hissed. She looked back at Jimmy Lee. "If you want me to go sit in the balcony, you'll have to carry me." With that, she folded her arms in defiance.

About that time something hit me in the forehead. It took me a second to realize what was happening, and in that second I heard Ruby cry, "Ow!" I looked over in Jed Mock's direction just as he and his ilk threw another round of Milk Duds at us. Ruby and I hunkered down and dodged, but one of them struck Wonnie in the cheek, and she cried out in surprise. Johnny Hart laughed like a mule again, except louder.

"Let's get out of here," I said as I grabbed Ruby's hand and tried to pull her free from her seat. She glared at me as she drew back her hand and folded her arms to match Wonnie's pose. Stunned, I froze in my seat, until another Milk Dud smacked into my throat. I felt a rage building as the hateful current of the crowd flowed around me. I felt the urge to scream and lash back at the hatred washing over me. I wanted to beat the snot out of Jed Mock and his bunch.

Samuel saved the three of us from being swept away by the growing current. He rushed down from the balcony, grabbed Wonnie by the arm, and yanked her out of

her seat. He looked like he was dressed in the same overalls, except he had a T-shirt on this time. He grabbed
her in his strong arms, threw her over his shoulder, and
hauled her kicking and screaming from the theater.

"I am not a second-class citizen!" she shouted as
Samuel carried her toward the door.

Johnny Hart yelled, "Git, nigger!" His mule laugh
echoed through the theater, accompanied by laughter from Jed, Stanley, Carl, and the rest of the ignorant,
white-trash gaggle.

Ruby stood and straightened her dress. "Take me
home, Stone," she pronounced. I stood and escorted her
from the theater feeling like a piece of driftwood washed
downstream against its will. We drove to her house in
silence. When I parked the car out front, I shut down the
engine and leaned my head against the steering wheel.

"I'm ashamed of you, Stone," said Ruby.

"What did I do?"

"Nothing. That's just the point."

"What was I supposed to do? Stand up to Jed Mock
and the ten guys he had with him?"

"He only had three or four with him, and you could
have at least spoken up for Wonnie when Jimmy Lee
Farmer came over and told her to move."

I smacked the steering wheel in frustration. "It's the
law! I can't change the world."

"No, but you can stand up for what you know is
right. The negros are God's children too, and they don't
deserve to be treated that way."

I poked my finger in her face and said, "If you feel
that way, how come there ain't any colored members at
your daddy's church?"

"It's the Methodist Church, and they choose not to
come, but they are welcome."

"By you maybe, but not by anybody else," I grumbled.

"Ezekiel Stone Molony," she pronounced, "sometimes all it takes to change the world is one person with conviction. Ghandi was one person. That's how Christ started too." She opened her door and got out. Before she closed her door, she stuck her head back in and declared, "Stone, have the courage to do what's right, even when the consequences are painful." She closed the door and walked up to the porch.

I was fuming as she walked away. I wanted to scream that it wasn't fair to blame me because the world was so twisted and mean. Instead of screaming I started the car and slammed it into first gear. I stomped the accelerator and the tires of the '49 Buick kicked up gravel as they spun up. When they hit the asphalt of High Street, the rubber let out a long peel. I was sure to hear about that from Pastor Tabor. I headed up High Street like a scalded dog and turned up the Old Burkesville Road toward Big Hill. I roared up the winding road, making the tires suffer at every switchback.

When I pulled into the parking lot of the Alpine Motel overlooking the town, several cars were there already. I thought about the loving couples in the other cars cuddled up together as they looked out over the lights. I never even shut off the car. I slammed it into reverse and raced back down the hill faster than I had climbed it. I slowed down a little as I came to the square, but the tires still squealed when I turned onto Main Street and cut off Willy McCoy in his old Ford truck. He laid on the horn, but I didn't even slow down. When I got to the edge of town, I floored it, and the old Buick came to life. About halfway down the straight stretch, almost to the turnoff for the old free ferry, I saw the headlights of an approaching car. Just as they got close,

I saw that it was a patrol car. He must have noticed my high rate of speed because he flipped on his lights just before we passed.

I swore and slapped the steering wheel. I began slowing immediately and could see him turning around in my rearview window. I let out a sigh and pulled over before he caught up to me. I watched him with dread as he pulled in behind me with the red light on top of his car going round and round. He left his lights on, got out of his car, and approached me with a flashlight in one hand and his other hand on his gun. I could tell by his height and perfect hair that it was Deputy Cortis Russel.

When he got close he shined the light in my face and practically blinded me. "Stone? Where you going in such a hurry?"

"Home," I mumbled.

"At the rate you were going, I thought you might be running moonshine down to Nashville," he said with a grin. "Slow down. We need you alive and in one piece for basketball season."

I let out a sigh of relief. "Yes, sir."

He lowered his flashlight and leaned against the car. "You gonna come play tomorrow morning?"

"Yes, sir, I'll be there," I said, nodding vigorously. "Nine o'clock over in Marrowbone."

He stood and smacked the top of the car. "Go on home now, son, but take it easy."

I eased the car back onto the road and watched the beam from his flashlight swing back and forth on its way back to his cruiser. My hands were still trembling on the wheel when I turned down our lane. I could see Mama rocking back and forth on the front porch, knitting, as I parked the car. She always waited up for me when I went to town on the weekend. I parked the car and took my time getting out.

"You're home early tonight," said Mama without looking up from her knitting. The rocking chair squeaked every time she rocked back.

I stopped with my hand on the door and hesitated. "Yeah, I didn't want to stay out too late since I've got to go play basketball over in Marrowbone tomorrow morning," I lied.

Mama continued rocking under the porch light, working her needles in rhythm to the squeaking rocker. "There's some leftover corn bread on the table if you're hungry."

I said, "Thanks," and went into the house. Daddy and Leck were sitting around listening to WSM on the radio, and just as I walked in, the National Life and Accident Insurance Company was running one of its ads claiming "We Shield Millions," the namesake for WSM. Leck looked up at me but didn't say anything. Daddy looked like he was drifting off to sleep. I just kept moving to the kitchen.

I grabbed a glass from the cupboard and crumbled up a big piece of corn bread on the table into it. I opened the icebox, grabbed one of the milk bottles, and sloshed it around until the layer of cream had disappeared back into the milk. Then I poured it over the corn bread until the glass was almost full. I sat there eating my corn bread and milk and stared at the empty kitchen, trying to figure out why my life had suddenly become so complicated.

The corn bread and milk didn't taste as good as usual. I figured my taste buds were tainted with the taste of shame. Ruby was right. I should've stuck up for Wonnie or at least offered her some protection. Instead, I had sat in my seat with a streak of yellow running down my back.

I finished the mushy corn bread treat and washed down my nagging guilt with another glass of milk before heading off to bed. When I got upstairs, I stretched out on my bed and stared at the ceiling. I could feel the music from the radio vibrating the springs in the mattress. Mama's rocking chair was still squeaking on the porch. I heard a car make a slow pass out on Celina Road. After all the excitement, I could feel myself drifting off to sleep with a belly full of Mama's corn bread. I didn't bother to get up and take off my clothes.

I don't know how long I had been asleep, but when Mama screamed, I bolted up in bed, wide awake.

"Billy! There's a drunk nigger coming up our driveway!" screamed Mama. I heard her quick footsteps on the porch followed by the slamming screen door.

I jumped out of my bed and raced downstairs. As I got to the front room, I saw Mama standing by the front window holding herself like she was cold. Daddy had grabbed the small Louisville Slugger he kept in the coat closet and was headed out the front door with the bat in his right hand. I rushed forward to the screen door as soon as it closed and looked out into the night as far as the porch light reached.

A figure struggled up our gravel lane still cloaked in shadow, but it looked to be the size of a man, and judging from the dull color of his skin in the dim light, he was a colored man. He was probably just drunk and turned around, but at this time of night it was good to be cautious. Before he could get any closer, Daddy brandished the bat at the top of the stairs and shouted, "What do you want, nigger? You been drinking?"

"Missuh Molony," came a familiar voice, "I . . . I been beat up. Please . . ."

Daddy lowered the bat. "Samuel? Is that you?"

The moment Daddy said his name it all came together in my mind—his features, his skin color, his overalls, his voice. I rushed out the front door just as Daddy dropped the bat and started down the stairs. We reached him about the same time. In the dim light cast from the porch, I could see dark stains on his T-shirt. I couldn't bear to look at his face yet, so I grabbed his right arm and slung it over my shoulder and started him for the house. Daddy got under the other arm, and we practically carried him up the stairs and into the house. I could feel his body trembling, and the sweat from his arm felt cold against my neck.

"Bring him into the kitchen and lay him on the table!" shouted Mama as we burst through the front door. "I'll heat some water."

We shuffled into the kitchen, focused on negotiating the doorway and moving the chairs out of our way. Daddy let go of him to clear the plate of corn bread from the table, and when he did I swiveled and picked him up and laid him down on the table.

When I stepped back, I got my first good look at his face. His left eye was swollen shut, with a big gash above his eyebrow exposing the pink flesh below his caramel-colored skin. His sharp nose was swollen and sat slightly askew on his face. His top lip was split and looked like somebody had shoved a grape into it. Red streaks of blood oozed from each of the wounds and had soaked his dirty white T-shirt around the neck.

I thought about his three older brothers who had been killed before my time. Each of them had met a violent and untimely death, and stories of their violent demise still swirled around them like ghosts that are never satisfied with staying dead. But I knew Samuel was different, yet here he was bleeding on my kitchen table. It made me wonder if the stories about his brothers were true.

Mama rushed back into the room with an old sheet in her hands and tossed it to Daddy. "Rip that into strips," she ordered. When she paused and looked at Samuel, her face went pale and she began shaking her head. I could see a flash of anger, but it was swallowed up with compassion almost as soon as it crossed her face. "Just relax, Samuel. We'll get you fixed up," she said.

I was standing there listening to the sound of ripping fabric, Samuel's wheezing moans, and running water, when I felt it. *Live; yea, I said unto thee when thou wast in thy blood, Live.* My head began to tingle with tiny lightning bolts and my hands felt suddenly warm. I glanced at Daddy and remembered his warning. I pushed the healing thoughts aside and stuck my hands into my pockets. I glanced up and saw Leck standing in the doorway, leaning against his crutches and watching me as if he could read my mind.

Daddy scooped up the strips of fabric and put them on the counter next to the stove. Mama grabbed a handful of them and shoved them into the large pot of water she was heating. Leck hobbled over on his crutches and leaned over Samuel.

"He ain't breathing right," said Leck. "Samuel, did they hit you anywhere else besides the head?" he asked.

Samuel kept his eyes closed, but let out a raspy reply. "My ribs," he said, bringing his left hand up to his side.

Leck reached down and started undoing the straps of Samuel's overalls. "Daddy, help me get a look at his ribs." Daddy stepped over and undid the other strap, and they gently pulled down the bib from his overalls.

"God help us," said Daddy.

I didn't have a clear view of Samuel's left side, but I could see a big red splotch of blood on the lower part of his T-shirt.

"It looks like they broke a rib or two," said Leck. "He might have a punctured lung." Daddy gave Leck a puzzled look. "I seen it before in Korea," explained Leck. The storm in my head surged again and the familiar scripture played over and over again like a broken record. Ruby's words about having the courage to do the right thing burned in my conscience.

"We need to get him to a hospital," said Leck.

I could see it in my mind—Samuel's face without a blemish, his nose straight as it ever was, his breathing back to normal. My hands burned in my pockets.

"You think they'll take him at the clinic in Burkesville?" asked Daddy. The nearest real hospital was over in Glasgow, and they probably didn't take colored patients.

"They have to," said Leck, "He might die otherwise."

When Leck said he might die, I couldn't hold back any longer. I pulled my hands from my pockets and stepped forward. The words from Ezekiel overwhelmed all my thoughts, and my scalp began to tingle with electricity. *Live; yea, I said unto thee when thou wast in thy blood, Live.* Without asking for permission, I reached past Leck and put both hands on Samuel's bloody rib cage and closed my eyes.

The storm in my head raged. Lightning bolts crisscrossed my skull with so much intensity that I thought my head might explode, but with each flash of lightning I could see Samuel's rib cage returning to a healthy shape. My hands felt like icy hot coals, almost like they were some artificial extension of my real arms. After a few moments, I knew that the ribs and lung were healed and moved my hands to his nose. The bolts of lightning gave me a vision of what his face would look like after I was done. My hot hands could feel his nose straightening under their touch. I put a hand over his eye, and felt the flesh reunite and come together as seamless dark skin. I put a hand on his lip and sensed the swelling leave. The storm raged more intensely. My hands burned and shook. Then all the energy gathered together in my chest and burst out like some gust of wind. I pulled my burning hands back and collapsed to the floor.

I could hear Mama shout, "Stone!" I could hear her rush to my side and felt her fingers caress my face, but the world was dark as Mammoth Cave when they turn the lights out.

"I'm here, Mama," I whispered. "I just can't see."

"Billy, help me get him to the couch," she said.

I felt Daddy's strong hands grab under my arms and lift me up. I tried to help as much as I could, but found myself weak and barely able to stand. With their help, I made it to the couch and collapsed. When I got comfortable I asked, "How's Samuel?"

I was surprised when Samuel himself responded, "Good as new, Stone, thanks to what you done."

They say that when you're blind your other senses become sharper. As I lay there I could hear Mama sniffle like she was trying to hold back tears. I heard Leck hobble into the room on his crutches and lean against the back of the couch. I heard Daddy's chair creak as he sat back in it. I heard Samuel breathing normally.

"I'll be fine in a few minutes," I announced, but I don't know where I got that idea since I had only been through this once. As I lay there relying only on my other four senses, I asked, "Who beat you up, Samuel?"

I could hear him shift his weight and shove his

hands into his pockets. "I don't rightly 'member. It was pretty dark."

"Where did it happen?" asked Leck.

"I's jest walking down Celina Road past the old free ferry road."

Remembering the incident in the theater tonight, I asked, "Where's Wonnie?"

"She caught a ride with some folks headed to Livingston after she . . . uh, left the theater," answered Samuel.

"It wasn't Jed Mock and his clan, was it?" I asked.

"No," he answered too quickly.

"Why would you think it was Jed Mock?" asked Mama.

"They were stirring up trouble earlier tonight at the theater," I told her, not wanting to give any more details.

"What kind of trouble?" asked Daddy.

I coughed. "Can I get a glass of water, please?"

I heard Mama hurry to the kitchen and bring me back a glass of water. "Sit up so you can drink it," she said as she took my hand and placed the cold glass between my fingers.

I sat there and sipped the water while I listened to the nervous breathing of everyone in the room. When I finished drinking, I began to make out obscure shapes in the room. I thought I could see the front door and the radio. "I think it's starting to come back."

"Thank the Lord," said Mama with a sigh of relief. Daddy's chair creaked, and Leck hobbled over to the end of the couch.

"Just like the stories," said Samuel.

Out of instinct I turned to look at him but only detected a dark shape. "What stories?"

I heard him shuffle, and the shape moved. "Some of the old folks say there used to be a woman that had the

healing gift and when she used it she would have to sit
for a while because she couldn't see."

"What was her name?" I asked. I blinked and Samuel
started to come into view.

"I think they just called her Miss Opal."

In my mind's eye, I could see the gravestone for Opal
Newby where I was found. I could read the scripture that
held such mysterious power over me. I imagined that I
traced my fingers over the inscription at the bottom—
May your healing gift continue forever.

"What else do you know about her?" I asked.

Before he could answer, Daddy cleared his throat
and said, "Now, Stone, don't go chasing old wives' tales
and legends. Can you see yet?"

I turned my head to look at him. He sat back in his
chair with an arm on each armrest and a stern and worried look on his face. "I can see," I announced.

Mama jumped up and gave me a hug. She had been
crying. "It's a miracle," she whispered. "A true gift from
God."

Leck reached out and patted me on the back. "Strong
work, Stone. Strong work." With that he hobbled off to
his bedroom, and I felt pity for him as I watched him
struggle. I still had no idea if my gift could heal him.

Daddy stood. "I'll go get the truck and take Samuel
across the river." With that he headed through the
kitchen and out the back door.

"Much obliged for all of your help, Missus Molony,"
said Samuel with a nod. Then he looked straight at me,
and I saw tears welling up in his eyes. Although his
T-shirt was covered in dried blood, there was no evidence in his face that less than an hour ago he had one
eye swollen shut and a broken nose. "And much obliged
to you and your healing gift, Stone." Then he bowed his

head like a penitent man leaving church and headed for the front door.

I followed him out the front door, and as he waited at the bottom of the porch for Daddy to pull up front with the truck, I asked, "What else do you know about that faith healer, Opal?"

He looked up and shrugged. "Just stories about how she used to come around and heal people from time to time. They say she used to go blind after she would heal someone, just like you." He flashed a big white smile. "Maybe she's yo' kin."

I wanted to ask more, but Daddy pulled up in front of the porch. Samuel waved as he climbed up in the back of the truck, and Daddy hurried down the lane and took a left turn onto Celina Road. I stood on the front porch for a few minutes listening to the crickets and thought I could hear the distant sound of the ferry motor as it powered across the Cumberland. I had no idea what I had set in motion by healing Samuel that night.

FIVE

I slept like a dead man after the excitement of the day, but my dreams were vivid as if I was awake. Daddy nudged me at the usual hour and told me it was time to get the morning chores done. I sat up and tried to get my bearings in the dim light of the dawn. I still had my clothes on from last night, and for a second I thought maybe I had dreamt everything that happened yesterday. But when I walked downstairs to the kitchen, the rags from the torn sheet were still sitting on the counter, and a drop of Samuel's blood had dried on the kitchen table during the night.

The steady rhythm of milking Jersey Girl seemed to restore some order to my world, and by the time I got the rest of my chores done and made it to the house, I was whistling and happy. I was glad that I had helped Samuel. I didn't understand my gift, but it felt good to know that I could heal someone.

I wasn't the only one in a good mood that morning. Mama seemed to glow as she served up our breakfast. Daddy, usually stern and sometimes dour, hummed as he walked through the kitchen door. Leck still appeared subdued but lacked his usual cynicism. It was if we were all benefitting from some sort of afterglow effect from helping Samuel last night.

After breakfast I grabbed my basketball shoes and gym clothes and started out for Marrowbone, the nearest indoor gymnasium since the Burkesville High School burned down a few years back. When I pulled up in front of the big brick building, Deputy Russel's car was sitting out front next to Coach Clark's old Chevy truck. I chuckled to myself as I thought about the ticket I dodged on the way home last night. I wondered what Ruby would say when I told her about what I had done for Samuel. Would she be proud of me now?

Coach and Cortis Russel were standing in the middle of the gym talking when I walked in. "Are you okay, son?" asked Coach Clark with a chuckle as I headed to the locker room. "It's not like you to be early."

"You're not still driving like a whiskey runner, are you?" teased Cortis Russel.

I just grinned, hurried to the locker room, and dressed out for practice. By the time everyone else started showing up, I was already shooting. Two of my best friends, Dewey "Dewdrop" Hazard and Willy McCoy, showed up already dressed to play and started warming up. "Where was the fire last night?" asked Willy as he dribbled onto the court. I gave him a sheepish apology and tried to stay focused on basketball.

I didn't pay too much attention as the rest of the team filed into the small gym until I heard Johnny Hart's distinct laugh. I stood still with the ball on my hip and saw him and Jed Mock amble onto the court from the locker room. "Hey, nigger lover," said Jed as he smacked the ball out of my hands and dribbled away with it. Johnny Hart bellowed like a mule.

"Just ignore 'em," said Dewdrop as he tossed me another basketball. I shook my head and tried to focus on the game, but the image of Samuel's bloody face and his broken ribs haunted me. I could feel my good mood giving way to a desire for revenge. Coach Clark interrupted my mood shift with his whistle. "Mornin', ladies. Let's start with some suicide sprints." We let out a collective sigh and lined up.

I was able to keep my cool during practice because Coach Clark and Cortis Russel kept us so busy running drills and playing ball that I didn't have time to focus on my anger. A couple of times during practice, I got an extra nudge from Jed as we jockeyed for position, and I could swear that I heard Johnny Hart's unusual laugh every time I got near, but I stayed focused on the game. When Coach Clark blew the last whistle and sent us to the locker room, the mood quickly changed.

"Hey, Johnny," said Jed loud enough for everyone to hear as he pulled off his basketball jersey. "Let's head over to the whorehouse in the colored part of town tonight. I hear Black Magic will give white boys a freebie if it's their first time."

Johnny laughed, and I felt my jaw tighten. "But, Jed, it ain't your first time. Don't you 'member that cat house over near Tompkinsville?"

My stomach fluttered and I wanted to hurry and get out of there, but since I had never been with a woman, my primal curiosity had also been pricked. It seemed like I wasn't the only one because the locker-room chatter stopped and everyone moved methodically while they listened.

"Oh yeah," said Jed. "We don't have to tell Black Magic about that. She'll never know. Besides I hear she only charges five bucks for five minutes and I know it don't take you more than two."

Johnny brayed and said, "In that case it'll only cost five bucks for the two of us." They both laughed like they understood the punch line of a joke that nobody else got.

Realizing that my sick curiosity had kept me listening to their twisted dribble, I grabbed my basketball gear and started for the door. "Hey, Stone, why don't you come with us tonight?" said Jed. "I know it's your first time and I understand you like dark meat."

I stopped but didn't turn around. I could feel my throat tighten. "No thanks," I said and started to leave again.

"C'mon! We know you ain't getting any from the preacher's daughter," said Jed as Johnny punctuated the insult with a guffaw. I could feel everyone's eyes on me. I dropped my bag and turned around. I clenched my fists by my sides and could feel my heart beating out of my chest. Jed tied his shoes and grinned, apparently pleased that he had managed to get my goat. He nudged Johnny with his elbow and said, "Maybe he's getting a little brown sugar on the side from that cute nigger girl sitting next to him at the theater last night."

I didn't wait for any more of an invitation. I let out a raging scream and lunged at Jed. He was ready for me and landed a jab on my jaw right before I barreled into him with my shoulder and slammed him against the lockers. I could feel him punching my back with fruitless swings as I picked him up and took him to the floor, barely missing the wooden bench. Using my size advantage, I wriggled on top of him as he tried to twist free. The wooden bench toppled over and the quiet locker room crowd, enthralled with the sexual escapades of idiots only moments before, burst into shouts.

I was just getting into a position to pummel Jed when Cortis Russel grabbed my arm. "That's enough!" he shouted. "Break it up, boys!"

I shook my arm free and stood with my fists still clenched. My breath surged in and out of my nose like some bull ready for the charge. I could feel my face red with rage and tried to break free, but Cortis Russel grabbed me again and held me back.

"You two get out of this locker room and onto the floor!" ordered Coach Clark as he pointed to the doorway. "The rest of you get cleaned up and get out of here. Now!"

Cortis Russel helped Jed up and shoved him for the door. I grabbed my bag and followed them. Everyone else started filing out of the gym to avoid the coach's wrath. Coach Clark was standing there at center court with his arms folded, waiting for an explanation when we got there. "What's all this nonsense about?" he demanded.

"Not sure, Coach," said Jed, putting on an innocent face. "I just invited him to go out for a little fun with us tonight, and he got all bent out of shape."

Coach Clark and Cortis Russel looked at me. I rubbed my jaw, suddenly feeling the punch that Jed had given me. "He insulted my girlfriend."

"Which one?" said Jed with an evil grin. "Colored or white?"

"That's enough, Jed," warned Cortis Russel.

"Well, it's true. He had 'em both sitting next to him at the Webb Theater last night," said Jed with a snort. "Everybody saw it."

Both Coach Clark and Cortis Russel gave me a puzzled look that I ignored. "So that's why you and your ilk beat up Samuel Wilburn on his way home last night?"

Now Jed looked at me like I had a third eye. "What are you talking about? We didn't go nowhere near Samuel last night," he insisted. He looked at Cortis Russel. "Honest!"

"Look, boys," said Coach Clark. "How are we supposed to build any team camaraderie if you two are fighting? You two need to shake hands and let this go."

I turned to Cortis Russel, who was staring at the floor, and stated, "Deputy Russel, I would like to report a crime." Deputy Russel looked up at me with a blank face like he knew what I was going to say next. "I would like to report that Jed Mock and his friends beat up Samuel Wilburn last night."

"What?" blurted Jed. "You ain't got no proof!"

Deputy Russel nodded and answered, "Okay, Stone. What evidence do you offer to back your accusation? A man's innocent until proven guilty, you know."

I swallowed hard realizing that the best evidence had been destroyed when I healed Samuel, but I kept going. "Jed and some of his friends were causing a ruckus at the theater last night involving Wonnie and Samuel Wilburn. Later that night Samuel showed up on our doorstep all busted up. We, uh . . . cleaned him and dressed his wounds."

"Okay, can he identify his attackers?" asked Deputy Russel, sounding more official with each question.

I charged ahead like a drunk man in a fight. "He said it was dark, but I'm sure it was Jed."

"How can you be so sure?" asked Deputy Russel, raising an eyebrow and making me feel more stupid with each question.

"Because they were throwing Milk Duds at us in the theater."

Jed shook his head and sighed. "We only threw Milk Duds at them because that colored girl was sitting in the white section of the theater, and last time I checked, that was against the law." He raised his right hand like he was swearing an oath. "Deputy Russel, I swear we didn't go anywhere near Samuel Wilburn last night."

Cortis Russel pursed his lips and nodded his head. "I believe you, Jed. Now go on home and keep your mouth shut in the locker room."

"Yes, sir," said Jed with a grin and trotted back to the locker room.

"Stone," said Coach Clark, "you can't let insults and badgering draw you into a fight. You gotta keep a cool head."

"And don't accuse a man of a crime without some hard proof," added Deputy Russel.

I stood there with my fists still clenched, trying to calm down. The good mood from this morning had vanished. I was ashamed for losing my cool over Jed's insults. I felt like a fool for making accusations I couldn't prove, but now I was wondering who had beaten Samuel within an inch of his life if it wasn't Jed. I hung my head to show contrition and said, "Yes, sir." Then I grabbed my gym bag and shuffled for the door.

When I shoved open the door, I was surprised to be greeted by Samuel and Otis leaning against Deputy Russel's cruiser. Otis immediately stood when he saw me, his face worried and tight. Samuel leaned against the car, picking his teeth with a toothpick, and waved like he owned the cruiser.

Before I could say anything, Deputy Russel came through the door behind me. As soon as he did, Samuel quit leaning against the car and stood at attention. Deputy Russel stopped with his mouth hanging open when he saw Otis and Samuel. Then after giving them a long look, he cleared his throat as if trying to regain his composure and asked, "Samuel, Stone says some boys beat you up pretty bad last night."

Samuel nodded without taking his eyes off Deputy Russel and said, "Yes, sir. I got beat real bad."

"Did you get a look at your attackers?" asked Deputy Russel.

Before Samuel could answer, Otis intervened. "It was awful dark, uh, Deputy Russel," said Otis as he bowed his head and shook it slowly. "He couldn't make out they faces."

Cortis gave half a nod. "That's too bad. What happened to your busted eye? How did it heal so quickly?"

Samuel's face slowly broke into a wide grin. "Stone here healed me with his healing gift."

"Stone?" said Deputy Russel with a wrinkled brow. "What in the devil is he talking about?"

I looked at the ground and shuffled my feet. I remembered Daddy's warning not to tell anybody about my gift, but what could I do now? I wanted to lie, but that didn't feel right. Part of me wanted to tell everybody and get it over with. After all, maybe I could help more people like Mama said. I was afraid of what people would say. I was afraid of being made fun of. Mostly, I was afraid of getting in trouble with Daddy, but I didn't see any way out of the situation. Right then I remembered Ruby's face as she leaned through the window last night. I could see her disappointment in my lack of courage, and the sadness in her eyes. I swallowed hard and, still looking at the ground, said, "He's telling the truth."

"You two ain't making any sense," said Deputy Russel.

I stood up straight and looked him in the eye. I was almost as tall as he was when I stood up straight. "It doesn't make much sense to me either, but it's true. Somehow, I have the ability to heal sometimes, and last night when Samuel showed up at our house all busted up, I was able to heal him." I felt relieved that I had told someone but was terrified about what Daddy would say when he found out.

Deputy Russel just stood there with a scowl on his face, scratching his head. Samuel chimed in, "That's right. I showed up with busted ribs and a swollen eye. Stone touched me with healing hands, and I walked out of they house as good as new." He stood there with his hands extended, offering himself as evidence of the event.

Deputy Russel looked at me and then at Samuel and just shook his head like he was trying to shake himself awake from some bad dream. "That's the craziest thing I've ever heard. Does your Daddy know you're telling these tall tales?"

I bowed my head and said, "He's seen me heal before, and he was there last night when I healed Samuel, but he doesn't want me to tell anybody."

"For good reason! People are going to think you're some freak of nature, or worse yet, some carnival sideshow."

"I'd thank you not to tell anyone," I said.

Deputy Russel just shook his head again. "Who would believe me anyway?" He waved me off and turned to Otis. "Go on home, Stone. I've got some business with Otis and Samuel."

I tossed my bag into the backseat and climbed into the Buick. I knew that my secret wasn't going to stay a secret for long. I cranked the engine and waited for Deputy Russel to pull out ahead of me. Samuel gave me a friendly wave from the back seat of the patrol car as they passed by. I didn't want to go home. I knew that I should tell Daddy what had happened, but I was afraid. I rationalized that Deputy Russel wouldn't tell anyone, and that nobody would believe Samuel either. I decided that telling Daddy wouldn't change anything.

Mama was in the kitchen fixing biscuits for dinner when I got home, but Daddy and Leck were nowhere in sight. I grabbed a glass of milk and sat at the table. "I saw Samuel and Otis in Marrowbone," I said.

"Oh?" she said without looking up from her work.

"He looks good. All healed." I finished the glass of milk and wiped my mouth with the back of my hand.

"Did it scare you when you healed Samuel?" she asked as she cut biscuits out of the dough with a glass.

"A little bit. I don't like going blind."

Mama wiped her cheek with the back of her hand and left a streak of flour. "Have you thought anymore about healing Leck?"

I twisted the glass nervously in my hands. "Yes, Mama, I've thought about it, but I don't know where to start."

"What do you mean?"

"Well, with Samuel I felt the power of the gift building as I watched him suffering on the table. I haven't felt like that with Leck." I shrugged. "I don't know. I don't feel anything from him. It's like he avoids me and doesn't want to be healed."

Mama put the pan of biscuits in the oven and leaned back against stove. "We've been good to you, haven't we, Stone?" She wiped her hands on her faded apron.

"Yes, of course."

"We've treated you like our son and raised you like our own child, haven't we?"

I nodded, feeling my anxiety build. I could see where this was going.

She looked straight at me and I could see tears building in her eyes. "If you have any gratitude in you heart for what we've done, please, at least try to heal Leck."

Her words stung. In my mind it wasn't just a question of wanting to heal someone. It was like the gift had a mind of its own, and when it was ready, it burst forth and took charge. I didn't understand why I had been able to heal Samuel, but I had never felt the first inkling of healing with Leck. I wanted to tell her that what she asked for was unfair and not completely in my control. Instead I bowed my head out of respect.

"I'll try, Mama. I'll try."

SIX

Daddy was honking his horn as I closed the front door and ran down the stairs of the front porch in my church clothes the next morning. He had the Buick in gear before I even got my door closed. I buttoned the top button of my shirt and clipped on my tie just as we pulled into the parking lot. Daddy hurried in to secure his pew like usual. I followed Mama and Leck to the door, looking for Ruby.

She was dressed in a pale yellow dress this week and looked like a ray of sunshine cast down through a gloomy gray sky. I swear I could almost smell the shampoo in her hair from the parking lot. I hadn't talked to her since Friday night, and I hoped she had forgiven me for my lack of courage. I wondered if I would get a chance to tell her about healing Samuel.

"Good morning, Mrs. Molony. Good morning, Leck," she said with a bright smile as she greeted us.

"Good morning, Ruby," said Mama.

Leck winked and broke into song as he hobbled past on his crutches. "You are my sunshine, my only sunshine . . ."

I mustered my courage and shook her hand. "Good morning, Ruby. You look wonderful in yellow," I offered, hoping for some sign that she and I were still together.

"Thank you, Stone. That's very kind of you," she answered. But that was it. No hug. No dinner invitation. Just a greeting and a handshake like everyone else walking through the door. I hesitated in the doorway and started to say something, but she turned to greet Old Man Riddle, who was walking up behind me. I slinked to my seat with a pit in my stomach.

As I approached our usual pew, I could see Cortis Russel leaning forward and whispering into Daddy's ear. When he saw me coming, he patted Daddy on the back and sat back. Daddy's face was red and his lips were drawn tight. Deputy Russel gave me a nod as I slid past and took my seat, and Shirley Mae looked down. I guessed that the cat was out of the bag, and Daddy would want to talk to me after church.

I sat hunched over with my head in my hands when Pastor Tabor started his sermon with a scripture. "In 1 Corinthians we read, 'Charity suffereth long, and is kind; charity envieth not; charity vaunteth not itself, is not puffed up, doth not behave itself unseemly, seeketh not her own, is not easily provoked, thinketh no evil.' To be true Christians, we must have charity."

I wasn't sure if I had enough charity to be a true Christian, but I was certain I was about to suffer long when Daddy got a hold of me. I was certain I was going to be miserable if Ruby and I were breaking up. After the sermon I hurried to Sunday School before Daddy could say anything to me.

I was the first one in the classroom and plopped myself down in the back row. Floyd Talbot was the next one through the door, wearing a big grin but no hat, and said something about the weather, but I didn't really pay any attention. He took a seat with me on the back row and leaned back in his chair. Then Ruby came in surrounded by Jo Anne Carter, Nina Faye Davidson, and Eula Shaw. Jo Anne gave me the evil eye with her coal-black eyes and whispered something to Ruby. Eula glanced over her shoulder through her black cat-eye glasses. Nina Faye winked at me. Ruby pretended I wasn't there. As everyone else came through the door, they gave me a look and picked the seats farthest from me. By the time Floyd's dad came in to teach the class, that half-wit Stanley Walsh was the closest person to me, other than Floyd, and Floyd seemed oblivious or apathetic to everyone's snub.

I stared out the window and wished I could just disappear. I didn't know why everyone was giving me the cold shoulder, but I guessed it was either because of Wonnie sitting next to me in the theater or word of me healing Samuel had spread. Maybe both.

When class was over, Ruby hurried out of the room still surrounded by her whispering gaggle. I slipped past everyone and caught up with her as she stepped outside.

"Hey, Ruby," I called.

She stopped, and the gaggle gathered around her. Jo Anne put an arm around her shoulder. Nina Faye and Eula closed ranks.

"Can I speak to you?" I asked. "Alone?"

She bit her bottom lip and looked around. The other girls huddled closer. She glanced at them and nodded. Reluctantly, they shuffled away about ten yards and stopped. "Of course, Stone," said Ruby. Her smile appeared as sweet as always, but there was something sour in her tone of voice.

"What's wrong? Are you still mad at me about Friday night at the theater?"

"No. Whatever gave you that idea?"

"Well, you seem to be avoiding me, along with everyone else."

The smile on her face faded, and she looked away. "I heard about what you did for Samuel. Everyone is talking about it."

"I thought you'd be proud of me. I did what you told me to. I showed some courage and made a difference."

"I think what you did was amazing!" She looked at the ground. "But . . ."

"But what?" I saw Pastor Tabor slip through the chapel doorway and stand there with his arms folded.

She let out an exasperated sigh and looked up at me. "My father says I can't date you anymore." I could see her eyes moisten. "I'm sorry, Stone."

I glanced over at her father. He looked like he'd been weaned on a pickle. "So all that talk about having the courage to do the right thing no matter what the consequences doesn't apply to you?"

She bit her bottom lip. "It's not like that," she whispered. "I can usually sweet-talk him, but on this matter, my father has been very persuasive."

"So that's it?" I asked. "We're not going steady anymore?"

She reached out and touched my arm. "I'm sorry, Stone."

I pulled my arm away from her touch. She pulled her hand back like she had burned it, then turned away and hurried over to the waiting gaggle of girls. I gave Pastor a glance, but he just slipped back into the chapel without even acknowledging our conversation.

I stood there for a moment with a hole in my chest and then started for our old Buick, feeling like I wanted to die. My limbs were moving, but I had no life in me. I was aware of people walking and cars driving away, but it was all a daze. I walked right past Mrs. Maggie

Owens and her daughter Hazel without even realizing they were there.

"Excuse me, Stone," said Mrs. Owens. "Are you okay?"

I nodded but didn't want to open my mouth. I noticed Hazel leaning against the car with braces on her legs and crutches tucked in her armpits. I faked a smile and hurried off to find everybody waiting in the car.

As soon as we got out on to the road, Daddy started lecturing. "Stone, I told you not to tell anybody about your gift. Did you not hear me?"

"How was I supposed to keep it a secret when Samuel is telling everyone?" I asked.

"Good folks would just ignore him, but when you told Cortis Russel, what did you think would happen?"

Mama intervened, "Now, Billy, it isn't fair—"

"Fair! Who said anything about fair? If the world were fair, we wouldn't have to have this conversation!" shouted Daddy. "He should've kept his mouth shut!"

"It ain't my fault that people gossip!" I shouted back.

"Why in God's green earth did you have to heal Samuel?" said Daddy.

"Billy!" said Mama. "You should be ashamed of yourself. Stone helped heal someone, someone who never hurt nobody, and all you can think about is what people are saying?" She shook her head. "Shame on you!"

It was a quiet ride the rest of the way home. Daddy jumped out of the car and slammed the door with the motor practically still running. He stormed off to the barn. Mama went into the house. Leck and I were still sitting in the backseat.

"You done the right thing, Stone," said Leck. Then he hoisted himself out of the car with his crutches and hobbled into the house.

I went to my bedroom and yanked off my tie and jacket. I stretched out on my bed and stared at the ceiling. Wondering if I should run away and join a circus, or maybe the army, I heard a knock at the front door. I looked out the window and saw Mrs. Maggie Owens's car out front. Her daughter Hazel was sitting in the front seat. I sat on my bed listening. I heard the muffled voices of Mama talking to Mrs. Owens, and then I heard her footsteps as she came up to my room. Mama knocked on the door and then poked her head in.

"Stone," she said meekly, "Maggie Owens from church is here to see you."

"Me?" I asked as if I didn't know why.

Mama just nodded and started back down the stairs.

I stood, straightened my shirt, and then went downstairs to the living room. I noticed that Mama and Leck were in the kitchen as I passed by. Mrs. Owens stood when I came in the room.

"Good afternoon, Mrs. Owens. What can I do for you?" I asked, pretending again that I had no idea why she was here.

For a moment she simply stood and wrung her hands like she was putting on lotion but then finally spoke. "I heard gossip about you today, strange and wonderful gossip." Her voice was shaky and strained. "Is it true that you healed Samuel Wilburn from . . . certain injuries?"

I shoved my hands in my pockets and answered, "Yes, yes it's true."

She opened her mouth to speak again, and I could hear the sound of her tongue unsticking from the roof of her mouth like she had been eating peanut butter. She hesitated at first but then finally managed to get the words out of her mouth by rushing her request. "Do you think you could heal my Hazel?"

I stood there with my hands in my pockets, staring at the floor, wondering what to do or how to proceed. I felt numb inside, like I didn't care what happened to me, or anybody else at that moment. I said, "Begging your pardon, Mrs. Owens, but I don't think I can do anything for your daughter. I'm sorry."

Her face fell, and I could see her lip quivering. She was holding back tears when she answered, "Thank you anyway." She nodded penitently and started out the front door. "Y'all have a nice day."

Just as she opened the door, I heard Leck hobbling from the kitchen on his crutches. "Hold on there, Mrs. Owens," he ordered. "My brother is being a bit humble, perhaps too humble." He glanced at me and then back at Mrs. Owens. "You bring Hazel into the house while I talk to Stone."

Mrs. Owens's face lit up and a tear trickled down her cheek. "Thank you kindly," she said as she slipped out onto the porch.

Before she got out the door, I was glaring at Leck. "What are you doing? I can't do anything for her daughter," I said. My voice had become a high-pitched nervous whine.

Mama had left the kitchen and stood behind Leck. She said, "Stone, we all saw what you did for Samuel. We believe you can do it."

"Believe?" I continued in my panicked voice. "I don't even know where to begin." I could feel a nervous knot forming in my stomach. I shook my head and said, "I can't do it!" I started for the stairs and up to my bedroom, but when I tried to pass Leck, he held up his right crutch and blocked my way.

"You gonna run away, you coward?" he snarled. His face looked like a drill sergeant dressing down a deserter.

"Do you know what its like to need crutches every day?" he asked, continuing his attack. "You get up every day and plant your feet on the floor without even thinking about it. When you run up and down the basketball court, does it ever occur to you that thousands of people don't have that privilege? Look!" he ordered, pointing to the front door with his chin.

I turned and through the screen door saw Mrs. Owens helping her daughter on crutches shuffle up the walkway.

"Don't you think she wants to run? Don't you think she wants to roll out of bed, plant her bare feet on the floor, and stand without help?" He hobbled closer and got right in my face. "Don't be a coward. You owe it to her to at least try. Why else would God give you a gift like that?" He pointed to the door with his head again. "Say the words and try," he hissed.

He stepped back and smiled as Mrs. Owens opened the door for Hazel. I turned and feigned a smile as well. Mama said, "Y'all take a seat on the couch. Would you care for a glass of water or some iced tea?"

Mrs. Owens shook her head and helped her daughter to the couch. They both looked like they just stepped into a Sears and Roebuck store with a twenty-dollar bill burning a hole in their pocket. Hazel looked up at me like I was the dress she had been saving up to buy for months.

I froze. It wasn't that I didn't want to heal her; it was that I didn't know where to start. Each time I had healed before, the power overcame me like a gathering storm. I heard the words in my head. I felt the lightning. My hands heated up and performed impossible miracles. But like a passing storm, I felt the wind on my face, smelled the coming moisture, heard the rolling thunder, saw the lightning streak across the sky. But I just experienced the weather. I didn't control it.

Leck pushed me with his crutch. I stumbled forward until I stood in front of them. They both beamed up at me and I gave them a weak smile. Mama and Leck stood behind the couch. "Afternoon," I said to Hazel.

"Good afternoon," she replied. She smiled and exposed crooked teeth to match her crooked legs.

I could see the braces clamped around her legs like manacles. I swallowed the lump in my throat and nervously asked, "Tell me about what happened to your legs."

"Well," she began, "when I was five I got real sick with fever. Mama thought it was just the flu. After a few days I had trouble standing, like my legs just wouldn't work right. I felt like my lungs didn't want to breathe." She looked over at her mother before she continued. "Mama rushed me over to the hospital in Glasgow. They hooked me up to a machine called an iron lung to help me breathe." She smoothed the flower-print fabric of her dress like straightening the fabric would somehow straighten her legs.

"She was in the hospital for almost eight weeks," continued Mrs. Owens. She caressed her daughter's hair and said, "I'm grateful we didn't lose her, but I ain't gonna lie. It has been very hard for her."

I felt a wave of compassion come over me, but still the haunting words from Ezekiel didn't come. "What about your father?" I asked.

Mrs. Owens said, "He died in a car accident when she was only a baby."

"I'm sorry," I said, feeling a sudden kinship with Hazel because of her father's death.

"Mama said you healed a black man from Coe Ridge," said Hazel.

I looked at the floor and nodded. "Yes, I did."

"Are you gonna heal me?"

I looked her in the eye. "I want to," I answered, "but I'm new at this and really don't know where to begin."

"Maybe if you come closer."

My nerves were jumping like crazy, and I hesitated. Mama nodded to me and motioned for me to move forward. I drew closer and knelt beside Hazel. She reached out, put her cold hands on my cheeks, and looked into my eyes like she could see straight through to my soul. Her deep brown eyes conveyed a sense of belief, and I could feel her faith. It was like some song playing on the radio in the other room that I could sense, but I couldn't make out the words or the tune.

She whispered, "I believe God is with you."

No sooner had she said the words than I felt the internal storm begin. I whispered, *"Live; yea, I said unto thee when thou wast in thy blood, Live."* The words just came out. My hands burned with healing heat, and I put them on her knees and concentrated.

Hazel drew in a sharp breath. I could feel the power working and her legs gaining strength. I could feel the effects of a disease that had ravaged so many people leaving her body. The storm raged. The heat pulsed in my hands. Just as before, all of the energy of the healing act gathered in my chest like a burning fire and flew away like a dove.

I fell back and sat on the floor, blind and weak. I heard Mama say, "Come on, Stone. Let's get you into a chair." She grabbed me under the arms and helped me up.

I could hear Mrs. Owens sniffling and crying. I could hear the straps coming off Hazel's legs. "Did it work?" I whispered.

"Yes," said Mama as she patted me on the shoulder. "It worked."

Hazel squealed and I thought I heard her jump up and down. "Look, Mama! Look, Mama!"

"Praise God!" said Mrs. Owens. "And Stone's healing gift."

I heard Hazel rush over to me and felt her squeeze my neck. She put her hands on my cheeks again and said, "I knew that God was with you." She hugged me again and whispered into my ear, "Thank you, Stone. God bless you and your gift!"

"It was your faith," I heard myself saying. "You believed in me, and that gave me the power to use my gift." Hazel squeezed my neck again, and I hugged her back as best as I could, still unable to see her.

"Can I pay you something for what you've done or offer you something for your help?" asked Mrs. Owens.

It was a tempting thought, but it didn't feel right. "No, thank you," I answered.

"Is he all right?" Mrs. Owens asked Mama.

"He'll be fine," she said. "Apparently each time he uses his gift, he loses his sight for a few minutes."

"Oh my!"

"It always comes back," reassured Mama as if she knew. I wondered if it would always come back. I wondered if other things were happening to me as well.

My vision didn't come back in time for me to watch Hazel walk out our front door without her braces and crutches, but when it did come back, I saw the discarded items on the couch. Mama sat next to them with her hands folded on her lap and a melancholy look on her face. I looked around for Leck, but he had slipped off to his room.

SEVEN

It was a busy week on the farm, and for once, I was glad. It kept my mind off what had happened with Ruby. Monday, right after supper, a man who identified himself as Mr. Bruce from Brownwood knocked at the door looking for me. He said he had been suffering from consumption and had heard that I had the power to help. His faith was strong, and it only took me a few minutes to draw upon my powers. He left with a clean bill of health.

On Tuesday Mary Glidewell, from Burkesville, showed up around lunchtime begging me to give her some relief from her arthritis. I sensed her faith, pronounced the words, and had her on her way in less than ten minutes. Each time I used my gift, it got easier.

On Wednesday some woman from over near Little Renox brought her son with a broken arm and wanted a miracle, but it didn't happen right away. I could tell that she, her son, or both, didn't really believe that I could heal his arm and wanted to test me. I said the words, but nothing happened. I told them that they didn't have enough faith yet and sent them away. They came back that night begging for help since they didn't have any money to get the arm set. I could sense their sincerity this time. I could feel their faith.

The boy was as good as new when they drove off in their old flatbed truck.

On Thursday evening, Samuel brought a couple of the black folks from Zeke Town, one with a hernia and another with fever, and knocked at the back door. They put so much faith in Samuel's story that I healed them both in one night right there on the back porch and sent them on their way.

Each time I learned a little more about the gift. Each time I felt more comfortable using it. Each time I was blind as a bat for several minutes after exercising my gift. Every time I healed someone else, I could sense Mama's frustration building, but Leck's faith was as elusive as ever. Daddy tolerated it all in silence. He said he didn't mind as long as it didn't interfere with our work on the farm, but I could tell that he wished he could turn back the clock. He seemed to take out his frustration by working me to death.

By the time Friday afternoon rolled around, I wanted to get off the farm. I had been working and healing people all week long and the only recreation I got was shooting a basketball at the hoop beside the barn whenever I was resting. Daddy let me borrow the Buick. So I got cleaned up and headed into town. I really wanted to see Ruby but didn't get my hopes up. If I was lucky, I might catch her at Walgreens and get a chance to talk to her alone, without Pastor Tabor butting in.

I parked Daddy's Buick on the square and sauntered into the drugstore trying to act casual. I ignored the looks that a few people gave me and looked around for Ruby. When I didn't see her, I headed over to the booth with Willy McCoy, Dewdrop Hazard, and Floyd Talbot. Floyd was nursing a bottle of grape Nehi. I grabbed an RC Cola and a bag of salted peanuts and slid in next to Willy.

"Look what the cat drug in," said Floyd with his head tilted back. "I ain't seen you all week."

"Been busy," I said. I took a sip from the soda and dumped the bag of peanuts into the bottle.

"Busy playing witch doctor," said Dewdrop with a snort. With dirty fingernails, he pulled a pinch of Redman tobacco out of his pouch and shoved it in between his cheek and gums. His daddy owned a machine shop, and no matter how hard he scrubbed, Dewdrop always had dirty fingernails.

I gave Dewdrop a blank stare but didn't respond to his dig.

Willy leaned forward and said, "We heard you healed Hazel Owens from polio and she don't even need crutches anymore. Is that true?"

"Yep, it's true."

"Dang!" said Willy. "Then all them stories are true." He shifted in his seat almost like he was afraid to sit next to me.

Dewdrop rolled his tongue over the wad of tobacco and spit into an empty soda bottle. "Told you," he said. Floyd just grinned.

I took a big swig from my drink and decided to set the record straight, "Look at me, fellas. Who do you see?" Floyd and Dewdrop glanced up at me, but nobody answered. "Dewdrop, when you caught that skunk in your trap lines, who brought over all those cans of tomato juice to get rid of the smell?"

Dewdrop spit into the bottle again and said, "You did, Stone."

"Willy, when you lit off that smoke bomb in the girls' bathroom last year, who covered for you and kept you out of trouble?"

"I appreciate that," said Willy with a shrug.

"And, Floyd, you've know me since first grade. Ain't I always been a good friend?"

"One of the best," said Floyd, still wearing a grin.

"Look, somehow I got this strange gift that lets me heal people, but I'm still the same guy. I still work on my daddy's farm. I still like basketball and fishing. I still like going to the movies." I looked at Willy. "I still like helping you play pranks on people." I sighed. "I didn't ask for this. It just happened."

They were all quiet for a moment and stared at their bottles of soda, but then finally Floyd spoke up. "What does it feel like? Does it hurt?"

"It feels like a tiny thunderstorm in my head, and my hands get hot, but it doesn't hurt. Well, except that after each time I heal someone, I'm blind for a few minutes."

"Whoa," said Dewdrop almost reverently.

"Why do you think that happens?" asked Willy.

I shrugged. "I don't know. It's kind of like getting the gift. I don't know how or why I have it. I just do."

"How does it work? Do you have to scream or shout Jesus's name? Do you have to say some special prayer?" asked Floyd.

I didn't answer right away but looked at their anxious faces. I felt defensive and on edge, but I could see that their questions were sincere. "C'mon, fellas," I said with a wave of my hand, "I came into town to get away from the farm and have some fun. I don't want to talk about it right now."

Willy loosened the lid from the salt shaker for the next unsuspecting customer. Floyd sat back a bit and pushed up his hat. Dewdrop spit. After an awkward pause, Willy said, "Hey, why don't we head over to that big tent revival? Tonight's their first night for public meetings."

Floyd pulled down his cap to the normal position

and peeked out from under the bill. "Somebody said they was gonna have snakes." We all laughed and slid out of the booth.

The big rectangle tent had a string of lights down the center that cast a dim light over the crowd. The place was packed with folks from all over the county, and probably some folks from down in Tennessee as well. I didn't expect to see Ruby, but I looked around for her and her friends anyway. Instead I saw Jed Mock and his bunch hanging out by one of the side entrances. When revival groups like this came through town, they offered preaching, salvation, and sometimes healing. Most of us didn't show up for the salvation or healing, but it was good entertainment. It didn't hurt that we got some preaching as well.

They were playing the organ when we slipped in and sat near the back. "Take off your hat, Floyd. You're in church," I reminded Floyd. He yanked it off and exposed his white forehead that rarely saw the light of day.

About the time we sat down, a man in a white shirt and a bow tie walked out onto the makeshift stage, and the organ stopped. He held up his hand and hushed the crowd before speaking into the loudspeaker. "Brothers and sisters, I am the Reverend Hines, and I want to welcome you all to the Holiness of God Revival. We will begin with a hymn and a prayer."

The organ started an upbeat version of a hymn I thought I recognized, and a couple of ladies in long dresses with their hair pulled up came out on stage and started smacking tambourines to provide a beat. You could feel the electricity building as everybody started singing. After the song a man came out and gave a passionate, and long-winded, prayer that everyone followed with a big "Amen."

Then the Reverend Hines came out and started preaching. He had a booming tenor voice that carried throughout the tent without the loudspeaker, but he used it anyway. He spoke in a cadence, almost like poetry, and moved with the cadence of his preaching almost like he was dancing. Every now and then his words would spark the crowd and someone would offer him support with a "hallelujah" or an "amen." Most of the audience was moved by his passionate preaching of the word of God, but we just sat and watched the entire spectacle for entertainment.

Willy nudged me with his elbow and whispered, "Ain't that Nina Faye up there with Ruby?"

Up near the front on our side of the tent, I could make out Nina Faye's blonde hair and probably Jo Anne's black hair next to her, but I couldn't make out if Ruby was with them. I thought I saw Eula Shaw with her cat-eye glasses, but a man's head blocked my view. While I was looking, Dewdrop said to Floyd, "I thought you said they would have snakes."

They ended the preaching with another lively hymn, and the audience stood to sing along. Then the man with the bow tie took to the loudspeaker again and announced, "Brothers and sisters, we read in Mark chapter sixteen, 'And these signs shall follow them that believe; In my name shall they cast out devils; they shall speak with new tongues; They shall take up serpents; and if they drink any deadly thing, it shall not hurt them; they shall lay hands on the sick, and they shall recover.'

"We believe in the power of healing, and tonight you will witness that power." He paused and pointed at the congregation. "If you have enough faith." Willy elbowed me in the ribs and made me flinch.

Someone handed the reverend a chair, and he placed it

in the middle of the stage. Then he placed the microphone for the loudspeaker in a short stand and stepped off to the side. As he left center stage, a tall woman with a knee-length white dress and hair black as coal pulled up on her head walked up onto stage. Her striking beauty caused an obvious stir through the crowd as the less-discreet men, like Floyd, let out an audible moan. The more discreet ones simply shifted in their chairs. But no one was blind to the striking figure as she walked onstage with a guitar and sat down. It was the woman from the travel trailer.

Without so much as looking at the audience, she began strumming the guitar strings and a man standing by the organ joined in with the fiddle. The chords were like rhythmic tears, and the notes from the fiddle sounded like a woman's cry. She drew close to the microphone and poured out a melody. "I'm just a poor wayfaring stranger, traveling through this world alone." Her voice was clean and hypnotic like that of a siren calling to passing sailors. Everyone hushed and sat mesmerized by the clear, melancholy tune. "There's no sickness, toil or danger in that bright land, to which I go. I'm going there to see my mother. I'm going there no more to roam."

It was like her presence and her voice cast a trance over the congregation. Even the young children sat still and listened to her ballad. I got chills as I listened and almost forgot that I was in a room full of people because it felt like she was singing just to me.

The fiddle wailed, and she sang louder. "I'm going there to meet my Savior, to sing his praise forever more. I'm just going over Jordan." Her cadence slowed and the fiddler drew out the notes like long laborious moans of someone finally getting relief from their pain. She drew out the last words with breathless precision. "I'm just going over home."

A blanket of silence covered the congregation like we were hoping that our silence would somehow help us linger in the memory of her voice. I heard a lady a few rows up from me sniffle. I blinked back the tears in my own eyes as well and noticed Floyd wipe his cheek. Reverend Hines brought us back to the present by announcing softly into the microphone, "Brothers and sisters, you have just heard from Sister Phoebe Webb." He continued in a low calm voice, "If anyone is in need of healing, come forward in faith, and she will heal you."

Willy elbowed me again, but I barely noticed. I had my eyes fixed on Phoebe Webb. She sat with her head bowed, her hands in her lap, and her legs folded neatly beneath her chair. She looked alone in a room full of people.

A man in the third or fourth row stood up with his crutches and hobbled up to the stage. I didn't recognize him, but he was dressed in a pair of Duck Head overalls with a white long sleeve shirt and a wide-brimmed straw hat that made it a little hard to see his facial features.

"What is your particular malady?" asked Reverend Hines.

"My foot got crushed by my tractor, and I can't walk without crutches," he said.

"Brothers and sisters, please maintain reverence as Sister Phoebe Webb lays her hands on this afflicted man."

Phoebe didn't leave her seat. In fact, she barely looked up as the man on crutches knelt down in front of her. She put her left hand on his head and I could see her lips moving, but it wasn't audible from where I was sitting. I wondered if she was saying the same words that came to me. I hoped that maybe I had found someone that could help me understand my gift.

Then the man began to shake like he was being

shocked. He shouted, "Hallelujah!" and stood up, leaving his crutches on the stage. He turned and faced the crowd and started doing a little jig. With a big smile on his face, he picked up his crutches and held them over his head like a conquering fighter and skipped off the stage.

"Dang!" said Floyd. "Is that what you can do too?"

I didn't say anything. I was busy watching Phoebe Webb. Something didn't seem right about that man's healing, but I couldn't put my finger on it.

Then, a woman about halfway back stood and started making her way to the stage. She had her right arm in a fabric sling. She went straight to Phoebe Webb and offered her bad arm. Phoebe reached up and put her left hand on the woman's arm and again her lips moved. The woman jerked upright all of a sudden, her mouth open in surprise. She yanked her arm free from the sling and moved it around, demonstrating that her arm was healthy and strong, and then walked off stage, twirling the cloth sling overhead.

I wasn't convinced. Both of them had physical ailments that could be easily faked. Both of the healings were a bit dramatic. It all seemed too convenient. I realized how I must look to other people when they hear about me healing someone. I was so disappointed that I was about to leave when I saw Old Man Riddle stand and make his way up to the stage.

Reverend stopped him and asked, "What ails you, brother?"

"I've got a cough that just won't heal," he said and then almost as if on cue fell into a coughing fit. Reverend Hines grabbed him by the arm and led him over to Phoebe, who still sat with her head bowed.

Old Man Riddle was still coughing when she put her

right hand on his shoulder. Just like before, I thought I saw her lips moving. After a moment her body seemed tense, like her muscles were suddenly more rigid. Old Man Riddle stopped coughing, and she dropped her hand back into her lap. She raised her head a little, but her stare passed right through the audience. Old Man Riddle clutched his chest and looked perplexed. Then, his chest heaved with a deep breath, and he shook his head in obvious surprise.

Now I was interested. I had to talk to this woman. I wanted to know about her gift. I needed her help. I glanced over at Willy, Dewdrop, and Floyd, and they were all looking at me with their mouths hanging open. I just shook my head and turned my attention back to Phoebe Webb.

I watched her heal three more people that night: a woman with a lazy eye, a baby with a fever, and a man with a festering toothache. Phoebe never moved from her chair. Her thousand-yard stare didn't change either. I didn't figure it out until after she healed the baby. She was blind.

"Brothers and sisters, that's all the Holy Spirit will allow for tonight," pronounced Reverend Hines. The organ began to play a soft easy tune that he could talk over. A man and a woman came out on the stage. The woman took Phoebe by the arm and led her off the stage, and the man grabbed the chair.

"God needs your donations for us to continue this important work," said Reverend Hines.

Several men appeared at the edges of the congregation with small metal buckets. One of them looked a whole lot like the man with the crushed foot. As Reverend Hines pleaded for money to continue God's important work, the buckets passed down each row and the music played softly in the background. I tossed in a buck out of guilt when it came past.

"Where are the snakes?" asked Dewdrop as they took the buckets of money away. Almost as if they had heard Dewdrop, two men brought out some sort of box covered in a white cloth. After setting down the box, they folded back the white cloth and exposed a glass case full of writhing snakes. The audience started to buzz, and Floyd said with a big grin, "Told you they was gonna have snakes."

"Brothers and sisters, tonight you will be witness to God's power as men and women exercise their faith in him by taking up serpents." The crowd got a little louder, and he held up his hand. "Please maintain reverence so that the Spirit of God can be with us as we take up these poisonous creatures."

The organ started to play a soothing tune, and one of the ladies joined in with a light beat on the tambourine. Reverend Hines rolled up his sleeves, opened up the top of the glass container, reached down into the mass of wriggling snakes, and drew out a large rattlesnake. We all held our breath as he caressed the snake and held it close to his face. A lady farther up passed out and fell into her husband's lap. Dewdrop's jaw dropped so far it was touching his chest, and he spit out the rest of his tobacco.

Then as the organ and tambourine provided the musical backdrop, Reverend Hines grabbed another snake. It writhed and wiggled as he pulled it free, and it immediately wrapped around his arm. He held them both just behind the head and raised his arms for the crowd to see. Then he released the head of the first snake he had picked up and moved his hand closer to his face. The snake coiled up farther onto his arm and drew back like it might strike. The crowd gasped, but when the snake didn't strike, everyone moaned in relief.

Two more men from the company came out and thrust their hands down into the ball of reptilian flesh and drew out snakes. They moved with the rhythm of the music and often looked up in praise. The hush over the crowd had broken and everyone began to murmur at the sight, like they had suddenly remembered how to talk. "How do they keep from getting bit?" whispered Floyd.

"Do you think those are real poisonous snakes?" asked Dewdrop.

I remembered Pastor Tabor's sermon and his dinner-time story. "Let's hope not."

Reverend Hines slipped the two snakes from his arms back into the glass container and picked up the microphone. "Brothers and sisters," he said quietly, "we invite anybody with enough faith to come join us on stage and show that God is with you."

The crowd murmured louder, but nobody came forward.

"I dare you to go up," said Willy to Dewdrop.

"No!" replied Dewdrop. His face had gone pale.

"Not enough faith?" chided Willy with a big grin.

"You go on up yourself," answered Dewdrop as he folded his arms.

"If anything happens, I'm sure Stone will fix you right up. Won't you, Stone?" asked Willy with a wink.

Before I could answer, I saw Ruby stand up. Willy had been right. She had been sitting next to Nina Faye. At first I thought that she was just getting up to leave, but when she got to the end of the row, she took a left turn and headed for the low stage. The crowd grew louder, and Reverend Hines asked for more reverence. Everyone complied except my heart, and it began to pound louder and louder with each step she took toward the stage.

Ruby stopped with her back to the audience a few feet from the glass container of snakes. Her arms hung limp at her sides, but her hands were balled up in tight fists. The two men still handling snakes nodded to her as an invitation. The crowd grew quiet, and she stood like she was looking over the edge of a cliff, trying to decide about jumping.

"Don't do it," I whispered to myself, and for a moment it looked like she was just going to watch for a moment and then go sit down, but then she stepped forward and jumped off that cliff.

Ruby brushed back her long brown hair, took two steps forward, and without hesitation shoved her hand down into that bin of vipers. With most of the crowd, and me, holding our breath, she pulled out a long timber rattler by the tail and held it dangling in the air in front of her with her right hand. One of the men handling snakes next to her gave her some apparent instruction, and she slid her left hand under the belly of the snake until she supported it in front of her with trembling hands.

Reverend Hines shouted, "Hallelujah!" The crowd started clapping. The music surged and Ruby's face broke into a relieved grin. She moved with the music and cradled the snake in her arms like some strange baby as she bounced to the beat of the tambourine. A strange energy surged through the audience, a feeling of relief, jubilation, and wonder all wrapped in one.

Reverend Hines invited others up, and soon Ruby was joined by a few more brave souls. Vince Frye left his seat next to Jed Mock and came running up on stage. Like Ruby he hesitated at first but then pulled out a small copperhead, like the one that killed Rusty, and carried it like he would a puppy. One of the old men who I always saw sitting and whittling in the square shuffled up and pulled out a couple of snakes like he was picking up baby chicks.

The crowd clapped and swayed to the music. Reverend Hines and several others from the traveling revival group joined him. Even Willy got into it and shouted, "Hallelujah! Praise the Lord!" I began to clap and hum along with the music, letting go of all of my own fears. I felt an enthusiasm and energy I had never felt. It made me feel strong, almost invincible. I thought that maybe I had found renewed faith. Maybe I found someplace that I could fit in.

Then the big timber rattler that Ruby was holding bit her on the neck.

Jo Anne Carter screamed first, but several other women in the audience followed suit. The organ and tambourine played on. Vince Frye threw his snake back into the bin and ran out of the tent. The rest of his gang followed right behind him. The old man from the square kept right on handling the snake, oblivious to Ruby's malady. Ruby winced and dropped the snake onto the low stage as she grabbed her neck. The snake slithered toward the front of the stage and cleared the first few rows as folks climbed over each other to get away from the stage. Reverend Hines rushed over to the snake, grabbed it by the tail, and gingerly dropped it back into the glass bin.

As the other handlers returned their snakes to the bin, Reverend Hines took Ruby by the shoulders and sat her on the front of the stage. The other two men quickly covered the glass container with the cloth and carted it away. The music stopped.

I stood and started for the stage, anxious for Ruby's

safety, but then I froze. Most of the town had heard rumors or gossip about my gift, but since I hadn't healed anybody in public, it was still just considered rumor. If I used it in front of this crowd, it would no longer be just rumor, and any hope I had for a normal life would probably vanish forever. More important than having everyone see me use my gift, I was worried that maybe I wouldn't be able to heal her. I remembered Rusty and wondered if my powers were limited when it came to snake bites. What if I couldn't feel her faith? Maybe she would reject my offer because she was worried about her father. I stood there like a statue.

Someone yelled, "Bring back the healer and heal her!" Several others echoed those sentiments, but the Reverend Hines shook his head and took the microphone. "Sister Phoebe Webb has done all the healing she can tonight. Besides, what makes you think that this young lady will have enough faith to be healed if she didn't have enough faith to handle the serpents without getting bit?" He shook his head with more emphasis and shook his finger at the crowd. "It is God's will."

When he pronounced those words, all the blood drained from Ruby's face. Her enthusiasm had turned to panic and fear. Someone else shouted, "Let's get her to a hospital!" Another answered, "It won't do no good. The bite is too close to her heart."

A few people scrambled for the exits likes rats from a sinking ship. Others moved closer to the stage. I'm not sure if they somehow wanted to help or were possessed with some morbid desire to watch Ruby suffer and die. I stood just outside of the crowd around the stage, still frozen by fear.

Old Man Riddle took charge. He looked at Nina

Faye Davidson and said, "Go get Pastor Tabor." Nina Faye nodded and ran for her car.

He looked back at Willy. "Willy, you got your truck?" he asked.

"Yes, sir, Mr. Riddle."

"Go to the hospital and tell them to send an ambulance, if they can." We only had a small hospital, and they didn't always have enough staff for the ambulance.

"Yes, sir," said Willy as he hurried from the tent.

Then as Reverend Hines, and everyone else, looked on, Old Man Riddle gently pulled Ruby's hand away from the bite for a better look. He reached into his pocket and pulled out his pouch of tobacco and shoved a wad into his cheeks. He worked it around in his mouth, building up a spit, then pulled the wad out and slapped it onto the bite.

"Hold that on the wound. It'll help draw out the venom," he said. "It's best if you lay down." He leaned her back, and one of the men from the revival slipped off his suit coat and made her a pillow. A streak of dirty brown tobacco juice dribbled through her fingers, down her neck, and onto her dress.

"Is she going to be okay?" asked Eula Shaw between sniffles.

"Hard to say," said Old Man Riddle. "Those big rattlers can pack a mean punch."

Eula pulled off her glasses and cried louder. "It's my fault. I dared her to go up." She began to sob like a baby calf looking for its mother.

Old Man Riddle looked up at Reverend Hines and asked, "Why can't that lady come out and heal her? She healed me."

"That, my good brother, is a delicate matter. You have to work up people's faith to get a healing like that, and she can only do a few healings each night." He shook his head. "I'm sorry. She's done for the night."

Before anyone else could speak, Floyd blurted out, "Stone can do it." Everyone turned to look at him. He had put back on his Dekalb Seed Company cap and looked out at the dubious crowd from under the bill. "Y'all ain't heard that he has the healing gift too?"

"Floyd!" I hissed as all eyes turned to me.

Jo Anne Carter glared at me with her coal-black eyes. "Everybody in town has heard the rumors that you healed one of the darkies from Coe Ridge. Is it true?"

I swallowed and nodded.

"He's done more than that," added Floyd. "He made Hazel Owens walk again. I seen her myself."

"Go on, Stone," insisted Dewdrop. "Heal Ruby before she dies." He shoved me forward, closer to the crowd.

"C'mon, son!" said one of the revival workers.

"Don't let her die!" cried Eula.

The small crowd erupted into shouts and pleadings. Some insisted. Others begged. I wanted to run. I shut out the crowd and looked at Ruby. Her chocolate eyes stared back at me, full of worry. I sensed her desperation but wondered if it sprang from the snakebite or from her fear of her strict father. I still loved her. I wanted to help, but I had never used my gift in an environment like this one before. All the noise and fear seemed to crush me.

"I remember what it said on the headstone," said Ruby. Everyone quieted down when she spoke. Her dark eyes pleaded. "May your healing gift continue forever." A tear trickled down her cheek and joined the brown streak of tobacco juice on her neck. "Help me, Stone," she whispered.

I walked over, sat on the stage, and cradled her head

in my lap like that afternoon up at Alpine Lodge. I closed my eyes and shut out the crowd. I pretended it was just me and Ruby. I caressed her soft corn-silk hair and its sweet smell overpowered the stench of wet tobacco. I remembered the wet kiss and the way she made me feel.

The words from Ezekiel came without coaxing. I felt the storm gathering in my head, and I could feel her faith burning. The flashes of lightning danced around my brain and the heat surged in my hands. She was holding the wad of tobacco on the wound with her left hand. I reached down, put my hand over hers, and whispered, "Live; yea, I said unto thee when thou wast in thy blood, Live."

At this point, I knew it was going to work. The storm raged in my head. My hands burned. I sensed the two small wounds left by the big timber rattler sealing up. I could sense the venom breaking down, losing its ability to harm. I could feel the steady beat of Ruby's heart. Then, just like always, all the energy gathered in my chest and flew away like some fleeting bird. I let out a heavy sigh and sat there in the darkness of my gift, still cradling Ruby's head in my lap.

I felt the soft touch of Ruby's fingers on my cheek. "Thank you, Stone," she said breathlessly. I felt her grab the back of my neck and pull me down into a kiss. Her lips were soft and her breath was sweet like honeysuckle. For a moment I forgot where I was and kept my lips locked with hers, but the shouts of the crowd brought me back to the vivid reality.

"I told ya he could do it!" shouted Floyd.

"Ruby?" asked Eula Shaw. "Are you okay?"

Ruby sat up and left me in the dark, longing for the taste of her lips.

"Look at my neck!" said Ruby. "It's like nothing ever happened."

"Except for the tobacco stain," said Dewdrop.

Everyone was cheering and celebrating while I sat there waiting to gain my vision back. I felt a hand on my shoulder, and the Reverend Hines whispered into my ear, "How long does it usually take for your vision to come back?"

"Five or ten minutes," I answered. He patted me on the shoulder like he understood.

"Three cheers for Stone!" shouted Floyd. Everyone joined him and shouted, "Hip hip, hurray! Hip hip, hurray! Hip hip, hurray!" After the shouts I heard the approaching siren and worried about how Pastor Tabor was going to react.

I gave a closed-mouth smile and waved in the general direction of the group, hoping nobody would notice that I couldn't see. I felt someone sit next to me and recognized it was Ruby by the smell of her hair when she gave me a hug.

"Thank you, Stone!" she said and planted a kiss on my cheek.

"All right, folks, let us through. Let us through!" commanded Deputy Cortis Russel.

"Ruby Ruth Tabor!" said Pastor Tabor, making me jump. "We were told that you were hurt. What is going on here?"

"It's my fault, Pastor," said Eula Shaw. "I talked her into coming tonight, even though she said you wouldn't approve. And then when they started handling the snakes, I dared her to go up and—"

"Ruby Ruth, you came here even after I forbade it?" said Pastor Tabor. "Young lady—"

Old Man Riddle cleared his throat. "Pastor, maybe you should just be grateful she's alive for you to fuss at. If it weren't for Stone here, you'd be looking to buy a coffin and a headstone."

"Stone? What did he have to do with this?"

I still couldn't see, but I could feel Pastor Tabor's eyes on me. I could imagine the stern and puzzled look on his face. I decided to speak for myself. "Well, sir, when she got bit, I was able to heal her." I looked in his general direction when I spoke, but I was only guessing.

"What? Look, will somebody start from the beginning and explain to me what happened tonight and why I was called down here to rescue my daughter from certain death only to find her alive and well?"

"Father," said Ruby with a sigh. "I know you told me, us, not to come to the tent revival tonight, but this town is so boring." A couple of people chuckled. "Well, after watching that lady, Phoebe, heal those people tonight, I was mesmerized. Then when they started handling the snakes and invited others with faith to come up, I wanted to try. I rushed up on stage and grabbed out a big timber rattler."

"You did what?" asked Pastor Tabor.

I blinked and could make out the string of lights overhead like stars in the night sky. My vision was starting to come back.

"I came up and took up a rattler. It was like nothing I'd ever felt before," swooned Ruby. "The mixture of fear and faith was intoxicating."

"Fear, faith, and foolishness," chided Pastor Tabor.

"It's a question of faith, brother," chimed in Reverend Hines from behind me.

"This is nothing more than a circus act," shot back Pastor Tabor. I could make out his shadow and could see him pointing his finger.

"O ye of little faith!" replied Reverend Hines.

Pastor started to continue the volley, when Deputy Cortis Russel stopped the argument. "You two gentlemen can continue your theological discussion another time. Finish your story, Ruby."

I looked at Ruby and everything came into focus again. She stood there with her hands folded in front of her, staring at the ground. Her neck and dress were stained from the wad of tobacco that Old Man Riddle had slapped on the wound, but other than that, her neck was perfect. No puncture marks. No redness. And she looked as pretty as she did every Sunday when she stood and greeted the congregation at the chapel door, as Leck would say, good enough to stop traffic.

"Well, while I was handling the snake, it suddenly lashed out and bit me on the neck." She tilted her head, exposing the brown spot, and pointed. "I froze with fear. I was paralyzed. I could feel the venom burning."

All the blood drained from Pastor Tabor's face. He took a seat in the front row.

"I thought I was going to die." She looked over at me. "Until Stone healed me."

Pastor Tabor shook his head but said nothing for a moment. Then he stood and straightened his shirt. He gave me a curt nod and said, "Thank you, Stone." Then he stepped over to Ruby and grabbed her just above the elbow. "C'mon, Ruby. Let's go home." He escorted her through the crowd and toward his car. She looked back at me and mouthed, "Thank you," before they got out of the tent.

Willy had come back empty-handed from the hospital, but he, Dewdrop, and Floyd stood beside me like proud parents. I sat there on the stage gathering my strength as several people filed past and shook my hand or patted me on the back. Even protective Jo Anne Carter gave me a hug. Some folks, like Eula Shaw, just stood back and looked at me, as if they were afraid to get near me. I wouldn't be able to hide behind rumors or gossip anymore. People were either going to believe in me, or fear me.

"Reverend Hines," announced Deputy Cortis Russel, sounding as authoritative as possible, "I reckon you best be shutting down this revival and moving on."

"Why? We have a permit for three weeks."

"In the interest of public safety. We can't have you endangering our citizens with poisonous snakes."

"Handling the snakes is strictly voluntary, sir. It is not against the law."

Deputy Russel straightened himself to his full height and rested his hand on the butt of his revolver. "I said you best be packing up and moving on."

"Are you the sheriff now?" asked a woman from behind the stage. Her clear strong voice was unmistakable. Phoebe Webb stepped out of the darkness and onto the stage. She wore a black silk robe over her dress, but her hair was still up. She strode to the front of the stage, folded her arms, and gave Deputy Russel a blank stare as if he were insignificant.

His mouth dropped open like he had seen a ghost. "Well, uh . . . You see . . ."

"What's the matter, Deputy? Cat got your tongue?" asked Phoebe Webb. She tapped her foot like she was impatient with the whole scene as everyone watched the exchange.

Deputy Cortis Russel opened his mouth again like he was going to speak but then blushed so much that his red face glowed like one of the light bulbs hanging overhead. Then he pulled his flat hat down over his eyes and hurried to his cruiser like a man running from a hornet's nest.

"I ain't never seen him act that way," whispered Willy.

"Me either," I added. I noticed that Phoebe Webb was still standing in the middle of the stage watching Deputy Russel's car drive away.

What was left of the crowd began to head home. I pushed myself off the edge of the stage. I wanted to do something that made me feel normal again. "C'mon, let's go down to Shorty's and shoot some pool," I said. Floyd grinned. Willy and Dewdrop nodded, and we all headed for our vehicles.

As I passed in front of the stage, I noticed that Reverend Hines was pointing at me and whispering in Phoebe's ear. I could feel her looking at me. I knew that part of the reason that I came tonight was to talk to anybody that might know about my gift, but right now, I just wanted to forget it all. I figured Shorty's would be a good place to unwind, and I hurried for the exit.

"Excuse me, young man!" It was her voice again, like a siren calling me, beckoning me. "Can I speak with you?"

Floyd, Willy, and Dewdrop all stopped and looked back at her when she spoke. I stopped but didn't turn around. They all looked at her and then at me as if trying to figure out where to place their allegiance.

"Y'all go on," I said. "I'll catch up."

For a moment I thought they didn't hear me, then Willy said, "Okay, see ya at Shorty's." They turned and continued, and I felt like the sailor that gets sacrificed to the sirens so the ship can pass.

"Yes, ma'am," I said as I turned around. I stuck my hands in my pockets and tried to hide my nervousness. I had wanted answers. I had wanted understanding. But now that I stood face-to-face with someone who might be able to give me both, I was afraid of what I might learn.

"Come on over to the stage," she insisted with a smile. "I won't bite."

I shuffled over with my hands still shoved deep into my pockets. Except for a few folks attached to the revival party, the tent was empty. Reverend Hines stood behind Phoebe Webb as if he wanted to protect his investment. She walked to the front of the stage and stood there with her arms crossed. At first she looked stern, but as I drew closer, she looked more puzzled and melancholy.

"What's your name?" she asked in her silky voice.

I felt like she was looking straight through me. "Ezekiel Stone Molony, ma'am."

"How old are you?"

"Around seventeen, but nobody knows my real birthday."

She pulled the robe more tightly around her, like she had suddenly felt a chill. Her steady eyes flickered and all the lines on her face drew taut. "You're tall. Like your father?"

"I never met my real father. Billy Molony is my step-father, and I'm already taller than him."

She examined me up and down while I stood there with my hands in my pockets. Finally, I gathered enough courage and asked, "Is your gift for real?"

My question seemed to surprise her, but I saw a hint of a smile at the corner of her mouth. "Yes, it's real."

"Then why did the first two people you heal have fake injuries?"

Her smile grew wider, and she glanced back at the Reverend Hines. He shook his head and mumbled under his breath, but I don't think it was a prayer.

"Sometimes," explained Reverend Hines, "we have to prime the well of faith. We use a few pseudo healings to help people believe. Then they will have enough faith for Sister Webb to heal those with real calamities."

"How did you know they were fake?" asked Phoebe.

I shrugged. "It's a small community. I didn't recognize them, and it all seemed a little too theatrical."

"Son," said Reverend Hines, shaking a threatening finger, "I urge you to use caution and discernment when you discuss this matter with anyone else."

I didn't respond to the threat but looked back at Phoebe and asked, "Do you go blind when you use your gift?"

She raised an eyebrow. "Yes, I lose my sight for a while when I heal someone." She relaxed her shoulders and slipped her hands into the pockets of her robe. "How about you? Did you lose your sight after healing the girl from the snakebite?"

I nodded. "The blindness lasts several minutes each time I use my gift."

"Do you know what power you possess?" she asked.

"Not really."

"Do you know how to use it properly?"

I shook my head, feeling embarrassed at the limits of my understanding. "I know I can heal people, that is, if they believe."

"Well, Ezekiel Stone Molony, you should be more careful using powers you don't understand." She turned and walked slowly toward the back of the stage. The sound of her heels against the wooden stage echoed through the empty tent.

I had come tonight in search of answers, and the person most likely to give them to me was walking away. "Wait! Can you teach me?" I blurted out.

She stopped just short of the back curtain and turned to look at me. Her face had clouded over with the look of a gathering storm. Her eyes were dark and brooding, and her brow creased with worry. She ducked through the back curtain without answering.

I jumped up on the low stage determined to go after her, but Reverend Hines jumped in front of me. "Not so fast there, young man," he said, grabbing me by the shoulders. "I think the lady's lack of a response is answer enough."

"But I have questions that only she can answer," I insisted.

"Look, son," said Reverend Hines with a gentle shake. "I'm very grateful to you for saving the young lady tonight, but I think it would be best if you didn't come back."

"What do you mean? Why not?"

"Let's just say, we already have one healer. A second one not affiliated with our revival troupe might have a very negative impact on the financial health of our mission. Besides, you understand how it works, and people don't often worship things they understand."

I couldn't believe what he was telling me. "Are you saying you don't want me coming back because you might not make as much money?"

"If you want to join us, I'm sure we could put you to work, but we don't need you as a competitor. Since you are underage and would need your parents' permission to join us, I think it's best if you just stay away. We'll be gone in a week or two."

I was being kicked out of a tent revival. For a moment I thought about punching the good reverend and heading through the curtain, but I kept my cool. I shook myself loose from his grip, jumped off the stage, and started for my car. I looked in the rearview mirror as I pulled out of the lot and saw Phoebe Webb standing in the door of her travel trailer, watching me go.

EIGHT

I could feel my frustration building as I drove over to the square and looked for a parking place not too far from Shorty's Pool Hall. I had gone to the revival hoping to get some answers, and instead I had been thrust further into the limelight. Not only that, but I had been snubbed by the person who I hoped would help me. I had just saved Ruby's life and still Pastor Tabor treated me like I wasn't good enough for his daughter. Daddy wanted to work me to death. Mama was frustrated with me because of Leck. The truth was, I was starting to feel a lot of pressure in my life. I was hoping to blow off some steam at Shorty's.

The front door of Shorty's was propped open, letting fresh air into the smoky pool hall. The sound of clinking pool balls and raucous conversation spilled out into the cool summer night. I think the jukebox was playing "Mr. Sandman." Shorty ran a tight ship. He offered pool, cold sodas, and cigarettes. A guy could unwind with a game of pool and lots of guy talk. Women never came into Shorty's.

Shorty gave me a nod from his tall stool in the corner when I walked in. True to his nickname, he was a little over five feet tall, but he had a voice like a foghorn that made him sound ten feet tall. If things started heating up in his place, a word from him would usually restore order, but just in case a word wasn't enough, he kept a pump shotgun full of rock salt under the back counter. I saw Willy and Dewdrop racking up for a game of eight ball on the middle table. Floyd sat off to the side drinking a root beer. I grabbed a cue off the rack and an RC Cola from Shorty and joined them. "I got winner," I announced. Floyd had his cap pulled down over his eyes again. He looked up at me from under the bill and just nodded.

Dewdrop broke the cluster of balls, and the six ball clinked into the corner pocket. "So what did the lady have to say?" he asked as he positioned for his next shot.

"Not much really. She just asked me a couple of questions about my age and my father."

"You think she's for real?" asked Floyd. "I mean, can she do what you did for Ruby?"

I sipped on my cola and tried to decide how much to tell them. "Well, according to Reverend Hines, the first few healings are fake. They use theatrics to prime the pump of faith, so to speak. But after that, she says they're for real."

"Dang it!" said Dewdrop as he missed an easy shot.

"If she's for real, then why didn't she come out and heal Ruby?" asked Willy as he positioned to sink a ball in the side pocket.

"She seems for real." I shrugged and took a swig of my soda. "Maybe she can only do so much." I wondered what she meant when she told me I had no idea what I was dealing with.

"It all sounds a little weird to me," said Willy. "Uh, no offense, Stone." He sank his shot. I just took another big gulp of my soda and nodded. I agreed. It was weird, but it was becoming my life. I sighed and watched Willy miss his next shot.

"Hey, healer boy!" shouted Jed Mock from Shorty's open doorway. "Come to fix a few broken pool cues?" Johnny Hart laughed like a mule.

I gave Jed a menacing glance and watched Dewdrop sink his shot in the corner pocket. I was in no mood to deal with those idiots. I just wanted to shoot some pool and forget about everything for a while. Of course, they had other plans.

Johnny Hart shouted, "Healer boy, I've got the green apple toots. Help me!" He farted so loud I could hear it over the music and everyone's ruckus.

"I've got a toothache," added Carl Ash, holding his jaw.

"It hurts when I pee!" said Jed Mock as he grabbed his crotch. Then they all laughed and sounded like hell's minions torturing the wicked. They grabbed cues off the rack and took over the table next to us.

"Y'all shut up!" shouted Floyd.

They all laughed louder at his demand.

Shorty's voice rumbled from the stool in the corner, "Easy, fellas."

"Just ignore 'em," whispered Floyd.

I turned and faced our table with my back to their insults. I was afraid that if I turned around, I wouldn't be able to control myself. I could feel the sweat building between my hand and the cue. My knuckles were all white with rage. I probably should have just walked back out to my car and gone home, but my pride wouldn't let me.

"Hey, healer boy, did you hear they arrested your colored girlfriend?" said Jed, ignoring Shorty. I spun around, brandishing the cue in my hand as a weapon. Jed leaned up against the next table, chalking his cue.

"Yep, she decided to sit in the white section of the theater again tonight, but you weren't there to save her this time." He puckered his lips and blew the excess chalk at my face. "The sheriff hauled her off in handcuffs this time." He grinned and the neon light from the front window reflected off his yellow teeth. "I must say she looked mighty inviting with her hands cuffed behind her back." He rolled his head to the left and snickered at Johnny Hart.

Before I realized what I was doing, I swung the pool cue with both hands. I hit him square across the nose above his pathetic mustache and broke the tip of the pool cue. His grin evaporated as blood gushed from his nose, and he covered his shocked face with both hands. He dropped to his knees, groaning, as drops of blood splattered the floor. Johnny grabbed his cue and jumped to his feet. Vince and Carl followed suit. I stood there with the broken cue in my hand ready to do battle. Willy, Dewdrop, and Floyd slid in beside me. Just as we were about to mix it up, I heard Shorty chamber a round in his pump shotgun.

"Awright, fellas," boomed Shorty. "The next one that moves gets a hind end full of rock salt."

We all froze. I could see Jed Mock hunched over with one knee on the floor still cupping his face with both hands and the blood pooling on the floor below him. Guilt crept in, replacing my rage, as I looked at my handiwork. The broken cue was suddenly heavy in my hand, and I was ashamed to be holding it.

The whole place got quiet except for Perry Como singing "Wanted" from the jukebox. Shorty strolled between us still holding the shotgun at the ready. "You boys put your pool cues on the table and your hands on top of your heads." We all complied without complaint, and Shorty lowered the shotgun. He looked down at Jed and saw the blood on his floor.

"Who started this mess?" demanded Shorty.

"They did, Shorty," said Willy. "They was making fun of Stone."

"Who took the first swing?"

I hung my head and owned up to the deed. "I did, Shorty."

"Stone?" asked Shorty with a puzzled look. Then he just shook his head and wrinkled his forehead like he was disappointed in what he had just heard. "Well then, you gotta clean up the mess and get him bandaged up."

"Yes, sir," I answered, ashamed at myself for losing control.

"The rest of you boys get out of here, and next time you come back, stick to shootin' pool." Shorty nodded at the front door with his head, and everybody but Jed and me left.

"Stone, go in the back and get the bucket from under the sink. Fill it with water and grab some rags to clean up this mess," commanded Shorty. I did as instructed, and when I came back, Shorty had Jed in a chair and was assessing the damage to his nose. A few guys were taking a look at my handiwork, but most everyone had returned to playing pool. Jed's nose was black and blue, and crooked as a dog's hind leg. The blood had clotted up in the sparse hairs of his mustache and dribbled onto his shirt. A wave of nausea swept over me at the sight as I realized the pain I had caused him. I got down on all fours and started wiping the blood up off the floor. The scripture from Ezekiel haunted me, but I ignored it. The burden of my violent act began to weigh me down like a millstone around my neck. With each drop of Jed's blood that I wiped up from the floor, my shoulders slumped. Before I finished, I was blinking back tears of guilt.

"Looks like you broke his nose," said Shorty. "You need to take him to a doctor."

I wiped my eyes and tried to hide my tears. I looked up at Jed sitting in the chair with his head leaned back against the wall and felt another wave of shame. He looked pitiful, and it was my fault. I forgot about all of his hateful teasing, lewd comments, and rude behavior. I saw a vulnerable young man, a lot like me, just trying to figure life out. I felt sorry for him. I longed to forgive him.

Jed raised his head and looked at me. The hatred in his eyes had been replaced with pain. "I heard what you did for Ruby. Can't you help me too?"

Then, without warning, the lightning storm kicked off in my head, and I knew what to do to ease my guilt. I put the rag in the bucket and stood up. I walked over and sat next to Jed. Shorty stood up and looked on in surprise as I put my hand on Jed's broken nose. Jed flinched at first, but then, as if he sensed what was coming, he closed his eyes and relaxed. The scripture raced around my head. My hands burned. The lightning storm raged. When I pulled my hand away, my knees buckled and I sat down on the floor, swimming in darkness.

"Da-ang," said Shorty, stretching the word into two syllables. "You fixed his nose."

I heard the clinking of pool balls from one of the other tables, but then Shorty's got quieter than I had ever heard it. Jed sniffled. Tennessee Earnie Ford was singing about Davy Crockett on the jukebox. Somebody sneezed.

"Your nose looks as good as new, Jed," said Shorty. "How do you feel?"

Jed sniffled again. "I feel fine. Like nothin' ever happened. How'd you do that, Stone?"

I sat there on the floor with my legs crossed Indian style, cradling my head in my hands and my elbows on my knees. "It's hard to explain, Jed," I started. "I have this strange gift for healing, but I'm not really sure how it happens. Truth is, I shouldn't have hurt you in the first place. I'm sorry."

Jed didn't say anything at first. I imagined him sitting there stroking his mustache wondering about what had happened. Finally he answered, "I didn't mean anything by my teasing. We was just havin' fun."

"Seems like you were trying to make me mad."

"Maybe so," he chuckled, "but you're so easy to get riled up."

"Maybe so."

"Hey, Shorty, I know you're gonna kick us out for fightin', but can we play a game before we go?" he asked.

"If you can play without fighting," said Shorty. I heard Shorty grab the bucket, mumbling something to himself about the craziest thing he'd ever seen, and head for the back room. The sound of pool balls slamming into one another filled the room again. Faron Young's voice started singing "If You Ain't Loving" on the jukebox. Everything was still dark.

"C'mon, grab a cue. You can break," said Jed.

I reached up, felt for the edge of the pool table, and pulled myself up. "Maybe you should break. I can't see just yet."

"What do you mean you can't see?"

"When I heal someone, I'm blind for a little while." I heard him light up a cigarette and smelled the smoke.

"That's weird," said Jed with a laugh. "Then I oughta be able to beat you."

"Give me a few minutes. It'll come back." I could just start to see the glow from the neon sign in Shorty's front window. I was a little baffled by Jed's change of heart, but I didn't want to waste his current goodwill. So I decided now might be a good time to clear the air a bit. "What do you have against colored people?" I asked.

"I ain't got nothin' against niggers. I think everyone should have one," he said with a laugh. I heard a cue ball crash into the group of racked balls. One of them dropped into a pocket. I blinked again and images started coming back as shadows. I felt my way over to a stool and sat down to let my vision return as Jed took another shot.

"Seriously, Jed," I continued. "Why should it bother you if Wonnie sits next to you in the movies?" My vision had almost returned to normal, and I could see that he was lining up for another shot at a corner pocket.

"Why can't she just sit up in the balcony where she belongs?" He missed the shot. "Dang it!" He took a drag from his cigarette. "Can you see well enough to shoot yet?"

"Yeah, barely. Stripes or solids?"

"You're stripes."

Things were still just a bit fuzzy, but I looked over the table and lined up my cue for a bumper shot. "Why do we treat the coloreds different anyway? They're just like you and me."

"No, they ain't just like you and me. Their skin is dark. They're dirty. They carry disease. They talk different. They're colored, and we're white."

I missed my shot. "Yeah, they're different and their skin is colored, but they're people just like you and me. Why can't they do the same things you and I can do?"

"'Cause they're colored folks, I guess." He sunk

another ball. "Look, I don't know why some things are the way they are, but I don't see no reason to go changing things either." He took another shot but missed. "Why do you care what happens to a bunch of coloreds anyway?"

I shrugged and struggled with my answer. "I guess . . . I guess I just don't think it's right the way they get treated, like they're not as good as whites." I lined up my shot and sunk a ball in the corner pocket.

"But they ain't as good as whites," he declared with his cigarette hanging from his mouth. "Half the coloreds in Zeke Town can't even write their own name. One or two of them is always in the jailhouse. I bet half of 'em don't even know who their real father is."

I missed my shot. I could feel myself getting frustrated and angry again. I found my RC Cola and took a long drink while he lined up his next shot. "What about Wonnie? She graduated from high school down in Birmingham. She's smart. She comes from a good family. She bathes regularly and doesn't carry disease. Why shouldn't she be allowed to sit in the white section of the movie theater?"

Jed sunk another ball. He was beating the pants off me. He looked up and grinned, and his yellow teeth looked even more yellow in the pool hall lighting. "Why do you like her so much? Is she really giving you a little brown sugar on the side?"

I blushed. I thought about how she looked the other day when I saw her on the front porch. I remembered how attractive she was. "No, it's not like that, Jed. I've known her since we were kids. My daddy's been delivering feed up on Coe Ridge for years, and I've been going with him. I guess I just see the colored folks different than you do."

"Well, my daddy don't want nothing to do with 'em," he said as he sunk another ball. "Unless he's looking for moonshine or a little nighttime company." He punctuated his statement with a wink and made a clicking sound out of the side of his mouth.

"What about your mom? Doesn't that bother her?"

The grin went away, and Jed looked out the front window of the smoky pool hall. "My mama died giving birth to my younger brother ten years ago." He tossed his cigarette butt on the floor and crushed it with his foot.

"Sorry, I didn't know that." I felt stupid for not knowing that about Jed, especially in such a small town. A lot of things about him suddenly made sense. The game got quiet for a few minutes as he sunk several balls in a row.

"Eight ball, corner pocket," he announced, and then he finished the game with a perfect shot. "Too bad we weren't playing for money. I would have taken you to the cleaners."

I nodded and chuckled. "You would've cleaned me out. I guess that means the game's on me." I put the cue back on the rack as he gathered the balls and racked them for the next players. We both stood there for an awkward moment next to the table until I stuck my hand out and said, "I'm sorry about what I did to your nose."

"Sorry for bustin' it or sorry for fixin' it?" he said with a grin as he shook my hand. "Shoot, I had it comin'. I've been picking at you for a long time." He released my hand and headed for the front door. "See you at basketball tomorrow morning, nigger lover!" he yelled over his shoulder with a laugh.

I shook my head at his comment. We had made our peace, but he was still the same bigoted troublemaker that I had whacked across the nose with a pool cue earlier. I guess I had hoped that my healing or my discussion about colored folks might change him at least a little, but it didn't seem to faze him. At least we weren't fighting anymore. Maybe in time he would change.

Shorty looked at me funny when I paid for the game and the pool cue I had busted over Jed's nose, but he didn't ask any more questions. I climbed into the old Buick and headed for home. It was after ten and I needed to get my chores done tomorrow morning before going to play basketball. I picked up speed as I headed out of town but kept it close to the limit. I didn't want Deputy Russel to stop me for speeding again.

The next morning Jersey Girl was restless, and when I got back to the house with the milk, Samuel was standing by the back porch. He was looking at the ground with his hands on his knees. Since he didn't have on a T-shirt, I could see his chest heaving up and down through the side of his bib overalls. Sweat was dropping from his forehead like he had been working out in the heat of the day.

"Samuel? What's goin' on?" I asked as I got close.

He stood up straight as soon as he heard my voice. "It's Wonnie. She's been hurt."

"Hurt? What happened? How bad?" I sat the milk container on the back step and looked at him. He was looking at the ground like he didn't want to look me in the eye. "What's going on, Samuel?"

"Somebody done beat her real bad." He looked up at me, and I could see his eyes full of tears and his lip quivering. "We need you to come and heal her."

I stood there in shock for a moment with my mind racing. Why would anyone beat up a girl? Who would have done such a thing? With my thoughts still churning,

I picked up the milk and hurried into the kitchen. "Give me a minute. I'll be out directly." Mama was fixing breakfast when I rushed in and set the milk on the table. "Mama, I've got to go up to Coe Ridge. Samuel's here and he says somebody beat up Wonnie."

"What?" She stood at the stove with her mouth open.

"I don't know what happened, but he says I need to go heal her." I grabbed the keys to the pickup truck from the hook near the back door. "Tell Daddy I'll be back as soon as I can." I rushed out the back door before she could answer.

We jumped into the truck and headed down the lane, but when we got to Neely's Ferry, I realized that I had forgotten my wallet. I convinced Cyrus, the ferry driver that morning, to let us pass because it was an emergency and I would pay him later. I burned up the asphalt with the old truck, but when we turned off the blacktop road, I had to slow down or risk ripping an axle loose on the miserable excuse for a road. "Tell me what happened, Samuel," I said, now that we had slowed down.

He had been staring out the window the whole time, and when I asked the question he only turned his head enough to make sure I could hear his voice. "We went to the movies again last night," he began. "Wonnie went down and sat in the white section again, but this time they called Sheriff Pace. He handcuffed her and hauled her away. I hung around for a while, but they told me just to go on home because they might have to keep her overnight." He started shaking his head and choking back sobs. "I shoulda stayed there. I shoulda stayed there."

I focused on the road and didn't say anything, waiting for him to regain his composure. After a couple of minutes, he let out a sobbing sigh and continued, "I hitched a ride on home and told Papa what had happened. He was madder than a hornet and said they had no right to keep his baby girl. He grabbed his gun, and we lit out on foot for town." He paused again and stared out the window.

We had started up the ridge, and I had the truck creeping along in low gear. I knew we would be getting to the Wilburn place shortly, but I didn't rush Samuel. He let out another sigh and continued. "When we was walking along the road almost to the blacktop road, we saw something in the road like a sack of feed that had fallen off a truck or something. Papa hurried over to it like he knew what it was, but I was afraid." Samuel started crying out loud, long sobs of anguish. "It was Wonnie," he said between cries. "Her face was busted up and one of her eyes was swollen shut. Her dress had been ripped down the front. Somebody done beat her and raped her and left her in the road like some dead animal." He put his face in his hands. "How could they do that? She ain't never hurt nobody," he wailed.

I felt the blood drain from my face and my empty stomach twist into knots. A wave of nausea swept over me, and for a moment I thought I might have to stop the truck and throw up. I gripped the steering wheel tighter and jammed on the gas to keep myself focused. The dizzying array of emotions made my head spin. I was worried about Wonnie. I was confused why anyone would do such a thing and so furious that I wanted to beat the snot out of whoever did it to her. I took a deep breath and tried to stay calm. I knew what I needed to do.

Samuel was still sobbing when we pulled up in front of the Wilburn's wooden shack. I set the brake, jumped out, and ran for the porch. Patsy Ann opened the door and ushered me into the house. "She's in her bed," said Patsy Ann. Her face was blank, and her eyes were dull like she was half-asleep.

We passed through the kitchen and hurried through the small wooden door to the bedroom she shared with Samuel. Otis was sitting beside her bed holding her limp hand. I wasn't prepared for what I saw. I cringed when I saw Wonnie's face and looked away out of reflex. I had to force myself to look back. My nausea returned, but I choked it back.

Both of Wonnie's eyes were swollen shut with huge black-and-blue half-moon bruises puffed up like a frog's chin when he's singing. Her top lip was busted near the corner of her mouth and bigger than a radish. The left side of her face was swollen so bad that she looked like she weighed three hundred pounds. Every time I looked at her I cringed and wanted to look away, but I forced myself to witness what they had done to her.

Otis looked up at me and said, "She ain't said a word since I picked her up on the road."

"She's our baby girl," said Patsy Ann, sounding like she was talking about a newborn.

I stood there in shock. I was so sure I could help when I left the house, but now that I stood here looking at the damage done to Wonnie, I doubted. I wanted to run. My anger surged and all I could think about was getting even for what they had done to her, all because she wanted to sit in the white section of the theater.

"Who did this to her?" I asked. I could feel my face red with anger.

Otis looked at the floor. "We don't know for sure," said Patsy Ann without taking her eyes off Wonnie, lying unconscious in the bed.

"We need to get the sheriff," I half growled. My jaw was tight, and my hands were balled into tight fists. "Whoever did this needs to be thrown in jail."

"You really think the sheriff's gonna do anything

about some bright nigger girl from Zeke Town?" asked Samuel from behind me. He must have come in quietly while I was focused on Wonnie. "Just like they did for each of my brothers? They'll file a report and pretend to care, but they ain't gonna find the sorry cusses that did this to my sister."

I turned around and faced Samuel. "Well, we've got to try! We gotta catch whoever did this to her and make sure they pay for what they've done."

Samuel snorted. "You ready to make them pay? The law sure ain't gonna do nothin'."

"They have to do something!" I shouted. "Look at her!"

Samuel nodded. "Oh, I seen her. Maybe it's you that needs to take a good look," he said, poking a finger into my chest. "She's a nigger."

"Samuel. Stone. That's enough boys!" boomed Otis's deep voice, loud enough that I could feel it. "Y'all can argue later. Right now we gots to take care of Wonnie." Samuel gritted his teeth like he was holding back his tongue, and then he lowered his head and nodded.

I tightened my jaw and blew air out through my nose, trying to calm down. "I'm sorry, Otis," I said. I turned and walked over to Wonnie with my emotions swirling in a mess of anger and anxiety.

"You think you can heal my baby girl?" asked Patsy Ann.

I nodded but didn't say anything. I was repeating the scripture over and over again in my head hoping that the storm in my head would start, but my mind was dominated by anger and my desire for revenge. I tried to clear my head, but every time I looked at Wonnie I cringed and felt helpless. I couldn't feel anything from her, like she was dead. I closed my eyes and tried to focus, but each time the image of her beaten face was all I could see. I mumbled the scripture to myself trying to find my gift. Nothing. I tried to see Wonnie's smiling face in my mind's eye, hoping that my gift would come. Nothing. I reached out and touched her, trying to feel something that would help me heal her. Nothing.

I stood there with my eyes closed, trying to focus. I heard Otis shift, and the old wooden chair he was sitting in creaked. Patsy Ann started singing in a low voice, "I'm troubled, I'm troubled, I'm troubled in my mind. If Jesus don't help me, I surely will die." I heard the screen door slam as Samuel went out onto the porch. Nothing came to me.

I opened my eyes and let out an exasperated sigh. "I can't do it," I said, shaking my head. "It ain't coming to me." I couldn't face Otis and Patsy Ann, so I just turned and headed out onto the front porch, sat on the bottom step, and put my head in my hands. I didn't understand why I couldn't heal her. I felt confused. I felt beaten.

I heard the screen door open slowly behind me. "You know, I remember when Miss Opal used to come around," said Patsy Ann as she sat on the top step of the rickety wooden porch. "She couldn't help everyone either. I remember one time she tried to heal my cousin Billy from the whooping cough, but she never could do it. She said there weren't enough faith."

"What happened to Billy?" I asked without turning around.

"Well, he got himself better, but it took him awhile."

I didn't know if Wonnie would recover from her wounds. I stood and rubbed the back of my neck. "Do you want me to take her to the hospital?" I asked.

"Before you go, come back inside and try one more time." She stood and glanced over at Samuel sitting at the end of the porch, staring off into the woods. "This time, we gonna help you. Come on, Samuel," she called. "Your sister needs you."

Patsy Ann turned and went back through the screen door. Samuel looked over at me with sad eyes and then stood to go inside. "Sorry 'bout yellin' at you, Stone. I'm jest all torn up about Wonnie."

I nodded and said, "Me too." I followed him back through the screen door and to Wonnie's bedside.

Otis still sat beside Wonnie holding her hand, but her face hadn't changed. Her chest rose and fell with each shallow breath, but other than that she could have passed for dead.

"Y'all gather round and hold hands," said Patsy Ann. Samuel slid up beside me, grabbed Otis's hand, and then offered me his. I took his hand as Patsy Ann grabbed mine. We all bowed our heads. Patsy Ann began to sing so low you could barely hear her.

I had always thought my gift came from God, but I didn't really know. Leck's explanation about me being an alien seemed just as plausible to me. I believed in God, but I guess I had never seen or recognized his power in a way that I could clearly attribute it to him. I stood there holding hands around Wonnie and prayed, hoping that if my gift did come from God, he would grant me the ability to save Wonnie. I asked for him to help me find who did this to her and see them brought to justice. Then I let go of my anger and begged for his help.

Lightning struck at the back of my neck. The scripture from Ezekiel went round and round inside my head. My hands began to burn. I let go of Samuel and Patsy Ann and put a hand on Wonnie's face. The storm raged worse than I had ever felt it before, almost like it was an angry storm bent on destruction. I focused on the scripture. I could see Wonnie's face without a bruise or swelling, but she wasn't smiling. I felt the energy flow from my hands like hot lava from a volcano that scours the ground as it spews out, and I could feel her broken body healing, but not her soul. Everything was working. I was healing her, but something was wrong. The unnatural energy flowed through me like I was a lightning rod catching every bolt of lightning during a summer thunderstorm as it passes by. Then, like always, all the energy gathered in my chest, but this time I felt it burn like hot wax, and I screamed as it flew away and left me blind and helpless on the floor beside her bed.

The next thing I heard was Wonnie crying.

Then Samuel said, "I'm sorry I left you, Wonnie. I'm sorry I left you."

I felt Patsy Ann grab me underneath my arms and start to lift me up. "Let's get you into a chair," she said as she guided me into the kitchen and sat me down. I heard her hurry back to Wonnie's side after she got me situated.

"Oh, praise the Lord!" said Patsy Ann.

I could hear Otis sobbing.

Then I heard Wonnie. "Y'all shoulda let me die," she said. "I don't wanna live!" she cried. "Y'all shoulda just let me die! I don't wanna live no more after what he done to me."

"Hush now, baby girl," said Patsy Ann, trying to calm her. "Everything gonna be okay now. Shhhh . . . hush now."

I could hear Wonnie wailing and crying like someone at a funeral. Short breaths punctuated her long wails. Over and over again, I heard her say that she wished we had let her die. I heard Patsy Ann and Otis try to comfort her, but she remained inconsolable as I sat there smothered by darkness in broad daylight.

I figured it took me almost thirty minutes to regain my sight. When I did finally recover my vision, Otis and Patsy were still hovering over their wailing baby girl. Samuel had removed himself to the front porch. I walked over and looked over Patsy Ann's shoulder to get a good look at Wonnie. Her face was without blemish. The swelling was gone. The cut on her lip was healed. The large blue bags around her eyes had disappeared. As best as I could tell by looking at her, she had been healed, but still she cried uncontrollably and wished to die.

When she saw me, she screamed at me. "Why didn't you just let me die? I don't want to live after what he did to me! Why did you save me?"

I looked at the floor, confused at the feelings of guilt and shame that came over me. Nobody had ever been upset with me for healing them. I wondered if I had done the right thing. Maybe God had meant for her to die, and I had saved her just so I could find out who had done this to her. "I'm sorry, Wonnie," I said.

Patsy Ann answered, "Don't you worry, Stone. She gonna be awright." Wonnie rolled over to face the wall, put her hands over her ears, and sobbed. Patsy patted her on the back and shushed her like a baby.

"You go on home now, Stone," said Otis. "We're much obliged for what you did, but you cain't do no more."

I started through the small kitchen for the front door feeling as if I was carrying a heavy load on my back when Otis stopped me. "Stone," he cautioned with a stern look, "don't go telling nobody about this. It ain't nobody's business but ours."

I nodded uncomfortably and then slipped out the screen door onto the porch as Wonnie continued to sob under the care of her parents. Samuel was sitting with his back up against the front tire of Daddy's truck, petting one of his hunting dogs, waiting for me. I trudged over to the truck, feeling spent like I had been working all day in the field, and his dog sniffed at my trousers and licked my hand. I scratched the dog's ears like I used to do to Rusty and then shoved my hands in my pockets, feeling numb.

"If she tells you who did this, will you let me know?" I asked.

"What for?" he asked as he stood up. "What you gonna do? Go after 'em?"

His tone surprised me again, but I was too tired to argue. "I'm going to tell the sheriff, so they can arrest them," I said.

Samuel just shook his head. "You don't know nothing about how things really work in our world, do you? This is Zeke Town, not Burkesville. The sheriff ain't gonna do nothing 'cept keep us in our place."

He put a hand on my shoulder and forced a smile. "You a good man, Stone, but they's a lot you don't know." With that he patted me on the shoulder and headed toward the barn with his dog trailing behind him. I climbed into the truck and started it, but I was so tired I don't remember the drive home.

NINE

⸎

I passed that night in and out of nightmares. I kept seeing Wonnie's disfigured face, feeling her pain, and hearing her cries. I woke up several times in a cold sweat hoping that the nightmares had passed, but each time I managed to get back to sleep, I was thrust back into a dark world of pain and anguish. I felt like I was experiencing the pain she had suffered first hand. I dreamt that when I woke up and looked in the mirror, my face was swollen and beaten. I woke up screaming several times, and by the time morning rolled around, I was ready to get out of bed and get my chores done.

Daddy was honking the horn ready for church when I hurried down the front porch with my tie and coat in hand. I climbed in the backseat, and he started down the lane before I got my door closed. I didn't see Leck beside me. "Where's Leck?" I asked.

Daddy scowled at me in the rearview mirror. Mama turned around and answered, "He doesn't feel well this morning. He says his back is bothering him." She turned back around and said almost to herself, "You'd feel the same way too if you had all that shrapnel in you."

I could tell that she was annoyed. We hadn't spoken about Leck for several days, but I figured it had to be because I had healed several other people, but not my own stepbrother. Truth is, I felt guilty also, but there wasn't anything I could do about it right now. I buttoned up my shirt and clipped on my tie.

I saw Maggie Owens walking in with her daughter Hazel when we pulled up in the church parking lot. I noticed Floyd's mom stop Hazel as they got to the front door and look at her legs. I could see the surprise on Mrs. Talbot's face as Hazel showed off her healed legs by jumping up and down. I hoped that she would speak well of me and my gift.

Daddy hurried in like always, but this time Mama was right beside him since she didn't have to worry about Leck. I got out slowly, still adjusting my tie, and tried to move nonchalantly for the door. Jo Anne Carter's family pulled up about the same time I got out of the car. Jo Anne gave me a big smile and wave. Her mother gave an equally big smile, but her eyes darted away from me, like she was nervous.

Ruby was at the door greeting, dressed in green this week. Any evidence of the snakebite was gone, and the skin of her neck was clean and radiant without blemish. She smelled clean and fresh from several yards away. I tried to think of some clever compliment, but nothing came to me.

"Good morning, Stone," she said, extending me her hand.

"Morning," I replied as I squeezed her hand.

She pulled my hand and wrapped her other arm around my neck, pulling me into a hug. "Thank you for saving my life," she whispered into my ear. I felt her soft hair against my cheek, and the smell of her clean hair filled my nose. Before I could respond, the embrace ended, and she was greeting the Carters right behind me.

I shuffled to our pew and slid in beside Mama.

"What happened to you yesterday?" asked Cortis Russel from the bench behind me. "Did your daddy have you working again so hard that you forgot about basketball?"

Daddy looked over at me and gave a snort. "No," I said, "I had to . . . um . . . I had to go to Coe Ridge to help somebody."

Cortis gave me a stern and puzzled look. "You went to Zeke Town instead of coming to basketball?" he asked in a raised voice. Mrs. Talbot was already playing the organ, but his voice carried above the music. His wife, Shirley Mae, stopped her conversation with Mrs. McCoy and both of them looked at me.

"Yes, sir," I said with a sheepish nod. He just shook his head in disgust.

I felt embarrassed all of a sudden, like I had done something wrong. It was kind of how I felt when I was up on Coe Ridge sometimes, just a little out of place. When I was up there, they were friendly and treated me well, but I was often reminded that I didn't understand what they went through. When I was here, everyone treated me and talked to me like an insider, like any other white boy, but even though I understood what they said, I didn't feel the same way they did. I felt like a stranger in a strange land. My gift only made it worse, or maybe it finally made me see the differences more clearly. I wondered if I would ever fit in completely or if I would forever remain that anonymous baby found crying in the graveyard that night.

We sang the opening hymn, and Old Man Riddle strode up to the altar to say the prayer. He looked ten years younger and took an obvious deep breath before starting the prayer. He didn't cough at all before, during, or after the prayer, and he wore a big smile on his face when he started back to his seat.

"Chastity, or sexual purity, is one of God's most important commandments," began Pastor Tabor. Once a year he gave a fire-and-brimstone sermon about the merits of sexual purity and the evils of promiscuity. To hear him tell it, anyone who even looked at a woman the wrong way was going to hell. He poured on the guilt and condemnation until I wondered how anyone ever managed to have children in his congregation.

I knew he was right about the evils of sexual desire, but it didn't keep me from feeling the desires nonetheless. I only hoped he wasn't right about the severe punishment that awaits anyone who even feels those carnal desires surge in his loins. If he was right, I figured every teenage boy in the world was going to hell, and a lot of grown men weren't far behind. I hoped for forgiveness and redemption, since I knew I was bound to be overcome with desire the next time I took a good look at his daughter. I was certain that if he had any idea how I felt, he would never let me see her again, but then I figured that he was speaking so strongly against sexual desire because he was a man, and he knew what it felt like. I half grinned to myself as I contemplated my human nature, but then I remembered that Wonnie had been raped. I shuddered. Suddenly, I saw the ugly side of the same coin I had treated lightly, and the grin fell from my face. Pastor Tabor was right. There was a warm spot in hell for the man ruled by his sexual desire, especially one who will quench his thirst by force.

Floyd and Willy sat next to me in Sunday School. Even Stanley Walsh was friendly. I figured that Jed had talked to him. Ruby sat a couple of rows up with Nina Faye and Jo Anne. I was sitting there only halfway listening, when Jo Anne slipped me a note from Ruby. *My father wants to talk to you after church,* it said. I wasn't sure I wanted to talk to him.

I caught Mama in the hallway and told her that I needed to talk to Pastor Tabor for a minute, but that I would be on shortly. She told me they would wait, and I left her talking with Hazel and Maggie Owens. I found Pastor Tabor putting away hymnbooks in the chapel.

"Pastor Tabor," I said with reverence, hoping to start on the right foot. "Ruby said you wanted to see me?"

"Yes, Stone, I do." He continued straightening the books in each row. "I wanted to thank you for saving Ruby's life." He focused on the books and only glanced at me from time to time. "Without you she would have died."

"You're welcome, but the way I see it I was just trying to use my gift the way God would want me to." I started helping him with the books. It seemed to help break the tension between us.

"About your gift," asked Pastor Tabor. "Do you think it's from God?"

I shrugged. "I'm not sure, but I would like to believe that it is."

"I have heard of such gifts, but they are rare and should be used with caution." He stopped and held up his finger. "Not like they do at that tent revival."

"Yes, sir," I said, not telling him what I knew about Phoebe Webb and the healings at the revival.

He stopped and looked directly at me. "Stone, if your gift is from God, then don't cast your pearls before swine. Treat it as something sacred that should be used with caution and thanksgiving, or God will hold you accountable for it at judgment day."

"Yes, sir," I replied. But I was thinking, *Oh great, something else God is going to hold against me.*

Pastor Tabor started back with the hymnbooks. "I have heard that attendance at the revival dropped off quite a bit after Friday night's events. It seems that someone has questioned the validity of their healer's gift." I helped put away a few more books but didn't reply. I remembered my offhand comment at Shorty's and wondered if it had gotten around that fast.

"Thank you for coming to talk with me," said Pastor Tabor as he put away the last of the books. "We'll see you next week," he said, signaling the end of the conversation.

I nodded and started for the door, but then courage, or my desires, got the best of me, and I stopped and turned around. "Can I see your daughter again?" I asked.

He looked at me, startled at first, like I had proposed something outlandish, but then he took a deep breath. "I suppose I can let you visit her on Sunday evenings after supper."

I smiled. "Great! Tell her I'll be by tonight." I turned and hurried to the car without waiting for a response. The parking lot was mostly empty when I got to the car, which was fine by me. It allowed me to avoid the funny looks and awkward interactions. When I got to the car, Daddy was staring out his window and Mama was staring out hers. I apologized for taking so long. Daddy just started the car and put it in gear. It was a long, quiet ride home.

I pulled up in front of Ruby's house about five thirty, nervous about Pastor Tabor, but excited about seeing Ruby again. When I knocked on the door, Pastor Tabor answered it. "Come in, Stone. She's just helping her mother finish the dishes," he said, motioning me to a couch in the living room.

The aromas of picnic ham and fresh biscuits still

lingered when I walked through the front door. My mouth watered, even though I had eaten before leaving my house. I sat at the end of the couch and tried not to fidget while Pastor Tabor sat in his easy chair and read the Bible. A few minutes later, Ruby came out of the kitchen, wiping her hands on her apron. She still had on her green dress and looked like she had just dressed for church that morning. Out of courtesy, I stood when she walked into the room. I knew I was buttering him up, but I needed all the help I could get.

"Good evening, Stone," she said with a coy smile.

"Evening, Ruby," I replied. Watching her walk into a room always gave me butterflies.

She turned her attention to her father and asked, "Daddy, do you mind if Stone and I go for a drive? It's a beautiful summer evening, and I would really love to get outside and enjoy God's creation."

Pastor Tabor looked up from his Bible and stroked his chin.

"I promise I'll be home before eight," offered Ruby with the smile of a little girl.

Mrs. Tabor appeared in the doorway of the kitchen and gave a nod to the pastor. He rolled his eyes and shook his head. "I suppose it will be okay," he said. Then he pointed his finger at me and added, "As long as you have her home promptly at eight."

I felt my stomach jump with excitement but tried not to show it. "Yes, sir," I replied, trying not to smile.

Ruby stripped off her apron and tossed it to her mother. She rushed over and gave Pastor Tabor a hug. "Oh, thank you, Daddy!" She grabbed my hand and pulled me toward the door. Just before we slipped out the front door, she looked back at her mother and mouthed a silent thank-you to her as well.

"Where do you want to go?" I asked as I started Daddy's Buick.

She looked at me and raised her eyebrows. "Let's go up Big Hill again."

We cruised up the winding road to the top of Big Hill and found the same parking spot as last time. A couple of families were picnicking, but nobody paid any attention as we pulled up. Ruby kicked off her shoes and stretched out with a sigh across my lap just like the last time we were here. "Thank you for rescuing me from death by boredom," she said, looking up at me with those chocolate eyes.

I smiled, looked down at her beautiful features, and stroked her cheek with my hand. The clean smell of her hair drifted up and tickled my nose. I moved my hand down to her neck and rubbed the spot where the big rattlesnake had bitten her. "Does it hurt at all?" I asked.

"The snakebite? No, not one bit," she said. Then she reached up and grabbed me around the back of the neck and pulled me down into a wet kiss. When we finally stopped, she said, "That was for saving my life." She pulled me down again, although I must admit that I didn't need to be forced, and we kissed again. "That was for saving me from death by boredom tonight."

On impulse, I reached down, slipped my hand behind her head, and pulled her up to me for another long and passionate kiss. "You're welcome," I said with a grin when I finally came up for air. We both giggled, like two kids that find some simple act of living suddenly tickling their funny bone. Ruby let out an audible content sigh. I put my hands on the steering wheel, looked out over the river, and forced myself to think about fishing. It felt good to be close to her again.

"What did you think when you saw me go up on stage and pick up that big snake?" she asked.

"I was nervous, of course."

She giggled again. "Oh, Stone, it was incredible! When I picked up that deadly creature and held it, my hands trembled, and my heart was thumping right out of my chest." She clutched her hands over her heart and let out a moan. "I felt . . . alive!"

"Alive? The dang snake bit you, and you almost died," I said with a frown.

"I know. I know, but the experience was like nothing I've felt before. Even just thinking about it makes me want to do it again."

"Do it again? Are you crazy?"

She reached up and stroked my worried face with the back of her hand. "I've got you to save me."

"Ruby, I can't always save people," I protested. "I think that it might even be wrong for me to save people sometimes."

Ruby sat up and spun around. She leaned back against the passenger door and plopped her legs across my lap. "Stone, have you thought about what you could do with your gift?" she started. "You could be famous! You could move to a big city like Louisville, or Nashville, and start your own church," she said, more animated. "Instead of traveling around like those tent revivals, we can build a big chapel and folks can come to us. We can sing gospel songs and preach the word. People will travel in from all over the country, maybe the world, to be healed by you. After they watch you use your gift, they will be more than happy to donate hundreds of dollars. We can buy a big house and—"

"Ruby," I interrupted. "I don't think I can do that."

"Why not?"

"I'm not sure I should use my gift like that."

"You'd be helping people."

"I know, but . . . it just doesn't feel right." I remembered Phoebe Webb's warning to me about not understanding the power I was playing with. "Besides, I barely understand how to use my gift."

"How many people have you healed already?"

"I don't know, ten or twelve maybe."

"Well, let's count them. Who have you healed?"

"Well, Rusty was the first one, if you count dogs."

"Okay. One," she counted it off as she held up a finger.

"Then Samuel Wilburn," I said.

"Two," she said, extending a second finger.

"Hazel Owens, who had polio."

"Three."

"A Mr. Bruce from over in Brownwood, who said he had consumption."

"Four."

"Mrs. Mary Glidwell, a boy from Little Renox who broke his arm, and two of Samuel's kin from Coe Ridge."

"Five, six, seven, eight," pronounced Ruby, counting them off like coins.

"Then I guess the next one would have been you."

"I'm number nine."

I remembered the pool hall. "Jed Mock after I busted his nose," I mumbled.

"You busted Jed Mock's nose and then healed him?"

"It's a long story," I said, shaking my head.

"Ten," she said without questioning it further.

"Then yesterday I healed Wonnie, Samuel's sister."

"You mean the one that came and sat in the white section of the theater?" she asked. I nodded. "What happened to her?"

"Somebody raped her and beat her half to death," I said without thinking.

As soon as I said it, Ruby's mouth dropped open with surprise, and her face went pale. I remembered Otis's warning. "Don't tell *anybody!*" I pleaded. "They don't want people to know."

"Stone, you can't just ignore a girl getting raped." She wagged a finger at me. "You have to tell the sheriff."

I shook my head and wished I had kept my mouth shut. "They said it was nobody's business. They said the sheriff isn't going to help them anyway."

"You mean to tell me that you would rather keep it a secret than stop a rapist on the loose?" Her eyes were alive with excitement and she pulled her legs under her and sat up. "Ezekiel Stone Molony, you cannot just sit there like some bump on a log and watch a young woman get raped! It is your duty to act! What if it were me?"

I looked at the excitement and worry in Ruby's eyes and remembered Wonnie's bruised and broken face. The thought of someone doing the same thing to Ruby made me sick to my stomach. I remembered Pastor Tabor's sermon and shuddered again at the ugliness I had witnessed. I knew there was a warm spot in hell for men like that, and if a man raped Ruby, I would be happy to send him there myself. I smacked my hand against the steering wheel. "What do you want me to do? They asked me not to go to the sheriff!"

"What's more important: doing what they asked you to do, or bringing a rapist to justice?"

I shook my head and let out a sigh. She was right, but I didn't want to talk about it anymore. "You're right," I consented. "I'll figure out a way to let the sheriff know."

I changed the subject, and we talked about going to college and rehashed local gossip. I got her home about seven thirty. She thought I dropped her off early because

I didn't want to catch the wrath of her father, but I was secretly planning to go see Phoebe again.

I drove by the revival with my window rolled down. The sun was beginning to set, and the cool evening air carried the sound of music playing and people clapping, but the parking lot only had a few cars scattered about. Attendance tonight must have been sparse again. The light in the travel trailer was on, and I hoped that maybe I would find Phoebe sitting inside if she was done with her healing for the night. I parked across the street, hoping that Reverend Hines would be too busy on stage handling snakes to notice me sneaking a look inside the tent.

Just like Friday night, several men, including Reverend Hines, were on stage handling snakes and singing along to the gospel music coming from a small band, but Phoebe Webb was nowhere in sight. Thinking she had probably healed several people and was suffering from the ensuing blindness that always came, I slipped around to the travel trailer and gave a gentle knock at the door, hoping to find her there.

I stood there biting my bottom lip until she opened the door. She was dressed in the same white dress with her black hair piled on top of her head and she stood in the doorway with a cigarette in her hand. She took a long look at me as she took a long drag on the cigarette and blew the smoke out of the side of her mouth.

"You coming inside, or do you just want to stand there and gawk?" she asked.

"Can I come in, please, ma'am?" I stammered.

She took another drag from the cigarette, and then sent it sailing into the evening air with a flick of her finger. "Come in and have a seat," she said, pulling the door open wider. "I've been expecting you."

I glanced back at the tent and then ducked through

the small door. It felt like I was inside a tin can, and the whole thing wobbled with every step I took. I imagined the novelty of living in this rolling tin can would wear off soon and understood why she sang about being a wayfaring stranger each night.

"Have a seat," she said, motioning to the small pop-up table. I slid onto the bench covered by tattered blue Naugahyde. A small overhead light struggled to illuminate the booth. The smell of stale cigarette smoke lingered in the cramped space. "Welcome to my mobile palace," she said as she slid onto the opposite bench.

Our knees bumped as she slid into position, and it gave me goose bumps. I felt a strange conflict of emotions, like two rivers running together. I was excited to finally talk to someone with the same gift as mine, but I was nervous about what I might find out. "How did the healings go tonight?" I asked, trying to break the tension.

She gave a crooked smile and said, "It was a slow night. Let's just say that I didn't go blind tonight."

Her answer confused me at first, and then I realized that she was telling me that she didn't heal anyone. I felt a little guilty knowing that I had something to do with that.

"I wanted to ask you some questions," I said. I was afraid to look at her and stared at my folded hands on the table, giving her only an occasional glance. "I want to know more about my gift."

She didn't answer right away. Instead she pulled out a cigarette and a book of matches. She lit the cigarette and took a long drag before she answered. "What makes you think I can help you?"

I stopped staring at my hands and looked up at her. When she had walked on stage the other night, her striking beauty had sent a ripple through the crowd. Here in the dim light of the travel trailer surrounded by cigarette smoke, I could see that her beauty was fading. Her heavy makeup covered the lines that were starting to show on her face and her red lipstick hid the sadness in her smile. Our eyes met, and even though the years were etched in the lines around her eyes, they were a deep green like the waters of the Cumberland on a hot summer day.

"You have the same gift I do," I stammered, still mesmerized by her eyes.

She took a drag from the cigarette without looking away. "I'll answer your questions, if I can, but you have to answer some questions for me."

I wondered what she could possibly want to know from me. "Okay," I agreed. "What does it feel like when you heal someone?"

"It feels like a thunderstorm in my head with lightning bolts dancing around my brain. My hands get warm and feel like they might burn people when I touch them, but it isn't painful. Of course, you know that when I'm finished with the healing, I'm blind for a while."

Happy that she had answered so candidly, I pressed forward. "How long do you stay blind after healing?"

"Uh-uh," she said, wagging her finger. "It's my turn to ask a question." She crushed out her cigarette. "Who are your parents?"

"Ada and Billy Molony are my stepparents," I answered and waited politely for her next question.

She pointed at me with her chin. "Your turn."

"How long do you stay blind after healing someone?"

"It depends on the severity of the sickness or wound that I heal," she said with a shrug. "It usually lasts five to ten minutes, but I have been blind up to thirty minutes a

Brock Booher

few times." She hesitated and then asked, "Do you know who your real parents are?"

"No, ma'am," I said, shaking my head. I grinned and added, "They found me lying on a grave in the cemetery one night. Sheriff George Pace heard me crying when he was sitting in his cruiser with the window rolled down. He found me on a gravestone with a scripture from Ezekiel and so they named me Ezekiel Stone." My comment about Ezekiel brought up another question. "Do you use any scriptures to help you heal?" I asked.

"The scripture from Ezekiel seems to be the key that everyone uses to unlock the power of the gift," she said.

"Everyone? There are others?"

"It's my turn," she said with a smile. "But, yes, I have met several others."

My mouth must have dropped open when she told me there were others.

"You seem surprised to learn that other people possess the same gift. When did you first learn of your gift?" she asked.

I shifted in my seat, trying to decide how I should feel about the fact that several other people, perhaps hundreds or maybe thousands, had a gift like mine. "Uh . . . I was mowing hay and cut the legs off my dog, Rusty." She cringed as I told her. "That scripture from Ezekiel kept going round and round in my head, and I just healed him."

"Were you very close to your dog, Rusty?"

"Yeah," I said, feeling his loss all over again. "I raised him from the time he was a pup. I spent hours training him."

"I'll bet you were glad when you healed him."

"Yeah, but he died later that day when a copperhead bit him."

"I'm sorry to hear that," she said. "You couldn't heal him from the snakebite?"

"No, it was like my mind was blank, and I couldn't remember the words."

"Maybe you weren't supposed to heal him."

I remembered how difficult it was to heal Wonnie. "Have you ever healed someone that you weren't supposed to?" I asked.

She nodded and looked out the window. "Yes." She turned and looked me straight in the eye. "Be careful. Sometimes, if people have enough faith and you want it bad enough, you can heal people that are supposed to die. It messes things up."

I gave her a puzzled frown.

She let out a sigh and continued, "I healed a man on his deathbed once. He begged me to help him. It took me several tries, but I kept trying because he seemed like such a good man." She took a deep breath and exhaled sharply. "Turns out he wasn't such a good man after all. A few months later he was caught molesting a young girl. When they convicted him, several more young women came forward." She shook her head and added, "If it don't feel right, don't use your gift." She lit another cigarette.

"Do you think it's a gift from God?" I asked.

"God?" she snorted. She blew out a long column of smoke. "Based on the things I've seen in my life, I'm not sure there is a God." She took another drag and let the smoke drift out of her nose. "I know the gift gets passed down from one generation to the next. I know the Bible scripture seems to be the key. I know that I can't heal someone unless I can feel their faith in my gift." She shook her head and added, "God? I hope and pray there's a heaven, but I don't know about God."

She took another drag on her cigarette and asked, "Have you started having nightmares yet?"

I remembered the last few nights. "Nightmares? Is that because of the gift?"

Someone gave a soft knock at the flimsy trailer door. Phoebe started to slide out of the bench and go to the door when it opened. Reverend Hines walked in without waiting for her to open the door or invite him in. When he closed the door behind him and saw me sitting there with Phoebe Webb, he narrowed his eyes and glared at me.

"What are you doing here?" he barked.

I considered shoving him aside and bolting through the door, but I froze. I was afraid I might have to knock Phoebe down as well since the space was tight.

Phoebe stepped between us and put a hand on his shoulder. "John, the boy just wanted to ask some questions."

He pointed at me and hissed, "He is the reason nobody showed up the last few nights!"

"Now, John," said Phoebe as she moved closer to him in the small space. "You don't have any proof. He's just a boy."

"A boy that needs to be taught a lesson," snarled Reverend Hines.

Phoebe caressed his face with her other hand. "Now, John, that isn't the Christian thing to do," she said in her silky calm voice. She had managed to move him a half step away from the door, giving me a clear path out of the trailer.

"You said this would be a good town for us," said the Reverend, focusing on Phoebe for the moment.

With Reverend Hines focused on Phoebe, I made a dash for the door. I felt his hand grab at my shoulder as I passed, and I shoved the door open so hard that it slammed into the side of the trailer. I put my long legs into motion and ran full speed for the car. Luckily nobody was coming down the road because I didn't even look when I crossed.

"If you come back again, I'm gonna teach you a lesson!" yelled Reverend Hines from the door of the trailer.

I didn't wait around to see what kind of lesson he had in mind.

Monday morning I got my chores done and helped Daddy repair some fence. Mama looked after Leck most of the morning since he was still in bed. After lunchtime, Daddy said he needed to go into town. I saw it as a chance to go see the sheriff and asked to tag along. When we got to the square, I asked him to drop me off and pick me up at Walgreens on his way back. From the square, I walked to the sheriff's office, trying to formulate my thoughts.

"Morning, Stone, can I help you?" asked Beulah Jean Davidson, Nina Faye's mom, when I walked into the sheriff's office with a knot in my stomach. It was easy to see where Nina Faye got her good looks. Mrs. Davidson had been a widow for years, and even though she could have had her pick of men, single or married, she had never remarried. Of course that made her the talk of the town among the women. Anytime some marriage fell apart, somebody would always blame her. She was the secretary and dispatcher all rolled into one and dedicated herself to her work and raising her only daughter.

"I need to see the sheriff," I said, trying not to sound nervous and trying not to notice the low-cut dress she was wearing.

"He's in a meeting right now with a revenue man," replied Mrs. Davidson as she freshened her red lipstick. Then she glanced over at the sheriff's closed door, covered the side of her mouth, and whispered, "Big Six Henderson."

Big Six Henderson was a famous revenue man that had busted up hundreds of moonshine stills and operations all over the state. I guessed he was making his rounds to Cumberland County, and I thought about Daddy and Leck's recent visit to Otis's barn. No doubt Big Six would be making a few trips to Coe Ridge looking for sources of white lightning.

"Deputy Russel is in," said Mrs. Davidson. "Would you like to speak with him?"

"That would be all right," I said. I thought that might even be better than talking to the sheriff. He knew Otis and Wonnie, and it would give me an opportunity to explain why I had missed basketball practice. I followed Mrs. Davidson's curvy figure down the hall to his office and reminded myself that she was old enough to be my mother.

"You've got a visitor, Cortis," she said as she knocked on the open door. She lingered just a moment in the doorway and then turned and went back to her desk with her heels clicking against the tile. I stood there in the doorway, too timid to walk in.

"Well, I'll be danged. What brings you here, Stone?" He motioned me toward the chair in front of his desk. "Come, sit down."

The office was small and stuffed with official-looking filing cabinets, except for the few trophy bass mounted next to the head of a twelve-point buck looming on the wall behind his desk. The trophy fish were bigger than anything I had ever caught, but the deer was quite a specimen. The hunting rifle he had probably used to shoot the prize buck hung just below the trophy head. Deputy Russel's desk was covered with stacks of files shrouded in green folders. He had a towel draped over his desk and was cleaning his revolver. I sat up straight in the metal chair and put my hands in my lap.

"What can I do you for?" he asked as he continued cleaning the gun on his desk.

"Where did you bag that buck?" I asked, trying to make small talk and calm my nerves.

"That little beauty?" he said with a glance over his shoulder. "I was in a deer blind up Little Renox when he crossed the ridgeline. He was a good two hundred yards away, but I put a bullet through his heart with one shot. Then it took me all day to hike over and haul his carcass out," he said with a chuckle. He put the revolver down on his desk and looked straight at me. "What's bothering you, Stone? I'm sure you didn't come here to talk about hunting deer."

"Well, sir," I said, shifting in my seat, "I need to report a crime."

He pulled a comb from the front pocket of his uniform shirt and pulled it through his perfect hair. "Not like the last time, is it? Is there a real victim and a real perpetrator this time?"

"Yes, sir. The victim is Wonnie Wilburn. She was beaten and raped," I told him as matter-of-factly as I could. "But I don't know who did it."

"Otis Wilburn's daughter?" he asked as he slipped the comb back into his shirt pocket.

"Yes, sir."

He picked up the revolver and spun the cylinder. "When did this happen?"

"Sometime Friday night."

He leaned down and pulled a box of ammunition from his desk drawer. "Well, the sheriff arrested her for sitting in the white section of the theater on Friday night. I reckon somebody wanted to teach her a lesson."

"Does that give them the right to break the law?" I asked.

"Well, no," he said as he started loading the revolver. He wagged a bullet at me and said, "But she was asking for trouble."

I felt the blood rush to my face. "Maybe so, but last time I checked, even raping a colored girl is against the law."

He set the revolver down and leaned back in his chair. "Look, Stone, I spend half of my time as a deputy either in Coe Ridge or over in the nigger part of town just below Big Hill trying to break up some drunken fight. Them colored folks are always getting drunk and raping each other or beating each other up." He shook his head. "The rest of the time I'm trying to catch whiskey runners from Coe Ridge trying to get their goods to market."

He pointed his long finger at me. "The way I figure it, one or more of her cousins probably got drunk and took advantage of her while she was walking home late at night. Did you know that there's at least five convicted felons living up on Coe Ridge right now?"

I shook my head. I knew that a few of the residents up on the ridge stepped on the wrong side of the law from time to time, but that was usually just running whiskey or getting into a fight in town. I didn't think that any of them would be capable of the really ugly crimes. "I don't know . . . I don't think they would do something like that to Wonnie."

"Don't be so naïve," he said. "Since I've been deputy, they've had three or four rapes that were reported and two murders."

His descriptions of the crimes shattered my image of the quaint life of the colored folks up on Coe Ridge. I had been going up there with my daddy since I was kid. I knew that they had their share of problems, but I had never seen it firsthand. Patsy Ann and Otis had always been so friendly. I guess I just figured everyone else up there was just like them.

"Tell you what I'll do," offered Deputy Russel. "The next time I'm up there, I'll do some snooping around and see what I can find out. How's that?"

I felt a pit in my stomach the size of a baseball as I wondered how Otis would take to Deputy Russel snooping around about Wonnie's rape. I nodded in agreement.

Deputy Russel closed the cylinder and slipped the revolver back into his holster. "How'd you find out about this anyway?" he asked.

"Well, Samuel Wilburn came by the house Saturday morning and told me." I hesitated to tell him the whole story because I remembered what happened last time I told him about healing someone but then decided that since I had come this far I might as well get it all out in the open. "He asked me to see if I could heal her," I answered. "That's why I missed basketball practice."

He folded up the towel on his desk and started putting the cleaning supplies into his desk drawer. "Were you able to heal her?" he asked.

"It took me a couple of tries, but, yeah, I healed her."

"Did she say who raped and beat her?" he asked, closing the drawer.

I shook my head. "No, she didn't say. In fact she told me that she wished I had let her die."

"Hmph," he grunted. "Probably one of her cousins, and she doesn't want to turn him in." He picked up a file from the pile on his desk. "Well, I better get back to my paperwork before Sheriff Pace finishes up his meeting with Big Six Henderson."

I stood to leave. "Thanks," I offered. "I'd be much obliged if you could find whoever did this to Wonnie. Can you do me a favor though and keep it discreet? Otis and Patsy Ann don't want people to know."

"I'll keep it hush-hush," he promised. I was almost out the door when he stopped me. "Hey, Stone, by the way, what kind of maladies can you heal?"

I shrugged and said, "I reckon I can heal anything that people have the faith for me to heal. Why?"

"Well . . . ," he said, rubbing his chin like he was hesitant to ask.

"Is everything okay, Deputy Russel?" I asked.

"Well, you see . . . my wife and I have never been able to have kids," he said, sounding almost embarrassed. "The doctor says there's something wrong with her plumbing."

I smiled and tried to put him at ease. "You talk to her. If she has enough faith in my gift, I'll see what I can do."

"Much obliged," he said with a nod as he went back to his stack of files.

Sheriff Pace's door was still closed, and Mrs. Davidson was painting her nails when I slipped past and headed back down to the square.

That night Mama served Leck supper in bed because he still didn't feel well enough to come downstairs. Daddy and I were finishing off some pork chops and butter beans when we heard a knock at the door. Daddy started to get up when Mama called from the stairs and said she would get it. I couldn't see the front door from my end of the table. "Who is it?" I asked Daddy between bites.

"Looks like Ada's cousin Bobby," he said, picking the last of the meat from the pork chop.

"The one that lives over by Eighty-Eight?" I asked.

Daddy nodded. I wondered what brought him all the way over here at this hour. I picked at my food and tried to hear the conversation at the front door since I had a feeling they were here to see me.

I heard my mother ask, "Good to see you, Bobby. What brings you here this time of night?"

"Evening, Ada." His voice sounded strained. "Sorry . . . world of pain."

"What happened?"

I heard him answer, but his voice was low and he seemed to be struggling with his words. ". . . can't even stand up straight."

"I'm sorry to hear that Bobby."

"I heard . . . Stone . . . heal. Is that true?" I was only catching some of what he was saying.

"Yes, he has been able to heal some people."

I heard him reply but couldn't make out what he said.

Mama said, "Sure. Come in. Come in. Just stretch out on the couch and try and get comfortable while I go get him."

I heard his boots scrape against the wooden floor. "Thank you kindly, Ada." He let out a sharp cry. "I'm in miserable shape, and I gotta have some relief."

"Well, I'm not sure he will be able to help you. He has healed several people, but not everyone." She sighed so heavy I could hear it from the kitchen table. "He hasn't done anything for Leck."

"I'm in so much pain that I'm willing to try anything." He let out another yelp as I heard him collapse onto the couch.

"You just relax here and I'll go get him."

I pushed my plate away and took a drink of water. Daddy sat at the other end of the table with his arms crossed, looking weary from the intrusions, when Mama appeared in the doorway.

"Stone, my cousin Bobby is here to see you." She sounded like a receptionist attending to a doctor's office, unemotional and unfazed by the trauma occurring in front of her. "He said he hurt his back." She sat back down at the table to finish her dinner. I wiped my mouth and headed for the living room while Mama finished her dinner and Daddy sat there with a scowl on his face.

"Evening, Bobby," I said as I sauntered into the room. "Mama tells me you hurt your back."

Bobby twisted his head to face me and grimaced in pain. "Yep, I've hurt it before, but never this bad. I can barely walk. I heard you have a gift for healing folks. Is that right?"

"That's right," I said with a nod. "I'll have you feeling good as new in no time." As soon as I said the words, my stomach sank. I sounded like Moses with the children of Israel when they were thirsty in the desert and he smote the rock to give them water. He took the credit for the miracle, and because of that God never let him enter into the promised land. I backtracked just a little, "Well, if you have enough faith."

Bobby groaned a bit as he shifted on the couch. "If you say you can heal me, I believe you."

In spite of my bravado and personal promotion, I could feel Bobby's simple faith. It was like a hot fire that cast its heat for several feet. He believed, and that belief was the energy I needed to make my gift work. Almost immediately the words from Ezekiel came pouring into my consciousness, and I felt the lightning start zapping at my scalp. A few minutes later, I sat on the same couch Bobby had been lying on listening to him say his good-byes to Mama and Daddy. He bubbled over with gratitude as he headed out the front door and left me sitting alone in the living room. I closed my blind eyes and listened to his truck drive away. When I finally got my vision back, I found Mama doing dishes in the kitchen.

"Where's Daddy?" I asked.

"He had to go check on the livestock," she said without looking up from the sink full of soapy water.

I felt the tension and frustration in the room lingering like the smell of the fried pork chops. Trying to be helpful, I joined Mama at the sink and started drying dishes and putting them away. She just focused on the dirty dishes and didn't say a word. We worked together in silence until she pulled the stopper and let the dirty water drain out.

"Do you think Leck would mind a visit from me?" I asked as I dried the last plate.

She glanced up at me as she rinsed out the sink. "No, I don't think he'd mind."

I put away the plate and closed the cabinet door. "Mama, I can't do anything for Leck if he doesn't believe."

She continued rinsing and cleaning the sink without looking up at me. "You told my cousin Bobby that you would have him good as new in no time. You've healed Samuel, Wonnie, Hazel Owens, and half the sick folks in the county. Why can't you heal your brother?"

"Mama I . . ." I didn't have an answer. It was true. I had used my gift to heal several people, but every time I even thought about healing Leck, my mind was clouded over and nothing came to me. "Okay, Mama, I'll go try." I headed up the stairs for his room.

I took a deep breath and knocked at his door.

"Door's unlocked!" shouted Leck.

I hesitated a couple of seconds and then turned the doorknob. I forced a smile as I entered his bedroom. He was propped up in bed reading *Life* magazine. "Hey, Leck, I thought you might like some company."

Leck turned the page of his magazine. "Sure, as long as you bring along a lady friend."

I grinned at his joke and sat in the chair beside the bed. He continued to focus on the magazine. The cover of *Life* was adorned with the bare back of a woman bathing in some exotic South Sea island called Tahiti. She had red flowers in her hair and skin the color of caramel, like Wonnie. I had to force myself to look away and noticed that the dinner Mama had brought him sat on the nightstand in front of the window. He had eaten the pork chop but barely touched anything else.

"We got that hole in the fence down past the barn fixed," I said, trying to make conversation. Leck just nodded and continued to read about exotic women of the South Seas. I decided I would have to say something a little more exciting to get his attention. "Did you hear what happened to Wonnie?" I asked.

"Mama told me she got beat and raped." He turned the page without even looking at me. "She said you healed her."

"I went and talked to Deputy Russel about it."

For some reason that got his attention, and he gave me a disapproving look. "Why'd you bother with that?"

I suddenly felt the need to defend my position and said, "Well, I thought he could catch whoever did it. We don't want a rapist on the loose."

"Deputy Cortis Russel," he articulated, "making the world a safer place." He thumbed another page of the magazine. "Who came to visit a little while ago?"

I hesitated and then answered, "Mama's cousin

Bobby Shelley from over in Eighty-Eight. He hurt his back real bad."

Leck turned another page. "You fix him all up?"

I nodded. "Yep." I didn't know what else to say, and an awkward silence followed, interrupted only by the sound of Leck turning the pages of the magazine. Finally, I decided just to ask, "Leck, why can't I heal you?" He put the magazine down and looked at me like he was annoyed that he had to have this conversation. "I've been able to heal a bunch of people, and most of them worse off than you, but why can't I heal you?" I persisted.

He held up the magazine so I could see the cover and asked, "What do you know about the women of Tahiti?"

I shrugged. "Nothing."

"And that's about as much as you know about me," he snapped. "You think you can waltz in here like God himself and make my problems go away, and you don't have any idea what I've been through or what I've done? If so, you've got another think comin'." He stuck his nose back into the magazine.

His words felt like cold water on my face. I sat there feeling embarrassed but not really understanding why. Why was it my fault? I didn't do anything except offer to help, and he dumps all his troubles on me. Frustrated, I snapped back at him, "Why are you always so mean to me? What did I ever do to you?"

He dropped the magazine on his lap and rolled his eyes. "Mean to you? I haven't even started being mean to you."

I stood up. "You used to treat me like a brother, but since you came home from the war, I swear you never have anything good to say to anybody, especially me."

"Yeah, and we all know it's all about you. What can *I* do to make *you* happy," he mocked.

I started pacing. "You make fun of me. You boss me around. You always have some snide comment waiting for anything I do."

"You're easy to make fun of because you're such an idiot," he said with a shrug.

"I'm an idiot?" I screamed. "You're just an unhappy jerk that wants to make everyone else miserable!"

"Suddenly you're an expert on my life?" he shot back. "Sit your butt down!" he yelled and pointed at the chair. I didn't move at first, but then he ordered again, "I said, sit your butt down!"

I clomped over and plopped myself down in the chair. He rolled up the magazine and smacked me on the head. "Since you don't know a thing about the way the world really works, I'll tell you why you can't heal me," he began.

"Once upon a time," he started, "I was a lot like you, except for the part about your healing gift. I had life all figured out. I had dreams. I had ambition. I was gonna take on the world," he said, waving his hand in the air. "Then, along came the world with other plans."

"These people on the other side of the world decided to make trouble for everyone else, and Uncle Sam couldn't stand for that. No, no, no, we had to show them who was boss. We had to teach them a lesson. We had to keep those yellow-reds from spreading communism throughout Asia. We had to stand up for truth, justice, and the American way." He put his hand on his heart.

"Next thing I knew, I was on a boat to an Asian peninsula called Korea. I was full of piss and vinegar, a regular GI Joe, a member of a mortar platoon attached to the 1st Cavalry. We were gonna push those commies all the way back to China with General MacArthur leading the way." I shifted in my chair, a bit uncomfortable with Leck's story. He had never talked about the war.

"Well, before we knew it, we got our chance to teach those uppity North Koreans a lesson, only they weren't very willing students," continued Leck. "They actually had the gall to fight back. They didn't seem to know, or care, who we were or what we wanted them to do." He shook his head and squeezed the rolled magazine in his hands. He stared at the opposite wall. "I watched my buddies die right before my eyes. I remember this one guy, Lebowski from Milwaukee. We heard the incoming rounds and sprinted for cover. He was a few steps ahead of me when the round hit. It knocked me off my feet and when I got up to start running for cover again, all that was left of Lebowski was his boots.

"One afternoon I was on guard duty. We had trenched in on a hill beside this muddy road full of refugees. They told us to watch out for any sympathizers among them since the enemy was on the other side of the road. I was scanning the passing stream of ragtag refugees with binoculars when I saw a little girl, maybe ten years old, break from the crowd and run for our position. She had a hand grenade with the pin out in her right hand." Leck's voice broke, and he started to cry. "I dropped my binoculars and shot her in the head. My sergeant started calling me names you don't want to hear, until the grenade in her hand went off and blew off half of her arm. Then he just muttered something like 'good shot,' and we never talked about it again."

Leck wiped his cheek with the back of his hand. "A couple of weeks later we got overrun on Hill 303. About fifty of us got taken prisoner. They tied us all together and marched us around in the dark. One fellow,

Contrell from Iowa, tried to escape. They caught him and chopped off his head with a trenching tool right in front of the rest of us.

"When our boys came to take back Hill 303, the North Koreans lined us up and opened fire. I just happened to be standing next to Martinez, a big Mexican fellow from El Paso. He was at least six foot three and over two hundred and fifty pounds. His body shielded me from most of the fire, and when we fell, I pulled him on top of me. They came through and riddled the bodies with bullets just to be sure, but Martinez saved me." He shook his head again and choked back a sob.

"I got hit eight times, and I thought I was going to die. I dreamt about sitting in Walgreens drinking a chocolate malt. I thought about casting my line into the deep green waters of the Cumberland and pulling out a catfish longer than my arm. I imagined I was mowing hay down by the river, and the smell of fresh-cut grass was so strong you could practically taste it. I was ready to die, but then I heard voices—American voices. With every last ounce of strength I had, I pushed Martinez off me and yelled for help."

Leck sat staring at the opposite wall. I realized that I was crying and wiped my eyes with my shirt. Neither of us said anything for a while. Finally, I picked up his dinner tray and started for the door. "Mama will want to get these dishes washed," I said as I slipped out and closed his bedroom door. I noticed my hands were shaking as I carried the tray downstairs and set it beside the sink.

I avoided Mama and went straight up to bed.

TEN

❦

Nightmares skirted my sleep again most of the
night, but I was too tired to give them any attention. I
remembered Phoebe's question about nightmares that I
didn't get to answer and wondered why she had asked
it. I piled out of bed and got Jersey Girl milked long
before breakfast. It was a clear summer day with only a
light breeze, and I should have been happy to see it, but
my cares were weighing me down. I gathered the eggs
and took care of my other chores before heading to the
house for breakfast. Leck was absent from the breakfast
table again.

"After breakfast, get cleaned up," directed Daddy
between bites. "We're delivering feed today."

I nodded but didn't say anything. We all hurried
through the meal like strangers, and I hustled off to clean
up and change into some nicer clothes. Daddy was waiting for me in the truck when I shuffled down the front
porch stairs. He cranked up the truck and threw it into
gear before I got my door shut.

Floyd was at the loading ramp of the feed store with
his Dekalb Seed Company hat pulled down over his eyes
like usual. "Hey, Stone. Did y'all get any rain over the
weekend?" he asked.

"Not a drop," I replied. I looked out over the town from the loading dock and added, "Looks like it's gonna be another hot one today, and not much of a breeze either."

Floyd nodded like he understood and spit. "Did you hear that the revival is packing up this week?"

I felt my stomach jump into my throat but tried not to show it. I thought about Phoebe. I was hoping they would be in town for a little longer so I could sneak another visit and ask her some more questions. "Naw, I hadn't heard. You gonna go another time before they leave town?"

"Probably not. Jo Anne Carter told me she went Sunday night and nobody was there. She said that the healing lady didn't heal a single soul." He tilted his head back and winked at me. "I guess faking a couple of miracles wasn't enough to get the crowd worked up that night." He laughed like he had told some knee-slapper. I laughed along with him to keep up appearances, but inside I was nervous.

Daddy walked out with his invoice in hand and started directing everyone how to load the truck the way he wanted it. We loaded bags of feed onto the truck until the springs just about bottomed out. Daddy hit the starter, and we eased down the road with the front end barely touching the asphalt, hoping that nobody would be foolish enough to pull out in front of us. We followed our usual route, sticking to the lowlands first. We delivered to a couple of small farms out on Crocus Creek Road and then over to Old Man Riddle's place to unload several bags of chicken feed. Being able to breathe normally again meant Old Man Riddle talked our ears off now. Daddy finally had to cut him off politely so we could finish delivering before sundown.

Daddy didn't whistle much that day. He wore a

constant worried look on his face and stared down the
road without making much conversation. Whatever he
was worried about made him forget about honking his
horn down on Lawson's Bottom Road. It wasn't until
we got to the other side of that narrow stretch and met
one of the Stearns boys on a tractor that we realized our
mistake. We were lucky we didn't meet him halfway or
most likely one of us would have ended up in the river.
We made our deliveries down in the bottom, and Daddy
was more careful on the way back.

We traveled with the windows down, each of us in
our own little world. I watched the passing scenery, and
my thoughts bounced between what had happened to
Wonnie and daydreaming about kissing Ruby again up
on Big Hill. I wondered if she and I would get married someday. Would she want to have children? Since
Phoebe said the gift was passed on from one generation
to the next, would one of our children turn out like
me? I shook my head in frustration. Could I ever have a
normal life again?

"What's the matter, Stone?" asked Daddy.

"Huh? Oh, nothing," I answered, trying to keep my
thoughts to myself.

"Must be a heavy load of nothing the way you were
staring out the window and shaking your head."

I turned away and stared at the passing scenery of
farms and forests and mumbled, "Just wondering if I'll
ever have a normal life again."

Daddy nodded his head and focused on the road
ahead for a moment like he understood and had nothing
to say, but then his lecture began. "You chose something
different than normal the moment you chose not to put
Rusty down with the rifle. From that moment forward,
normal was a thing of the past."

"I guess you're right," I answered.

"The truth is that nothing about you has been normal from the day you were born," Daddy said with a chuckle. "How many other people do you know that was found in a graveyard?"

I had heard the story from Mama, but Daddy and I had never talked much about where I came from. "Do you know who my real parents are?" I asked.

"Sheriff George Pace found you in the graveyard May 16th, 1938," he stated like he was reading from the newspaper. "You were in front of Opal Newby's headstone wrapped up in some blankets." We were coming up on an intersection and Daddy downshifted, and the engine let out a throaty moan as it slowed the heavy load.

"I know that part of the story," I said, "But do you know anything about my real parents?" I had never asked anything about my real parents before. My whole life Billy and Ada Molony were my real parents. I even thought sometimes that the graveyard story was just some make-believe yarn to keep me entertained. I think my question caught him off guard.

Daddy checked for traffic, slapped the truck into first gear, and lurched into the intersection. He answered my question with a question. "Why do you want to know?"

I frowned and said, "Well, because I think my gift might have been passed down to me by my real mother or father." I shrugged and added, "And I want to know the truth."

He deflected with another question. "Where do you think your gift comes from?"

"Well, at first I thought it might come from God, but the healer at the revival said it was passed from one generation to the next."

"You spoke with the healing lady from the revival?"

"Yeah, Sunday night after I dropped off Ruby."

"What else did she tell you?"

I was a little surprised at Daddy's questions, but I figured he was just trying to protect me. "She told me what it feels like when she uses her gift and warned me to be careful how I use it."

Daddy nodded. "That's good advice. You have the power of life and death in your hands. You don't want to treat it lightly or use it carelessly. You can cheapen your gift and may do more harm than good."

"What do you think about my gift?" I asked.

Daddy was quiet for a moment and then answered, "Do you know the story of Moses and Jethro, his father-in-law?" I shook my head. "Well, Moses was trying to govern the children of Israel by himself, and they were working him night and day, running him into the ground. Jethro, his father-in-law, told him that if he kept that up it was going to kill him. He told him to delegate and not spread himself too thin."

"Daddy, I can't delegate my gift," I chided.

"No, but you don't have to try and heal the whole world. You don't need to spread yourself too thin. You need to use your gift sparingly, with wisdom and thanksgiving. You don't have to say yes every time somebody comes knocking at our door."

I just nodded at his advice. I knew he was right, but I also knew that I didn't have the heart to turn anyone away.

"I spoke with Leck last night," I said, trying to change the subject. "He told me some war stories."

"He did?" Daddy seemed as surprised at that as he did about discovering I could heal people. "What did he talk about?"

I hesitated, worried that maybe the stories were

meant just for me, but then I continued, "He told me about how he was captured by the North Koreans, and when they started shooting them, he was saved by a big Mexican guy."

Daddy pursed his lips and nodded, like the story was some sort of bad-tasting medicine that he was forced to take, but he didn't stop me. "What else?"

"He told me about shooting a little girl with a hand grenade in her hand in order to save his platoon." It dawned on me at that moment why I couldn't heal Leck. "Do you think that's why I can't heal him, because he feels guilty?"

Daddy downshifted again and turned the truck down the Moody's dirt road for our next stop. "My older brother, Henry, went off to World War I a carefree country boy. He came home a troubled drunk. He never talked much about what happened, and he died in a car accident long before you were born." Daddy pulled up in front of the barn and turned off the truck. "The war will always be with Leck. That takes a different kind of healing than you can offer, Stone." With that he opened his door and greeted Mr. Moody with a smile.

The truck was running smoothly with most of the load gone, and our day on the road seemed to have lightened our load as well. Daddy was back to whistling his favorite tunes. I was flying my hand in the passing wind and daydreaming about Ruby again. When we turned down Zeke Town Road, he broke into singing the chorus of Webb Pierce's hit "In the Jailhouse Now" so loud that I was sure everyone within a hundred yards of the road was gonna hear it. Just as he reached a crescendo, we rounded a curve and almost ran into a black Buick parked halfway in the road.

A tall, lanky white man with a sidearm on his hip was leaning up against the driver's side door of the car with his arms folded. He wore khaki pants and a drab green short sleeve shirt. He barely moved when we rounded the corner, as if he knew exactly where we were going to stop and he didn't need to waste any energy on unnecessary movement. He held up a hand like he had the power to bring that hunk of metal to a grinding halt without breaking a sweat.

The truck skidded a bit on the loose gravel road as Daddy complied with the command of the almighty hand and brought the truck to a stop right next to the Buick. The man let the dust blow past before he pushed himself away from the car with his hand on his black sidearm and stepped up to my window. He was tall enough that I was almost looking straight into his turquoise eyes.

"Afternoon, fellas," he said, like he was greeting an old friend. "What brings you to Zeke Town?"

"Afternoon, Big Six," replied Daddy. "We're just delivering some feed and a few bags of shelled corn," he added with a chuckle.

A grin broke across Big Six's face and he asked, "Who you delivering to?"

I found it hard to believe that this affable man was the dreaded Big Six Henderson that had put away more moonshiners than any other revenue man in Kentucky history. He was so famous at his job that girls on the playground would jump rope and sing, "My mama told me to watch the still, in case Big Six comes over the hill," and yet he carried himself like he was the Fuller Brush man just passing through the neighborhood selling his wares with a smile.

"We're headed to the Wilburn place," said Daddy. I

gave Daddy a cautious glance, thinking it unwise to give up so much information, but he didn't look worried in the least.

"Give Otis and Patsy Ann my regards," Big Six said with a cordial nod. Then his face turned serious, and his bright blue eyes darkened. "Best be careful, though. Folks around here are mighty skittish right now. I heard rumors that somebody's been stealing their product before they can get it to market. It's got 'em all a little jumpy and trigger happy."

"We're just delivering feed, but we'll keep our eyes open for trouble," said Daddy.

Big Six cocked his head a little and focused on me until I was uncomfortable. "Son, is your name Stone?"

My jaw dropped so low I had to pick it up off the floorboard. "Yes, sir," I said, wondering how he would know who I was.

He looked me over again like he was scrutinizing a wanted poster and then nodded. "Yep, I've heard about what you can do." He turned and smacked the side of the truck a couple of times with the palm of his hand. "You boys stay out of trouble and harm's way," he said, and then he propped himself against the black Buick like he was waiting for the next visitor.

"Y'all have a good afternoon," said Daddy, and he shoved the truck into gear and headed down the dirt road to the Wilburn place. As the rutted road twisted up the ridgeline, I saw a boy perched up in one of the big oak trees at the top of the ridge. When he saw our truck, he stood up on the limb and hollered out, "Fire in the hole!" I knew that his warning would be echoed down the line.

When we passed the first rusty-roofed homestead, the dogs were the only ones that came out to greet us this time. The same colored man that we passed last week smiled at us and tipped his straw hat, but I noticed that he had a shotgun or rifle across his lap this week. Daddy waved and acted calm, but I could tell he was bit nervous. A young man with a rifle slung over his shoulder was leaning up against the porch of the next shack we passed. Daddy waved, but the young man didn't wave back. It was the same scene each time we passed a dwelling—dogs barked and chased us, but the only people we saw were old enough to carry a gun, and most of them had a gun of some sort on their shoulder or lap.

We forded the creek and headed up the hill to the Wilburn place. I expected to see Samuel out front playing with the dogs, or maybe Patsy Ann hanging out the wash with Wonnie helping her. Instead, Samuel was standing by the barn like a sentry with a shotgun. Daddy eased up in front of the barn and turned off the truck.

"Afternoon, Samuel," said Daddy, sounding business as usual.

"Afternoon, Missah Molony," said Samuel with a nod, but he didn't smile.

After an unpleasant pause, Daddy said, "I've got some shelled corn and some dog food."

"I ain't sure about the corn, but I needs some dog food. Daddy'll be along d'rectly," said Samuel. His eyes darted from side to side like he was expecting some booger to come out of the woods.

"How's Wonnie?" I asked.

He shook his head. "Her body's awright, but I ain't so sure about her head."

I didn't like the sound of that. "Is she up at the house?" I asked.

"Naw, she's sitting down under the hickory tree. You know, the one with the swing."

Talking as much to Daddy as I was to Samuel, I asked, "Y'all mind if I pay her a visit?"

Daddy gave me a look and wrinkled his brow, but he nodded as if he understood that I had to go see her. Samuel just shrugged and said, "Suit yoself. She ain't much to talk to these days."

Before I could open the door, Otis rounded the corner of the barn. Samuel jumped just a bit and then looked ashamed for being so jumpy. Otis waved and said, "Afternoon, Missah Molony." His rich baritone voice practically vibrated the truck windows.

"Afternoon, Otis," replied Daddy. "I got stopped by Big Six on the way up."

Otis grinned and said, "Is that so?"

"He told me to give you and Patsy Ann his regards when I dropped off my delivery," said Daddy as he opened the truck door and slipped out of the driver's side.

"Maybe he'll stop by for supper," said Otis. Thunderous laughter erupted from deep in his chest. Samuel and Daddy relaxed and laughed with him. I was confused by his reaction. I got out of the truck and circled around the front to join in the conversation.

"Afternoon, Stone," said Otis, still chuckling as I rounded the front bumper.

"Afternoon, Otis," I offered, but my face must have given my confusion away.

"You look a might bit confused," said Otis. "What's vexing you?"

"I thought you'd be worried about Big Six stopping by to see you. I don't understand how you can find it so funny."

"Big Six ain't caught me yet, but if I was to get caught by a lawman, I hope and pray it would be Big Six. He good at catching shiners, but he's a fair man." He grunted

and spit like he was trying to get rid of a bad taste lingering in his mouth. "That's a lot more than I can say for
some other lawmen."

Daddy cleared his throat and said, "Otis, you want
any shelled corn this week?"

"Yessuh, I could use a couple of bags. Let me help
you unload 'em." With that Daddy unlatched the tailgate on the truck and started climbing up into the back
to unload the bags. Samuel stood there still watching
the woods. I turned and hustled off to find Wonnie, still
shaking my head at the image of Big Six Henderson sitting down to supper with Otis and Patsy Ann Wilburn.

I found Wonnie sitting right where Samuel said she
would be. When I came with Daddy as a boy, I loved
stopping at the Wilburn place. Samuel would show me
his dogs. Patsy Ann would give me some homemade
treat fresh out of her oven. Best of all, I would play with
Wonnie. Our favorite place was the old hickory tree out
at the edge of a high bluff overlooking the Cumberland
River.

It was a big tree with limbs low enough to grab onto
and climb. Otis had tied a rope to one of the big low-
hanging boughs and attached an old barn plank to the
end for a seat. It made for the perfect swing. With a little
help from Wonnie, I could swing so high I thought I
would launch to the moon if the rope were to break at
just the right moment. The rope was a rough hemp and
the board could put splinters deep into soft skin, but we
didn't mind because the swing made you feel like you
could fly.

Wonnie was drifting back and forth in the old swing
when I walked up. She kicked her bare feet against the
ground just enough to propel herself a few feet backward,
and then let herself drift forward again. She looked lost

and detached like the rope swing was the only thing keeping her from floating up to heaven. She had her back to me and seemed to be looking off into the forest like she was cloud watching. She spoke before I could say anything. "Come to save me again, Zekie?"

I stopped a few feet from the tree and watched her drift back and forth for a moment before answering. "I just wanted to see how you were doing," I said.

"Doing? I wish I was dead. How's that for doing?" She kept staring listlessly out into the trees and drifting back and forth.

"I'm sorry about what happened to you," I said.

"About what happened to me? You mean what some-one did to me."

I was nervous and nudged the green-husked hickory nuts lying at my feet. "If you know who did it, why don't you go tell the sheriff?" I asked.

She gave me a glance over her shoulder and then shook her head. "Sure, Zekie. I'll waltz into the sheriff's office and tell him all about how I was raped and beaten like a good little nigger girl, and he'll ask, 'Where's the bruises? Where's the broken bones? Where's the damage to your private areas?'" She snorted and continued to drift back and forth.

I felt my face go flush with anger and, for some reason, a measure of shame. I was the reason she didn't have any evidence, but her blaming me was hardly fair. "You would've died if I hadn't healed you," I snapped.

She continued to drift back and forth in the swing. "I'd be better off dead," she mumbled without even giving me a glance.

"Look, I know the deputy sheriff pretty well. He goes to my church—"

Wonnie feigned a look of surprise with her hand on

her face and interrupted me, "Oh lawdy! A churchgoin' deputy gonna come to my rescue!" She shook her head in disgust and pushed her bare feet against the barren ground to set herself adrift.

I watched her drift for a moment and then foolishly continued to talk about getting her help. "He promised me he'd ask around next time he was up here and try and find out who did this to you," I tried to explain.

Wonnie drifted back and forth at the end the rope and continued looking through the trees and down the bluff. "You mean you've already told him?"

I shoved my hands deep into my pockets and kicked the hickory nut I had been nudging around with my toe. "Yeah, I told him. I couldn't just let them get away with what they did to you."

She stopped kicking with her feet, and her whole body went limp. She looked like some rag doll propped up on the rope swing just waiting for someone to come along and push her off. Tears started streaming down her cheeks.

I bit my lip and stood there about as useless as tits on a boar hog. I had no idea what to say to make her feel better. I wanted to put my arms around her and hold her close. I wanted to protect her. I wished I could somehow heal the pain she felt on the inside like I had healed the wounds on the outside. Instead I stood there lifeless as the hickory nuts that covered the ground around the tree.

Wonnie wiped her cheek with the back of one hand and looked through the trees. "I wish I was a mermaid," she said. She sounded like the little girl I used to play with. "Then you could push me in this swing so high that I could fly into the air, through those trees, and land in the river at the bottom of the bluff. Then I could swim all the way to the ocean and never come back."

She looked over at me with her eyes full of tears. "Push me, Zekie."

I let out a sigh and pulled my hands out of my pockets. Her comments felt even stranger since I knew that she couldn't swim. I leaned into her and put my palms on the small of her back. It wasn't the same back that I pushed against when we were both younger. She had become a young woman, and I could feel her tender skin beneath the cotton dress give way like soft clay beneath the bones in my hand as I gave her a push. She giggled as she raised her feet high and let her dress slide up above her knees just before she started back down. I felt her laughing as I put my hands on her supple back again and pushed her higher. She squealed with excitement, like the little girl from so many years ago, as I catapulted her back into the air.

"Higher, Zekie!" she shouted. "I can see the river!"

I pushed her higher than I thought I should. I could just imagine the old hemp rope breaking and watching her fly out over the trees and into the river. Instead, she came back to me each time. When I touched the small of her back, I could feel her laughing. It was like a strange electricity, and I started to laugh myself.

Then her laughter stopped. Her body was quiet, and I sensed a stark change in her mood. I felt her shudder as she began to sob and her laughter turned into hopeless wails. The electricity I felt before turned to a dull ache. Her skin felt cold and lifeless beneath the cotton dress. I stopped pushing her, and she drifted back and forth, sobbing on the old hemp rope.

I heard Daddy start the truck and knew he was ready to go, but I didn't want to leave Wonnie. I felt my own tears rolling down my cheeks and tasted the salty taste of sadness on my lips. Daddy honked the horn. I walked around in front of her, cupped her face in my hands, and kissed her on the forehead. Then I ran for the truck, wiping my tears as I went.

It was a quiet ride home, and when we crossed the Cumberland at Neely's Ferry, I wondered if any mermaids were swimming around in that deep green water along with the catfish. I worried about Wonnie and felt frustrated by my gift. I thought I understood how to use it now, but I was wondering if I should use it at all. I thought I might be doing about as much harm as I did good. I wondered if it came from God at all, and if I was somehow interfering with God's will by using it. I gave myself a headache thinking about it. I naïvely wished I could go back to the day I cut off Rusty's paws with the mowing machine and put him down instead of healing him.

Mama was on the front porch when we turned down the lane, and she hurried down the steps as we pulled up in front of the house. She had her hair pulled back and several strands fell across her forehead, giving her a frazzled look. When she jumped up onto the running board of the truck and stuck her head into the window, her face was pale and worried. "Leck needs to go to the hospital, Billy," she said.

"What's wrong?" asked Daddy.

She glanced at me. "He's got fever and seems delirious. We need to go right away."

Daddy put his rough hand over hers and nodded. Then he looked over at me. "Wash your hands and help me carry Leck to the car."

"Yes, sir," I said and jumped out of the truck. I ran to the kitchen and washed my hands while he parked the truck down by the barn and came in the back door with Mama right behind him. I waited for him to wash his hands, and then I followed him upstairs.

Leck's room was stale and smelled like sweaty sheets. He lay there with his eyes closed and his mouth open. His head was tilted to the side, and I thought at first that he might be dead, but he moaned and moved his head. Daddy propped the door open with the chair and then pulled back the covers. Leck lay there with his pale legs at an unnatural angle, dressed in his boxers and a T-shirt. He looked thinner than I remembered.

"You get between his legs and grab them at the knees like this," said Daddy, showing me what to do. "I'll grab him at the shoulders. You go down the stairs first, but take it slow. C'mon."

I took my position like Daddy had shown me and slipped my hands around Leck's knees. His legs were limp, but hot as fire with fever. I waited for Daddy to get into position, and then we lifted him off of the bed and carried him out the bedroom door. I don't know if it was the adrenaline or if Daddy was doing all the heavy lifting, but he felt light as a feather as we made our way down the stairs. Mama held the front door open for us and then ran to open the car door.

"Swing around, Stone, and let me put him in head-first," directed Daddy. Mama ran around the car and cradled his head and body as we slid him into the back seat. We folded his legs so he would fit and shut the door. "Go close the front door and let's go," said Daddy as he slid into the driver's seat. I hurried back up the porch steps and pulled the front door shut. Then I bypassed the steps and jumped off the porch in one jump and ran to the car. Daddy had the car started and was heading down the lane before I could get my door shut.

We hit a hundred miles an hour on the straightaway between our house and Burkesville. The wind whistled against the mirrors and roared through the open windows like a freight train, but Daddy didn't let up until we got close to town. When we got to the hospital, I started to jump out and help unload Leck, but Daddy stopped me. "You stay in the car," he demanded with a pointed finger. "The last thing I need right now is people asking to be healed and creating a scene." He opened his door and looked back at Mama before getting out. "I'll go get somebody to carry him in properly, Ada."

I sat there feeling helpless as he hurried through the glass doors and into the hospital in search of some proper help. I wanted to offer some words of sympathy or hope to Mama, but my tongue stuck to the roof of my dry mouth. I thought about my gift, but after my conversation with Wonnie, I was afraid I might do more harm than good. I sat there confused and worthless as my stepbrother was dying in the backseat.

A few minutes later Daddy came through the doors followed by a couple of nurses pushing a bed on wheels. I jumped out of the car and started to help, but Daddy shook his head at me. I just stood back and watched them maneuver Leck out of the backseat and onto the rolling gurney. Mama was holding his hand as they rolled him into the hospital. After they got through the front door, Daddy leaned against the front fender and said, "Why don't you go on home and take care of the stock. You can come back and pick us up in a couple of hours."

I wanted to stay. Leck may have become cynical and testy after the war, but he was the only brother I had. I thought that maybe if I was there and he had a change of heart about my gift, I could end his misery, and we could all go home happy. I started to argue but decided that I would be more useful to Daddy if I just did what he asked. At least I could take care of the livestock without ruining anyone's life or possibly interfering with the will of God.

"Why don't I just hitchhike home, and you and Mama can bring Leck home when they release him?" I offered. I knew they probably wouldn't be releasing him anytime soon, but I didn't want to say it.

Daddy stood there staring at the hospital door like he was looking for Leck to come walking out with Mama at any minute. I had seen him outwork men half his age, but he suddenly looked like one of the old men that sat on the square and whittled with a far-off look in their eyes. I closed the car door left open by the nurses with a thump and brought him back to the present.

He faced me and nodded. "Okay. Make sure you check on the cattle, and feed the baby calves some grain. Don't forget—"

"I'm seventeen years old, Daddy. I can take care of the stock," I said with a grin. He stood there with his mouth open for a moment, like he wanted to say something, but then his lip started to quiver, and he just grabbed me in a big hug. I hugged him back and held back my own tears. The hug lasted just long enough for me to feel that he loved me, and then he released me and spun on his heel and started around the front of the car.

"I better get this car parked and go check on your mother," he said over his shoulder. "Be careful."

"I will," I replied, but I didn't waste any more time standing there. I turned and headed for the square, hoping he wouldn't see the tears on my cheek for the second time that day.

I didn't figure anyone would pick me up until I got past the square, but I walked along with my thumb dangling out as I walked along Glasgow Road with the scant hope that someone I knew might come along and give me a ride. I hadn't gotten too far when I heard a car slowing down behind me. I turned and saw Sheriff Pace in his Chevy Bel-Air cruiser pulling over to give me a ride. He stuck his head out the window and yelled, "Jump in, Stone."

"Thank you, sir," I said as I climbed into the front seat and closed the door.

"You headed down to Walgreens?" he asked, putting the car into gear and easing it back onto the road.

"No, sir. I'm trying to get home. Daddy and Mama had to stay at the hospital with Leck."

Sheriff Pace kept his eyes on the road and both his hands on the wheel. His gray crew cut and steely-eyed stare gave him an air of authority, in or out of uniform. People said he was a bit of a hothead, and I remembered the time one of the Newby boys got drunk and spit on the sheriff when he got hauled in. The Newby boy ended up with a broken jaw. But Pace had been elected sheriff three times over the past twenty years. He had just announced that he wasn't going to run again.

"That don't sound so good. What's wrong with Leck?"

I shook my head and shrugged. "I guess he's just suffering from the effects of his war wounds. He's in pretty bad shape."

His jaw tightened, and he nodded like he understood all too well how violence left a mark on a man in more ways than one. "I've been needing to talk to you," he said. "How 'bout I take you home so we can talk a spell?" It was structured as a question, but I could tell that the answer was a forgone conclusion.

"Well, sir, that's fine by me," I answered, but I felt uncomfortable and fidgeted in my seat. "What did you need to talk to me about?" I asked. I wasn't sure if he had questions about my gift or maybe Deputy Russel had told him about Wonnie, but I wanted to know what he was going to ask me in the worst way.

"Do you go up to Coe Ridge with your Daddy very often?" he asked. His tone was soft and even, but I detected just a hint of interrogative authority in his voice. He was probably used to getting answers, and I was sure he could spot a lie just by the look on someone's face.

I nodded and answered truthfully since I knew I didn't have anything to hide. "Yes, sir. We go up there almost every week. In fact, we were up there today delivering feed to the Wilburn place."

He didn't nod or even take his eyes off the road. He just asked another question like he had already catalogued the answer to the last question for future reference. "Have you noticed anything unusual lately?"

"Just about everybody today had a gun in their hands. Big Six said that somebody was stealing their product before they could get it to market."

He glanced at me when I mentioned Big Six. "Big Six stopped you?"

"Yes, sir. He told us to be careful."

"Good advice. Zeke Town can be a dangerous place."

We passed through the square, and I felt everyone's eyes on me as we drove past Walgreens and Shorty's, but I kept my eyes straight ahead. "Anything else unusual?" he asked.

"Well, of course, you've heard about Samuel Wilburn getting beat up and Wonnie Wilburn getting raped and beaten," I answered. I assumed that Deputy Russel had told him about both incidents, but from the sheriff's reaction, I could tell that I was mistaken.

He took his eyes off the road for a good ten seconds and looked straight at me. "Did you say rape?" he asked.

I nodded sheepishly and answered, "Yes, sir."

"How do you know about it, and why didn't you report it?" he asked.

"I talked to Deputy Russel about it. He promised me he would look into it," I insisted. "I did ask him to be discreet, but I figured he would tell you."

He frowned, and his bushy white eyebrows twisted in concern. "I see. Tell me what you know about the rape." The veins on his forehead were popping out of his creased skin and his jaw was tight.

"Well, apparently somebody beat and raped Wonnie Wilburn Friday night, after you released her. Remember? You arrested her for sitting in the white section of the theater." I tried to keep my voice even and calm. I didn't want him getting angry with me.

He nodded and said, "I remember. I released her without charging her around nine fifteen. She said she would hitch a ride home and started walking. How do you know that she was raped?"

"Well, sir, Saturday morning Samuel, her brother, came to my house and told me she had been beat up. He asked for me to . . . ," I hesitated. I didn't know how much the sheriff knew about my gift or if he had just heard rumors. I was worried about his reaction, but I continued. "He asked for me to come see if I could heal her."

"You mean like you did Ruby Tabor?"

"Yes, sir," I answered. I didn't want to get mired down in the workings of my gift or my doubts and troubles with it.

"What did you find when you got to the Wilburn place?"

"Wonnie's face was busted up pretty bad. They told me they had found her in the middle of the road raped and beaten. She was unconscious."

He took in a deep breath and exhaled through his nostrils like a bull does when it's getting angry. He was getting angry again, but I wasn't sure why. "Did she regain consciousness while you were there?" he asked, articulating his words.

"Yes, sir." I didn't offer him the details of healing her, and he didn't ask. We turned off Celina Road and down our driveway.

"Did she say who attacked her?"

"No, sir."

He snorted like a bull again. "Do you know how Wonnie is doing now?" He pulled up in front of our house and shut off the car.

"Yes, sir. I saw her today. She seemed all right physically, but she's still a bit troubled emotionally."

He twisted his eyebrows and wrinkled his forehead in confusion again. "Have her wounds healed?"

"I was able to heal her," I offered, "like how I healed Ruby Tabor."

He raised his eyebrows in surprise. "Oh, ain't that something," he said, but then he immediately frowned again and wrinkled his forehead. "So she shows no signs of the attack now?"

I bowed my head, feeling strangely ashamed. "No, sir," I said. I remembered what Wonnie had said earlier that day about not having any evidence of the crime. I raised my head and offered, "But I think she knows who did it to her."

"I'll have to look into that." He started the car. "Let me know if you see anything else unusual next time you go up there."

I nodded and got out of the car. Before I closed the door, I realized that I was missing a valuable opportunity. I stuck my head back into the car and asked, "Sheriff, what do you know about my real parents?"

He twisted his eyebrows again. "Nothing really. Somebody left a note on my car window telling me they had abandoned a baby at the cemetery, and I was supposed to deliver it to Billy and Ada Molony to raise." He scratched his short white hair and continued, "Just like the note said, I found you in the graveyard, crying your lungs out. I did like the note said, but I did a little snooping as well." He shook his head. "I'm sorry, Stone. I never figured out who left you there, but at least they picked a good home for you."

I stood up straight and looked up at the empty house. "Yes, sir, they did."

He said good-bye and put the car in gear. I closed the door to his cruiser and walked down to the barn to check on the livestock.

ELEVEN

I took care of all the livestock and found some left-overs in the icebox for dinner. I thought about going back to the hospital but decided that Daddy still didn't want me there. Instead I turned on the radio and sat there in the living room listening to WSM. I watched for lights coming up the driveway, but I eventually realized that they weren't coming home. I left the light on in the front room and went to bed.

I woke the next morning right on schedule without Daddy's help. I peeked out the front window and saw the car sitting there, but I didn't hear anybody up. I rolled out of bed and headed outside to get the morning chores done. I took care of all of the chores, including the ones Daddy usually did. Jersey Girl seemed glad to see me, and I got her milked pretty fast and headed for the house with fresh milk.

The kitchen normally smelled of fresh biscuits and crispy bacon by the time I got back to the house, but that morning it was cold and smelled like day-old scraps. I put the milk away and lit the stove. Then I took the scrap bucket, emptied it into the chicken pen (much to the delight of the chickens), and headed back to the house to see if I could make myself a hot breakfast. I found Daddy at the stove with a skillet in his hand. I wasn't sure he knew what to do either, since I had never seen him cook.

"Morning, Daddy. How was Leck when you came home?" I asked.

Daddy stared at the skillet like fresh-cooked bacon might suddenly appear. "No change," he said. He sounded tired.

"I lit the stove, but I don't know how to make biscuits. Is Mama home?"

Daddy opened up the icebox and grabbed out the eggs. "Nope, she stayed the night at the hospital. You want some eggs?"

"Sure. Scrambled. We got any bacon?"

"Should have. Check and see," he said with a nod toward the icebox. I found a slab of bacon and sat it on the counter beside the eggs. Since neither one of us knew enough about cooking to make biscuits, we ate a big breakfast of bacon and scrambled eggs.

When I finished my breakfast, I grabbed my dirty dishes and washed them in the sink. Daddy was still sitting at the table. He had finished his breakfast, but he just sat with his hands in his lap and stared at the other end of the table. He looked up at me when I picked up his dirty dishes and said, "Thank you, son. I'm sorry I'm not much on conversation this morning."

I nodded my understanding and starting washing the rest of the dirty dishes while Daddy sat at the table staring off into space. "Are you headed back into the hospital this morning?" I asked as I finished cleaning the last of the dishes.

Daddy sighed heavily and shook his head. "No, in times like these I find it best to be out working with my hands. I figured we could plant that acre we partitioned and plowed a few weeks ago. I need to stay busy with my hands."

Every year we fenced off an acre or two and planted a combination of soybeans, corn, and pumpkin. We wouldn't try and harvest it in the fall. Instead we would buy some shoat pigs and turn them loose on the plot. They would hog it down and fatten themselves at the same time. That would give us bacon, pork chops, and ham for the winter. I wasn't excited about working that day, but Daddy was right. Something about keeping my hands busy with productive work was therapeutic. Staying close to the rich soil that provided life was good for the soul.

"Do you want me to go hook up the disc and start disking?" I asked, trying to be helpful.

"You do that, and I'll get the seed ready."

Daddy seemed to take on new life in one breath. It was like the thought of planting something and bringing life into the world with the sweat of his brow gave him a reason to live. We both put on our boots, and I started out the back door for the barn with Daddy right behind me. Before I could get to the bottom of the back porch, I saw Samuel cutting across the field headed for our house. I thought I heard Daddy groan. We both stood there waiting for the trouble Samuel was surely bringing on his back.

"Morning, Samuel," said Daddy, trying to sound upbeat. "What brings you 'round here today?"

He looked at the ground and stuck his hands into the bib of his overalls. Sweat was beaded up on his forehead and dripped off his nose. He tried to talk but then choked up and closed his eyes for a moment. I started to say something, but Daddy put his hand on my arm and I knew he wanted me to wait.

After struggling for a couple of minutes, Samuel cleared his throat and wiped his eyes with his hands.

He stood up straight and let his hands hang limp by his side. "Missah Molony, Mama sent me to tell you that they found Wonnie drowned in the river this morning." After he delivered his message, his knees buckled and he collapsed onto the ground and began to sob.

Daddy swore under his breath and kicked at the dirt.

I felt the blood drain from my face and lowered myself to the bottom step of the back porch before I collapsed like Samuel. I felt my head spinning and my stomach churned. I wanted the tears to come, but instead I felt like I was trapped underwater and couldn't breathe.

"Samuel," commanded Daddy, "tell us what happened."

I started breathing again when I heard his stern voice. Samuel continued sobbing on the ground.

"Samuel," repeated Daddy. His voice wasn't harsh, but it carried weight. "Tell us what happened. Where did they find her?"

Samuel was lying on his back now with his arm covering his eyes. His chest was heaving up and down, but his sobs were mostly silent and unprofitable. "They found her in the river down near the ferry at Turkey Neck Bend this mornin'."

Daddy squatted down beside Samuel and patted his arm. "Any idea how it happened?" he asked, still calm and deliberate.

"No, suh. Yesterday afternoon she went for a walk a little before sundown and never came home," answered Samuel. He had stopped crying, but he still covered his eyes with his bare arm. His black skin had goose bumps and he started to shiver slightly. "Me and Pa went out looking for her and searched half the night, but we didn't find nothing. Mama just sat on the front porch in her rocker praying and crying most of the night. Then this morning we got up at first light. Mama said to check down by the river. So we figured we'd go down to the ferry at Turkey Neck Bend and work upriver." He wailed and cried his way through a few breaths, and then he added, "The ferryman had already fished her out of the water, and she was lying on the ferry with a blanket over her. I guess the river currents had pushed her up into a pile of driftwood nearby. Lord have mercy on her."

Daddy stood and rubbed the back of his neck like he would after a long day's work. His eyes were sunken and hollow and he looked ten years older at that moment. He paced back and forth for a few moments while Samuel just lay there breathing deeper and deeper with each breath. I stared at them without seeing them and felt like I was sinking in the deep green water of the river myself.

I guess it was the strength developed by years of toiling with the soil to make a living, or maybe just the years themselves and all the pain and hurt they can bring to a man, that gave Daddy strength. He stopped pacing and stood where he could face us both. The haggard look on his face had vanished, replaced by the hard look of a determined man. "All right, boys, listen to me," he said. "We'll have time enough for crying and moping on another day. Right now we've got work to get done." He walked over to Samuel and extended his hand. "Samuel, get up and wipe your face. Your folks are gonna need a lot of help from you over the next few days." He shook his extended hand and insisted, "Get up and wipe your face."

Samuel slid his arm away from his face and looked up at Daddy standing over him. He blinked back the tears and wiped his eyes before grabbing Daddy's hand and pulling himself to his feet. When he got to his feet, Daddy didn't let go. Instead he pulled Samuel into an embrace and patted him on the back a couple of times.

"God gives and God takes away. Blessed be the name of God," said Daddy as he released Samuel. His conviction surprised me. I always thought he just went along with Mama when it came to religion, but now I could see that his faith wasn't all about going to church and singing in the choir. He was a man of quiet faith, a man who would rather preach by his actions.

He turned to me and put his hands on his hips. "Stone, I need you to disk that field and then change the disk for the seeder and plant corn, soybeans, and pumpkins, just like we did the last few years. Do you remember how?"

"Yes, but—" I started to protest. I wanted to go see Wonnie. Somewhere in the back of my troubled mind I thought that maybe my gift might still work on her and restore life to her dead body. I had some crazy notion that maybe it was all just some twisted mistake and that I was going to find her swinging underneath the hickory tree.

Daddy held up his hand and stopped me. "I know that you want to go see Wonnie. I know you think that maybe somehow you can help." He shook his head and added, "She's gone, Stone, and the best thing you can do is take this burden off my shoulders so I can take Samuel home and check on Otis and Patsy Ann. Besides, the work will help take your mind off all your troubles."

Nothing seemed real at that moment. I felt like this was some sort of bad dream that I was going to wake up from and find everyone healthy and happy. The last thing I wanted to do was disk the field and plant the crops, but Daddy stood there like a rock. I bowed my head and consented.

"Good," said Daddy. "Take your time, and be careful. Keep the rows straight. I know we're not gonna harvest these crops, but that don't mean you can let yourself get sloppy with your work. You should be done by the time I get back." He looked at me expectantly, like he was waiting for me to go get started.

I sat there on the back porch, trying to find the will to get my body to do what he asked me to do. Even though I knew I should stand up and start heading for the barn, I just sat there and started crying. They were quiet tears, not the sobbing and wailing like Samuel, but simple involuntary tears rolling down my cheeks without any apparent passion.

"C'mon, Stone," said Daddy as he stepped toward me and extended his hand. "We've got work to do."

I looked at his extended hand and then up at his face. They seemed so far away and almost imaginary, but I was surprised to find his hand very real when I reached out and grabbed it. He pulled me up, and just like Samuel, he pulled me into an embrace. I hugged him back and felt my will coming back to me.

"Everything has a season," whispered Daddy. "There's a time to live and a time to die. You extended her time a little bit, just like you did Rusty's, but you can't keep people from dying, son." He released me and put his hands on my shoulders. "There is also a time to plant. Even though we know that in the end those plants will die, we plant them anyway. Life is one continuous cycle. We play our part in the cycle, but we can't stop it." He shook me gently. "Go and plant."

When he released me, it was like he restored my will. It was a feeble pulse at first that willed me to nod and start walking for the barn, but with each step it grew. By the time I climbed onto the tractor, my mind had pushed everything away except the task at hand. I had work to do, and I couldn't stop living because death had claimed a friend.

As I prepared the soil with the disk, the smell of the fresh earth and the even hum of the tractor motor put me into some sort of a trance. My limbs operated without thought and allowed my mind to examine the events of the last few days. I looked for some sort of pattern to the events, some sort of common thread. The only one I could find was my gift. I wondered what would have happened if I hadn't healed Samuel. Did I somehow upset the cycle of life Daddy had mentioned every time I healed someone? I began to worry again that maybe I was interfering with fate and doing more harm than good, but I remembered the other people I had healed—Hazel Owens, Bobby Shelly, Ruby, and even Jed Mock. They hadn't met with any tragic ending, yet.

I finished disking the field and started planting the corn. I replayed each of the healings in my head, the situation, the wounds, and the power as it surged through me and into their troubled bodies. I thought about Leck and how powerless I was to heal him. I understood the basic mechanics of my gift, but I had no real grasp on its power or its purpose. The only person that knew how I felt and could answer my questions was Phoebe Webb, and she was off limits because of Reverend Hines.

I focused on the front wheels of the tractor as I planted the rows of corn, soybean, and pumpkin. When those plants came up, I wanted Daddy to pat me on the back and tell me how good of a job I had done. That's how I felt about my gift. If there was a God, and he had given me this gift, then I wanted him to be proud of how I used it. I decided that the only way that was possible was if I understood it better. I decided that I had to go see Phoebe Webb again.

When I finished planting the pumpkin seeds, I stopped at the end of the field and surveyed what I had done. There was no immediate evidence of the work I had done except for the tractor tire tracks and the lingering smell of dirt, but I knew that in a few days those seeds would germinate and break the soft ground with their leaves as they struggled upward looking for sunlight. A warm wave of satisfaction came over me and I began to weep. The tears left clean tracks on my dusty cheeks, but they weren't bitter tears. Daddy was right. Planting the field had helped me deal with Wonnie's death, and in a few weeks life would spring forth to replace death, and the cycle would begin all over again.

Daddy pulled up in the truck about the time I was putting the seed away. He smiled at me as he looked down at the field and recognized that the job was done. I was a little embarrassed that evidence of my tears was obvious on my face, but he didn't seem to care.

"When's the funeral?" I asked.

"Saturday morning, at the chapel next to the schoolhouse. I suspect it'll be packed with every family from Coe Ridge," he said. "Patsy Ann is taking it the worst. She's in bed and won't talk to nobody, but several women were there to take care of things. Otis is down at the barn trying to stay busy, and Samuel is working his dogs." He let out a heavy sigh and shook his head. "They ain't strangers to death, but that don't make it any easier."

I put the seed back into the storage room and closed the door. "Did she drown?" I asked as I knocked the dust off my hat.

Daddy's forehead wrinkled up and he frowned. "That's what it looks like, but nobody can figure out how she got into the water." He shook his head and his frown became more serious. "They think she may have fallen, or jumped, into the river from the top of one of those bluffs."

I thought about her comments yesterday at the swing but didn't say anything about them. I figured they wouldn't bring anyone comfort. "Are you going back to the hospital this evening?" I asked.

"As soon as I take care of a few things."

"Can I go to town with you?"

He gave me a puzzled look at first, but whatever bothered him about my request must have been swallowed up by his compassion. "Go on to the house and get cleaned up. I'll be ready in a little while."

I walked back to the house trying to figure out a way to get past Reverend Hines and see Phoebe Webb again.

Daddy wouldn't let me go into the hospital again. He dropped me off at the square and told me he would swing by and pick me up at eight thirty in front of Walgreens. I didn't argue. The hospital was the last place I wanted to go tonight. I needed some help getting to Phoebe, and I was hoping I could recruit that help at Walgreens. I figured that since it was a Wednesday evening, I might catch Floyd and Willy before they headed to midweek church. Dewdrop didn't usually come into town until the weekend.

The first person I saw when I walked in was Jed Mock with an unlit cigarette hanging out of his mouth. He was holding court with Stanley Walsh and Johnny Hart. I immediately felt my stomach turn over, but Jed just grinned and gave me a nod. Stanley and Johnny glanced up but went right back to their conversation. I guess they had decided I wasn't worth bothering anymore.

Most of the booths were empty, and I ordered a cherry smash and slid into the one furthest from Jed. I thought about his exchanges with Wonnie and wondered if they were the ones that had beaten her and left her in the road last Friday night. I started to get worked up about the possibilities, but then I remembered that I was playing pool with Jed until late Friday night, and the other boys didn't have the backbone to do anything without Jed. I was Jed's alibi. Someone else, maybe one of her cousins like Deputy Russel suggested, had committed the deed, and now Wonnie was dead. She would never be able to identify the pond scum that did it to her.

I was beginning to get worried that I was on my own when Floyd and Willy walked in together. I hailed them with a wave and sipped at my cherry smash while they grabbed something. Jo Anne Carter and Nina Faye Davidson came through the door right behind them. I thought about Ruby for the first time that day and wondered if she would show up as well.

"What brings you in here on a Wednesday?" asked Floyd from beneath the bill of his hat as he and Willy slid into the booth. "We figured we wouldn't see you until we got to church."

I looked away and fumbled with the tabletop jukebox, trying to muster my words and tell them about Wonnie. "They found Wonnie Wilburn in the river down by Turkey Neck Bend this morning," I said. I pretended to look through the selection of songs and hoped that they wouldn't see the tears welling up in my eyes. I blinked and tried to keep from crying.

"Is she the colored girl that got arrested last Friday for sitting in the white section of the theater?" asked Floyd, almost in a whisper. I nodded and took a sip from my drink. I still couldn't look at them.

"She lived that close to the river and didn't know how to swim?" asked Willy.

I sniffled and coughed to hide the fact that I was on

the verge of tears. "A lot of the colored folks never learn how to swim. It's a shame to see people die so young," I said, shaking my head. They both nodded in agreement but didn't say anything. I let the issue die in that moment of silence.

"I need help with something," I said.

Floyd tilted his head back. "Whatcha need help with?"

"The revival is leaving soon, right?" They nodded. "I need to talk to Phoebe Webb again before they leave, but Reverend Hines ran me off last time I went to see her." I took a sip from my cherry smash. "I need you to help me sneak in to see her again . . . tonight."

Willy grinned and rubbed his chin. "That sounds like more fun than church, but what do you want us to do?"

I shrugged. I hadn't thought it through and didn't have a plan. "I don't know. I need to sneak into her trailer so that when she comes back from healing, I can talk to her while the Reverend is still busy with the services."

Willy laughed. "I can help with that," he said with a wicked smile. He usually had some fireworks lying around, and he was the mastermind behind sneaking a pig onto the Monroe County football team's school bus last year. "I've got a few cherry bombs and a couple of smoke bombs. As soon as they take her off stage, I'll light off a couple of those M-80s followed by a smoke bomb. That will keep Reverend Hines busy for a while."

Floyd's eyes lit up, and he wiggled his eyebrows so much it made his hat wiggle. "I could be your lookout," he offered.

I grinned and said, "I like the idea, but what if we lit them off in the middle of Reverend Hines preaching?" I must admit that deep down in my soul I wanted a little revenge on the reverend for the way he had treated me, and I could just see the shock on his face when Willy lit off the first cherry bomb. I thought Floyd was going to wiggle his hat right off his head he got so excited at my suggestion.

A little while later we were in position. I was poised to make a run for the trailer door on Floyd's signal. Willy was loitering on the other side of the tent with his pyro-technics at the ready. We figured I would have about ten minutes or so once I got into the trailer. I could hear the congregation singing and gave Floyd a thumbs-up. He peeked into the revival tent and looked up at me like a deer in the headlights. Before he could give me a signal, I heard the first explosion. I didn't wait for Floyd's signal and made a dash for the trailer. I was afraid that if Phoebe was in the trailer, the noise might bring her out. I wanted to make it to the door before she opened it.

My long legs and adrenaline carried me to the trailer faster than I expected. The lights were off inside, and she hadn't opened the door to see about the noise. The thought crossed my mind that she might not be in her trailer, but I was committed now. I would go into her trailer and wait until she came back. I figured it might be my last chance to get some answers.

The tin-can trailer rocked as I stepped onto the metal stair. I flung open the flimsy door and jumped deep into the cramped dark space, pulling the door closed behind me in one motion. I stood by the small table and tried to let my eyes adjust. Something brushed against my ankle. I shuffled forward and stepped on something. I looked down at the floor, trying to focus my eyes in the dark. The floor seemed to be moving. I heard a rattle. My heart jumped into my throat as my mind raced to under-stand all the clues it had been given. When the first snake bit me on my right leg, the situation was crystal clear in my mind's eye. I was standing ankle deep in snakes.

The first bite started burning immediately. I side-stepped, trying not to step on another snake, but it was futile. I felt a second bite on the same leg. I danced on my toes and turned to find the door. I got bit in the left leg and felt the sharp fangs dig into my flesh. I jumped for the door and landed on another one and took another strike to my left leg. I grabbed for the door handle and kicked at the pile of snakes at my heels. I was told later that I got bit seven times, but I don't remember the other bites. Finally I got the door open and half jumped, half fell out of the trailer door.

I got up and ran blindly out of panic. Just like before, I ran across the road without looking for traffic. I would probably have kept running until the venom killed me, except Floyd and Willy grabbed me somewhere on the other side of the road. They were laughing at the practical joke and probably at the panic they saw on my face until I just collapsed on to the ground in shock.

"C'mon, Stone," said Willy, still laughing at his handiwork. "We gotta git before the reverend finds us." He reached down to pull me up. "I guess you decided not to talk to the healer lady after all since she had just come out onto the stage."

My heart was racing. My legs were burning like they had been stung by a hive of hornets. All I could say to Willy and Floyd was, "Get me to the hospital!"

Willy must have noticed the panic on my face because he froze for a second. Floyd chuckled nervously like maybe this was all just part of the elaborate joke, and he wasn't in on it. "The hospital?" he asked, almost mocking my request.

"I've been bit by a rattlesnake!" I shouted. I could

feel the skin around my ankles beginning to stretch. The burning sensation was moving up my legs. I felt a cold sweat coming over me, and I shivered on the ground, probably more out of shock than real pain, but I swore I could feel myself dying.

"Get him up!" said Willy as he took off running. "I'll get my truck!" he shouted over his shoulder as he sprinted away. Floyd pushed his hat back on his head, exposing his wide eyes and wrinkled brow. He reached down and pulled my hand away from my chest and helped me stand up. Then he tucked himself underneath my arm and held me up.

My feet felt like burning rocks as the venom seeped into my toes. It was strange facing death. I had saved others from pain and death, but looking at death from my own eyes made it much more vivid and real. I hadn't considered my own mortality, and the thought of dying made me shiver and shrink like a coward. I thought about Leck on a hill in Korea hiding under a dead soldier wondering if he would take his last breath so far from home. I understood the fear that must have gripped him. I caught a glimpse of the guilt he must have felt when he survived while so many around him passed from this life in violence.

I shivered, and Floyd reassured me that they were going to get me to the hospital. "Hang on, Stone," he whispered.

Willy roared up in his Ford truck and screeched to a stop. "Put him in the back! It'll be quicker," he ordered.

I hobbled to the back of the truck with Floyd's help. He dropped the tailgate and jumped up to help me lie down in the bed of the truck. Right before I collapsed, I looked back at the trailer. The door was open and I thought I saw Phoebe Webb standing just outside in the waning light, staring in my direction. I fell into the bed, and Floyd pulled me in.

"Go! Go! Go!" yelled Floyd as he banged on the back window. Willy burned rubber and raced to the hospital while I jostled and bumped on the dirty truck bed watching the last remnants of daylight disappear in the evening sky.

We got to the hospital in less than five minutes. Willy pulled up in front of the glass doors and hurried inside looking for help while Floyd jumped over the side of the truck and starting pulling me out of the back. I'm not sure what Willy told them, but they were loading me on the gurney before I could spit. Everything began to seem distant, like I was watching it all in a movie. I began to drift and felt like I was floating through the hallway under the bright lights. The only thing that felt real was the pain throbbing in my legs and pushing up into my chest.

I felt a needle prick my arm, and a few minutes later the room began to spin. I closed my eyes and let myself drift with the current. I could hear commotion. I could feel the hands that cared for me as they cut my pant legs. I could hear the urgency in the voices. I wanted to concentrate on what they were saying, but I felt like I was drifting downstream in the middle of the Cumberland and everyone else was speaking to me from the banks. I panicked as I felt the current carry me farther and farther downriver and away from reality, but all my attempts to swim to shore were futile.

I drifted toward a light so bright that I had to shield my eyes. I felt like other people were there on the shore waiting for me, but I couldn't see anyone. All the tension and panic left me, and I stopped struggling against the current. I was overcome with the desire to reach the shore and felt renewed strength as I began to swim for the nearest bank of the river. I could make out figures in white, but I didn't recognize anyone. I kicked harder and as I got close, one of the figures stuck out a hand. I looked up at the face and thought I saw Wonnie. I hesitated like I understood that once I grabbed her hand I couldn't go back, but then I reached for it.

My hand never reached hers. I felt myself yanked back upriver by some invisible rope. The pain and panic rushed back into my frame. I heard the commotion of voices again. Bright lights flickered overhead. The scripture from Ezekiel rumbled through my thoughts like an old friend. I felt warm hands touching my head. Then all the burning pain left me.

When I finally had the courage to open my eyes, Phoebe Webb was sitting on the edge of my bed, looking off in the distance. Her eyes were glazed over. Floyd and Willy were standing near the doorway looking spooked, like on the night we were fishing down by Neely's Ferry and reeled in a snapping turtle. A nurse was taking my pulse, and Doctor Williams was standing beside her with his hands in his lab coat pockets. Everyone seemed surprised and relieved at the same time. After a moment, I realized what had happened. Phoebe Webb had healed me.

TWELVE

"Welcome back, son," said Doctor Williams as he patted me on the shoulder. "What's his blood pressure?" he asked the nurse.

The nurse pulled the cuff from my arm. "One twenty-five over eighty," she said as she tucked the stethoscope and cuff under her arm.

"A little high but much better than where it was headed," he said as he examined my ankles. "No sign of the bite marks anymore either." He looked up at Phoebe and shook his head. "I've been a doctor for a long time, but that beats anything I've ever seen. If I hadn't seen it with my own eyes, I wouldn't have believed it." He shook his head again and held up his hands like he was surrendering. "Truth is, I'm not sure I believe it even after seeing it. How did you do that?"

Phoebe didn't look at him but continued to stare off into the distance. "It is a strange gift that is often misunderstood and sometimes misused," she answered. "I'm just glad I got here in time."

"So am I. He was bitten at least seven times, and for some reason his body had an allergic reaction that compounded the effects of the venom. We were losing him when you walked through the door." Doctor Williams walked around to face Phoebe's distant stare. "Are you okay, ma'am?" he asked.

"I will be shortly," she answered.

Doctor Williams just shook his head and started for the door like he wasn't sure he wanted to know anymore. The nurse gave me a satisfied smile like she understood things Doctor Williams never would and practically skipped out of the room.

The burning in my legs, the swelling skin, the throbbing veins—all the pain was gone. I wanted to get up, but the vision I had seen drained me of most of the energy I had left. Besides, Phoebe Webb, the person I wanted most to talk to right now, was sitting on the edge of my bed, and she wasn't going anywhere until she could see again.

"Thank you for saving me," I said.

"You're welcome." She sat with her hands folded in her lap and her eyes still fixed somewhere in the distance.

"How did you know I was here?" I asked.

"When those two yahoos lit off those cherry bombs," she said with a nod in Willy and Floyd's general direction, "I headed back to my trailer to check on things and found the door open with snakes practically falling out of it." She shook her head like something didn't make sense to her. "Apparently somebody had emptied the revival's box of snakes into my trailer. I saw them load you in the truck, and I had a hunch. So I commandeered a vehicle and followed you here. Good thing for you I did."

Floyd and Willy looked at the floor like they were ashamed somehow, but I certainly didn't blame them for what happened. "They were trying to distract Reverend Hines so I could come talk to you."

Phoebe shifted as if getting more comfortable. "Well, I'm here now. Let's talk."

I was about to ask my first question when Mama burst through the door. She pushed past Floyd and Willy with the worried look she normally reserved for Leck these days. "What happened? Are you hurt?" she asked, almost breathless.

I saw Daddy stop in the doorway when he saw Phoebe. "I'm all right, Mama. I was hurt, but this woman healed me," I said, nodding at Phoebe.

Mama stood there looking frazzled and confused. Her unkempt hair was pulled back, but several strands fell into her face. After sitting with Leck in the hospital, her face was gaunt and her eyes had dark rings under them. Her eyes darted back between me and Phoebe. "Thank you, Miss . . . ," she said in an unsure voice.

Phoebe didn't turn and look at Mama, but kept her eyes fixed in the distance and said, "Phoebe Webb, and it was the least I could do."

Daddy must've decided to join Mama at my bedside and walked into the room. His boots were heavy against the floor, and Phoebe turned her head like she was listening more intently. "Hello, Billy. It's been a long time," she said.

Daddy stopped next to my bed and looked down at the floor. "Hello, Phoebe. Looks like the years have been good to you."

I'm not sure who looked more bewildered and confused at that moment, me or Mama. Floyd told me later that my mouth was hanging open so big he thought I was going to start catching flies. Mama's eyes darted faster and more frequently between everyone at the bedside. Daddy just stared at the floor.

Phoebe blinked hard, and I knew her vision starting to come back. "Looks like you've raised my son well. He's become a fine man."

I felt the air rush out of my lungs, and I don't know how long it was before I started breathing again, but when I did my breaths came fast and shallow for a while. I'm not sure if it was Floyd or Willy, but one of them mumbled, "I'll be danged!"

Mama clutched at her chest and put her hand over her heart like she was afraid it might stop beating any second. "Your son? You're the mother?" she asked. Before anyone could answer, she looked at Daddy with yearning eyes. "Billy, is that true?"

Daddy kept looking at the floor and just nodded his head.

"Why didn't you tell me?" she asked. Her voice wavered and squeaked. I could see her lips start to tremble.

Daddy let out a heavy sigh and raised his head to face her. "That was part of the arrangement," he said.

"Arrangement?"

"Yes, the arrangement," he said in a soothing voice. He reached out to her and put his hands gently on her shoulders. "When the doctor said you couldn't have no more children, you were devastated. Nothing eased your pain." Tears welled up in his eyes. "I was afraid I was going to lose you." He sniffled and continued, "Then one day while I was delivering feed up on Coe Ridge, I met Phoebe."

"I was already pregnant when I met your husband," added Phoebe emphatically. She was looking at everyone when she spoke now, so I figured her vision must have come back. "I was hiding from the father because the circumstances surrounding the conception were . . . shall we say, violent." She stood and began pacing as she spoke. "Patsy Ann told me that you couldn't have any more children, but that you wanted more. I was young and didn't think I could raise the child, not to mention the pain I felt because of his father. So we made an arrangement."

Mama slid closer to Daddy, and he put his arms around her like he did when she was cold. Phoebe stopped at my bedside again and faced Billy and Ada. "I would deliver the baby in secret and leave it in the grave-yard on my aunt's grave. Sheriff Pace would find it and offer it to you and Billy. Then I would disappear."

Mama sat on the edge of my bed. I was afraid that she might collapse right on top of me. She looked at me and then back at Phoebe. "You're his mother," she whispered.

"No," answered Phoebe, shaking her head. "I gave him life, but you're his mother."

"Who's my father?" I blurted out, still trying to catch my breath. I looked back and forth between Pheobe, my birth mother, and Billy, my stepdaddy, for an answer.

Billy shrugged his shoulders and shook his head. Phoebe tried to smile at me, but instead her face looked pained and melancholy. "Some secrets are best carried to the grave," she said.

"But—"

Phoebe held up a finger and cut me off. "You ain't gonna understand all of this tonight," she said.

"But you're leaving with the revival," I whined. For once in my life I was getting some straight answers about who I was, and the person that knew the most was about to leave me again. I must have sounded pitiful because both Phoebe and Ada put a hand on me to comfort me.

Phoebe looked at Ada and pulled back her hand. "No, I'm not leaving," she said. "I've decided to come back home for good. The revival is leaving, but I'm moving back into my aunt's old farmhouse out near Judio." She nodded at Billy and Ada and started for the door. "Billy, you know where the place is. Have the boy come see me."

"Wait!" I shouted before she could get past Floyd and Willy. "Who put all those snakes in your trailer?"

She gave me a pitiful smile and slipped out the door.

I heard Phoebe's footsteps as she disappeared down the hallway, and I felt like the hospital bed had become a sinkhole in the ground, swallowing me up. I grabbed at the sheets like some lifeline and hung on until my knuckles were white so I wouldn't slip into that black hole and drown. I must have looked panicked because Mama put her hand on mine and asked, "Stone, is everything all right?"

I tried to nod but just stared at the only face I had ever known as my mother. From my earliest recollection it was her face that came to me when I was scared at night or comforted me when I got hurt. It was her face that I saw when she rocked me back and forth in the front porch rocker as I watched the fireflies on hot summer nights. It was her face that smiled at me when I came running to the dinner table hungry. It was her face that lovingly scolded me when I tracked dirt into the house or forgot my manners around visitors. It was the face of the only mother I had ever known, and yet it wasn't the face of the woman who gave me life.

"Stone, honey, are you feeling okay?" she asked again.

I swallowed the feelings of panic and nodded. "I just wanna go home, Mama," I heard myself say. It almost felt like another person. It was like someone tore me in half inside, like a piece of paper. Right now the person I had been raised as was in control, and the other person, the one who was abandoned years ago in a graveyard, was lurking and watching for an opportunity to take over.

I swung my legs away from Mama and climbed out

of bed. The floor was cold against my bare feet. They must have removed my shoes somewhere along the way, and my pants were cut off at the knee, but I didn't care. I started for the door because movement kept me sane at that moment. Floyd and Willy were both watching me like some freak show attraction. I slipped past them without even thanking them for bringing me to the hospital. I didn't even wait to see if Billy and Ada were following me and started down the hall for the exit.

When I found the car in the parking lot, Daddy was with me. "Your mother will be along directly," he said. "She needed to check on Leck before she went home."

I climbed into the back seat without responding and sat there alone in the dark as Daddy leaned against the front fender and waited. After tonight I wasn't sure whether to call him "Daddy" or call him by his name. I wasn't sure he deserved to be my father after lying to me all these years, but he was the only father I had ever known. Mama came along in a few minutes, and we drove home together like three familiar strangers.

THIRTEEN

I didn't wake up the next morning until long after the sun had come up. Daddy must have let me sleep and done the morning chores himself. By the time I got downstairs, I found a plate of biscuits and a note. He and Mama had gone back to the hospital to see about Leck.

I nibbled at the biscuits and drank a glass of milk. The quiet house felt like a prison cell. So I slipped on my boots and headed outside. I whistled for Rusty, something I hadn't done for days, and then chided myself for being so stupid. I wandered down by the barn and past the patch of land I had seeded the day before. I moseyed out through the pasture to check on the cattle, and after a while I found myself down by the river, just a few yards from where Rusty got bit.

I plopped myself down at the top of the muddy bank and watched the river drift by. The current moved past this bend like molasses—thick, deep, and in no hurry. I grabbed a piece of driftwood at my feet and tossed it into the casual current and watched it meander downstream. I grabbed another piece of wood and hurled it into the deep. It drifted aimlessly at the mercy of the river until it was out of sight. At that moment I felt just like that driftwood, dead and detached. I wanted to join it. I wanted to toss myself in and drift away, like Wonnie had done. I sat there hurling unloved pieces of useless wood into the river over and over again until the sun hung low in the afternoon sky.

The kitchen light was on when I got back to the house. I could see Mama through the kitchen window working as I walked up. I decided to avoid her and walked around the house to the front door. I rounded the corner and found Daddy sitting on the front porch.

"Evening, Stone," said Daddy. I hesitated and then started up the stairs with every intention of passing him by and disappearing up to my room. "Sit down with me," he said, signaling to the chair next to him. "Mama'll have supper ready in few minutes." The word *supper* made my stomach growl, and I took a seat. We both stared down the lane and watched for any passing cars. "Where you been all day?" he asked.

"Down by the river."

He nodded like he understood, waited a few seconds, and started saying the things I expected he would say. "What happened to Phoebe Webb ain't our fault. It's not your fault either. She had her reasons for not wanting to keep you, and you can go talk to her about that if you want to. But we have loved you and cared for you like our own from the moment we got you."

A part of me knew he was right, but I was still angry. I just wasn't sure who I was angry with. The abandoned baby inside of me cried out for answers. "Why didn't you tell me the whole story sooner? I feel like my whole life is some sort of lie," I snapped.

"That was part of the arrangement. I gave my word that I wouldn't tell a soul who your mother was."

"You didn't think I had a right to know?" I shouted.

Daddy fidgeted in his seat, and his jaw got tight like

it did when he was getting upset about something. "I gave my word," he insisted.

"All these years I've wondered about my real mother and father and you knew all along!" I pounded my fist on my knee and stuck my finger in his face. "You should have told me!" I had never raised my voice to Daddy, and I wasn't sure how he was going to react to it. For a second I was afraid he might reach across and grab my finger, but he tightened his jaw and took it. Not wanting to risk the rising confrontation, I jumped up and started through the door but found Mama standing just inside wiping her hands on her apron.

"Supper's ready," she said meekly.

Hunger brought me to the table, but I wasn't much on conversation. The only noise was the sound of silverware against plates. I shoved the hot food into my mouth and stared at my plate. Before I could finish, someone knocked at the door.

"I'll get it," said Daddy before Mama could get up.

I picked at my food and tried to listen to the conversation at the front door. I could tell by Daddy's tone that it was a stranger.

"Evening, what can I do for you?"

"Evening, sorry to bother you. I'm Roy Cornet from over near Eighty-Eight. I heard from Bobby Shelley that your son has the power to heal people." His voice wavered like a nervous man.

"Yes, sir," answered Daddy. "He has been able to heal a few people, but it ain't a good time right now."

His denial got my dander up, and the anger I felt earlier returned with a vengeance. I started to get up and Mama put a hand on my arm to stop me. Her eyes pleaded and she shook her head.

At the front door, Mr. Cornet continued to plead

also. "I understand, sir, but my son, Archie, here has been in this wheelchair with palsy since the day he was born. Don't you think you could spare an hour on his behalf?"

"I'm sorry, not tonight," answered Billy firmly. "Maybe another time," he said as he started to close the door.

I shook off Mama's hand and stood up from the table. I was sick of being everyone's pawn. I wasn't going to let Daddy, Mama, Phoebe, or anybody else, tell me when I could and couldn't use my gift. I stomped into the front room and grabbed the closing door from Daddy's hand. "Did you say you needed somebody to heal your son?" I asked through the screen door.

Mr. Cornet stood behind a wheelchair in a pair of overalls and a hat that had seen better days. He was a big man, and his size made the wheelchair look like some tinker toy that he could snap with his fingers if he wanted to. His son, Archie, sat curled up in the chair with his head cocked to one side like some grotesque bird. His hands were withered and useless—like chicken feet. He jerked and squawked like some hen after she laid an egg.

I wasn't prepared for the extremity of his condition and my confidence left me, but my pride and anger pushed me forward. I put on a hospitable face and stepped past Daddy and through the screen door. "Let's see what I can do for you," I pronounced.

Mr. Cornet took off his hat and held it in front of his chest. He bowed his head slightly and said, "Much obliged to you, son."

I looked down at the twisted and pitiful form of the human being in the rickety wheelchair in front of me, and my heart sank. The angry confidence that I had felt a few moments ago melted away in front of such a daunting disease. I tried to focus, but all I could see was the feeble arms and legs of a nimble soul trapped in this wretched excuse of a body. Fear grabbed ahold of me, and any faith I had felt was gone.

I smiled nervously at Mr. Cornet. I worried what a scorned man his size could do to me if I failed to cure his son. "Sometimes it takes a few minutes for me to feel the necessary faith," I offered. "Do you believe that your son can be healed?"

"I know you healed Bobby Shelley," he said. "And I heard you saved a girl's life from a rattlesnake bite." He shrugged his broad shoulders. "I reckon if you can do those things, you might be able to help Archie here."

His simple faith seemed sincere, but I couldn't muster even an ounce of my own. It was like someone had shoved my gift into a closet and locked the door, and I couldn't find the key. I closed my eyes and tried to focus on the scripture from Ezekiel. Nothing came to me. I tried to remember the lightning storm that usually surged in my head, or the burning hands that carried the power to the sickly. Nothing happened. I felt like the heavens were sealed, and my gift was behind some hidden door locked away by my own pride and anger. I attempted to force it for almost fifteen minutes, and I might have continued embarrassing myself in front of that crippled boy and his mountain of a father if Daddy hadn't interceded.

I was standing there with my eyes closed when I heard Daddy open the screen door and walk out onto the front porch. I opened my eyes as he laid a gentle hand on my shoulder and spoke on my behalf. "Mr. Cornet, I've seen Stone heal several people. I know that on another night he might be able to heal your son." He patted me on the back. "But like I said when you came to the door, tonight ain't a good time." He stepped forward and stuck a hand out to Mr. Cornet. "I'm real sorry. Maybe another time," he offered.

Mr. Cornet put back on the ragged hat he had been clutching at his chest as he waited for me to perform some sort of miracle. He wiped a tear with the back of his left hand as his right hand swallowed Daddy's outstretched hand. After the handshake he picked up his son, wheelchair and all, carried him down the front porch stairs, and then rolled him over to an old flatbed truck.

I stood there like a broken statue as he loaded his son into the front seat and then tied the wheelchair onto the flatbed truck. When his taillights disappeared down our lane, Daddy patted me on the back and quietly went back inside. I'm not sure how long I stood there feeling empty, but eventually I slinked upstairs and fell into bed with my clothes on.

The next day Daddy woke me up at the usual time. I didn't bother changing clothes when I got up and started for the barn to milk Jersey Girl. My head ached and the last place I wanted to be was milking some dumb cow. I was a little rough with her that morning, nothing that would hurt her, but I didn't talk to her or soothe her with my voice as I got her ready to milk. She responded by smacking me upside the head with her tail a couple of times. When I got mad and yelled at her for it, she just looked at me with those big dumb eyes as if to say, "What's your problem?" I just shook my head and felt stupid for talking to a cow.

When I got back to the house for breakfast, the kitchen was filled with the rich aromas of Mama's cooking. It only took a couple of days for me to miss her touch in the kitchen. Daddy blessed the food, and we ate in peace, but with Leck missing and everything that had happened the last few days, the mood was a mixture of somber and tense. I felt like I was at the free throw line with a big game in the balance as the butterflies swirled around my stomach.

Daddy finished first and pushed himself back from the table and cleared his throat. "Stone," he began, "your mother and I are going to the hospital this morning. I have several things I need you to do while we're gone." I nodded reluctantly and kept eating. I didn't really feel like going anywhere, but I wasn't thrilled about working all day either.

"Hook up the cultivator and cultivate the patch of corn first," he instructed. "When you're done with that, grab your hoe and hoe the tobacco. Be careful not to damage the lower leaves." That was enough to keep me busy most of the day, but he wasn't through. "While you're resting, I need you to grease the baler, but be careful not to overgrease it."

I sat up straight and dropped my fork onto my plate. Mama shrunk just a little and looked at her plate like she was afraid of the two of us at opposite ends of the table. "With Leck in the hospital and all the commotion this past week, our work's been piling up on us," declared Daddy sternly. He leaned forward and shook a rough finger at me. "You can be angry about the past all you want, but we put a roof over your head, clothes on your back, and food in your mouth. It won't hurt you none to help out around here."

I wanted to pick up my plate and throw it at him, but the next thing he said caught me off guard. "Tomorrow is Wonnie's funeral. I want you to take the truck and go to the funeral and represent our family. When it's over, go see Phoebe." He glanced at Mama. "Maybe she can help you understand some things."

I looked at Mama sitting there with her hands in her lap and her head bowed like she was at church, and my heart sank. I was angry at Phoebe and Daddy. They had both known what they were doing. Mama had simply been a willing, and loving, unknowing participant in the whole scheme. She had taken in an abandoned baby and raised it as her own. She had been there to answer life's questions and offer me solace from life's trials. Now, when I needed answers, when I needed solace, she had to let me go to the very person that had abandoned me. Out of respect for her selfless love, I swallowed my anger and consented. "Cultivate the corn. Hoe the tobacco. Grease the baler. Got it," I said. "How do I find Phoebe's place?"

Billy sat back in his seat again. "Just ask Otis or Samuel. They know."

An awkward moment passed before I pushed myself from the table and headed out the back door. I passed the day working on the assigned tasks. It was hot, and several times I thought about dropping everything and going back to the shady riverbank to fish or watch driftwood, but the work kept my hands busy and let my mind work on the puzzle that my life had become. I finished several hours before dark, and when I didn't find anyone at the house, I headed down to the river.

I thought about what I would say to Phoebe. Why did she abandon me? Didn't she love me? Who was my father and why didn't he want me? Where had she been all these years? Did I get my gift from her? It was almost dark by the time I got back to the house, but nobody was home. Mama had left me some corn bread on the table. So I had some with milk, ironed my Sunday shirt, and took a bath. Daddy wasn't home by the time I was ready for bed, and I didn't wait up.

Daddy got me up at the usual time on Saturday morning. I got my chores done, and we ate oatmeal and day-old biscuits for breakfast with little conversation between us. I cleaned up and pulled on my Sunday pants and shirt and a dark clip-on tie. When I went to find the truck keys, I found him sitting at the kitchen table.

"Give our condolences to Patsy Ann and Otis. Tell them we'd be there if Leck wasn't in the hospital," he said. He didn't look at me but traced his finger aimlessly back and forth across the table. "You have a right to be angry at me, and maybe Phoebe, but Ada ain't done nothing but give you love." I nodded but didn't say anything. I knew he was probably right, but I just didn't want to talk to him right now.

He dangled the truck keys from his finger for me to grab. "I hope you get some answers, Stone, and I hope you are ready for the truth you might find."

I grabbed the keys and headed for Wonnie's funeral.

FOURTEEN

I had never been to a colored church before, let alone a colored funeral. I figured it would be a lot like the Methodist funerals I had attended, but it wasn't.

I pulled up in Daddy's Ford truck just as people were starting to arrive at the church. It was a small, one-room church made from lumber they had harvested from right there on Coe Ridge. The whitewash was thin in several places and the red mud had splashed up on the bottom of the wall, giving the old white church a skirt of red stain. A small fenced graveyard sat out back, and I noticed the fresh pile of dirt and the new grave that had been dug for Wonnie.

I slipped into the church, trying not to draw any attention to myself, even though I didn't see another white face in the gathering congregation. The small windows were open, but the chapel remained dark and musty. The candles and coal-oil lanterns cast their dim light on the wooden pews. When my eyes adjusted, I saw Wonnie lying in the rough wooden casket at the front of the chapel.

Several suspicious eyes watched me as I made my way to her side. She was dressed in a white cotton dress that made her look angelic, like she had looked in my dream just a couple of days ago. I'm sure they had done their best to make her face look nice for the funeral, but her skin was pale, and her lips were puffed up. It was difficult to look at her. I could still see the image of her walking down on her porch steps with a big smile on her face, and her image from my dream was still vivid in my mind. All at once the church felt damp and cold, and I shuddered. I shoved my hands into my pockets and trudged to a seat in the back, holding back the flood of tears that pushed against my eyes.

I ignored the gathering congregation around me, and they returned the favor. I sat on the last pew with my head in my hands and let the occasional tear drip onto the worn wooden planks of the floor until the funeral started. Everyone stood when Otis and Samuel escorted Patsy Ann into the church. They each had an arm and practically carried her to the front pew. When they passed by Wonnie, Patsy Ann wailed and tried to break away from Otis and Samuel, but they held on to her and sat her down between them on the front row.

The preacher, dressed in a white shirt and black tie, stood to start the services. I sat up out of respect and saw that I wasn't the only white person at the services. Phoebe Webb sat a few rows up from me. She had her hair pulled up on top of her head and wore a black dress that exposed her white shoulders and neck against the sea of black. Her presence puzzled me even more.

The funeral was a journey of sadness and grief. The congregation sang an emotional and slow-paced version of "Amazing Grace" that resonated in the humble chapel and made it feel small. The preacher spoke from Corinthians chapter fifteen about the resurrection, but even though the words were intended to uplift, the sting of death was all too real at that moment and wasn't swallowed up by words from the Bible. A heavyset woman stood and sang "Precious Lord" as she swayed back and forth with the tempo of the song. The dam broke when the congregation sang "I'll Fly Away" to end the services, and I was wishing I had a handkerchief as I wiped the waves of tears from my face with my shirtsleeve. They ended the services by ringing the church bell one time for each year of Wonnie's life—seventeen short years.

When the services in the chapel were over, Otis and Samuel took Patsy Ann at each arm and escorted her to the graveyard. Everyone else filed outside after them and stood around the open grave. The smell of fresh earth reminded me of the planting I had done the day Wonnie died, and I remembered Daddy's words about life and death. At the moment, they didn't bring me much comfort, but later that summer I would think about Wonnie each time I passed by the tall corn and remember how she had changed my life.

I recognized some of the faces of the six men that carried Wonnie's casket from the church, but I didn't know their names. They moved methodically toward the dark hole, never missing a step or faltering. When they got close, they set the wooden box across three ropes. Each of the men took up positions at the end of the ropes, lifted Wonnie up, and held her over her final mortal resting place. For a moment they levitated her above the anxious grave like they were offering her soul to heaven.

Otis's rich baritone voice sang, "Swing low, sweet chariot, coming for to carry me home." After the first line, everyone began to sing along, and the pallbearers lowered Wonnie into the waiting earth. I thought I had cried all of my tears, but I broke down again and bawled like a baby.

After the hymn, Patsy Ann stepped forward and grabbed a handful of red dirt and sprinkled it on top of the casket. Otis and Samuel followed suit. Then one by one everyone filed forward and took a somber handful of dirt and began the process of burying their beloved Wonnie. I went last.

As soon as I tossed in the handful of dirt, several men with shovels began to fill the gaping hole. The sound of the sharp metal against the soft earth took me back to Rusty's burial. I could hear the sound of Daddy's shovel all over again as it sank into the rich river-bottom soil to bury my trusted friend. I didn't think I would ever feel as sad as that day again, but I was wrong. Once again, untimely death had claimed someone I cared about, someone I had healed.

I started for the truck and tried to compose myself before approaching Phoebe Webb. She found me before I could get my eyes dry. "Colored funerals are almost always a lesson in tragedy," she said as she lit up a cigarette. "As hard as their lives are, you'd think they'd be happy about someone finally escaping the injustice and hardship, but instead the whole service seems to symbolize the pain they all feel on a daily basis."

"Do you know the Wilburns?" I asked.

She took a drag from her cigarette and exhaled sharply. "I used to live up here when I was a little girl."

"Here? On Coe Ridge?"

She nodded, took another long drag on her cigarette, and then tossed it to the ground. "Can you give me a ride home?"

I was trying to get my mind around what she had just told me and almost forgot my manners. "Yes, uh . . . Yes, ma'am." I opened the door for her and then climbed into the driver's seat. A few minutes later, we headed down a washed-out road on our way to her house near Judio.

At first I was too shocked to remember any of the questions I had for her. Phoebe Webb, my biological mother, sat next to me, and my mind was blank. I stared out the windshield and navigated the sorry excuse for a road while she peered out the passenger side window and gave me occasional directions.

After a few minutes of traveling together in silence, she took control of the conversation. "I know you must have a lot of questions," she started. "Why don't you drive and let me tell you a short history of my life. After that, you can ask questions. I won't promise to answer all of them, but I'll try and answer some of them. How's that sound?"

I stared out the windshield ahead and nodded.

"My mother's name was Wanda Groce. She had a sister Opal who married one of the Newby boys. That's why you ended up on her graveside," she began. "Their father was a strict and harsh man, and when Wanda, my mother, was about sixteen, he beat her for kissing a boy in public. Well, my mother got angry and spiteful and ran away to Coe Ridge to live. She did it to hurt her father, but while she was there she fell in love with my father, Calvin Coe. Even though they were never married, I was born about a year later."

I focused on the road. I gripped the steering wheel so tight my knuckles were white. She was telling me that my real grandfather was a mixed-breed Coe from Zeke Town.

"I don't remember anything from living there as a little girl because we left when I was about two years old." She pointed to an upcoming lane and directed, "My house is a couple of miles down that road." She chuckled and returned to her story. "Apparently, Calvin had a knack for fathering children, by women other than my mother. So she decided to pack us up and move to Bowling Green with a friend. I spent most of my childhood watching her struggle, trying to keep food on the table and bouncing from boyfriend to boyfriend. Then one day when I was about fifteen, we got word that her parents had died in a car wreck, and within a few weeks we were living in their old house in Burkesville."

"So your father is Calvin Coe?" I asked. I couldn't bring myself to say that he was my grandfather yet. I knew I was talking about my heritage as well as hers, but when I spoke about it from her perspective, it didn't seem so personal.

"The one and only," she said with a shake of her head.

"Who's my father?"

She didn't say anything right away but looked out the window at the passing trees along the dirt lane. "I adjusted to life in Burkesville pretty well. Everybody thought we were from Bowling Green. Because Calvin was almost a quarter Cherokee, and a quarter white, I grew up looking like any other white girl with jet-black hair. Nobody knew about my past." She pointed to a small house sitting off the dirt road. "That's the place."

I pulled in front of the small farmhouse with a rusted tin roof. It sat back from the road in a small horseshoe-shaped valley. A sluggish stream hugged the lane. The steep ridgeline surrounding the house on three sides didn't leave much land for farming, and the place looked like it had sat fallow for several years. An unpainted outhouse sat back behind the house almost into the tree line.

When I stopped and turned off the truck, she didn't get out right away but continued her story. "The most popular young man in high school fell in love with me.

I must admit that I was head over heels for him as well, but that was before I knew what he was capable of." She fumbled in her purse and pulled out another cigarette. Her hands shook as she lit the cigarette and tossed the match out the window. She didn't speak again until she had taken a couple of drags. "Somehow he found out who I really was. He took me to a party out at the Reeder place, not too far from here. After a few sips of moonshine, he slipped me off into the woods away from the house." She puffed again at the cigarette in an apparent attempt to calm her nerves, but her hands were still shaking. "When he tackled me to the ground, I thought it was just in fun. But when he straddled me and held me down, I could see the fire in his face. He said he knew who my father was, and if I didn't do everything he told me to that night, he would make sure everybody in the school knew I was nothing more than the daughter of some nigger trash from Zeke Town." She spit out the words like they were bitter on her tongue and tossed her cigarette.

"I fought some at first, but it was useless. He was strong, athletic. I guess I felt guilty too, like I deserved what he was doing to me, like somehow it was my fault. He left me half naked and lying in the dark woods. We never spoke again."

Growing up on a farm around animals, you don't need a parent to explain the birds and bees to you. You just know. As she spoke about her rape, I just knew. I knew that my father was the rapist.

"Out of shame, I went to live with my half sister, Patsy Ann. She was pregnant with Wonnie at the time." She laughed to herself and shook her head. "Poor Otis stuck in that small house with two pregnant women."

I still clutched the steering wheel with both hands,

and she put a hand on my arm and looked right at me. "I remembered how my mother had struggled to take care of me. I remembered the hungry nights, and the strange men that visited us from time to time. I wanted you to have a better life. So I made an arrangement with Billy, and here we are." She drew back her hand and slipped out of the truck.

I watched her from the truck as she trudged up the porch of the old farmhouse and then turned to look at me. I saw Wonnie. I saw Ruby. I saw a vulnerable woman full of secrets, and I felt sorry for her. A part of me wanted to protect her, but another part of me simply wanted to know more about who I was. Before she could open her front door, I jumped out of the truck. "Is that it?" I asked.

She turned around and crossed her arms. "I've already told you more than you need to know."

I took a few steps forward and shook my finger at her. "You owe me."

She cocked her head and put her hands on her hips. "I owe you?" She shook her head at me, and I started to feel like a new student on the first day of school trying to tell the teacher how to run her class. "I may not have been around to be your mama and teach you much, but let me teach you something now—life don't owe you nothin'. I don't owe you nothin'. I gave you up because I wanted you to have a family, and you got one." She waved her hand like she was swatting flies. "Go on home." She turned to go into the old farmhouse.

"No!" I shouted. She turned and gave me a stern look, and I softened my request. "No," I begged. "You're the only person I know that understands my gift. I have so many questions." I stepped onto the first wooden plank leading up to her porch. "I need someone to teach me, please." I stood there halfway up her porch stairs, hoping to get some answers.

For a moment she just looked at me but then let out an exasperated sigh. "You're too stubborn for your own good," she said. The front door groaned as she shoved it open and walked in. "Come on in." She left the door open, and I followed her in.

The old farmhouse didn't have much in the way of modern comforts. An old wooden table with a couple of chairs sat in the front room that also served as the kitchen. The walls were papered with old newspapers that had yellowed over the years. Sunlight struggled its way through the small dirty windows. There were no signs of running water, and an old wood cookstove sat against the back wall. Everything except the table and chairs was covered in several years of dust. An acoustic guitar, probably the one she had played at the revival, sat in the corner.

She tossed her purse on the table and grabbed a bottle and a glass from a small cabinet. She set the bottle of whiskey down with a thump and took a seat. "Have a seat," she said as she poured herself a glass. "Want a drink?"

Mama had preached against drink for years, and I had never seen Daddy drink, even though I knew he sipped a little white lightning with Otis from time to time. I had seen some of my buddies get drunk, and right at that moment it sure looked inviting, but I decided it was not the time to start experimenting with liquor.

"No, thank you," I answered. I pulled off my clip-on tie, set it on the table, and unbuttoned my top button. I tried to relax and think, but the wobbly wooden chair I was sitting in kept me off balance.

She shrugged and tossed back the shot of sipping

whiskey. Then she fumbled in her purse and pulled out a cigarette and matches. She lit another one up, took a long drag, and flicked the ashes on the floor. "So, what do you want to know?"

"Why did you come back if you don't care about me?"

"First of all, I gave you up because I cared for you. Second, I didn't come back because of you."

"Why did you come back then?" I asked.

She took another drag on her cigarette. "Look, the less you know about me, the better. I thought you wanted to talk about your healing power."

"I do, but . . . I'm just trying to understand." At the time I wasn't exactly sure what I was trying to understand, but looking back, I can see that I was trying to get a grip on my past. I wanted to know my history. I wanted to know why my mother had left me and why she had come back. I waited and hoped for an answer, something I could hang my hat on.

She chewed at her bottom lip and then answered, "Patsy Ann sent me a letter. She told me they'd been having trouble."

"Trouble?"

"Apparently a crooked lawman is putting the squeeze on them. Big Six owed me a favor. So he agreed to come see what he could do if I came back and helped. Then when I came back, it felt like I had come home, and I decided to stay." I must have looked like a deer in headlights I was so shocked. "I can see you're confused." She reached out and patted my hand. "Don't worry. The less you know, the better."

She got up and tossed her cigarette butt out the front door and grabbed the guitar. She sat back down and started strumming and picking at the strings, filling the abandoned farmhouse with music. "What do you want to know about your gift?" she asked as she continued to focus on her guitar.

I set aside all the new questions she had sparked in my mind and focused on trying to understand my gift. "How did I get it?"

"They say it's a spiritual gift that's passed from generation to generation, but it usually doesn't show up in men," she said as she continued to pick out a melody. "My aunt had it, but not my mother. Childbirth, or some other traumatic or emotional event, seems to bring it out." She stopped strumming the guitar and looked at me. "What was it you said happened to you? You killed your dog?"

"Yeah, I cut off his legs with a mowing machine."

She nodded and went back to picking at the guitar. "I'll bet that tore you up. You had the power lying asleep inside of you, and when that happened, the gift came alive."

I liked that explanation better than Leck's speculation that I was from outer space. "Why won't it work all of the time? I mean, I can heal some people, but others I can't."

"Like I told you before, it works on people's faith. Typically, they have to have enough faith to be healed. I've learned that you can force it sometimes, when you have enough faith in yourself." She hushed the guitar strings with the palm of her hand and looked up at me. "That's usually when I get the nightmares, when I force it. But sometimes you feel like you don't have a choice. You feel like God has thrust you into the lives of these desperate people, and you are the only hope they have. So you find the will, and faith, inside of yourself to fix their problems, even if maybe they don't deserve it."

I thought about Leck. "You mean if I believe enough in my ability, I can heal people that don't believe?"

"Yep, but like I said, it comes with a price." She began strumming a new melody and humming along with the guitar.

"Why did you join that traveling revival?" I asked.

"Let's just say that I'm not an expert at picking men."

I remembered the way she had spoken with Reverend Hines when he caught me in her trailer. That reminded me of stumbling into a trailer full of poisonous snakes. "Did they ever figure out who put the snakes in your trailer?"

She shook her head and said, "Nope, but I have a pretty good idea."

"Reverend Hines?"

She laughed. "He may be a charlatan, but he's not a killer."

"Then who did it?"

She stopped playing the guitar and leaned it up against the table. She poured another shot of whiskey while I waited for an answer. "Stone, you're young, naïve, and full of life. You think everything is so black and white, so cut and dry." She took a sip of whiskey and stared right through me. "Life is nothing more than a series of messy choices between the lesser of two evils. No matter how hard you try, you can't heal the whole world." She tossed back the rest of the whiskey shot and slammed the glass onto the table with a loud thump. "If you want to be happy, go on home to your mama. Forget about your gift. Forget about me. Go marry that preacher's daughter and have lots of babies." She poured herself another drink.

At that point, I almost asked for a drink myself, but decided Daddy would skin me alive if I showed up driving his truck with whiskey on my breath. I could see that at the rate Phoebe was drinking, I wasn't going to get any good answers for very long, and based on her attitude toward the whole situation, I probably would never get the answers I wanted.

She started playing "Wayfaring Stranger" on the guitar and humming the melody, and I felt myself beginning to drift again. Here I sat with my real mother that I had never known, trying to understand myself, trying to understand this strange gift that had somehow come to me, trying to understand my past and what it meant to me, and yet I felt more detached and alone than ever. Maybe she was right. I was better off forgetting her and getting on with my life, but I was too stubborn to just walk out the door without some more answers. "Who's my father?" I asked.

She stopped strumming the guitar and silenced the strings with her fingers. She stood and put the guitar back in the corner of the room. She fetched another cigarette and lit it as I waited for any answer. After she took a long drag and exhaled the smoke at the ceiling, she pointed at the door with her long finger. "I think it would be best if you left now."

I stood. "Please, I just want to know who my father is."

"Like I told you before, some secrets are best carried to the grave. It's safer for you if you don't know, especially right now." She pointed toward the door again. "As far as you're concerned, your father is Billy Molony and your mother is Ada Molony. Now go on home to them and don't look back."

"But—"

"I said go on home!" she shouted. Her words stung like a swarm of hornets, and I thought I was going to start crying right there in the front room of that ratty old farmhouse, but she didn't give me any time or sympathy. She grabbed me by the arm and shoved me for the door. "I said get out of here! Don't make me chase you off with my shotgun," she threatened.

I stumbled through the front door and hurried to the truck in a daze. I felt like some lost calf without a mother being herded out of the barn and into the pasture to die. I climbed into the truck, hit the starter, and headed down the lane. In my rearview mirror, I could see my birth mother, Phoebe Webb, standing on the front porch, lighting up another cigarette.

FIFTEEN

I drove back out the way I came, still trying to get my bearings. Tears stung in my eyes and made it so hard for me to see that I stopped at the first intersection before continuing. I sat at that crossroads for a few minutes with my head against the steering wheel, trying to get control of myself enough to keep driving. I felt like I had a gaping hole in my chest that made breathing a chore. Nothing seemed certain. Something deep inside of me just wanted to go back and beg her to love me.

After a few minutes I wiped my eyes on my shirtsleeve and tried to gather my bearings. I knew turning left would take me back up to Coe Ridge. For a moment I thought maybe I belonged there, but I turned right and headed out toward Judio Road and eventually Neely's Ferry. When I rounded the next corner, I met a logging truck kicking up dust. After we passed, the dust in the rearview mirror caught my attention, and for a moment it seemed so appropriate. I was leaving my past in the dust. While I was looking in the mirror, I realized that I had forgotten my clip-on tie. Now, I didn't really care about that tie, but I began to rationalize that going back for my tie might give me one more chance to fill that black hole in my chest. I turned around and headed back into the dust.

About a half mile later, I met Deputy Russel's cruiser flying down the lane with his lights on. He must not have seen me coming in all the dust, and he almost ran me over. I swerved the truck onto the shoulder and managed to avoid the ditch. It scared me so much I stopped, and I thought he might stop to check on me since he ran me off the road, but he kept on moving and kicking up a bigger cloud of dust than before.

In my head I rehearsed all the things I wanted to say to Phoebe Webb when I got back to her farmhouse. I would tell her that I didn't care about all the bad things that had happened in her life or any of the wrong choices she may have made. She was my mother, and I needed her to love me. I would promise to come see her from time to time. We could get to know one another. Maybe someday she would come visit her grandkids and tell them stories while she rocked them on the front porch of my house. I would make it impossible for her to refuse.

The first thing I noticed as I drove up was that the front door was still standing open. I figured that she left it open to let a little air into the place, since I knew how much it needed it. I pulled up in front like before and climbed out of the truck. I didn't see her until I started up the rickety front porch steps.

Phoebe lay sprawled across the rough wooden boards of the porch right where I had last seen her in my rear-view mirror. When I first saw her lying there in her black dress, I stopped and blinked, like it was some sort of mirage. When I opened my eyes again she was still lying motionless with her hair falling over her face, but this time I saw the blood on the dirty boards of the porch.

"No!" I screamed. I rushed over to her and fell to my knees beside her. I pulled her head into my lap and brushed the long black hair from her face. I put my hand on her neck and checked for a pulse. It was weak, but she was still alive. The blood had soaked the front of her dress, and it looked like she had been shot in the chest just above the heart. I immediately summoned my gift by reciting the scripture from Ezekiel out loud. I closed my eyes and concentrated on the power I knew was inside of me. I had just started to feel the gathering electric storm inside of my head when she reached up and put her hand on my cheek.

Her touch startled me so much that I lost all my concentration for a moment. I looked down at her face and her eyes were half open. "Don't save me. Let me go," she whispered. Blood had colored her lips, and her face was pale.

I choked back my tears and shouted at her, "No! I can't let you die." I closed my eyes and started to focus again, but she reached up and caressed my cheek.

She coughed and whispered, "Please, son, show me some mercy. I'm goin' over Jordan. I'm just goin' home."

I recognized the words from the song immediately and knew that she just wanted me to let her pass, but that aching hole in my chest throbbed and demanded that I heal her. I also knew that if she died she would take her secrets with her, and I would never know who my father was. I closed my eyes again to concentrate on the scripture. I could feel the electricity building again when she grabbed my arm.

"Let me go," she begged. "I'm tired."

I wasn't sure what I wanted from her, but I knew I didn't want her to die. I had too many questions. "I can't let you go. Besides, if you die I'll never know who my father is."

"If I tell you, will you let me pass?"

This was not a decision I wanted to make. I wanted

to ignore the request and heal her anyway. I was sure that if I healed her I could get to know her and eventually get her to tell me who my father was, but when I looked in her eyes I saw nothing but sadness. I remembered that night at the revival how her singing brought tears to our eyes, and I realized that to her it wasn't just a song—it was her soul's desire. I felt my tears begin to flow again. "Are you sure that's what you want?" I asked. "Why can't we do both? If I save you—"

"If you heal me," she interrupted, "I'll leave and never come back. Promise to let me pass, and I'll tell you who shot me too."

I sat there cradling her head in my lap with the healing storm rumbling in the back of my head, deciding what to do. I figured she would make good on her promise of leaving. She had left me once before. That would be worse than watching her die. I knew that she wanted to leave this world, and that she would take her secrets with her to the grave. I felt like I didn't have a choice, or at least a choice I liked. I calmed the coming storm in my head and pushed it back. I choked back my sorrow and said, "I promise to let you pass."

She tried to smile and a look of peace came over her face. "Your father is Cortis Russel. He's also the one who shot me."

I stared down at her in disbelief. The building storm abated completely and all my efforts to focus were useless. The hole in my chest doubled in size and my head spun out of control like some whirling dervish. I shook my head in denial, but all the clues fell into place like pieces of some morbid jigsaw puzzle. I cradled her head in my lap and watched her eyes grow dim just like Rusty's had.

She reached up and wiped a tear from my cheek. She

whispered, "I'll wait for you, son . . . In that bright land to which I go."

They say at the moment of death you can hear a death rattle, but I didn't hear anything when my mother died with her head in my lap that day. She simply looked up at me with half-open eyes and crossed over Jordan to that bright land free of toil and danger. After soaking her pale face with my tears, I reached down with my fingers and closed her eyes.

I'm not sure how long I knelt there on the porch with her head in my lap, but judging by the fact that my knees throbbed and my legs were asleep, I must have been there a while. I knew I couldn't leave her like that on the porch, so I laid her down gently, went inside, and grabbed the thin blanket off her bed. I took great care with her as I wrapped her from head to toe in the blanket and carefully loaded her into the truck. I laid her across the front seat and put her head in my lap so I could drive.

I drove straight to the sheriff's office, and Mrs. Davidson about had a heart attack when I walked through the front door with blood all over me. She called the sheriff, who had been over near Coe Ridge on patrol, and I was standing outside by the truck when he came roaring up with his lights flashing and his siren blaring. I was afraid to tell him what I knew because I thought he might be in on it all. I just told him that I found her dead on the front porch when I pulled up. He took me inside, gave me a coke, and took a statement. Then he told me not to worry and sent Nina Faye's mom to get my parents over at the hospital. I sat there numb and detached until Daddy picked me up and took me home.

SIXTEEN

"Just toss all your clothes out into the hallway, and I'll throw them away," said Daddy as he ran me a hot bath. "We'll get you some new Sunday clothes."

I nodded in agreement as I stripped everything off and tossed it into a pile just outside the bathroom door. The hot water was nice, and even though I felt like crying, all my tears were gone. As I sat there soaking in the warm water, I began to see things clearly. My biological mother, Phoebe Webb, had just been killed by my biological father, the rapist, Deputy Cortis Russel. I reckoned that he must also be the crooked lawman that she had mentioned. It made sense now. I was tall like him, and all of a sudden, I could see the resemblance. He was always cruising the road to Celina looking for moonshine runners and would have plenty of opportunity to take a cut from the shipments, and he ran me off the road near Phoebe's place just before I found her on her front porch with a bullet hole in her chest. He didn't lose any sleep over Wonnie's rape either.

Wonnie's rape. I didn't want to accept it at first, but I figured that most likely he was the one responsible for that as well. I was so disgusted that I'm sure I would have thrown up if I had any food in my stomach. I remembered the burning place in hell reserved for a man who chooses to fulfill his sexual desire by force, but I'm sure the temperature would go up several thousand degrees because of murder. My disgust transformed into resolve, and I started trying to figure out how to send Cortis Russel to his designated reward sooner instead of later.

My anger and enthusiasm quickly gave way to fear and doubt. I didn't know who I could trust. I wanted revenge. I wanted justice. But I had never killed a man. I couldn't even put a suffering dog out of his misery. Yes, I had killed while hunting, and even killed snakes and possum raiding the henhouse, but that was a far cry from killing a man, especially one who would most likely fight back. I knew I was out of my league. I realized that I needed help. The sheriff thought that I found Phoebe dead on the porch. So neither the sheriff nor Deputy Russel knew that I knew. I was afraid to tell anyone else, because that might put them in danger. The only person I knew with experience in such weighty matters of life, death, and killing was lying in a hospital bed in Burkesville. I had to go see Leck.

I drained the bathwater and got dressed. Daddy was sitting in the front room listening to the radio when I came downstairs. "Daddy," I said. His title sounded good on my lips. "Can I go visit Leck?"

He rubbed the stubble on his chin and asked, "Seems to me like you've had a pretty rough day. Are you sure you're up to it?"

I nodded. "Yep, and I think it will do me some good."

"Okay. You can drive the truck home, if the sheriff's done with it," he added as he stood. He motioned for the front door, and we headed for town. We stopped by and retrieved the truck. Only Mrs. Davidson was at the sheriff's office, and I was glad I didn't have to face

Sheriff Pace or Deputy Russel. I followed Daddy over to the hospital.

I ignored all the sick and injured people we passed on the way to Leck's room by keeping my eyes on the floor. The hospital wasn't busy, so he had a room to himself. Mama jumped to her feet when she saw me and wrapped me in her tender arms for the longest time. I was through crying at that point, but I hugged her back and remembered what Phoebe had said about her being my true mother. The hole in my chest shrank a little bit.

Leck had undergone surgery yesterday. They were trying to remove some shrapnel that had lodged itself in his spine. Apparently it hadn't gone well, and he hadn't been coherent for over twenty-four hours. His gaunt face reminded me of Phoebe just before she passed on, and I worried that Leck might not be far behind.

"I'm so sorry about Phoebe," said Mama. "Do they have any idea who did it?" I shook my head. "What is this world coming to? First Wonnie and then this . . . it beats anything I've ever seen," she said, wrapping her arms around herself like she was suddenly chilled.

"Any change in Leck while I was gone?" asked Daddy.

Mama frowned like she was going to cry. Daddy's face fell and he seemed to age a few years right before my eyes. "Why don't y'all take a break?" I said. "I can sit here with Leck for a few hours. Y'all go on home for a while and get your mind off things."

Mama cast a worried look over at Leck and bit her bottom lip. Daddy stepped over and wrapped his arms around her. "Come on, Ada. Let's head on home for the night. There ain't much we can do anyway." He moved her toward the door and looked back at me with a grateful nod.

After they left I closed the door to Leck's hospital

room and took a seat beside his bed. He had tubes and wires running down to his arm and chest, and he looked like something out of a horror comic book. I sat and watched him for a few minutes until he reminded me too much of the death I had seen earlier that day, and I stood and looked out the window. The afternoon sun was falling low in the sky, and as far as I was concerned, the sooner today was over, the better, but I did have one more thing to do before the day was done.

I stood beside Leck and started talking to him as if he could hear me. "Leck, I know that maybe you don't believe that you deserve to be healed, but I'm in a tight spot. They buried Wonnie today, and Phoebe Webb was shot and killed. I think I know who did it, but I'm afraid. I need your help. So, if you're in there listening, come on out so we can talk, please." I knelt down beside the bed and leaned my head against the side rail.

I was startled when Leck said in a dry voice, "I was really hoping to wake up to some Tahitian beauty, not your ugly face."

I grinned and told him, "Well, if you promise to get better, I'll see what I can rustle up, but you might have to settle for some spinster from Tompkinsville."

He tried to laugh and coughed instead. "What are you doing here? I thought Daddy didn't want you putting the hospital out of business with your healing powers."

"I sent them home to take a break." I glanced at the door and said, "Truth is, I wanted to talk to you about something."

"Can't you see I'm kinda busy?"

"I'll try and keep it short then," I said with a smile, but my smile soon left me. "Did Mama tell you about Wonnie?"

He nodded and asked, "How was the funeral?"

"Sad."

"You didn't come here just to tell me that a funeral was sad, did you?"

I took a deep breath and let it out slowly as I tried to keep my emotions from overwhelming me again. "After the funeral I went to see Phoebe Webb at her old house near Judio. She wasn't real talkative, but I learned a little more about her and the gift we both have."

"What's that got to do with me?" he asked.

"She told me that the gift works best when people believe they can be healed, but if I have enough faith in the gift I can sometimes force it." I looked him straight in the eye and asked, "Why don't you believe that I can heal you?"

Leck looked away from me and closed his eyes. I thought for a moment that he might just ignore me and go back to sleep. Finally he answered, "I didn't want to go off to war, but I'd done some things I was ashamed of and thought that volunteering to go fight might atone for those sins. It didn't really turn out the way I thought it would."

"Do you still believe in God?" I asked.

Leck opened his eyes but looked away and stared out the window. "They say there are no atheists in foxholes. I'd have to say that's true. I didn't stop believing in God, but I did stop believing that he cared about me." He let out a big sigh and looked like he was trying not to cry.

"Why would God stop caring about you?" I asked. I knew he had become unpleasant to be around, but I never thought of him as a bad person, unworthy of God's love.

"I ain't exactly been a saint," he snorted.

"You mean during the war?"

He glanced over at me and shook his head but

continued to look out the window. "No, I ain't sorry about killing those commies. They was trying to kill me."

I wondered what Leck could possibly have done that would keep God from loving him or at least make him feel unworthy of it. "What did you do?"

He waved me off with a weak hand. "It don't matter. I ain't worth saving."

I could see him sink farther into that hospital bed like he just wanted to be swallowed up. I decided that if I was going to get his help, I needed to shift gears. "I need your help with something," I said.

"Well, I guess you're out of luck then, unless you need someone to lie around and say mean things to you. I'm not much good at much else anymore."

I tried to find the right words to tell Leck what had happened. I tried to think of some graceful way to tell him why I needed his help. Nothing clever came to me. So I decided just to tell him straight up. I glanced at the door to make sure it was still closed, lowered my voice, and said, "Phoebe Webb was shot and killed today, and I know who did it."

His sluggish nature changed instantly, and he gave me a wide-eyed stare. For the first time in a long time he didn't make some snide or cutting remark. "You mean the healing lady from the revival?"

I nodded. I didn't know what he had been told. I wasn't sure if Mama had been keeping him up to date on all the things happening in our little world. "Did Mama tell you that she was also my mother?"

"Yeah, she did. I guess you're not an alien after all." He sat up and stared past me for a moment, like he was organizing all the information I had just given him. Then he nodded his head in understanding and said, "Okay then, who shot her?"

I gave another glance at the door. "Deputy Cortis Russel," I whispered.

"Dang," he whispered. "Looks like things finally caught up to that sorry cuss." Then he came to himself and added in a low voice, "I'm sorry about Phoebe."

It felt good to hear the compassion in his voice. "It's okay," I answered. "She hasn't been my mother since the day she left me in the graveyard. She was ready to go."

Leck nodded and continued speaking in the same low voice, "Are you going to tell the sheriff?"

"I was afraid to do that. I thought he might be in on it. You're the only one I've told."

"Why are you telling me?"

I shrugged and said, "I figured that because of your war experience, you'd know what to do."

"Hmmm . . . well, I can think of a few things," he said, looking out the window at the setting sun. "But I ain't in no position to do any of 'em."

This was the moment of truth for me. I closed my eyes and remembered each of the healings I had done. I searched for that spark of divinity and supernatural power inside of me, that one gift that somehow had been passed on to me by my mother, hoping God wouldn't judge me too harshly if I happened to misuse it. Somewhere in my jumbled up feelings of grief, inadequacy, and desire for justice, or revenge, I found it.

I opened my eyes and said, "That's about to change, brother."

He flinched just a little when I put my hand on his chest. I sensed his doubt, but also his desire to be whole. I forced the scripture from Ezekiel into the forefront of my mind and felt the oncoming storm. Unlike the random power of before, it was like the bolts of energy bent to my will and my hands began to warm at my beckoning.

I'm not sure if it was caused by my heightened emotional state, or because I had learned to control the gift better, but the storm inside my head was more spectacular than with any of the other healings. I felt the surging electricity fill my head and race down my arms until my hands burned like white-hot coals. I could feel the dark festering wounds deep inside of Leck fill with light and the mangled flesh take on healthy form. I sensed the twisted shrapnel lodged in his spine and pushed it free with my will. I pushed it out of his body and healed the tissue behind it. He screamed in pain. I screamed in effort as I cast out the offending piece of metal and healed my brother's broken and twisted body.

When I was done, the power gathered in my chest and rushed out of me like hot steam from a boiling pot. I collapsed across Leck's chest and was only aware of his heavy breaths when I heard a nurse come rushing into his room.

"Mr. Molony, are you all right?" she asked.

Leck patted me on the back. "Well, Nurse Hankins, it's been years since I've been this good," he answered. "How 'bout you Stone? You okay?"

I pushed myself up from the bed and fumbled my way into the chair. I was exhausted, and as usual, I was blind as a bat. "I'll be okay in a few minutes," I said as I tried to grin.

"Nurse Hankins, will you unhook me from all this stuff?" asked Leck. "I'm going home."

SEVENTEEN

It took almost twenty minutes for the nurse to unhook Leck and for Dr. Williams to release him, but it took even longer for me to recover my sight. While I sat there waiting for my vision to come back, I listened to Leck argue with Dr. Williams about letting him go home.

"I'm telling you, Doc," said Leck, "this is the slug that was lodged in my spine. You know, the one you couldn't get out."

"And I'm telling you, that's impossible," answered Doctor Williams.

"Possible or not, it's the honest-to-God truth. My brother healed me and pushed it out of my body." I heard the bed squeak. "Now whether you believe it or not, or whether you release me or not, I'm going home."

"You shouldn't leave until you have completely healed."

"I am healed! Just watch me. I can jump. I can walk. I can bend over. What else do I need to show you before you're convinced?"

"Leck, I'm not sure where you got that piece of metal," said Dr. Williams, sounding more flustered by the moment, "but the surgery must have worked. That's why you're feeling better. Now you need to recuperate a few days before—"

I heard a rustle of fabric and a short gasp from the nurse. "If that's the case," asked Leck, "then where are my previous scars? And where is the scar from your surgery?"

Dr. Williams cleared his throat and said, "Mr. Molony, no need to expose yourself." He sounded even more flustered than before. "Lower your gown."

I could just imagine Leck standing there with his hospital gown yanked up into his armpits. He probably winked at Nurse Hankins while he was at it. I smiled at the scene, even though I was still waiting for my eyesight to come back. It was nice to have my playful brother back.

"Tell you what, Doc, you check out his eyes while I get dressed," offered Leck. "Nurse Hankins, can you bring me my clothes?"

"Of course, Mr. Molony." I could almost hear the smile on her face as she slipped out of the room through the squeaky door.

I heard Dr. Williams fumbling in his pockets right in front of me. "Stone, can you see anything?" he asked.

"Nothing."

"How do you feel?"

"Tired, but other than that, good."

"Can you lean your head just a little? I'm going to shine a light into your eyes."

"Okay." I leaned back and opened my eyes, but everything remained in darkness. I felt his finger against my cheek and tried not to blink.

"What do you see?" he asked.

"Nothing."

"I just don't understand. Everything looks normal."

"I don't understand it either, Dr. Williams, but it will come back." I tried to sound reassuring even though it was taking a lot longer this time. I figured it must be because I had learned to force my gift just a bit. I wondered if the nightmares Phoebe talked about would haunt me tonight.

I heard the nurse come back through the door. "Here are your clothes, Mr. Molony. I would offer to help you dress," I could hear her smiling again, "but I'm not sure you want help . . . getting dressed."

"Much obliged, ma'am," said Leck. "I'd love to stay and chat, or play a game of cards, but we need to get on home." I could hear him slipping on his pants.

"I should probably keep you both under observation," said Dr. Williams.

Leck said, "Sorry, Doc. No can do." He grabbed me by the arm and told me, "C'mon, brother. I'll drive you home." I let Leck guide me out of the room and into the hallway. Even though I couldn't see the people in the hallway, I could feel their eyes on me as we headed for the exit. Occasionally, I heard whispers. I almost expected someone to stop us, but in a few moments we had walked through the hospital door and into the cool evening air. I could hear the crickets and tree frogs starting to sing.

I directed Leck to the truck and he cranked it up and started for home. I swear I could feel the grin on his face, and I could hear him humming over the truck engine. By the time we turned down the lane and I heard the gravel crunch under the truck tires, I started to worry that my sight wasn't coming back at all.

"I can't wait to see the look on Mama's face when we walk through the front door," said Leck. "Can you see yet?" I shook my head. "Hang on. I'll guide you," he told me as he brought the truck to a stop and shut down the engine.

I thought about me and Daddy carrying Leck down the stairs and shoving him into the backseat of the car just a few days earlier. Now here he was helping me out of the truck and up the stairs. When we got to the top of the stairs, I heard the screen door hinges squeak.

"Dear God!" said Daddy. "Ada, get out here! It's Leck!"

Leck hurried me through the front door and sat me down on the couch in the front room. The radio was blaring the Grand Ole Opry on WSM so loud I barely heard Mama's footsteps, but I heard her squeal with delight and say, "Praise the Lord! Praise the Lord!" as Daddy's laughter transformed into pleasant sobbing.

I smiled as the sounds of the joyous reunion washed over me. Faron Young was singing "Live Fast, Love Hard, Die Young" with the sounds of Mama and Daddy swooning over Leck and crying tears of joy. Like a breaking thunderstorm, I began to cry as well, and all the emotions of the last week came flowing out of me like a downpour. No sooner had the tears started than I began to see shadows and shapes. Within a few seconds, my vision returned, and I saw Mama, Leck, and Daddy all hugging each other and crying like they hadn't seen each other in several years.

I sat there feeling awkward as they continued the warm embrace, but I figured it was overdue. I remembered the almost cold reaction when Leck first came home from the war. They were happy to see him, but they seemed to love him from a distance like they couldn't quite come to grips with the fact that this crippled form was their son. They were finally getting to welcome home the son they had waved good-bye to so many years before.

I wiped my eyes and Leck must have seen me. He broke away from Mama and Daddy and hurried over to me. "Did your sight finally come back?" he asked. I nodded as I still wiped the tears from my face with both hands. He tousled my hair and let out a comforting laugh. "I figured it would."

"What changed? How come you were able to heal him now?" asked Mama.

Leck answered before I could. "I took the kryptonite out of my pockets," he teased. Then he winked at me. He was keeping our conversation about Cortis Russel private.

Daddy walked over and turned off the radio. "Well, whatever the reason, let's give thanks to God that we got our son back," said Daddy. "Will y'all join me in prayer?"

We huddled together and held hands. Daddy offered an emotional prayer of gratitude. I felt a warm energy passing through us like my chest was going to explode, but in the back of my mind, I worried that the good feelings smothering me now would give way to the nightmares Phoebe warned me about. I set my worries aside for just a few minutes and basked in the moment, hoping that they would carry me through any trouble ahead.

After the prayer, Daddy turned back on the radio. He and Mama danced to the music as Leck clapped his hands. I clapped along for a while, but it wasn't long before I felt like I was carrying a sack of flour on my shoulders and my eyelids were made of lead. They were still clapping, dancing, and singing along as I excused myself and headed upstairs to bed. I had to force myself to strip off my clothes before I crawled between the sheets, exhausted by the events of the day.

Phoebe was right after all. The nightmares came

with a vengeance that night. I found myself in a hospital bed with Leck sitting beside me. I was crippled and racked with pain. When I tried to cry out, I felt like I was yelling through a mouth full of cotton balls. When I tried to reach out to him, my limbs wouldn't obey the commands and lay there lifeless beside me on the bed. At one point I realized that it was all a dream but was unable to wake myself up. I simply gave up and accepted that this was a small price to pay for helping Leck and happily endured the experience. I don't know how long the dreams lasted, but Daddy must have let me sleep because when Leck finally woke me up, the sun was pouring through my window, and Mama and Daddy had left for church.

"Hey, sleepyhead," said Leck as he nudged my shoulder with his foot. "Don't expect me to do your chores for you every morning." He stood over my bed with a huge grin across his face and a fishing pole in his hand. "I told Mama and Daddy that you and I needed to rest instead of going to church this morning. I figured we could try our hand at fishin' instead. C'mon, we're burning daylight." He turned and headed downstairs.

I shook off the images of the night and pulled on some clothes. I grabbed a glass of milk and wolfed down the plate of food Mama had left me as Leck sat patiently on the back porch whistling, with fishing poles in hand. The dew was almost gone as we headed down the dirt lane to the river. It was mostly small talk and fishing stories until we got our lines in the water, and then Leck got right to the point.

"What do you want to do about Cortis Russel?" he asked.

"I want to send him to hell." The venom in my voice surprised me.

"What proof do you have that he killed that healing lady, your mother?"

I shook my head and shrugged. "Well, he almost ran into me with his cruiser out near Phoebe's place right before I found her shot on her front porch, and before she died, she told me that he was the one that shot her," I added emphatically. "I'm not sure I can trust the sheriff either."

Leck shook his head and said, "That might be enough to get him investigated, but that's about it. Any idea why he would want to kill her?"

"She said she came back to Cumberland County as a favor to Big Six and to Patsy Ann. She said something about a crooked lawman taking a cut of the local moonshine business by force. If Cortis Russel is the crooked lawman, then he would want to stop her."

"That still ain't enough to get him for murder."

I didn't really want to tell Leck about Phoebe's rape, but I figured he needed the whole picture. I stared out at my red and white bobber against the green water wishing again that I was a fish with nothing more to worry about other than living. "About seventeen years ago Cortis Russel raped Phoebe Webb and got her pregnant," I said without looking at him. "He's my father."

About that time Leck's bobber sank below the water, and he jerked his pole to set the line, but came up empty. As he reeled in the line to check the bait, he said, "I'm not doubting your story, but good luck proving it. Phoebe's dead and the only other witness is Cortis."

I was beginning to the think twice about asking for Leck's help. "I healed you so you could help me, not shoot my story full of holes," I said angrily. "What do you think I should do? I can't let him just get away with murder."

I sat and stared at my bobber, waiting for an answer while Leck put some more stink bait on his hook. Finally he said, "Catching Cortis Russel is like trying to catch these big catfish that have been avoiding the frying pan for years. He's hard to snag."

Frustrated, I asked, "How do you know so much about him all of a sudden?"

He stood up and cast his line into the deep green water and then sat down to wait for another chance to set the hook in one of those big monsters that lurked in the deep. "You gotta remember that he helped coach my basketball team too. He's the reason I went off to fight in the war."

"What do you mean?"

"You are so naïve. I swear sometimes you act like you've been living under a rock. I mean he ain't the law-abiding citizen everybody thinks he is. He's guilty all right, but you have no idea what you're up against."

His comment stung a bit. I didn't think of myself as naïve. I brushed it off and asked, "But what does that have to do with you joining the army?"

Leck picked up a nearby stick and started digging at the dirt with it. "When I graduated from high school in '49, one of my basketball buddies invited me to a party at some abandoned house out near Turkey Neck Bend. I thought it would be fun, so I showed up. When I got there, it was the starting five from the basketball team and Cortis Russel. He told us it was initiation night. He told us we were all going to be men by the end of the night. He broke out a jar of moonshine and started passing it around. Then while we were drinking, he slipped out and brought in a colored girl. She couldn't have been over sixteen. He said she was some whore that owed him a few favors, and he was gonna let us collect tonight.

I'm not sure what gave him power over her, but he told her to take off her shirt, and she stripped to the waist right there in front of us. He told us we could each have ten minutes with her and then took her to one of the bedrooms.

"We drew straws and I got to go first. Everybody whooped and hollered as I went in with her and shut the door behind me. Truth is, I was scared since I'd never been with a woman. She was lying on an old metal bed. The only light in the room was a candle on the mantle of an empty fireplace. When I got close I could see that she was crying. She just looked up at me with big scared eyes waiting for me to pounce on her. I pulled my trousers off and started to climb on top of her, but I couldn't do it." He threw the stick into the river downstream of our bobbers.

"I wanted to run. I wanted to bust her loose and get her out of there. Instead, like a coward, I just pulled on my trousers, waited a few minutes, and then gave her up to the next guy in line. They all patted me on the back and shouted when I came out of the room. I got drunk as fast as I could, hoping to forget, but the next morning the images of her were just as real as the night before."

My mouth hung open like some dumb fish when he finished. "Why didn't you tell somebody or try and stop him?"

Leck shook his head and stared at the rising bluff across the river. "It would have been everybody else's word against mine, and besides, he was Deputy Sheriff Cortis Russel, hometown hero. Naw, I slinked away to war trying to atone for that night." He exhaled like it was his last breath and added, "It didn't really turn out the way I hoped."

I wondered how all this had happened right in front

of me without me seeing it. Leck was right. I had been living under a rock. The images he described were almost impossible for me to imagine, and picturing him as a part of something so ugly was painful. It was like staring at some optical illusion where your mind thinks it knows what it's looking at until the real picture is suddenly clear. All the lines were there, and now they formed a picture that was uglier than I had ever imagined.

"You don't believe me, do you?" asked Leck.

"I believe you," I said with a nod. "I wish I didn't, but I believe you."

Neither of us said anything for a while. We both just stared at the passing river. My mind drifted through my memories of Wonnie, and then Phoebe. I scanned my happy childhood as a Molony for clues of the trouble I was staring at right now, but all I came up with was images of working the farm together, eating meals together, and sitting around listening to the radio. I sat and wished that I could somehow turn back the clock and see the world through my innocent eyes again, but I knew that it would be easier to hold out my hand and stop the river.

Finally I looked at Leck and said, "You don't have any proof of your story either, unless some of the other guys decide to talk, and it doesn't solve Phoebe's murder."

He nodded and said, "Good luck getting anybody to talk. They would just be hanging themselves. I know it doesn't give us any hard proof about the murder, but at least it ought to be enough proof to do what needs to be done."

"What's that?"

"Kill Cortis Russel."

"I can't do that," I objected.

"He's guilty, ain't he?"

"Yes, but—"

"He murdered your mother, didn't he?"

I was okay with playing judge and jury, but when faced with the task of executioner, my confidence left me. My gut told me that he was guilty, but I couldn't stomach carrying out the sentence. "I'm pretty sure," I said.

"Pretty sure?" shouted Leck. "A few minutes ago you were ready to send him to his appointed place in the fiery pits of hell, and now you're just pretty sure?"

"You're talking about killing a man!" I shouted back.

Leck jumped to his feet. "He needs a killin'!" His eyes were dark and determined. I had come to Leck because he had experience in these things, and I could see that he had no problem with his course of action. These matters of life and death were cut and dry for him, but I was still stuck in the no-man's land of indecision and inaction. I looked away and stared at my bobber again, feeling my resolve leave me. "Maybe we should just go to the sheriff," I offered.

Leck grabbed his fishing pole and started reeling in his line. "Yeah, sure, let's go tell the sheriff that the hometown hero parading around as a deputy is really a rapist and a killer. When he asks how we know, we can tell him that a dead woman told us." He flicked the stink bait off his hook and secured the hook to his fishing pole. "Maybe what we ought to do is just move a few counties away and leave this mess behind us." He scrambled up the bank and left me staring at the passing waters of the Cumberland.

EIGHTEEN

I wanted to go see Ruby in the worst way Sunday night, but after missing church, I didn't think Pastor Tabor would allow me to visit her anyway. I missed her touch and the clean smell of her hair. I resigned myself to sitting on the front porch, watching traffic pass by as Mama and Daddy swooned over Leck.

Monday it rained. Leck and I didn't talk much, and I avoided being alone with him. Mama was just so happy to have her son back, she floated about the house like she didn't have a care in the world. A world of worry seemed to have been lifted off of Daddy as well. I guess he figured that with two sons the work around the farm would get a lot easier. Leck and I spent the day straightening up the barn and helping him grease the baler, since I didn't get to it the other day.

I halfway expected somebody to come looking to be healed, but I was glad every time I looked up the lane and didn't see a vehicle coming toward the house. I wasn't sure I was up to the task at the moment. That afternoon, just as the rain was starting to slow down a bit, I looked up and saw Sheriff Pace coming down the lane in his black and white Bel-Air cruiser. I was pretty sure he wasn't looking for a healing.

We all stopped working as he got out of his car and walked up to the barn. "Afternoon, Billy," he said without coming in out of the rain. "Do you mind if I talk to Stone for a few minutes?"

Daddy gave me a funny look, and I tried to fake a look of confusion. "We can spare him for a few minutes," said Daddy with a nod. "Is he in trouble?"

"Well, no, I don't think so," answered the Sheriff with a wave and a wink. "I'm just trying to solve a crime." He nodded at his cruiser and said, "C'mon, Stone, let's you and me go for a ride."

I looked at Leck, but he had busied himself with the baler again. My stomach jumped into my throat, and I tried to hide it with a smile and a joke. "Okay, Sheriff, but don't keep me too long. I wouldn't want to miss out on any work." Nobody else laughed, and I followed the sheriff down to his cruiser and climbed into the front seat. I thought I saw Mama looking out the front window of the house as we drove off.

When we turned onto Celina Road, the sheriff got right to the point. "I'm headed up to Coe Ridge. Who can tell me about Wonnie's rape?"

My throat was tight, like I could barely breathe. I cleared it and said, "If she told anybody about it, Patsy Ann would be the most likely one."

"Did she ever tell you?"

"No, sir."

We turned off onto Jackson Hollow Road instead of heading into town. "You've had a few days to think about it now. Did you think of anything else that might help us figure out who shot Phoebe Webb?" he asked.

It was like he knew that I wasn't telling him the whole story. At first I started to lie and tell him the same story I had told before. I figured he couldn't be that close to a crooked deputy without knowing something was going on, and he was most likely in on it. But then again, we had been sitting next to him at church for years, and nobody there seemed to know. Maybe the sheriff had been fooled as well. After all, Cortis Russel was a local hero, and his marriage to the local beauty queen and former mayor's daughter only elevated his status. In spite of all that, I decided that since I didn't have the stomach to do what Leck recommended, I would have to risk trusting the sheriff.

"I think I know who shot her," I said, "but you may not believe me."

Sheriff Pace raised a bushy white eyebrow but kept his eyes on the road. "Just tell me what happened, and let me figure out what to believe," he said.

I wiped my sweaty hands on my trousers. "Phoebe Webb was still alive when I found her on her front porch," I began. He nodded but didn't interrupt. "I wanted to heal her, but she wouldn't let me. Before she died, she told me that my real father was Cortis Russel." I looked up at the sheriff to see how he would react to that news before I continued. His eyebrows were knitted into a fuzzy mess, and he pulled over the car and stopped on the side of the road.

He kept both hands on the steering wheel like he was bracing for a head-on collision. "What else did she say?"

I blurted out the rest like I was some kid caught in a lie. "She said that Cortis Russel shot her." I held my breath, braced for impact.

Instead I watched the sheriff wilt with disappointment. He looked like a tire going flat right before my eyes. He shook his head and then rested it on his steering wheel. He sat that way long enough for me to worry that he might just be upset because now I knew their secret, and he didn't want to kill me. I moved my hand to the door handle and wondered if I could make it into the woods before he could get a bead on me.

Finally he raised his head and looked at me. His eyes were wet. "It's my fault. I saw some signs that he wasn't on the up and up, but I just couldn't bring myself to believe them. Then Big Six came snooping around my office and telling me that somebody was crooked. He even accused me at first." He shook his head and rubbed his temples with his fingers. "I heard gossip and rumors, and some of the clues were right in front of me, but I didn't want to believe them."

He threw the car in gear and spun it around. The driving seemed to help him regain his composure. "You can't tell anybody about our conversation. Understood?"

"Yes, sir," I replied, but I wasn't sure I could keep that promise.

"I'll try and gather some hard evidence. You just lie low." His normally commanding demeanor was lackluster and he sounded like he was just going through the motions. I suspected that this information had hurt his pride quite a bit.

"Sheriff," I asked, "you really didn't know that Phoebe Webb was my real mother?"

"As God as my witness Stone, I had no clue."

I knew that the sheriff had years of practice catching folks in their web of lies, and I figured that that kind of practice might make him an able liar himself, but it didn't sound that way to me. If he had no clue that she was my mother, then he certainly didn't have an inkling that Cortis Russel had fathered me during his heinous act. My past was still a secret, and that might be an advantage to me.

The sheriff didn't get out of his cruiser when he dropped me off. He pulled up to the house and told me, "Remember not to talk about this to anyone." I nodded and climbed out into the drizzle. I saw Mama come to the front window as he was driving off, but I hurried back up to the barn.

As soon as I got out of the rain, Daddy asked, "What was that all about?"

"He asked me about Phoebe," I said.

Leck looked up from his work and our eyes met for a moment. Daddy asked, "What did you tell him?"

"The same thing I told him the other day," I said with a shrug. I glanced over at Leck, but a glance was all it took for me to see that he didn't believe me.

The rain let up, but it was too wet to get anything else done, so we knocked off work early that afternoon. I got cleaned up and asked Daddy if I could borrow the car and go call on Ruby. He was still in such a good mood about Leck that he gave me permission and even told me not to worry about coming home for supper if I wanted to stay longer.

I was happy when Mrs. Tabor answered the door instead of Pastor Tabor. "Good afternoon, Stone," she said with a polite smile. "We missed you at services yesterday."

"Yes, ma'am. The events of the last few days drained me," I answered.

"Well, no better place than church to energize the soul and find rest from trouble."

I doubted I would have found much rest for my soul sitting next to Cortis Russel, but I just smiled and said, "Yes, ma'am. Is Ruby home?"

"She's reading in her room," she said, opening the door further. "Come in while I get her for you."

I prayed that Pastor Tabor wouldn't be home to throw any guilt on me and stepped across the threshold. Mrs. Tabor disappeared down the hallway, and I found myself alone, thankfully. In less than a minute Ruby appeared, looking like she was dressed for a date, not like she had been reading in her room. Her essence arrived a half second before she did, and I breathed in that clean fragrance as though I was standing next to honeysuckle in bloom.

"Good afternoon, Stone," she offered as she gave me a cursory hug. "I'm so sorry to hear about Wonnie," she said with a sigh and shake of her head. "And Phoebe," she added. "You've had a very rough week. I didn't expect you today."

I wasn't sure how to react to the comments. So I bowed my head and nodded at her condolences.

She glanced at Mrs. Tabor, who was standing at the edge of the room, still lingering in the hallway. "What brings you into town on this rainy afternoon?"

"We knocked off early because of the rain," I explained. "I was hoping maybe you and me could go for a drive."

She put on her best Sunday-greeting smile like she was welcoming me into her father's chapel, but her eyes flitted from side to side like some nervous critter. "Oh, I see," she said. "Well, I didn't know you were coming, so I, um, made other plans."

I opened my mouth to respond, but nothing came out. I stood there tongue-tied and looking foolish until she spoke again. "Can we step out onto the front porch, please?" She brushed up next to me and pulled my arm. I let her lead me out the front door and onto the porch.

I finally found my voice again when the front door closed. "Are you going out with someone else tonight?"

I asked. It was strange. I didn't feel angry or even jealous; I just felt like I was watching the whole scene on the movie screen. It was someone else's life, and I was just watching the drama unfold.

She grabbed my hands and looked up at me with her chocolate eyes. "Stone, I'm sorry, but with all the gossip swirling around you right now, Daddy practically forbid me from dating you for a while." She lowered her gaze as if she was afraid to tell me the rest. "He said I should date other young men and pushed me to go on a date with another pastor's son from over in Albany."

I nodded like I understood completely, but I felt like I had been kicked by a mule and all the wind had been knocked out of me. I managed to find enough wind to whisper, "Okay, I guess I'll see you later." I let go of her hands and started for the car, trying to catch my breath. She called after me again, but I was in a daze and ignored her.

Instead of going home, I headed up Big Hill Road and parked the car overlooking Burkesville, but without Ruby this time. The low clouds were swirling along the ridgeline, and the streets had a thin sheen of water on them. The river was taking on a muddy color as the runoff carried the soil from surrounding streams into the normally green river. I sat there, still trying to catch my breath. That huge hole in my chest had come back.

I realized that I had parked near the marker for Captain Jack McLain, a decorated Union officer who committed suicide after accidentally killing his best friend. He said he wanted to be buried up here because it was the closest to heaven he would ever get. It didn't feel so heavenly to me right now. Seeing Captain McLain's marker made me wonder how easy it would be to kill myself.

Right at that moment, I didn't want to go on. What was the point of living? What did I have to look forward to? I started the car and gripped the steering wheel. I thought that if I just stomped on the accelerator, I could send the car flying over the bluff, and maybe people would think it was an accident when they found me dead at the bottom in the wreckage. My hands trembled, and my white knuckles ached as I squeezed the steering wheel and looked out over the bluff at Burkesville several hundred feet below.

I let out a scream and then leaned my head against the steering wheel like I had seen the sheriff do earlier today. I banged my head against it a few times and started to cry again. All the emotion of the last week poured out of me like water from a fire hose. I cried for Wonnie. I cried for Phoebe. I cried for Ruby. I felt like a big crybaby, and I was glad nobody was there to see how big of a wreck I was.

When I was all out of tears and I looked out over Burkesville again, the car was still running. The clouds had broken just a bit, and the afternoon sun had managed to send a shaft of sunlight down onto the fields across the river. The light seemed to dance and sparkle on the wet crops as it burst through a hole in the dark rain clouds. I wasn't sure if that was an answer to a prayer, and I didn't even remember uttering a prayer, but I decided to take it as a sign from God that my life should go on. Life went on even after Captain McLain took his life, but the only difference was that he wasn't around to enjoy it anymore. I figured that even though my life was a bit stormy right now, I might as well stick around and hope for a break in the weather. I put the car in reverse and drove on home, resolved to live another day.

When I got home, Leck was sitting on the front

porch, going through his weekly ritual of cleaning his M-1, but this time he had his ammo out as well. He didn't say anything when I walked up the porch and sat down beside him. I decided to break the ice. "I told the sheriff what Phoebe said. I told him about Cortis Russel."

He looked down the barrel and jammed the bolt back into place. "I figured as much," he said without looking at me.

"Do you think it will do any good?"

He started loading a magazine with ammunition. "Probably not, but we'll find out pretty soon. I don't imagine it will take long for things to break one way or another." He slapped the magazine into the gun and closed the bolt. He slung the rifle over his shoulder, picked up his things, and left me sitting alone on the front porch.

NINETEEN

I woke up early the next morning and was already dressed when Daddy tapped on my door. That gaping hole in my chest was still there, but the motion that life required helped me deal with it. The chores went faster with Leck's help. All I had to do was milk Jersey Girl, and she seemed happy to see me that morning. I was glad to see that not all the girls in my life were abandoning me.

Breakfast chatter was more lively than normal, except for me. Daddy, Mama, and Leck chatted about old times and told funny stories. I smiled and laughed along without feeling anything. After breakfast I piled into the truck with Leck and Daddy, and we headed into town to start our weekly feed deliveries.

Floyd was waiting for me at the loading dock with the bill of his hat pulled down low. The truck engine had barely stopped turning when he jumped on the driver's side running board and asked, "Y'all headed up to Coe Ridge today?"

Daddy gave him a puzzled look and said, "We usually do."

"Well, you might want to reconsider that today," said Floyd. "Sheriff Pace was shot and killed up yonder yesterday afternoon."

Daddy gave me a concerned look, and I just stared back in shock. Leck just nodded his head like it was expected news. "Let me go talk to your father," said Daddy, and Floyd jumped down so Daddy could get out and go inside.

I jumped out on my side so I could find out more from Floyd, and Leck slid out after me and sauntered inside like it was any ordinary day. "Tell me everything you know, Floyd," I demanded.

He tilted his head back so he could see me from under the bill of his cap. "Well, apparently the sheriff was headed up to Coe Ridge yesterday for something, and his car got stuck in the mud about halfway up the ridge. They found him about a hundred yards up the hill from the cruiser with a bullet through the chest."

"Did they arrest anybody yet?"

"Nope, but Nina Faye said she overheard Deputy Russel talking about Otis Wilburn."

I felt a chill run down my spine when he said Deputy Russel's name, and I started thinking that maybe it was time to move to another county. I wondered if Otis had finally had enough after losing Wonnie, but I didn't think he was capable of killing a man in cold blood. I just shook my head and kept my secrets to myself.

Floyd continued to pile on the good news. "Hey, I saw Ruby at Walgreens with some other guy yesterday afternoon. Are you two still together?"

I blew out an exasperated sigh and said, "I guess not."

He gave me an understanding nod and changed the subject. "How much rain did y'all get yesterday?"

I shrugged and chuckled at how he could always move the conversation back to the weather or some other mundane topic. When the end of the world came, Floyd would want to know about the weather on the other side of the county. "I don't have any idea," I answered.

About that time Daddy came back out with Leck right behind him. It was clear that the happy mood that had possessed him the last few days had waned a bit. We loaded up the truck, minus the usual load for Coe Ridge, and headed out for our deliveries. More than once I thought about telling Daddy everything, but each time, I felt Leck's eyes on me, like he was telling me to keep it a secret. Based on the outcome from my last confession, I figured that was a good idea.

When we pulled up to cross Neely's Ferry that afternoon, Samuel appeared out of the trees by the road and surprised me when he jumped on the running board next to me. "Afternoon, Missuh Molony, I figured you wouldn't be comin' up our way, what with all the ruckus over the sheriff gettin' shot yesterday. Would you mind if I talk to Stone for a while?" he asked. "In private?"

Daddy seemed a bit taken back by the request. "Y'all can go on home," I said. "I'll cross the river and walk home when I'm done." Daddy nodded, and I hopped out of the truck and started to close the door, but Leck held it open.

"Mind if I tag along?" asked Leck as he slid out of the truck.

Samuel was surprised to see Leck walking without crutches, but he just looked at me and grinned big enough for me to see every white tooth in his head. "Naw, I guess that would be awright."

Leck waved Daddy on, and we walked up the ridge overlooking the river just a bit and found a log to sit on. "What's going on, Samuel?" I asked as soon as we sat down.

Samuel looked around, like he was expecting

somebody to come out of the woods, but when nobody did, he started talking. "I saw who shot the sheriff. I know they's saying that Pa did it, but it wadn't him."

"Who was it then?" asked Leck.

Samuel looked around again, like he was sure somebody was just waiting to jump out from behind a tree. "It was my turn on lookout, and when I saw the sheriff's car comin', I sounded the alarm, like always. Then his car started sliding in the muddy road, and he couldn't get up the hill. I figured he would turn around and head back down, but instead he got out of the car and started walkin' up. He hadn't walked far when I heard a shot, and the sheriff fell to the ground. I thought about climbing down and running to check on him, but I was scared of gettin' shot myself, so I stayed hid up in the tree."

He shook his head and continued, "I figured I knowed who done it anyway, and sure 'nough a few minutes later, Deputy Russel came strollin' out of the woods with a rifle slung over his shoulder. He checked to see if the sheriff was dead, looked around to see if anyone seen him, and then he hightailed it out of there."

"What makes you so sure it was Deputy Russel that shot him?" I asked. "Did you see him fire the shot?" I figured Samuel was right, but I was just trying to shoot holes in the accusation, like Leck had to me.

"'Cause it wadn't a bunch of white boys that beat me that night you healed me," said Samuel. He looked at the ground like he didn't want to tell me. "It was him that done it."

Leck just leaned against a tree, casually taking all this in like none of it was surprising, but I stood up and began to pace back and forth waving my arms as I spoke. "Why didn't you tell us? Why would he do that to you? Why didn't you go to the sheriff then?"

"I'm sorry about lyin', but y'all don't understand," said Samuel, shaking his head.

"Why? Because I ain't colored?" I said with a snort. "In case you haven't heard, or don't already know, my grandfather was Calvin Coe."

Samuel gave me a puzzled look, and even Leck raised an eyebrow. "Naw, it ain't that," said Samuel. "Deputy Russel has been puttin' the squeeze on us for years, making us give him a cut if we wanted to get our product to market without any trouble. He seemed to know where all our stills were, but he promised to keep the sheriff off our trail, if we gave him a cut. At first, he didn't want too much, but after a while, his price kept goin' up. A few months ago, folks up on the ridge got together and decided we would rather take our chances with the likes of Big Six than be slaves to Deputy Russel. Pa was the one that got elected to tell him. He laughed in Pa's face, said we'd be happy to start paying him again when he was through."

I continued pacing. "But why didn't you go to the sheriff, or somebody?"

This time Leck intervened. "Sure, they waltz into the sheriff's office and say, 'Hey, Sheriff, we need some help because we can't get our moonshine to market.'" He shook his head. "You really have been living under a rock."

I paced back and forth a couple of times, trying to come to grips with the situation. "What did Deputy Russel do? Bust up a couple of the stills?"

"Naw," said Samuel, shaking his head. "He busted me up."

I stopped pacing and let my hands fall to my sides. "But then, why did you and Otis go see Deputy Russel the day after I healed you?"

"They sent Pa to make a deal, but the deputy just raised the price again." Samuel shook his head and added, "When Pa refused, he told us we'd be back to see him soon."

"Wonnie," I said as the picture came into focus.

Samuel nodded, and I could see that he was struggling not to cry. "She wasn't the first, but he didn't beat the others half to death."

I squatted down and picked at a fern growing at my feet. Leck still leaned against the tree like he was impatient with all this talk. I figured the whole conversation only served to make him more confident in his chosen course of action. Maybe he was more confident, but I was only more confused. "Why are you telling me all this? What do you expect me to do?"

"We was cleaning out Wonnie's stuff and found this." Samuel pulled a wrinkled envelope from his back pocket and extended it to me. "You gonna wanna read it. It's from Wonnie."

My hands were practically shaking when I took the envelope. Samuel stood there patiently as I pulled out the letter written by Wonnie's hand.

Dear Zekie,

I am writing to you because I know that my suicide will trouble you. I told you I was going to change some things around here. I tried, but I guess I underestimated how much trouble change could bring to a person. I wanted to thank you for healing Samuel with your wonderful gift and trying to heal me. The truth is that I was dead from the moment that Deputy Russel raped me that night, and nothing you could do was going to change that. You were able to heal me physically, but he damaged me in ways that even your healing powers couldn't fix. I didn't want to live anymore in a world where a man could do that to a woman and get away with it. I've gone to find the mermaids and swim to the ocean.

Wonnie

"What's it say?" asked Leck.

I hesitated to give it to him at first, but I knew I couldn't talk about it either. I surrendered the letter to him.

While I stared out over the Cumberland where Wonnie had taken her life, Leck zipped through her suicide note. When he finished, he carefully folded it back into the envelope and handed it to me. I took it back and looked at Leck for guidance, but he just shrugged and said, "Don't look at me. This only tells us what we already knew. You know what I think we need to do." He pointed his finger like a gun, fired his thumb like the hammer, and said, "Pow."

I was beginning to think he was right, but I still couldn't bring myself to accept his solution. I pondered Wonnie's words and realized that her suicide note and Samuel's testimony might help us convince someone that Deputy Russel was guilty. "What if we set up a meeting with Big Six? Everyone knows he's an honest revenue man, and he could get us some help from the state police," I said. "Do you think Otis would talk to Big Six?"

"I s'pose so," said Samuel.

"How about tomorrow afternoon? Maybe around one o'clock?" I asked. I wanted to get this over with in the worst way. Samuel nodded in agreement. Leck just shrugged like this was delaying the inevitable. "Where should we meet?" I asked.

"We can't meet in town, and it can't be up on Coe Ridge 'cause he might be watching like he was with the sheriff," said Samuel. "It'll have to be someplace private. Someplace we can get to on foot."

All of us, including Big Six, knew the location of Phoebe's old farmhouse. It was isolated, and Samuel and Otis could get there on foot. I realized that it might be the best place to meet, but I shuddered at the thought of going back to that ratty old farmhouse and the scene of Phoebe's death. I set aside my fears and said. "Why don't we meet at the house where Phoebe was living when she died, I mean, got killed?"

Samuel mulled it over for a second and then nodded in agreement. "That oughta work. Pa knows that place, and we can walk there. Can you get word to Big Six?"

I looked at Leck hoping for approval, but he just turned and spit. I still wanted his help so I asked, "What do you think Leck?"

He picked at the tree bark with his fingernail like he was bored and said, "Sure, might as well give it a shot. I reckon waiting one more day to bring justice on his head ain't gonna matter in the long run." Then he looked at Samuel and added, "Y'all watch your back until then, and come locked and loaded to the meeting."

We walked down the ridge, and Samuel disappeared into the woods on the other side of the road. Leck and I hopped the ferry.

"Do you think we should tell Daddy?" I asked, staring down into the passing water of the Cumberland.

Leck shook his head and said, "Daddy's been sitting next to Cortis and Shirley Mae at church for years. He wouldn't believe us even if we did tell him. Even if we could convince him, he wouldn't approve of us getting involved. It's best just to leave him out of this." I didn't want to believe it either, and I wasn't sure that leaving Daddy out was the right thing to do, but I trusted Leck and nodded in agreement.

Leck asked, "Is it true that your grandfather was Calvin Coe?"

"Yep," I said as I examined the envelope still in my hand. I wasn't sure how people would react if they knew I was part colored, but I was beginning not to care. Leck hit me in the arm playfully like brothers do and said, "I could have sworn you was an alien from outer space." We both laughed.

After supper Leck told Daddy he wanted to go shoot some pool down at Shorty's. That gave us an excuse to go to town and see if we could deliver a message to Big Six, if he was still in town. We drove by the Sheriff's office to see if anyone was still there, but the place was dark.

"Now what?" asked Leck.

I knew where Nina Faye lived so I said, "Let's go see Mrs. Davidson. She can probably help us get a message to Big Six."

We headed over to their house on Baker Street and knocked on the door. Nina Faye was a bit surprised, but her blue eyes lit up when she answered the door and saw us on her front porch, "Hey, Stone. What brings you here?"

"Hey, Nina Faye. We need to speak to your mother," I said. "Is she home?"

The request seemed to puzzle her more, but she went and got her mother from the bedroom. Mrs. Davidson came out putting on earrings and dressed in a black dress without sleeves that highlighted her more womanly parts. I saw Leck give her a long once-over when she came into the room.

"What can I do for you fellas?" asked Mrs. Davidson as she fiddled with the earrings.

"Well, ma'am," I said, "we need to get a message to Big Six regarding, uh . . . some information about a moonshine still." I glanced at Leck hoping for some help, but he just smiled and enjoyed the view while I did all the talking. "Is he still in town?"

She finished fiddling with her earrings, struck a pose with her hands on her hips, and said, "He's supposed to be in tomorrow morning. I can give him a message if you like." Her smile was accommodating, and her lipstick was perfect. Nina Faye was standing behind her and rolled her eyes at her mother's obvious expression of femininity.

I wasn't sure what to do, so I glanced over at Leck. He was smiling back like no matter what she asked for he would be obliged to do it. I cleared my throat and said, "I guess we could do that. Do you have a piece of paper?"

She patted me on the arm and said, "Hold on, dear." Then she disappeared into the kitchen as Leck followed her with his eyes.

Nina Faye broke his trance when she looked at Leck and asked, "Is it nice to be back to normal? I mean, health-wise?"

Leck came to himself and said, "Yep, it sure is."

"How did it feel?" she asked.

"Kind of like when you get shocked by electricity, but much stronger."

Nina Faye put on a coy smile and asked, "Is it true you flashed Nurse Hankins?"

Leck laughed and said, "I reckon I did, but they wouldn't believe me when I told them I was healed. I had to do something so they would let me go."

Nina Faye giggled and winked at Leck. "I wish I'd

been there to see it." I could see that even though Nina Faye had rolled her eyes at her mother's charm, she was also a student of the feminine arts.

"Here you go, fellas," said Mrs. Davidson as she handed me a pen and paper. "Just write down your message, and I'll get it to Big Six tomorrow morning."

I wasn't sure how much information to give in the message. If I didn't give enough, he wouldn't think it worth his time and might not show up. If I was too clear and someone else saw the message, we'd all be in danger. I opted for clear and wrote, *We know who shot the sheriff. Come to Phoebe Webb's old place tomorrow afternoon around one o'clock.* Then I folded it. "Do you have an envelope?" I asked. I didn't want anyone else but Big Six to open it.

Mrs. Davidson found an envelope, and I stuffed the message inside, sealed it, and addressed it to Big Six Henderson. I was still nervous when I handed it over to Mrs. Davidson. "Make sure he gets it first thing tomorrow morning, please."

"And make sure nobody but Big Six gets it," added Leck, suddenly trying to sound helpful.

"Don't you worry, dear," she said to Leck as she patted him on the arm. "I've been working for the sheriff's office for over ten years. I'll make sure the message is delivered confidentially." She pulled the envelope from my fingers.

TWENTY

Even though I had stayed up late reading the letter from Wonnie over and over again, I was already dressed when Daddy tapped on my door early the next morning. My stomach had been in knots all night worrying about everything, and for once in my life, I didn't have much of an appetite. Jersey Girl was pretty calm that morning and made life easy for me. Even after finishing my morning chores, I didn't have much of an appetite and had to force myself to eat breakfast so I didn't raise suspicion.

"Daddy, I figured if you didn't have any extra work, Stone and I would go huntin' this afternoon over on Pleasant Hill," said Leck, as cool as a cucumber. He chuckled to himself and added, "I figure I've given them squirrels enough of a break."

Daddy seemed all too happy to see life getting back to normal in his house and said, "That'd be fine by me. I'm sure your Mama wants you home for supper." He grinned and pointed at us with his knife, "But don't expect her to go cleaning up any game you shoot." We both nodded and smiled. I couldn't tell about Leck, but my stomach did a summersault and rumbled like thunder.

A little while later we drove away in Daddy's Ford truck with Leck at the wheel whistling "River of No Return" by Tennessee Earnie Ford. We had the Winchester and the shotgun hanging on the gun rack in the window, and Leck brought along his M-1 with plenty of ammo. I stared out the window and hoped that Big Six would show up today so we wouldn't have to use any of it, but it was just a hope.

It was a few minutes after noon when we drove down the lane to Phoebe's old place. The front door was still ajar when we pulled up, and I felt a chill run down my spine as the scene from a few days ago replayed in my mind. I could still picture her in the rearview mirror as I drove away. I preferred that image to the one of her lying in a pool of blood on the front porch.

Instead of stopping in front of the house, Leck drove the truck around back and parked it behind the house, out of sight from anyone driving up. "We want to keep the element of surprise if we can," he said. When he climbed out, he surveyed the surrounding area. "I don't like the ridgeline on three sides. It leaves us vulnerable if somebody gets up there, but it also gives some natural protection." He grabbed the M-1 from the truck and started through the back door of the house. I looked over my shoulder at the ridgeline and followed right behind him like a shadow.

"Grab the Winchester," he ordered.

"I thought we were just gonna talk to Big Six," I said.

Leck stopped in the doorway and looked at me. "You really think pretty Mrs. Davidson gave that note to Big Six?"

I was surprised at his question. "She said she would."

Leck shook his head. "You are by far the most trusting, naïve person I have ever seen. The way I see it, we got about a fifty-fifty chance. Either she took it to Big Six or she took it straight to Deputy Russel."

"What?" I screamed. My voice became a nervous whine. "If you thought she was going to talk to Deputy Russel, why did you let me give her the note?"

"Well, I didn't *know* that she would do that, and she might have taken the note to Big Six, but I'll lay odds that she took it straight to Deputy Russel. I figured that if she took the note to Big Six, we could have us a sit-down, just like you wanted. And if she took the note to Deputy Russel, it was the easiest way to bring him to the fight. Either way, we ought to get some resolution today." He nodded at the truck. "Grab the Winchester."

My bowels turned to water as I looked back at the rifle hanging in the back window of the truck. I still wanted to believe that Big Six was going to show up and everything could be worked out. "Look, I don't want to shoot anybody unless we absolutely have to. Right now, I just want to talk to Big Six."

Leck stopped on the back porch and looked back at me. "Suit yourself," he said. He shook his head as he chambered a round and slipped in through the back door.

The ratty old farmhouse was much the same. Sunlight struggled its way through the muck on the windows, and the open bottle of whiskey Phoebe had been drinking a few days ago still sat on the table with the cork out. My clip-on tie was gathering dust on the table. Leck put the rifle on the table and pulled up a chair where he could watch the lane coming up to the house through the dirty front window. He sniffed at the bottle and took a swig.

I closed the front door and took out the envelope that Samuel had given me as evidence and set it on the table. I was so nervous that my head was spinning and my stomach was in knots. "Do you think Big Six will believe us?" I asked.

"If he's the one that shows up, I reckon he will," said Leck as he took another swig and then corked the bottle. "Question is what's he gonna do once we tell him what we know." He patted the rifle. "I got a feelin' that Lady Justice still might need a little help with this problem."

I paced the floor while Leck sat like a sentry, watching the window. The groaning in my bowels got worse, and I realized that there was no way I could hold back the explosion that had been brewing in me all night long, and all morning. "I gotta go to the outhouse," I said. I did have the presence of mind to grab a piece of old newspaper off the wall before I went running out the back door. I didn't figure I'd find a roll of toilet paper or even a Sears and Roebuck catalog waiting for me in the outhouse when I was finished with my business. I hurried into the rickety privy trying to hold my nose, but it was pointless. I sat on the hole doubled over in knots as my bowels emptied themselves over and over again and I wished I could hurry and finish up. I hadn't been this nervous since my first high school basketball game, but that time I was able to get everything under control as soon we started playing. I wished Samuel and Otis would hurry and get here. I hoped Nina Faye's mom had delivered our message to Big Six.

When I finally finished up and was pulling up my trousers, I heard tires on gravel. I peeked through the cracks in the outhouse door and saw a car coming up the lane—it was the sheriff's black-and-white Bel-Air cruiser. It took a few seconds for that to register with me. The sheriff was dead, so the only person that would be driving his cruiser would be Deputy Russel. By the time I realized what I was seeing, it was too late.

I was scrambling to get my trousers zipped up when the car skidded to a stop in front of the house with the passenger's side closest to the front door of the house. From the outhouse I could still see the cruiser, and I watched as the driver's side door swung open and Deputy Russel threw something at the house, something on fire. I heard glass shatter. I heard a shot from the house and watched the window in the passenger door shatter. I saw Cortis fire his revolver into the house. I smelled smoke.

I froze. Not twenty yards from me two men were locked in a mortal combat, and I was watching from an outhouse like some chicken in a chicken coop. My first reaction was to just hide there in the outhouse until it was over. Leck knew how to handle himself. He was good with a gun. I could just stay there and wait until he had finished the job. My second reaction was to make a beeline for the trees and climb the ridgeline, but then if Leck didn't win, I might be a sitting duck, and I knew that Cortis was a pretty good shot. I liked my odds better if I stayed hidden. So I stood there in the putrid smell of an old outhouse on a hot summer day and watched the fight unfold through the cracks in the wood.

About that time I saw the flames reach the roof. The old house was a tinderbox, and Leck was still inside. Cortis was still hidden behind the cruiser waiting for the smoke and fire to flush Leck out. I started to worry. Then I saw Leck burst through the back door with one hand over his mouth coughing like a man with black lung and the rifle clutched in the other hand. I almost ran out of the outhouse to help, but he looked over my way and held his hand up for me to stay. Then he started creeping around the other side of the burning house to outflank Cortis. I worried that the truck was too close to the fire, but there wasn't much I could do about it right then.

I saw Cortis poke his head up and take a look around, but then he disappeared again. I was thinking he must be reloading and would pop up again to shoot at any second when I heard three shots. It was hard to tell, but the first shot sounded like it came from the M-1, and the next two from the revolver. The shots were so close together, and it was hard to tell which was which with the fire starting to roar as it devoured the ratty old farmhouse. Just then I remembered the envelope that I had left on the table. The best piece of evidence we had against Cortis Russel was going up in flames.

The gun battle had gone silent. I figured the time for hiding had past. Either Leck had gotten the drop on Cortis and I was safe, or Cortis had gotten the drop on Leck and hiding wouldn't do me any good for much longer. Since Cortis had shown up instead of Big Six, I figured that Otis and Samuel weren't coming. I had to make a decision.

I remembered the Winchester hanging in the truck. I prayed for help, and forgiveness, and then I burst through that outhouse door and ran for the truck. The fire was hotter than I expected, and the rifle was warm to the touch when I grabbed it from the rack and knelt beside the truck. I chambered a round. I figured that they had both circled around the house the same way and met each other, so I decided to circle around the other way in hopes of finding Leck alive, or if not, I hoped I could outflank Cortis and get the drop on him. The truth is, I wasn't sure what I would do if I did face Cortis. I wasn't sure I could pull the trigger.

I skirted the burning house and ducked behind the cruiser. I peeked around the side of the car and saw that Cortis was gone, just like I suspected. Using the car for cover, I crawled to the front and looked around the bumper to see who was alive. There was Deputy Cortis Russel—pillar of the community, hometown hero, my father by blood—dragging an unconscious Leck toward the burning house.

I jumped from cover and raised the Winchester with my finger on the trigger. "Pull him away from the house!" I yelled. I rested my elbows on the hood of the car to steady my aim and felt the heat from the fire as it engulfed the old farmhouse.

Cortis stopped with a handful of Leck's shirt still in one hand and a revolver in the other. He looked up at me and smiled like he knew something I didn't. I kept my sights aimed at his chest and repeated my demand. "Pull him away from the house!"

He still held the revolver above his head and started pulling Leck's limp body away from the burning building with the other hand. I kept him in my sights, hoping that I wouldn't have to pull the trigger. I couldn't tell if Leck was still alive, but I wanted him away from the fire. When he got far enough from the burning house that I thought Leck would be safe, I yelled, "That's far enough. Now drop your gun!"

He let go of Leck's shirt and stood there with one hand at his side and the other hand still over his head with the revolver in it. It hadn't dawned on me at the time, but he was holding the revolver over his head in his left hand, but he was right handed. About that time, the roof of the old farmhouse caved in with a loud crash and distracted me for just a second. I glanced over at the house, and when I looked back, Cortis was pulling a gun from the holster on his right hip while he still held the other one over his head in his left hand.

I pulled the trigger.

Even good marksmen blink when they pull the

trigger. It is a simple reaction to the sound and force of the recoil. I blinked as the rifle discharged its deadly load. I opened my eyes just in time to see the bullet tear a hole in his chest and knock hometown hero Deputy Cortis Russel off his feet.

I remembered the first deer I shot. It was a small buck, only about six points, that I had tracked to a clearing. One minute it was standing there with its chest puffed up full of life, and the next minute it was falling to its knees. Leck had taught me to always chamber another round and shoot again. I heard his voice again, inside my head, coaching me, and I reached up and chambered another round, but I didn't shoot again.

I knew I had hit him, but I could see that he wasn't dead. I kept the rifle leveled at his writhing body as I moved forward. I could feel the heat from the burning house as it continued to collapse. Leck was lying far enough from the fire to be out of danger, if he was still alive. He was on his side and it looked like he had taken a round to the left shoulder. Blood was also trickling down his face, and it looked like he had been hit in the head. I feared the worst. I wanted to check his pulse, but I could hear Cortis Russel's moaning over the sound of the burning house, and I didn't know if he was still armed. Trying to keep one eye on Cortis, I knelt and felt for a pulse in Leck. I couldn't feel anything, but then again my own heart was pumping so loud I thought it would pop out of my chest. I decided it would be better to disarm Cortis before I checked on Leck again.

Cortis was clutching at his chest with both hands. He had dropped the revolvers when he got hit and they were lying near his feet. I kicked them out of reach and stood over him with the rifle still pointed at his chest. He was a pitiful sight.

"Please don't kill me," he begged. "I don't want to die."

I had shot him in the chest below the heart and so much blood was seeping out between his fingers that I figured he wouldn't live long without a doctor. Realizing this was my handiwork, I felt a sudden rush of guilt, just like I did after busting Jed Mock's nose at Shorty's. All the evidence told me that this man bleeding on the ground in front of me deserved to die for the things he had done, but instead of feeling justified, I felt only guilt.

"Stone, don't let me die. I know you can heal me," he said in a raspy voice.

I steadied myself and tried to focus, but tears welled up in my eyes. Any rage I had felt before was melting. "Why should I save you? You raped and beat Wonnie. You raped and killed Phoebe Webb. You killed the sheriff."

He began to cry. "I know. I know, but don't let me die like this. Heal me. I know you can do it. You have your mother's gift."

When he mentioned my mother, I felt that big gaping hole rip through my chest again, just like the day I left Phoebe standing on the front porch. Tears clouded my vision. The thought of losing Phoebe, my mother, and now my father, made that hole in my chest begin to throb. The old farmhouse was burning up the last pieces of her pitiful life. Without my intervention, his sorry life would be over soon as well. I didn't consciously summon it, but the scripture from Ezekiel flooded my mind.

"If you heal me, I promise to turn myself in. I'll spend the rest of my life in prison, but please, don't let me die." He reached up and tried to touch me, like the lady Jesus healed when she touched his garment. "I know you can heal me."

There was no doubt he had the faith to be healed. I could feel it pulsing, calling me. That gaping hole of emotion was so strong that I forgot about Leck lying just a few yards away from me. The words from Ezekiel went round and round in my head, and I could feel the gathering storm. I had shot him, and I knew he would die before I could get him to a hospital. In spite of his obvious sins, his blood weighed heavy on my soul. I began to rationalize that God wouldn't let me heal him if he was meant to die. How could my gift work on him if he deserved death? Who was I to deny this man life? After all, he was my father.

I pushed my doubts and fears aside and embraced the storm building inside of me. Lightning danced inside my head with vicious fury. My hands began to burn. I began to whisper the words from Ezekiel. I lowered the gun and knelt beside Deputy Cortis Russel, my father. He looked up at me with faith in his eyes, and I dropped the rifle and put my hands on his bleeding chest. The storm raged inside my head, and my hands burned like hot coals. I could feel the flesh coming together again. I could sense the blood stop flowing as the wound closed up. I healed, and sealed, the gaping hole my bullet had inflicted as the lightning in my head danced. Then as I finished healing his wound, just like always, all the burning energy gathered in my chest and flew away like a dove. I collapsed to the ground exhausted, and blind.

I could feel the heat from the house on my back. I could hear the burning wood as it popped and spit. I could taste the ash in the air. I could feel the rough ground against my face. But the world around was dark as midnight.

I sat up and listened for any movement from Cortis Russel. I heard the bolt action of the Winchester as someone checked the chamber. I heard him laugh. "You must have got your brains from your mother, 'cause you're about as stupid and naïve as they come."

I didn't see the rifle butt coming, but it felt like an explosion when it hit me upside the head. I fell face-first against the ground and clawed at the grass as the pain in my head throbbed. I didn't want to believe what was happening, and the shock overwhelmed me. I healed him, and now he was going to kill me. Why had God let this happen to me? I had tried to do the right thing. I had been merciful and used my gift to help someone. Why had he let me use my gift to save someone that only wanted to kill me? I rolled over on my back and tried to get my bearings. The pounding in my head was over-whelming, but I managed to ask, "Why are you doing this? I showed you mercy. I healed you."

"Simple," he said. "You two were gonna go to Big Six and ruin everything." His voice moved in a circle around me like he was stalking his wounded prey.

I could tell that the heat from the smoldering fire was distorting his voice, but he had stopped circling. I thought that maybe I could stall him until my sight came back. I wondered if he had picked up the revolvers.

"Samuel saw you shoot the sheriff. He'll go to Big Six anyway," I said, trying to rattle him any way I could.

"I took care of him already."

"Like you did last time?"

"I didn't have to. Big Six already picked him up this morning cooking whiskey up on the ridge. Oh, and he found the rifle that shot the sheriff at the still. Like I've been trying to tell you, you gotta have evidence." He laughed.

I got the feeling that he was running out of patience, and that the game was all but over. So I decided to take one last shot. "How did you find out?" I asked as I searched the ground around me with my hands, hoping to find one of the revolvers he had dropped. I figured I knew the answer, but maybe it would buy me enough time.

"Do you think I'd work with a looker like Mrs. Davidson all these years without sampling the merchandise?" he said with a laugh. "Let's just say that the lovely Mrs. Davidson and I have an arrangement. After today I'm sure I'll have to do a little persuadin' to make sure she keeps our arrangement, but I'm sure I can manage."

"You gonna persuade her like you did Phoebe Webb?"

"Phoebe Webb," he pronounced her name like he was reminiscing some long-lost love, not the woman he had raped and then eventually shot in cold blood. "She was quite the handful, and deceitful to boot. I should have put two and two together and figured you were her son a long time ago. What'd she tell you? That I forced myself on her?" He snorted.

"I've got evidence that you raped her, just like you did Wonnie," I lied, hoping to catch him off guard. "Like you've been saying, don't accuse anyone unless you have evidence."

"You're lying. You ain't got nothing," he said, but he stopped laughing.

"I've got a letter from Wonnie that says you raped her," I sat up and strained to overcome my blindness. "Let us live and maybe we can make an arrangement as well."

"Sorry, but the only arrangement I have in mind is to put a bullet in you an' toss your bodies into the fire."

"You can't shoot me!" I pleaded. "I'm your son!"

"Don't flatter yourself. Phoebe was easy, just like every other nigger whore I've known, and I've known my share." His voice sounded closer. He grunted. "I'll bet I ain't even your father. You ain't nothin' but the bastard child of a half-colored whore." I heard a clicking sound as he pulled back the hammer of the Winchester.

When I got bit by the rattlesnakes, I had slipped into unconsciousness, but this time I was facing my demise wide awake. It was an unusual feeling, with a mixture of panic and serenity. My body was racked with the fear of pain and death, but my soul was serene. I was at peace with myself and the way I had lived my life. I wasn't absolutely sure there was a God, but I figured that if I died at this moment, and there was a God in heaven, I could stand in front of him and tell him I had tried to do the right thing. I wouldn't have to explain why I had the blood of Cortis Russel on my hands.

I was still blind. I bowed my head and waited for the bullet. I heard a shot ring out but felt no pain. It took me a second to realize that I was still alive. I could hear the crackling of the fire and sense its heat on my skin. My head still throbbed from the blow of the rifle butt. I smelled the smoke from the burning house and gunpowder. I was still alive.

I heard Leck say, "He ain't a bastard child. He's my brother."

"Leck?"

"Yep."

"Is he dead?"

"Unless he can live with a bullet hole clean through his head, he's dead."

I had forgotten how tough Leck was, and how much of a survivor he could be. I collapsed on the ground, and I started to shake and shiver. I stretched out on the grass, and even though I couldn't see, I stared up into heaven and said a prayer to God, thanking him for sparing me.

"I don't suppose you could heal me again, could you?" Leck interrupted. "I took a round through the shoulder, and it's bleeding pretty bad. He knocked me cold with his revolver, and my head feels like ten hangovers. I know you can't see me, but I'm in a bad way over here. One thing's for sure, I *do* have the faith to be healed."

I gathered my strength and crawled toward his voice. Still blind, and with my own head pounding, I knelt beside Leck and summoned the healing storm. I could feel Leck's faith surge like power from a dynamo. I felt the heat from the burning farmhouse on my back, and my hands became torches of healing power. The scripture from Ezekiel played over and over again in my head as the lightning storm danced inside me. I laid my hands on my brother and healed him again.

By the time my sight came back, Leck had gathered the guns, including the ones Cortis Russel had brought. He had pulled the truck around front away from the burning house. We were lucky that it hadn't been damaged. He left the sheriff's cruiser and Deputy Russel right where they were. He was just sitting and watching the fire when I finally got my vision back.

"Took you a while this time," said Leck, still staring at the smoldering fire.

"I don't usually heal gunshot wounds back to back like that. It really walloped me good." I looked over at Cortis Russel's lifeless body and asked, "Do you think we did the right thing?"

"The way I see it," said Leck with a shrug, "he needed a killin', and we gave it to him."

"You mean you did. After I shot him, I felt so guilty that I healed him. I figured that God wouldn't let me heal him unless I was supposed to. You're right. I'm so naïve that I thought that if I healed him, he would turn himself in. After all, he was my father." I felt ashamed and looked at the ground. "I'm sorry."

Leck shook his head and spit. "Well, he never was your daddy. No need to be sorry. You did what you thought was right." He shrugged and added, "Who knows? Maybe we both did what God wanted us to do. Maybe God gives us talents and gifts, and then he just sits back and watches us to see what choices we'll make. You probably made the right choice for you. I know I made the right choice for me. Otherwise, I would have lost a brother."

I never figured Leck for much of a religious philosopher, but his words were as wise as a proverb.

TWENTY-ONE

It's been over a year since the day Rusty died and I discovered my gift. I guess you could say I grew up a lot during those few weeks of turmoil, but I grew up even more in the last year. Time has allowed me to turn things over and over again in my head. I haven't been able to make sense of everything, but I have understood well enough to make a few choices.

After the blindness left me, Leck and I piled into Daddy's truck, drove into town, and told Big Six everything. He believed us, but only after interviewing Otis and Samuel separately and hearing the same story. I also think he believed us because he trusted Phoebe.

Mrs. Davidson laid on the charm when we walked in, but Big Six broke her too, and she admitted to giving Deputy Russel the letter. She lost her job at the sheriff's office, but she avoided going to jail since the only thing she was guilty of was sharing secrets between the sheets. She opened up a beauty parlor and is still brokering secrets, and breaking hearts, and marriages.

Daddy was fit to be tied when he found out what Leck and I had done behind his back. He did something he almost never did. While we stood there on the porch, he yelled and screamed at us both about how we should never have taken the law into our own hands and how we could have both been killed and sent our mother to an early grave from grief. Then he practically collapsed into a chair and sat there crying for a few minutes while Leck and I just stood there with our heads bowed. After a while he wiped his eyes and hugged us both at the same time. I have to admit that I shed a few tears myself.

My mama, Ada Molony, took the news quietly. When we were done, she slipped away to her room for several minutes, and when she came back her eyes were puffy and red. She sat us down at the kitchen table and told us how proud she was that we had stood up for justice. I always thought she was frail and weak, but she showed how strong and resilient she was that day.

Big Six was lenient on Otis and Samuel. He busted up their still and charged them a fine, but they didn't have to do any jail time. Before the summer was over, a relative from Indianapolis sent them some money and word about jobs. They gathered all their belongings into a few suitcases and took the bus north. Samuel stopped by the house around Christmas dressed in a new suit and dropped off a country ham. He said he had come back to convince some more folks to join them in Indianapolis. Most of the folks listened, and by springtime Coe Ridge was mostly a ghost town of old shanties.

We buried Phoebe in a plot not too far from where the sheriff found me. Besides my family, the only people that showed up were the Wilburns from Coe Ridge and Old Man Riddle. I wondered how many people she had healed over the years. How many lives did she save? Where were they now, and if they knew of her passing, would they show up to pay their respects? I figured she was happier now, on the other side of Jordan. I made sure that the same inscription was chiseled into her head-stone—*May your healing gift continue forever.*

With both the sheriff and the deputy gone, the county held a special election. Several able men put their name out there for the position, but none were more qualified than Leck. He won by a majority and was gracious enough to hire Harold Guffey as his deputy, even though he ran against Leck as a Republican. He set things right in the county and even hauled in Jed Mock for throwing a rock through an old colored woman's window and threatening her because she had the audacity to drink out of the white water fountain. When I asked him about it, he said he was just trying to win the colored vote in the next election, but I could see that he had changed, at least a little.

The gossip about me spread like a wildfire all over the county and into a few of the neighboring counties. I couldn't go anywhere without whispers and stares for a long time. After a couple of weeks I went to see Pastor Tabor and asked permission to date Ruby again. He wasn't keen on it, but they had me back over for dinner a few times, and eventually he let us go out again.

I'm not sure if it was the changes in me, or in her, but it was never the same with Ruby again. Hoping to regain some of the magic we felt, I took her back up Big Hill one more time to look out over Burkesville. Just like before, she kicked off her shoes and looked up at me with those chocolate eyes. Her hair still smelled like Prell shampoo, and her lips were just as inviting as before, but it never felt the same again. Instead of magic, it was awkward and rigid like we were just going through the same motions as before but without any real feeling. We never really broke up. We just stopped dating and went on with our lives. I haven't dated anyone else since then.

I haven't healed anyone since that day at Phoebe's old place. I've been approached many times, but I've turned them all away out of fear. I wasn't afraid that I wouldn't be able to heal them. I was afraid that my gift would become trivial, or that I might heal someone that I shouldn't. I wasn't ready to play god with the gift God had given me. Several times I have felt the healing storm surge inside of me and have listened to the scripture circle my thoughts, but I have held back. I figured that I needed some time to grow and understand. I didn't want to become a circus act like Phoebe and die a lonely, unappreciated death. It was hard at first because my fame had begun to spread, and I didn't like to see people suffer, but over time folks stopped showing up on our doorstep.

My life returned to working on the farm, fishing, and basketball. Work on the farm was a lot easier with Leck around, but when it came time to haul hay I missed Samuel and Otis. I missed going up to Coe Ridge with Daddy and delivering shelled corn. I missed Wonnie. I focused on my schooling and my basketball, and we made it to the final four but lost by one point. I was voted the most valuable player by the other teammates, and several college scouts introduced themselves.

As the year progressed, I grew restless. My dreams of marrying a pretty girl, buying a farm in the river bottom, and raising a family kind of drifted away. The small-town charm wore off, and I longed to find someplace where I could disappear in the crowd and be invisible again. I got several letters and brochures from far away universities inviting me attend. I felt drawn to one in west Texas—Texas Western College in El Paso. The basketball coach sent me a personal letter asking me to come play. I figured it was far enough away that I could start over. I hoped that maybe I could figure out a way to use my gift without drawing so much attention, but I'm not sure I'll ever use it again.

Mama was the one that insisted I write these things down. She said that over time I would forget the details, and the events would become fuzzy in my mind. I couldn't see how that was possible, but I took her advice. At night I would sit in the front room and scribble my story into notebooks while Daddy tapped his foot to music from the radio and Mama knitted.

Now that I'm done, I feel a sense of relief. I feel like no matter what happens, or no matter where I roam in this world, my story will live on. When I'm done traveling through this wilderness like some wayfaring stranger and cross over Jordan, I'll have left something behind for people to remember me by.

EPILOGUE

Stone downshifted as he started up the Glasgow Road with Burkesville, Kentucky, in the rearview mirror of his Ford Tudor Sedan. He had several days of travel ahead of him on his way to El Paso, but today he just wanted to make it to Little Rock. He had a map with his route all planned out on the front seat beside him and almost everything he owned crammed into the trunk and backseat of the car he had scraped and saved to buy. He was nervous about leaving home, and he could feel the butterflies he always felt before a big basketball game tickling his insides. He topped the hill and started to accelerate when he heard a siren and saw a flashing light in his rearview mirror. He grinned and pulled over. Instead of waiting, he jumped out of the car and started walking toward the black-and-white Bel-Air as the sheriff came toward him adjusting the gun on his hip and holding a small box.

Stone smiled and said, "What are you gonna do? Arrest me so I can't leave town?"

"I ought to throw you into the loony bin," said Sheriff Leck Molony. "I think you're crazy for going so far away from home. None of the schools in Kentucky were good enough? You know we do play basketball in Kentucky, don't you?"

"C'mon, Leck. You know it's not that."

Leck nodded. "I know, but I still think you're crazy." He held the box out to his brother. "I wanted to give you this."

Stone wrinkled his brow and took the box. It was small but heavy. He pulled off the lid and saw a black revolver inside with a small container of ammunition. He put the lid back on and tried to hand it back to his brother. "Leck, I don't need this. I'm going off to college, not a gunfight."

Leck rolled his eyes and shook his head. "Still naïve as ever I see. You're about to cross three states, including Texas, and spend your nights camped on the side of the road. A man should have himself a little insurance in those situations."

Stone realized that it was no use arguing and tucked the box under his arm. "Thanks for watching out for me, again. You could have just given me this at home."

Leck grinned and said, "If I had done that, you would have accidentally forgotten it." He punched Stone in the shoulder like brothers do and said, "Now get out of here before I write you a ticket." Then he turned and started back to his cruiser. Just before he opened his door, he looked back and said, "Godspeed, brother." Then he climbed into the Bel-Air, turned it around, and sped off toward Burkesville, leaving Stone standing there on the side of the road with the heavy box under his arm.

Stone shoved the box behind the driver's seat and drove off toward Glasgow. He knew he had to make good time in order to make it to Little Rock before bedtime, but he had to make one more stop in Eighty-Eight before he could focus on the road ahead of him.

He stopped and asked directions at the general store on Eighty-Eight and soon found himself pulling down the dirt lane of Mr. Cornet and his son, Archie. The house was adorned with a rusty tin roof and faded yellow paint with red dirt stains around the bottom. The small column of smoke rising from the chimney told him that somebody was probably cooking in the kitchen. He glanced up at the porch and saw a barking dog and a young man twisted by disease, sitting by himself in a rickety wheelchair.

He stopped the car and said a silent prayer. When he got out, the pitiful dog stopped barking and lay back down like he was too tired to care anymore. Archie jerked his head to look up at Stone and squawked. Nobody else came out of the house or up from the barn.

Stone hesitated at the bottom of the porch stairs and looked around for Mr. Cornet, almost afraid that the big man might not be so cordial as last time. He thought about the box that Leck had just given him and almost wished he had the gun tucked in his belt just in case. He took a deep breath and focused on Archie sitting patiently in the wheelchair. That was why he had come. That was why he was here.

He stood up straight and marched up the stairs. He pushed the fear from his mind and began to pass the scripture from Ezekiel in front of his mind's eye over and over again. His gift didn't come at first, and he struggled to focus when he remembered the last time he tried to heal Archie. Just as he was about to give up hope, he felt a spark of faith from the boy in the wheelchair. The storm began to gather inside his head, and he smiled as the energy began to flow to his hands. Lightning crackled and tingled his scalp. His hands burned like fire. He reached out and put both of his ardent hands on Archie, who wriggled and jerked so much that the wheelchair rocked.

Stone could feel the muscles and joints take on healthy form. He could sense the dark disease leaving the boy's body. In his mind, he could see the healthy young man that he could now become. The storm raged. His healing hands burned. Then, all at once, all the energy gathered in his chest and flew away, leaving Stone weak and unable to see.

He felt his way to the porch stairs and sat on the top step, waiting for his sight to return. He wondered what the young man would look like when the blindness passed. He heard the creaking seat of the wheelchair and soft steps against the wooden planks of the porch. The dog whimpered. The boy laughed. Then the steps came faster, and he was almost knocked over as Archie threw himself onto Stone's shoulders and hugged him.

The disease had robbed Archie of the power to speak all of his life, and even though the muscles and joints functioned normally now, it would take him some time to learn how to talk. He expressed himself by squeezing Stone's neck and wetting his shoulder with tears. Stone began to cry as well. They sat there crying silent tears of joy until Stone began to recover his sight and stood to see the healed boy.

The young man before him was whole. His limbs and joints were weak from lack of use, but they were healthy. His eyes danced with delight, and his face beamed. He was no longer in a twisted shell of human form. He was a vibrant human being capable of living life without the boundaries of a debilitating disease.

Stone held his finger up to his lips. "Please don't tell anyone," he said as he started down the stairs toward his car. "I don't want everyone in the country chasing me down looking to be healed." Archie nodded as if he

understood, but Stone knew it was an impossible promise to keep.

Stone glanced up at his rearview mirror and saw
Archie jumping and waving from the porch next to the
barking dog. Stone pulled down the dirt lane and headed
west down the country road in search of a new beginning. He still hoped to make Little Rock by nightfall.

DISCUSSION QUESTIONS

1. If you were given Stone's power to heal, how would you choose between whom to heal and not to heal? Could you walk past someone in need and not help?

2. Why do you think Stone couldn't heal Rusty the second time? Is there a higher purpose to Rusty's healing and subsequent death? Does death ever have a higher purpose?

3. How would you react to discovering that you had a unique gift? What gifts are you capable of but are afraid to use?

4. How does Wonnie change the way Stone understands race? How have you been affected by the prejudice of society or individuals? What have you done to overcome that?

5. How did you feel when both Ada and Billy Molony reacted negatively to Samuel as he approached the house in the dark after being beaten? Do you consider Billy and Ada's behavior as a whole racist?

6. Do you believe in spiritual gifts? How do you feel about the outward display of those gifts, such as snake handling?

7. Can you feel, or have you ever felt, the faith of another person? What role has faith played in your life?

8. Billy Molony had a unique way of coping with Wonnie's death. How have you coped with the passing of a loved one? How does that compare with Billy Molony's technique?

9. Why did Stone heal Cortis Russel? Given the same choice, what would you have done?

10. Would you take another person's life in the name of justice? Do you feel that Leck was justified?

11. Why couldn't Stone stay in Burkesville? Have you ever changed so much that you felt compelled to move or at least change scenes?

12. What should Stone do next with his gift? What would you do?

ACKNOWLEDGMENTS

It isn't easy to write a novel. It's impossible to write a novel without help from a lot of people.

I started my writing journey out of sheer arrogance. I read a book from an author that I usually enjoyed, and it wasn't that good. I turned the book over and saw that it was a *New York Times* bestseller.

"I could write better than that," I mumbled to myself. So, I decided to try. Of course my arrogance soon faded.

It took me a year to write the manuscript for this novel, and another thirteen months of submissions to publishers before I finally found someone who enjoyed it enough to give me a contract. It was a journey full of lonely days in front of my computer hacking away at the keys, and anxious days waiting for letters and emails from agents and publishers, most of whom replied in the negative and several that didn't bother to reply at all. None of this would have been possible if it weren't for the loving support of my wife, Britt. My parents inspired the story, but my wife believed I could actually tell it.

My writing partner, Kevin Whaley, held me accountable throughout the process. His feedback and encouragement got me through the rough spots when I wanted to quit. He is a gentleman and a scholar.

Since this is my first novel, the most difficult thing to obtain was good feedback. It took a long list of beta readers to make the manuscript better and keep me from abandoning hope when the rejections piled up. Here's to the beta readers: Britt Booher, my wife, who always stroked my ego and made me feel good. Monica Whiting who begged to read the manuscript as soon as I printed it off. Alt Flo Lewis, from Cumberland County,

326

Kentucky who gave the text authenticity and detail. My parents, Eddie and Jeanetta Booher, who told me stories of 1955 and filled my head with imagination. My in-laws, Brent and Dorothy Hancock, who treat me like their own son. My sister-in-law, Jennifer Hancock, whose soft-spoken opinion I value. My high school friend Jane Barbee Lewis, who gave me a much-needed point of view. Carolyn Hanchet, whose wisdom and expertise added to the story. Joel Bikman, whose humble counsel steered me through the publishing maze. Dalynn Albright, who gave me feedback while cutting my hair. My sister Tassie, who read the manuscript out loud to her daughters, Brie, Mirette, and London, while her husband, Randy Earnest, drove for hours. Katie Kunzleman, who gave the search for a publisher new hope with her enthusiasm for the manuscript. Deneen Wilson, my neighbor and friend, who has supported my family through thick and thin. My writing buddy, Jimmy Jo Allen, who took the time to give me critical feedback from long distance. My friend, Kim Aguilar, who gave me much needed editorial feedback when the story was in its inception stage and I wasn't sure where to go with it or how to get it there. My sister Tahlee, who brainstormed with me and helped me flesh out ideas. My sister Ada, whose love for reading mirrors our mother. Of course, my Granny (who recently celebrated her ninetieth birthday), who breathed some authenticity into the text. And Angie Workman, the acquisitions editor who believed in the manuscript enough to offer me a contract.

This journey would not have been possible without my family, both immediate and extended. All of my children, brothers, sisters, aunts, uncles, cousins, nieces, nephews, and in-laws have been kind enough to read the things I write, and encourage me to keep writing.

This is a work of fiction. I have shamelessly stolen ideas from overheard conversations, magazine articles, oral stories, and the works listed in the bibliography. Because it is a work of fiction, I have usually twisted those ideas and shaped them to fit the story. Don't hold me accountable to complete honesty in this work. I am, after all, a fiction writer.

BIBLIOGRAPHY

"1955 in Country Music." Wikipedia. November 18, 2013. Accessed January 07, 2014. http://en.wikipedia.org/wiki/1955_in_country_music.

Coe, Samuel S., and R. A. Adams. *Chronicles of the Coe Colony, Pea Ridge, Kentucky.* Burkesville, KY: Xerxes, 2007.

Cohn, Beverly. *What a Year It Was! 1955.* Marina Del Rey, CA: MMS, 1995.

"George Went Hensley." Wikipedia. May 01, 2014. Accessed January 07, 2014. http://en.wikipedia.org/wiki/George_Went_Hensley.

"Grand Ole Opry History." Home. Accessed January 07, 2014. http://www.opry.com/history.

Guffey, Billy N. *Fire in the Hole!: An Oral History of Moonshine and Murder in Cumberland County, Kentucky.* Burkesville, KY: Xerxes, 2007.

"Hill 303: NK Murder of Prisoners." *Hill 303: NK Murder of Prisoners.* Accessed January 07, 2014. http://www.koreanwaronline.com/arms/hill303.htm.

Montell, William Lynwood. *Don't Go up Kettle Creek: Verbal Legacy of the Upper Cumberland.* Knoxville: University of Tennessee Press, 1983.

Montell, William Lynwood. *The Saga of Coe Ridge: A Study in Oral History.* Knoxville: University of Tennessee Press, 1970.

Wigginton, Eliot. *Foxfire 3.* Garden City, NY: Anchor Press/Doubleday, 1975.

Wigginton, Eliot. *The Foxfire Book.* Garden City, NY: Anchor Press/Doubleday, 1972.

BROCK BOOHER grew up on a farm in rural Kentucky, the fourth of ten children, where he learned to work hard, use his imagination, and believe in himself. He left the farm to pursue the friendly skies as a pilot and currently flies for a major US carrier. A dedicated husband and father of six children, he began writing out of sheer arrogance, but the writing craft quickly humbled him. During that process, he discovered that he enjoyed writing because it is an endeavor that can never quite be mastered. He still gladly struggles every day to improve his writing and storytelling skills.